International Vixen

Welcome sisters of the light!
This Vixen guidebook has powers as yet unknown to you.
It is invaluable in the success of being a Vixen.
Use it wisely and guard its secrets with your life.

THE VIXEN'S SECRET HANDBOOK SERIES

Book 2

International Vixen

DEFYING DATING RULES

By

KM Chapman

International Vixen

Dedicated to the memory of my wonderful editor, Marian. Even with the toughest of feedback, Marians' kind heart shone through, to make me a better author. Missed by many more than she will ever know.

Contents

Preface

The information contained within these pages is for the eyes of Vixens only. We cannot give away the secrets of the Vixens, so be alert and guard these words with care, sisters! Read on and take delight in the awakening of your own inner Vixen. Draw her into the light. Have fun, be playful, and light-hearted. Share around the delights of your mystical Vixen love!

BUT do not share the most sacred of all ... "The Vixen's Secret Handbook" Shh! Don't even utter the words aloud as yet, make sure you are alone first! Read on, dear sisters and willing purveyors of the path of Vixendom, as your lives will be changed forever ...

IF YOU DARE!

The Vixen's Secret Handbook

Vixen Coven Commandments

- Everyone's time is valuable, so do not waste a moment on anything or anyone unworthy of receiving the wondrous gift of a Vixen's precious time and attention.

- At all times, Vixens remain respectful, kind, and mindful of others' feelings. Vixens are not rude to unwanted Marks either online or in person. Even if you are horrified or revolted at what you hear or see, remain outwardly calm and extract yourself from the situation with grace and kindness, for it costs nothing to be kind to others, and this is the Vixen way.

- When in play mode, ensure each man chosen meets one of the major 'unsuitability' points previously determined by each Vixen. This is to prevent a Vixen's heart from being affected negatively and to help her to stay conscious of the fact she is currently in Vixen play mode, not marriage mode.

- Thou shalt not knowingly play with or ensnare any man who is married or in a monogamous relationship. Such underhanded behaviour is beneath the Vixen. (Failure to adhere to this rule will result in more headaches, heartaches, and issues than it is worth, so stay vigilant on your dates.)

❧ Never covet or play with another Vixen's established Mark. Vixens are not in competition with each other, rather a supportive sisterhood taking a break from the rollercoaster of emotions that traditional relationships can be. There are many more potentials available than there are Vixens, so if you come to realise another Vixen has already ensnared a Mark, step down.

❧ Know ye well the Vixen's Secret Handbook! Yes, it will enable you to protect your heart for a while and indulge in light-hearted play and adventure … but there will come a time when these lessons and dates will serve you well.

❧ When the Vixen life no longer suits your needs, do not be afraid of this revelation, instead recognize this change within, and see if your inner light is strong enough to withstand the search for the love and connection, we all yearn for at some stage of our lives.

❧ Be prepared, oh Vixens, that this living Book will morph as needed, so constant consultation of its pages is recommended, even if you transition into hunting a love-match

CHAPTER 1

Holiday Fever

Lingering between dream land and consciousness, I drift. To return to the sex-filled dream I was enjoying is proving elusive. Wait. What's today? A broad grin spreads across my face. My inner energy dances in excitement.

Holiday, finally you are here! My eyes fly open. What's the time? Phew! It's still early, I can relax. My legs twitch, eager to face the day and start my well-deserved break. Three hours left of Sydney before I fly to a beautiful tropical island! I can't help myself. The twitching in my legs turns into an enthusiastic horizontal wiggle-dance involving my entire body.

Happily, no one is here to witness this.

I laugh out loud at my silliness. Instead of a solo holiday, I could have asked a friend or one of the guys I'm currently dating to come with me. But this time I want to go alone. A few years ago, the thought of holidaying solo would have been scary. But now I can't wait! I need massages, rest, relaxation, and retail therapy. It's not always possible to do that with every friend, or with one of my guys in tow.

'What's that?' I hear you say, in response to my claim of dating several men. Yes! It's true. And they all know about each other too. Total honesty, that's how I do it! Hey, did you like that? I *knew* you were thinking, 'Surely these men can't know she's seeing other guys!'

I've been working on my intuition... as well as using my secret weapon! Umm, what? Are you serious? If I told you what it was this early in, how would it stay a secret? You never know who has picked up this book to leaf through the pages... Any random flicker could come across these words! Yet it's only for the chosen few to know. When I feel you can be trusted I will share it with you.

A picture of thirty-six-year-old Krystian appears in my mind. He is the first one in my collection of men. Tall, handsome, emotionally intelligent and he definitely knows how to treat a lady. Also a player in the dating field, we often compare our dating stories accompanied by drinks and laughter.

An original Polish gentleman, Krystian is thoughtful, interesting, and fun to hang out with. Our friendship grows stronger daily, and I genuinely enjoy spending time with him... Plus he also owns a wicked heated outdoor spa!

The essential deal-breaker that ensures I won't accidentally fall into a relationship with him, is his association with a biker gang. Oh, and the fact that he owns a satanic bible which is kind of opposite to my beliefs.

Roshan the second hot guy I'm dating pops into my head.

His cheeky grin and twinkling eyes are only topped by his rock-hard chest and washboard abs you could scrub clothes on. Not yet thirty, Roshan is mature for his years, with a sense of naughty mischievousness that's catching. Sri Lankan with tanned skin, shaved head, and perfect gym-toned physique, he remains hard to resist. So, I don't!

All the men I date must have deal-breakers though. Roshan's is the huge age gap between us and the fact that he is only one inch taller than me. I prefer to be able to wear heels without towering over a guy.

The third man in my current dating collection Darz, is a gym junkie. His brooding sexy eyes drew me in at the beginning, as did the pictures of his smooth, naked chest online. Smart and switched-on career-wise, he is on the fast track towards becoming a millionaire. His lickable body is delicious, and he owns a large thick cock to match. Adventurous in nature, this Czech man likes to push sexual boundaries. The biggest deal-breaker for me with Darz is that he really wants to have children and being over forty, I definitely *don't.*

But these are the reasons for having Krystian, Darz, and Roshan in my life. I don't want to marry any of them. Ever! I just want to date all three, and perhaps add a couple more to my list. I have none marked for hunting yet, but who knows what I may find on my travels?

To be honest, I'm not expecting to be attracted to any of the local men on holiday. I literally look down on guys there although I'm only five foot six inches! Even if I do find a Balinese man taller than myself, I'm rarely attracted to their features.

In previous Bali holidays, I had to strike Aussies off my list of men to date. Football club trips and boys on holidays with mates equal drunken Australian idiots! Plus, I can date someone from my own country at any time.

Come to think of it, none of the guys I'm currently dating are Australian. Maybe I prefer European men? No, wait. Roshan is Sri Lankan so *that* theory is shot. I just ruled out other Aussies and locals to Bali. Oh no. My holiday fling possibility list is getting shorter by the second!

Hmm... What's a Vixen on holiday overseas to do? Seek sexy international men of course! There are a lot of countries in this world. Even though the majority of tourists in Bali are Australian, there must be some hot international men there too. French hotties, or smooth-talking, sexy Greeks, or Italians. A tall handsome blond Swede perhaps.

What a perfect idea. An international hunting ground for this Vixen. I will give this some thought and attention between massages and pedicures. Internet dating sites are worldwide so there will be a plethora of Marks to choose from. Now I'm even more excited about my upcoming trip.

Dammit! Thinking about men has wasted almost an hour of my time. I finished my packing last night, so I just need to get ready and make it to the airport in time. Yippee! Anticipation builds within as I imagine myself sprawled on a sunbed sipping cocktails by a sparkling pool. Water at the perfect temperature to sink straight into and hot men to perve on. The perfect place for a Vixen on holiday!

Before I know it, my phone is buzzing to let me know my taxi is here. After a last-minute check of all the doors and windows, I pull the front door closed. Double checking that it's locked securely before I head away for my two weeks of bliss, I step towards the waiting car pulling my suitcase behind me.

The airport is buzzing with the excitement of travellers. I'm early. What a relief! You can never be sure with Sydney traffic. I stand patiently in the growing line at the check-in counter and people watch to pass the time.

Harassed parents are dragging their crying children towards the security check. A group of teenagers in private school uniforms mill close by; their exuberant chatter drowning out the yowling kids. Several businessmen stand in stiff suits sporting bored expressions — a stark contrast to the eager holidaymakers in their comfortable travel wear.

Finally relieved of my suitcase by a smiling attendant I head through security, boarding pass in hand. My tummy growls, reminding me to find food before passing through customs. I plan to sleep for as long as possible, and hate being disturbed by the hostesses with food mid-flight. As I bin the wrappers and empty drink bottle, the call to board my flight echoes through the terminal.

A quick glance around confirms my suspicions. There are at least ten small children to board. Fingers crossed; none are seated near me! Almost seven hours in the air drag on *much* longer with a crying child nearby.

I feel empathy for the parents. How challenging to manage a hysterical kid while surrounding passengers glare at you! Often, they seat families towards the back of the plane.

I check my boarding pass again. My seat number is 6A. Perfect! Right near the front of the plane. I can see more action at the gate now and feel the energy of the waiting passengers rise. We surge forward, all eager to be off to whatever adventure is planned. Bali, here I come!!

The air hostess calls for those seated towards the back to board first. Happily, every child in sight is pushed towards the boarding counter. This tells me I will have a peaceful, child-free flight. It was worth asking for a front window seat! Biding my time, I board when requested and settle into my assigned seat.

The drone of the engine starting signals we are ready to leave. I can't wait! My favourite part of flying is the take-off and landing. I look calm on the outside, but my energy is sparkling excitedly within. Next to me remains an empty seat. I'm praying to be the lucky passenger who can spread out a bit, and not be rubbing shoulders with a stranger.

Yes, the stranger might be tall, dark, and handsome ... But really, what are my chances of *that* happening?

The younger woman on the other side of the empty seat smiles gleefully at me.

"I think we won the seat lotto with a free one between us!"

I grin in return. "You're right! I'm amazed — I did request the seat be free, but you never know until you're ready to leave hey."

"I'm Deanna." She says.

"Nice to meet you, Deanna! I'm Arleia. Are you also flying solo on holiday?"

"Yes! This is about my twentieth time in Bali, so I'm used to it!"

Wow, that's a lot. What draws her back so often? I don't really want to talk, but my curiosity gets the better of me.

"Do you stay at the same place each time?"

She laughs. "Yes, I do, but that's because my cousin and I rent a villa year-round in Bali, so I always stay there. It would be silly not to. The rest of the time we sublet the property out to holiday makers."

I'm surprised. An idea like that had never entered my head before... but what an excellent business idea! The price of a yearly rental property in Bali compared to prices in Australia would be peanuts. It makes sense to rent it out for half of the year to pay the rent, then holiday there for free for the rest of the year. Perfect!

"That's incredibly smart! I can't say I've ever thought of doing that. So, are you just going there to check everything's still ok with your rental property?"

"No... The main reason I'm heading to Bali is for work. I developed a natural skincare range, and my manufacturers are in Bali."

I'm impressed. That's *two* great entrepreneurial ideas that she's carried through with and turned into reality. What am I doing wasting my time working in an office?!

"Wow, that's amazing! Good on you, Deanna!"

How cool. What made her decide to take this path? It takes a lot of strength and courage to create something new. What could I do instead? Something I can start part-time and build on would be great.

Our conversation is interrupted by the flight attendant's voice over the loudspeaker, demanding our attention.

Here we go! My fingers clenched the arms of my seat in excitement, as I watch the ground drop away from us. Bali, here I come!

CHAPTER 2

Hellooo Bali

The faint buzz of conversation surrounds me, awakening me from a deep sleep. I frown in annoyance. Do people on a plane have to talk so loudly? Squeezing my eyes tightly shut, I try to recapture unconsciousness. Nope. Sleep has deserted me. My neck aches. I reach to adjust my pillow and realise it's my travel pillow. I open one eye to see Deanna grinning at me.

"How was your snooze, sleeping beauty?!"

"Wow, did I sleep the entire flight?"

Wiping the sleep out of my eyes, I stretch and yawn simultaneously.

"We have about thirty minutes until we land! The pilot just announced the start of our descent — I can't wait!"

I laugh at her eagerness – but I feel the same. The unopened paperback shoved in the pocket of the seat in front reminds me to gather my things in readiness to leave the plane. My butt aches in protest after being seated for such a long time.

The wheels touch down with a screech, and we all lurch forward as the brakes are applied hard. We're here! I can't wipe the smile off my face as I peer out the window at the familiar surroundings. Miniature men below run around with stairs and baggage carts, ready to unload.

Warm, humid air hits my face like a furnace immediately as I step off the plane. The faint smell of incense hangs in the air welcomes travellers to Bali. Deanna and I squash into the closest waiting bus that ferries us to the international terminal. Excited chatter fills the bus.

Filing through customs is surprisingly fast – lucky for us no other flights arrived at the same time. The longest wait is at the baggage carousel. I might have felt uncomfortable standing here alone, but Deanna and I band together and chat while we wait.

In the past, I have always holidayed overseas with friends. Or with different romantic partners, a lifetime ago. My friends' reactions to my proposed solo trip were priceless. Everything from being worried about my safety, to asking me how I would cope with eating alone in a restaurant. Their unfounded concerns amuse me, but at least they care!

They projected their own fears of the unknown onto me and imagined how they would feel. Many people are afraid of spending too much time alone. They think alone means feeling lonely. That is not the case for me now. Since my last long-term relationship ended six months ago, I love to be alone! To have the complete freedom to do what I want, when I want to, is bliss to me.

Spotting my bag, I hoist it off the carousel. Deanna's bag

appeared moments before, so we make for the exit together. During our wait, we discussed sharing a taxi to travel to our respective accommodations. Agreeing to travel together, we ready ourselves for the bombardment of options upon exiting the terminal.

Signs with handwritten prices are propped next to grubby car windows. Hordes of men beckon from every direction with calls of "Taxi! You want taxi ma'am?" Sweaty hands try to grab at our suitcases until firmly told "NO!" Deanna and I grin at each other. As return travellers, we are used to this chaos.

Arguing with a taxi driver because the price he quoted was different from the price written on his sign, Deanna shakes her head.

"What a dickhead! When will Uber set up here? These drivers get worse every time I come here. As if I'm going to pay one hundred thousand Rupiah more than what's written on his stupid sign!"

I nod in agreement. This was a common problem on arrival. The taxi prices were always jacked up to ridiculous rates compared to their regular flag fall and fare. Sometimes it's better to walk a bit further from the airports' exit and barter with an independent driver for a better price.

We walk towards the car park, ignoring several offers from hopeful drivers. One was persistent in his pursuit of a fare.

"Ma'am, please! I do you good price! Special price for you! You come to Bali many time. I give you best price. Thank you for visit Bali again. Ma'am? Ma'am!!"

Deanna and I exchange glances and stop.

"We are going to two places. Kuta and Seminyak. What is your best price?"

He pauses for a split second. I can see him calculating in his mind what we might be willing to pay.

"I can do for two hundred and fifty thousand ma'am!"

Deanna's slight head shake alerts me to the fact she thinks that it is too expensive, as do I.

"I don't think that's your best price!"

I smile in a teasing fashion – it is the best way to get a better price. Bartering is common in the tourist areas of Bali, and if you aren't good at it, you can easily find yourself paying way too much! I rev up the bartering and throw in a cheeky smile.

"Come on.... give us better price! You know we love Bali so much... you want us to come back? Or cry because taxi driver makes us so sad? We pay you one hundred and fifty thousand. That's all!"

I slip into shortened Bali English naturally. I know what his dramatic response will be and wait for it to be unleashed.

"Ohhhhhh! You kill me! Oh my God! One hundred and fifty thousand! Ma'am, please! Little bit more. Just little bit. You pay two hundred thousand. Ma'aaaaaaaaaaam!"

Anyone else may have caved in at this point, but Deanna and I are seasoned Bali travellers. She picks up the good cop bad cop routine like a pro.

"I come here four times a year! Always I pay only one hundred thousand! This time, you have two stops, and we will pay fifty thousand more. I will have to tell all my friends that taxis are too expensive for Australians to come to Bali now."

Shouldering her bag, she pretends to walk off. Man, she is good! That's what you must do to get what you want here sometimes.

"Ok ok ok! OK. One hundred and fifty thousand. I will do. Wait here please!"

He hurries off to find his car in the throng of parked vehicles nearby. Turning to each other we hit a high five and grin. Yes! This is exactly what we want. A reasonable price for our taxi ride to our accommodation... Not a price that's a higher fare than Australian taxis would charge!

Frantic beeps and waving catch our attention as he pulls up in front of us. Loading our luggage into the car, he gestures for us to get in quickly so he can clear the lane for others. Dozens of cars clog up the exit, all eager to leave the airport. We settle into the air-conditioned car in comfort, glad that the difficult part of bartering is over.

Arriving at my hotel first, the driver hops out and retrieves my bag. Deanna and I exchange numbers so we can keep in touch and catch up again some time. I wave goodbye as the taxi lurches straight back into the traffic mayhem, beeping as it goes.

Well. That's it then. I'm in a foreign country alone. Yippee, I made it! I drag my case behind me as I head towards the massive reception desk to be welcomed by the friendly staff.

A high thatched style pitched roof covers the open-air reception desk, flanked by two massive tropical flower arrangements. The three receptionists each have frangipani tucked behind their ears, and their orange Balinese style uniforms look fresh and cool despite the humidity. After a complimentary check-in drink, my bags are whisked away from me, and I'm shown to my new home for the next two weeks.

Gesturing that I should enter first, the polite porter brings my bag in for me and explains the workings of the key card, air conditioner, and features of my room. Finally, he leaves, and I breathe a sigh of relief. I clap my hands in glee as I survey the room. It's spacious, with a huge flat-screen TV and modern décor, but with a traditional Bali feel. The king-size bed's bamboo headboard gleams with two inbuilt lights for reading, and I find the minibar hidden behind a traditionally carved wooden cupboard underneath the TV.

I step into the bathroom. Spacious and sparkling, the shower is huge with a silver rainfall shower head. Next to the two sealed bottles of water at the gleaming basin's edge along the long, marble benchtop sits a selection of local designer bath products in a bow-topped wicker basket.

I turn my attention to the toilet. What would be the trick with this one? Would it sport a side sprayer for washing your butt, or something more modern? Leaning to each side I looked for the hose. Nope! No spray visible there. But wait. What's this extra button on the cistern? Stepping back cautiously, I press it.

A stream of water shoots out of the top of the toilet bowl. The force is so great it splashes into the bath opposite. Holy crap, I wasn't expecting that! Thank God I wasn't in the firing line when I pressed the button, or I'd be drenched with toilet water. I couldn't help but laugh. I might have to video this bottom sprayer for my friends at home!

Walking back into the bedroom I flop on the bed and sprawl out happily. At last, I'm here. Now what?

The pool! Since I upgraded to a pool access room, it should be right behind those wooden shutters. Sliding the shutters open I gasp in delight. With the water shimmering in the sun invitingly, the pool is literally only four steps from my private terrace. It's a long, wide pool so I don't feel like the rooms across the other side are too close for comfort either.

First things first! I throw on my bathers and step into the water. It's warm enough to sink into without a cold shiver. Ahh, hello paradise! As I float on my back looking up at the tops of the palm trees dotted throughout the lush tropical garden surroundings, I contemplate my next move.

There are so many options and no one else here but me to decide. This may be harder than I thought. My stomach growls in a reminder that it has been forever since I last ate. I guess that's the deciding factor for my next destination!

Drying quickly once I exit the water, I change into shorts and a tank top to head out of the resort in search of food. Straight away I'm hit by sticky humidity in the street. Calls of 'Darling, hello darrrrling! Massage! You want massaaaaaage?' echo behind me as I quickly weave through the slow-moving shoppers.

I can see at least six warungs from here, which is the Balinese equivalent of a small restaurant. My mouth waters as I inhale delicious smells wafting past me. Choosing one at the end of the street I step inside, dodging the other shop owners trying to pull me in to look at their wares.

I hardly glance at the menu. Mi Goreng! My favourite

Indonesian dish. I order and relax into the cushioned wooden chair. The restaurant is open-air style, with big wooden ceiling fans circulating the still air. A dozen square wooden tables with mismatched coloured chairs crowds the small space. Local art adorns the bamboo walls, while the waitress shoos away a curious cat scavenging for food. There are a few other tourists eating here as well as the cat, so the food should be safe enough!

My meal appears in five minutes flat. Inhaling deeply, my mouth waters at the smell wafting up from the steaming noodle dish topped with egg in front of me. I am almost three-quarters of the way through eating before I even realise that I'm sitting solo in a restaurant and loving it.

I feel empowered and proud of myself for taking the leap of traveling alone. A feeling of accomplishment and growth even. I finish my meal and head back towards the hotel, stopping to buy extra snacks and drinks. Now back to my room for some holiday comfort!

Propped up on plump cotton pillows I try to watch a movie. What a long day. I can hardly keep my eyes open now — despite the long plane nap. Maybe my body needs to catch up on all the sleep missed by too many recent late dates? I drift into sleep with a smile on my face. I'm excited to see what the next two weeks will bring.

CHAPTER 3

Lazy Days

My days fall into an easy pattern. Get up early and walk along the beach. Have a quick dip in the pool. Shower and get dressed, pull my hair back in a messy ponytail, and with the barest flick of mascara and lip gloss I'm ready.

I try every dish possible at the resort's enormous buffet breakfast. At first, I could only stomach western breakfast food choices. However, as time went by it became more reasonable to add fried rice, stir-fried vegetables, or sweet and sour chicken in for breakfast.

After my hearty late brunch, I step out to explore. Each time I go in a different direction to discover something new. Unique treasures like tiny jewellery shops are well hidden between repetitive clothes shops.

Ridiculous slogans on tank tops by the thousands wave in the breeze. 'Genuine fake' clothes, underwear, purses, and handbags hang along every path. Hundreds of fascinating lasers, miniature drums, and untreated wooden products line shelves. However, the latter would be confiscated upon return to Australia!

Every year there is a new trend in the shops here. One year it was white dream catchers. This year it's macramé themed items. Daily I pass skin-eating fish spas, huge carved wooden penises, and live frogs displayed in aquatic tanks.

Heat from the uneven sidewalk rises to mingle with the humidity and incense in the air. Every day is warm here. Some days, however, are more humid than others.

With Deanna's influence, my vague thoughts of my own business have solidified into selling local Balinese jewellery designs online. I've found five different designers as future sources for my jewellery business idea, and love walking the streets to discover these hidden gems. The occasional blast of air conditioning hits me as I wander, but most of the tiny open-front shops have only fans to cool the air. Sweat drips from every tourist I pass, but some look hotter than others.

Each afternoon is spent relaxing since it's the hottest part of the day. I read books on my terrace by the pool, punctuated with dips in the water to cool off. Or enjoy an indulgent massage or facial at my favourite spa nearby.

Being a quarter of the price compared with back home, a massage is great value. Add a facial and pedicure, and an indulgent afternoon of pampering in air-conditioned comfort flies by. The best thing is that I can afford to enjoy this self-pampering every day here — not just on special occasions.

I sprawl on my huge bed with room service watching a movie. Or flick through the sixty television channels on offer hunting for the English-speaking channels. Cosseted and relaxed on my solo holiday, I squeeze in an occasional sneaky nap and return messages to my three sexy men or friends back home.

Evenings are spent watching the sun set over the water. My toes curled in the warm sand; I lounge on a brightly coloured beanbag under an umbrella sipping a cocktail. Some shopping, followed by a late dinner, and voila, another sunset fades on the horizon! Before I know it, five days of my holiday have already passed.

Not once have I felt lonely. I can't help talking to people here. The locals *force* me to. With comments like, "Where are you from? We love Australian! I know you! Sexy lady come in my shop! Free for looking... same-same, but different! Maaaa'aaaam... Just looking, ok? Cheap morning price... good luck for me! You buy? How much you pay? Cheaper for three... I give you good price!"

Some days it is a relief to get back to the peace and quiet of the resort. Almost a week in and I am happy, content, and peaceful. Everything I have wanted to do, I've done. This holiday is different. It is relaxing, but not adventurous. Enjoyable, but not *exciting*! Don't get me wrong, I love being by myself. But I don't laugh as much as usual.

An interesting revelation! What to do about this? I've been so used to exciting dating adventures for the past six months that I'm missing them! Granted, some of them have been disaster dates, but still adventures. Dating? I can feel the colour drain from my face as I come to a realization. Oh. My. God. I forgot to bring my magical, secret dating weapon. Damn! How will I fare meeting guys here without it?

Yes, I know you are *dying* to know what the hell it is. Look. You're still here. So maybe it's safe to tell you now. I don't have it with me anyway, so I can't show you yet. But I can tell you. You had better be trustworthy though, *or the wrath of Karma will descend upon you!* Or something like that.

It's a book. But not just *any* book. It is The Vixens' Secret Handbook. Shush! Don't say it out loud for God's sake! You don't know who may be listening. Keep your voice down! If you are reading this in a library, you will be kicked out for sure. Remember men are not to have any knowledge of this book.

If you can manage to keep quiet, I will explain. This handbook was given to me over ten years ago. I was at a psychic fair when a mysterious gypsy approached me. She told me that I was the rightful owner she had been searching for, as she pressed the worn leather book in my hands. I didn't know what to make of her. Meanwhile, my friends had vanished down the next aisle, so I was a captive audience.

The book started to glow in my hands, and I freaked out. What the hell? She told me it was a secret Vixen handbook for women on successful dating, that had been passed down for generations. I didn't know whether to believe her or not, but the bloody book *glowed*. It was worth hearing her out.

She explained to me how to use it. But I was confused. How did she know it was meant for me? Was she crazy? Who owned it before me? Where are they now? Before I could get the answers to these questions and more, she had vanished.

I kept the book hidden in the top of a closet for years, unused. Forgotten. Until *that* day, about six months ago. The day my long-term boyfriend cheated on me, and I was thrust back into the world of singledom. After a deep meditation on which direction to take, I was drawn to the book.

It was the perfect solution for me. The handbook details how to successfully date several men at once. *When I remembered to follow its advice!* The few times I forgot to check it before a date, I missed the red warning glow of caution. Of course, there was something wrong with each man... which resulted in some disaster dates! Forced to use prearranged exit strategies to escape, I swore I'd never go on another date without consulting my guide again.

But now, here I am. On holiday alone — without the most essential tool I own. I don't want to miss this opportunity to meet men from around the world. They are right here on my doorstep! I contemplate the idea. It's not like I'm looking for a relationship. Nothing can continue beyond this holiday, but it would be interesting to meet a guy for a drink and chat with someone new.

Now is the time for action. I update my location on a dating site to see who is nearby. Swiping left for no; and right for yes, I alter my location to Legian Beach and start perusing the market.

Hundreds of choices appear before my eyes. Many are local guys so they're easy to decide on — an immediate no. But there are also men online who do fit my international smorgasbord criteria!

Although it's getting late and I'm tired, I have a quick flick through the menu. No, no, no, no, no, no, no... Yes! That seems to be the pattern. About one in every twenty is worthy of a swipe to the right. Of course, that is considering my criteria which is: no local Balinese men or Australians.

Within minutes I add a hot Italian and a Frenchmen. A few guys that look Nordic slip through. I'm not currently into the fair-haired boys since my last long-term relationship was with a blonde — but what the heck! I'm on holiday. A couple more look Latino-ish, and lastly a few guys that I can't determine their origin.

My eyelids are heavy. The screen is too bright now. I close them for a second and I'm asleep before I can drop my phone, dreaming of tomorrow's possible adventures.

CHAPTER 4

Vixen Mode

Not until breakfast the next morning, did I remember what I'd done the previous night. The dating site! How could I have forgotten? There could be multiple messages from hot men waiting for me right now! The thought makes me snigger into my freshly squeezed orange juice.

My stomach growls in reminder of the most important task at hand right now, which is choosing from the delicious delights in front of me! I add banana pancakes with maple syrup drizzled over them, with the blob of whipped cream sliding off the top. I stop it from mingling with the fresh fruit on the side then pop a tiny blueberry muffin in my mouth.

One of the best things about this resort is that the chefs make everything in miniature! This is especially important if you can't decide between the lemon curd cheesecake, layered chocolate mousse cake, or an apricot and custard pastry.

Usually, I only allow myself one choice. But here? At the buffet of heaven, you can have it all. Bite-size miniatures are available in every flavour of cake, pastry, or slice with new flavours to entice me daily. Even the freshly cooked mini pancakes change flavour every day. All that to choose as well as the rice dishes, eggs, curries, noodles, *and* the more conventional western fare.

Normally I wouldn't dream of eating so much for breakfast. A protein shake or fruit smoothie is my idea of morning food. On holiday I feel so decadent and spoilt for choice; I want to try it all.

I'm getting so carried away with this mouth-watering food that I totally forgot about men. That's *not* like me! All those massages and relaxation must have addled my mind. Even that thought, however, can't stop me from finishing everything on my plate.

Now to check my messages! I connect and immediately several alerts sound. Well, that didn't take long. Now to see if there are any hot men with brains here! An intelligent conversation with some humour and laughter thrown in would be a great start to a holiday dating adventure.

After half an hour of scrolling through the list of messages, I narrow it down to five possible men to meet. Glancing around me, I see that the open-air restaurant is emptying fast. The temptation is too great. I decide to splurge on another plate before the food is whisked away. The beauty of a great buffet breakfast is that when you eat around late morning, you really don't need lunch!

I head back to the comfort of my room to contemplate my choices. The first option I look at is Marco, an Italian sex god by the look of his picture! His cheeky grin and perfect white teeth are framed by dark shoulder-length curls atop a tanned bare chest.

Taking the plunge, I reply to his message. I don't expect a reply from him immediately, but I wait a few moments, just in case! I reread his profile, but he hasn't divulged much information there. He is thirty-four, five foot nine, has no children, and loves to travel.

On to the next prospective Mark! Sorry, have I explained what a 'Mark' is yet? I'm in the habit of referring to my men like that now! Hmm, I think you can be trusted. There's a whole section in the handbook about Marks. I don't have time now to give you the details but let me give you the gist of it.

Vixens hunt men they call 'Marks'. For consideration, a guy must meet the basics of a Vixen's personal list of requirements. Things like emotional intelligence, honesty, and respect are vital. Attractiveness is also high on every Vixens list! However, there is *one more* criterion they must meet: the 'unsuitability' criteria!

They *must* possess at least one characteristic that will be a deal-breaker. Remember what I told you earlier about my regular guys? Having deal-breakers ensures that I can separate 'Casual Fun Man', from 'Relationship Man'.

These two types of men are incredibly different but can appear the same on the surface. That's why women get so confused. Some guys promise second dates and seem extremely keen, only to vanish into the night — never to be seen or heard from again!

Others seem like they are great casual partners at first. Until you start receiving hourly texts asking if everything is ok ... since you didn't reply to his last ten texts yet. *Or* the letter he shoved under your windscreen wiper.

Becoming a vixen has reminded me of my awesomeness. Once that spark of light inside us is found, it dares us to change and grow and *anything* is possible!

Unfortunately, most women doubt their own fabulousness. Self-doubt is a bitch. Every media outlet screams daily that we are inadequate. That we are not enough. The measurements are in and apparently, most of us don't measure up.

How did we become a society that judges on looks alone? Are physical looks everlasting? Why can't we change this shallow measurement of each other?

Imagine if we were measured by acts of kindness by thoughtful actions instead. Or by the love we show to those dear to us, or to a stranger. Or by being brave in the face of change.

We would be forever beautiful! Growing the inner light that we all possess, produces more beauty in the world than any expensive face cream ever could. The best thing is — it doesn't cost a cent! Once we have rediscovered our inner light, we can grow it.

All it takes is kindness to ourselves and others. Then voila! Our inner glow can be seen on the outside, no matter what our age. This is a well-kept secret. If word got out to the masses that all we need to be the most beautiful version possible, is to grow your inner light... Imagine what would happen. But that is some of what I've learnt as a Vixen.

My phone chimes with a new message alert. It's from Marco... the only guy I've managed to reply to so far. I flop onto the bed and open his message. Apart from calling me 'Hun' (an unacceptable term of endearment to me) his message has a playful happy tone, so I decide to reply:

A: Hey Marco, how's your holiday going? How long are you here for?

M: I have another few days here Bella! We should meet up for a drink!

A: That might be fun yeah. When are you free? Tomorrow?

M: Ahhhh tomorrow I go to Lombok Island babe.

A: Hmm, that's a bit far from where I am to come and meet you then! Hahaha

M: I stay two days there Bella, but I come back. We go for drink then, sexy woman!

Damn. Two days before I can meet him. Now that I am back in Vixen mode, I really want to meet a man tomorrow. I need to send out messages to the remaining short-listed Marks and see if anyone's free to meet sooner than in forty-eight hours. Marco can be put on the backburner for now.

I make an excuse to the handsome Italian, promising a drink with him upon his return. Free to pursue other potentials, French man Gabriel is the first to catch my eye. Cropped brown hair frames a strong jaw. Broad shoulders and a cute friendly smile are enough to sway me.

He converses well and is funny and respectful. Traveling alone for a month, he has braved the traffic chaos here and hired a scooter. I'm impressed. With the traffic accidents for moped riders extremely high here, I'm not game to risk it.

We chat a bit longer, and he suggests we meet for a drink.

Tonight. Woah, I was thinking tomorrow, but there's no reason to put him off until then. I throw caution out the door and agree to meet him.

The only problem with meeting men while on holiday is that now I have to put effort into my appearance. My blonde hair is frizzing in waves and has forgotten its usual sleek smooth style without the straightening iron. My face is bare, and more freckles have appeared in the last few days.

It's such a chore to spend time on grooming when in holiday mode. A vacation shouldn't include blow drying my hair unless someone else is doing it for me. Now that's a great idea! The humidity here is not my friend, so leaving it to the professionals will be a welcome addition to my spa treatments this afternoon before my date tonight.

Successful Selection of a Mark

Vixens target men who are unsuitable for long-term relationships only. Henceforth men deemed suitable for vixen play are known as 'Marks'.

Essential Criteria for Mark Selection:

* Hot, sexy, and single
* Treats women well and with respect
* Playful nature and likes to have fun*
* naughty sense of humour
* High level of emotional intelligence*
* Quick-witted with a curious mind
* Interested in exploring fantasy play
* Out of your social circle
* Has at least two deal-breaking flaws

*Note: You may think emotional intelligence would not be needed - but men without this are too easy to access and will not be able to hold your attention or fully appreciate your vixenly ways.

CHAPTER 5

French Foray

The perspiration on my neck makes it difficult to keep my hair straight for tonight's date. For the first time this week, I have put some effort into my appearance. A light application of makeup and my hair done is enough though. At least I managed to find something sexier to wear than the same shorts and tank top I've been living in for days!

Since both Gabriel and I are not familiar with nearby bar names, we decide to meet at my hotel. From there we can cross the road to a tiny round open-air bar I spotted earlier. It takes

Fortunately, on holiday time I'm not a stickler for men being on time. Back home, more than ten minutes late without a text would be considered rude and disrespectful. Gabriel and his scooter far longer to get here than expected, even with a map. I am sprawled next to the pool reading my book, so it takes me thirty minutes to realise he is late!

In his defence, the traffic is so chaotic here that it is hard to arrive *anywhere* on time in Bali. Tucking my book away I wander out the front of the hotel to see if I can spot a cute Frenchman on a bike looking lost.

Twice in one minute, I am asked if I want a taxi. Waving them away, I see a man with a scooter who might be Gabriel. I approach him with a smile and say hello. He smiles in return and greets me. It takes less than a sentence to tell me this isn't Gabriel at all... no French accent. *Oops.* Wrong guy!

I excuse myself and turn away, glad the increasing darkness hides my flaming cheeks. I fan my face to cool down before the real Gabriel arrives. A few minutes later I see a second potential Gabriel cruise up on a bike. Please let this be him! He takes his helmet off, looks over at me and smiles.

"Arleia?"

"Hi there... Gabriel?"

I am still a bit cautious after the first case of mistaken identity.

"Oui! Yes... I am so sorry I run so late Arleia. It is hard to umm... find. No Wi-Fi on my bike!"

He leans in towards me for a hug in greeting and unexpectedly does the cheek kissing thing. No Australian man ever does that! I feel glad I have opened myself up to a new experience. I've never been on a date with a Frenchman before.

"That's ok, I understand. I was wondering if you would struggle to find the resort!"

"Mmm... I not speak English good. I better typing! Can you repeat this, please? More slow?"

I laugh and nod, repeating my words slowly. It's easy to forget how fast Australians talk. We also tend to use a lot of slang, so Aussies can sometimes be hard to understand.

"Ahh yes. Resort hard to find. No matter. I am here. You want we go to bar?"

"Yes. The small bar over there is good. Not too loud so we can hear and understand each other!"

His eyes follow my pointed finger to a small, round, thatched hut. The bar looks exactly as you'd imagine a tropical island beach bar. Bamboo poles, a gleaming wood-topped bar set in the centre with rows of colourful cocktail bottles on display. High wooden bar stools facing outward to view the water and passing foot traffic. Eighties music serenades us through invisible speakers, but not so loud that we can't hear each other.

We order a couple of drinks from the bar and find a seat nearby. He's nervous, I can tell. I would be too if I were about to have a conversation in anything but my native language. I learnt high school French for three years. You may think I could remember more than a few phrases, but now I realise that I can't!

The only French words that come to mind are basic things like: My name is Arleia. Or where is the toilet? I can name a few body parts and tell you that your hair looks beautiful, but those phrases are not going to be helpful in a regular conversation! I probably can't even count to ten in French.

Looking over at Gabriel, I give him an encouraging smile. Maybe I should start the conversation. *Slowly.* As I am about to speak the barman interrupts us with our drinks. Tonight is definitely a night for alcohol. In moderation, it can help loosen tongues and dispel nervousness. Gabriel's not the only one who's feeling slightly nervous!

It's been a long time since I went on a first date with someone new. Since I have fallen into the pattern of seeing Krystian, Roshan and Darz regularly I've become slack in finding new Marks.

I've forgotten that first dates can be scary. It is usually 'fear of the unknown', like what if I don't like them? Or if he doesn't like me? Fear of rejection is a strong motivator to avoid dating.

And if the attraction is mutual, then what? Do we make another date? Is a hug, cheek peck, or a passionate kiss on the lips to follow? What will he expect and what do I want to happen? The stress of the unknown is enough for anyone to consider cancelling a date and stay in their comfort zones!

Why are we afraid? What needs to occur for us to take a leap into the unknown? Confidence is a behaviour, so when we act that way for long enough, we become more confident.

What you think about, you bring about.

Talking of bringing things anywhere, I need to bring my attention back to this date! I slow my word speed down, smile, and turn on the charm.

"So, Gabriel, how much longer do you have in Bali on holiday?"

He tells me he's already been here for a couple of weeks and has twelve days to go. This is his third holiday alone in a foreign country since he split from his long-term girlfriend three years ago. His friends think he is crazy to travel alone, and they don't understand why he would want to do this.

"If I listen to my friends, I not challenge myself. I have no new experience. And I not meet such beautiful Australian woman like Arleia!"

We both laugh and any remaining tension dissolves. With Google translate on hand, it's far easier when he gets stuck for the right English words. This doesn't bother me in the slightest. I'd rather he understands what I say!

The hardest word for me to convey is jellyfish while talking about the ocean off the coast of North Queensland. Trying to explain marine stingers without pictures is hopeless!

By this time, we are almost falling off our seats in laughter. I pick up my drink and realise the glass is empty. A glance towards the bar is all it takes to have the attendant rush over to us.

"Yes ma'am? Can I get you some drink? You want same? Vodka with the coke? Mister, I get you something?"

We agree on two more of the same. Despite the language barrier he is doing surprisingly well at understanding me, and vice versa. But after two hours of conversing slowly, I'm exhausted.

The language barrier is something I will have to consider in my future hunts. No comprehensive English skills? No date! Regardless of how attractive he looks. Unless it's just sex and no talking that I'm after. *Then* I'd consider it!

Mwaaahaaahahahaaa!

Gabriel is a nice guy, but there is no spark between us. I've had enough conversation and laughter to last me another day or two, and I am now restless in my seat. I'm not interested in a goodnight kiss. Hopefully, he doesn't try planting one on me.

Gaging from his body language he feels the same way. He

enjoyed the evening and conversation, but there's no further attraction. What a relief! We wander across the road towards my hotel where his scooter is parked. I hope I read his non-interest correctly.

With a massive, stifled yawn from me, he gets the hint.

"It was so lovely to meet you Arleia! I had very much fun talking with you. Thank you for meeting me. *Tu es tres belle mademoiselle!* You are a very beautiful lady."

I amaze myself by understanding his French sentence thrown in. Maybe there are more French words lingering in my memory than I thought?

"Thank you, Gabriel! It was great to meet you too — I enjoyed meeting you too!"

He grins and comes closer. Please let it be for just a hug! Picking up my internal vibes, he gives me a big bear hug with kisses on each cheek. I happily return the hug, relieved that we are on the same page. Sliding his helmet over his shortly cropped hair he swings his leg over the bike and starts the motor.

With friendly waves amid wishes of a remaining great holiday, he putters off. A huge sigh of relief escapes me. I didn't realise how difficult it would be to hold a long conversation with someone whose English skills are limited.

Walking back towards the lobby, I pass a security guard.

"Hello, ma'am! You have good night?" he asks me with a smirk. I smile noncommittally as I hurry up the stairs and slip past the glowing pool sparkling with floating candles without speaking to anyone else. Once in the sanctuary of my room, I sprawl across the bed in relief.

I've done it! My first 'International Mark Hunt' was a success. Sure, I wasn't attracted to him physically and probably won't ever see him again. But who cares? The date was still much better than other disasters I've had in the past, and without help from the magical handbook.

If the opportunity arises to meet another hot French guy, I will take it. But only if he can speak English well enough. Or is so damn hot that I won't care. Their accents are so sexy!

I congratulate myself on a reasonable date without the guidance of the book. With its help, I may have made a better choice, but there are plenty more men on my list to explore tomorrow.

Optional Criteria Suggestions for Mark Selection:

* Broad minded and open to new things
* Meets your age requirement: 5 to 15 years younger, or 10 years older
* Different nationality
* Body and face which is attractive to you
* Possesses a cock worthy of your attention
* Meets the minimum height requirement determined by you
* Can converse easily in your language

CHAPTER 6

Steamy Skyping

After sleeping later than normal, it's busier than usual along the beach pathway. Usually the cooler, still morning air is only disturbed by a few other tourists exercising. Some walk, others jog. A few are on bicycles and others are surfing.

This morning however, merchants line the path. Assorted shells for sale on neatly lined blankets are laid out on the sand. Hand-made jewellery thrust before my face as I pass between offers of massage or hair braiding. My morning greeting to other walkers passing is lost. Instead, I am focused on avoiding eye contact with aggressive sellers or voicing that I have no money with me.

Undeterred, they press on. "You come back later Ma'am? I give you cheap price!"

There are only so many times you can say 'no thank you' in an hour! Perhaps a bicycle is the key. At least then I would be sailing past them faster than they could register. Tomorrow I will hire a bike and ride along the seafront path instead if I'm later than usual.

Relieved to get back to the peace of the hotel, I shower grab my phone, and head towards the restaurant. Too tired to look last night after my date, I also didn't check my messages this morning before my walk. Sitting at a leisurely late breakfast is the more attractive option to catch up on new men.

Balancing my plate piled high with tiny portions of everything new, I return to my table. A cool breeze whips up and snatches away serviettes before rustling through the leaves of lush gardens nearby.

I sigh happily. The immaculately green garden, bursting with brightly coloured tropical flowers, is so beautiful. I could stare at it all day. Workers trim the fast-growing plants here daily. Even the frangipani flowers drifting down from the trees are scooped up immediately.

I wonder how long it would take nature to reclaim the hotel grounds here if people suddenly vanished. The humidity and heat coupled with the abundant rainfall might mean a timeframe of only a few months! I draw my attention away from my surroundings and back to my messages.

Holy shit! I'm greeted by a total of twenty-five messages. Each one is from a different guy. Thank God I remember something from my handbook and am brilliant at whittling down my choices! Well, I hope I am. I've had enough practice in the past, but that was *with* the handbook's guidance.

Here goes. My first selection criteria for deleting messages is nationality. All the short Balinese men and Bali Bogan Aussies (a common term for loud beer-drinking, badly behaving men in Australia who take frequent trips to Bali) are on the chopping block. There may be some hunks who aren't in holiday 'Bali Bogan' mode, but I doubt it.

It takes an hour to whittle down my choices to a manageable quantity. Ok. Let's look at my final possibilities. Firstly, there's Raza, a twenty-eight-year-old Persian with black hair and a nice smile.

Next is thirty-three-year-old gorgeous Georgios, a Greek hunk with an infectious grin. I can tell by his sentence structure that he speaks English well. His messages are intelligent and funny. His interests in philosophy and yoga match mine. At least I would have a fun time with him. After last nights' slow conversation, I need to find men I can chat with easily!

Prez is the next possibility. At thirty-two he is of Indian and Spanish heritage. A shaved head, tanned skin, and a sparkling grin that might entice me to meet him. Wait a second. He lives in Australia! But he fits my criteria of an international man perfectly *except* for living on the Gold Coast.

Undecided, I chat to him longer. He doesn't appear to be like the usual drunk Aussie guy on holiday. Maybe I will make an exception to my rule. If I had the Vixens handbook here these decisions would be easier.

His humour and chattiness win me over, and we arrange to meet after dinner tonight. This is his first time here on holiday, so he's unfamiliar with the streets. Prez and his mates are staying in a villa complex on Poppies Lane, so that's easy to find.

His friends do sound like they belong in the Bali Bogan

drunk hall of fame though. None of them have surfaced yet from a night of partying and excessive drinking. In contrast, Prez is a great communicator, and we have some interests in common. Plus, he understands Aussie accents easily.

I think briefly about the Italian, Marco that I spoke to yesterday. He's touring around Lombok Island today. However, that hasn't stopped him from sending a few cheeky messages containing a strong sexual tone that I roll my eyes at. Yeah, whatever, mate! Nice that you want to lick me all over, but how about we meet first? I don't bother replying to his last message.

An alternative contender on my list is Amar, holidaying here from Malaysia. Another tanned guy with a shaved head — this is becoming a pattern! I wonder how tall he is. Malaysian men I've met before were not that tall. I guess he's in with a chance!

Amar tells me he is off sightseeing to visit Balinese temples today with his mates. But maybe we can meet up later? I'm not going to divulge to him that I've already got a date lined up for tonight. Anything is possible, so I just agree to 'see what happens later'.

Wow, having this many conversations online at once is exhausting! Chatting to the three men I'm already dating is easy. We know each other. We've spent time building our friendships. No more 'getting to know you' questions where I have to constantly repeat my answers.

Each one knows I'm on holiday and has been sending me at least a message or two a day. I appreciate their thoughtfulness - it makes me feel cared for. Just as I'm thinking of my regular boys back home, one of them, Roshan sends me a message.

Roshan: Hey sexy woman! What are you up to now?

Arleia: That's a great question! I can't decide if I want to go for a swim or another massage! Hahaha

Roshan: Aww, I'm so jealous. Lucky you! Shame I'm not there to give you that massage, sexy.

Arleia: Yeah, you will have to wait until I get back. You owe me one now mister cheeky!

Roshan: Mmm yes, I do. In fact, I'm just about to have a shower. Shall I video call you? Heh heh.

His suggestion ends with a devil face emoji. Hmm. Naked Roshan in the shower. Soaping up his delicious body... Or stroking his hands along his hard cock. Do I really have time to watch that? Hell yes! This could be a far more interesting sight than most of the options around me.

I send a triple smiley face emoji followed by an angel, and my phone immediately rings.

"Hey, babe."

A naked Roshan smiles up at me from the screen. I can see he's walking toward the bathroom, so his flatmates must be out.

"Hey sexy butt! Mmm, naked chat, I like it. It's almost like live porn!"

He laughs in reply as he turns on the shower taps, and steam begins filling the room. Propping up his phone in the corner on the shower's shelf leaves both his hands free. He picks up the soap and runs it lazily over his chest towards his penis. My eyes follow his hands down.

Roshan stroking his balls from underneath is mesmerizing to watch. Soap-suds bubble around his smooth hairless skin. His flaccid cock bounces left and right. He continues to massage his balls slowly, his dick stirring.

"Let me see your breasts, baby."

His request is fair. It's not like he hasn't seen them before in person. But this is different. Naughty. I smile and agree. Slipping my breasts free I cup the jiggling flesh and my rosebud nipples harden. He groans in approval and his cock jumps to full attention.

"God your breasts are beautiful!"

He smiles and slowly strokes himself. I can't look away. Roshan has the most beautiful dick that always makes me want to lick it! His hands move faster. Up and down. Rhythmically. His moans get louder.

"Oh, baby! I'm going to cum!"

Just as he grunts out the words his hard cock pulses. His eyes are closed. One hand still slowly stroking himself, while steam billows around the shower cubicle. One last guttural moan breaks the silence. Water streams down his body washing away the sticky residue.

Holy crap, that was hot! I squirm uncomfortably on the bed, wishing he were here in person to continue. Roshan laughs. Completely at ease with his naked body, he blows me a kiss.

"Gotta run babe! Can't wait for you to get back... I want the first date!"

Agreeing I return his air kiss as he disconnects. I know he would love me to say more than I do, but I can't. Sex talk feels awkward. Usually a talented communicator, I'm often struck mute in the bedroom.

Shocking I know. It's not like I don't get any practice! As much as I enjoy sex, I prefer the physical act rather than just talking about it. If the man turns me on with conversation first, then that's enough conversing for me.

If I'm using my precious concentration and energy for the act of sex, I concentrate on the feelings generated. My mind isn't in the 'let's have a chat' mode. My body is in feel-good mode and doesn't always need words.

Sure, there are times when my body forces me to say, "To the left!" Or "Press harder! Now softer!"

Or to the over-enthusiastic nipple biter: "Ouch! That hurt, you numbskull!"

One time a guy slapped my butt cheek so hard I promised to punch him in the face if he ever slapped me that hard again. He didn't get a return invitation. I know he was just over-enthusiastic, but it crossed the line from pleasure to pain. The previous enjoyment of his company disappeared after that incident.

How many women talk like porn stars in the bedroom? I don't know any women who do what the directors of porn expect. A hundred 'Oh my God's' punctuated by 'harder baby' and interspersed with 'Oh yeah, oh yeah... oh yeah!' is far from reality. Plus, it's unrealistically loud for suburbia.

Even if a woman *wants* to scream out: 'Yes, yes! Oh my God, yes!' she's probably stopped by the children in the next room. Or the nosy neighbours next door. Unbridled passion is not really something you want the world to hear! Some things are better kept private.

I can't believe the entire morning has gone. I book in for a relaxing massage, swim then shower before dinner. By then I'll be ready for my date with Prez!

CHAPTER 7

Try Again

During my two-hour massage this afternoon, I fell asleep. Normally that's not a bad thing, and I do feel refreshed after my snooze. But apparently, I snored. *Loudly.* According to the lovely masseuse I saw.

Surely a lot of people fall asleep halfway through a massage. Don't they? Not during the remedial sort where they poke fingers into sore spots, of course. You can't drift off with the pain of that! I've experienced the benefits of this type of massage when my muscles are tight or knotted and it's great. But I prefer relaxing massages on holiday.

The only time I have not enjoyed a massage here is when the masseuse rubs my chest. Yes, you heard right. A 'booby' massage! There is no warning, girls! One second, you're lying face up with a sarong over you, completely relaxed. The next minute... Hello, bare breasts!

Those girls whip the sarong from chin height to your waist

as if it's nothing unusual. Their hands then massage your boobs in a circular motion. The problem is that all relaxation vanishes the second they do this. Awkward! Why do some spas teach their masseuses to do this? Believe me, there are no muscles in that area that need massaging. None! (Except if a hot man is massaging my chest with my consent of course. Haha!)

All my girl friends who have experienced this phenomenon agree with me. Guys probably wouldn't complain, though!

A male friend once told me he was offered a 'happy ending'. It happened towards the finish of his massage. I was shocked! Of course, I had heard of this happening. But I thought that kind of offer only occurred in really seedy joints, and he had chosen a reputable spa.

Even he was surprised at the suggestion. But being a typical man, he didn't decline. He said she told him the extra fee – around ten Australian dollars. Agreeing, he relaxed back into the massage bed while she set to work. For a moment bartering with her popped into his mind, he told me, but he thought that might be rude.

I laughed so hard when he told me her tiny hands made his dick appear even bigger! He said it was all over in five minutes. Then had to point out to me he *was* already half-hard before she started. *Sure thing*! I knew he didn't want to give me the impression that he could only last five minutes.

A couple of trips ago, someone told me you could get a 'yoni' massage here in Bali. I was like... What the heck is a yoni?? Google to the rescue! I was stunned to find out that yoni was a term used for vagina.

A *pussy* massage! Do women really go to someone and *pay* for that service?! Is there a course the therapist has completed to be qualified to massage vaginas?

Incredulous that such a thing could exist, I did some further research. Apparently, it does! And there are Yoni masseuses here in Bali. My face screws up in distaste. I don't know how I'd feel going to a stranger to have my vagina massaged... and pay for the privilege! Usually, my chosen men do it for me for free.

Mwaahahahaaahahahaa!

I can't imagine feeling comfortable with that level of intimacy when I'm not into the dude. Us women don't spread our legs for just any old guy!

OK. There are exceptions to the rule. There's childbirth. That's a big one. Also, the Brazilian bikini wax. There's no dignity there, and having a beauty therapist smear wax around *those* lips is never going to be painless. Believe me.

It seems that everything women have professionally done down there is painful. Pap smears, gynaecology appointments, and waxing! None of these are pleasant. Maybe we *do* need a few sexy men to take up the calling to become Yoni masseuses! Not just in Bali — around the entire world.

A lot of men are clueless here. They think licking out a girl is a literal act. No. We don't want your tongue inside our vagina. What's this going to do for us? It's the clit you need to aim for... if you can find it. If a guy's not hitting the right spot, he may as well give up.

It's about as pleasurable as waiting in a queue. You hope for satisfaction eventually, but it can be a long boring wait with no guarantee. Sometimes the self-serve queue is more satisfying... And a damn sight faster!

Uh-oh! I'm getting horny thinking about this. Just as well I have a date with Prez soon. I'm optimistic about our date. He seems to be an interesting guy, as well as sexy. I need mental stimulation as well as the physical attraction to consider being intimate with a guy. It could be his lucky night! *Or mine.*

Night descends and my stomach is reminding me it needs food soon. Taxis are the fastest option to get where I'm going, but I choose to walk after a lazy day. All I did was chat online, swim, and doze during a massage, so it seems forever since my morning stroll.

Heading out of the hotel I make my way towards where Prez is staying. Fairy lights twinkle from the trees lining the street. I decline eager offers of dining from enthusiastic restaurant hosts pushing their menu in front of me, and sidestep other tourists meandering along the path.

Shopkeepers call out to every passer-by, attempting to lure them into each shop. I weave past prams, shoppers, and locals. The footpaths are uneven here, so I watch where I'm walking more carefully than in Sydney.

My stomach rumbles loudly in protest as I decline another invitation to shop. The Balinese shopkeeper hears it and dissolves into laughter. I can't help but laugh with him.

"Ohh, you hungry ma'am! You need food, not t-shirt! Come back later, hungry belly! You eat now!"

My face feels redder than normal as I hurried away. Any

other time no one would hear that. But nooooo. I pray he doesn't remember me on the way back.

I realise I'm close to where Prez is staying now. Examining a few menus as I wander past restaurants, I choose a tiny place that offers my favourite dish. The décor isn't fancy. Painted wooden tables are paired with a kaleidoscope of mismatched metal chairs. Intricate wooden carvings adorn the walls next to a miniature religious altar. Traditional fruit offerings and burning incense sticks perch at the top.

Choosing a table near the street, I check out the menu. The prices seem exceptionally cheap here. Converting currencies, I work out that my main course would cost less than a pie from a bakery back home.

Service is fast, and my spring rolls arrive first, steaming hot and filled with fresh vegetables. My stomach groans in delight as the first mouthfuls arrive. The faint grumpiness I feel due to lack of food dissipates.

Once I'm satisfied, I text him. Prez answers my message immediately. Yes, he's free to come and meet me now! Can I please take a photo of the restaurant where I am so he can find it easier? Phone out, I snap a shot and send it across.

My main course arrives. Mouth-watering, I inhale the smell of the noodles, vegetables, and chicken. The yolk of the egg on the top wobbles as I poke it with my fork. Perfectly cooked! I tuck into the food with gusto.

I want to be finished eating before Prez arrives. Imagine if an unknown dribble of yolk ran down my chin. Not exactly the type of first impression I'm hoping to make. Not with any man!

Relaxing into my chair, I survey the people passing while finishing my meal. A quick check of my face assures me I have nothing green stuck in my teeth, or egg on my face. What a relief. Lipstick refreshed, now I'm ready!

As I finish the thought, he appears. Shaved head, nice smile, and laughing eyes are my first impression. He's wearing cargo shorts and a tank top, so I check out his biceps next. He passes my Vixen tests in all areas thus far.

I stand to greet him and gesture for him to sit with me. Since the restaurant is quiet, the waitress rushes over. He orders us both a drink. We exchange mutual grins as she returns before we can start a conversation.

"It's so great to meet you Arleia! Thanks for sending me that photo – it made it easier to find you since I'm not great with directions here yet. How was your dinner?"

"Thanks for meeting me, Prez! Oh my God, the food here was delicious! My stomach is in heaven right now."

We fall into an easy conversation punctuated with lots of laughter. I had forgotten how much easier it is to chat with someone who speaks English well! Prez tells me of his holiday experiences filled with monkey attacks, Hindu temples, and partying hard.

Time flies by. Only when the waitress starts packing up the chairs around us, do we realise we've overstayed our welcome. Prez pays for both our drinks *and* my meal. Thanking the girl, we step onto the street.

"What shall we do now?"

Bars and clubs are of no interest to me. Music is played so loudly there that it will be impossible to carry on a conversation.

"Why don't we just go for a walk and see where we end up?" I suggested.

He agrees and we slowly wander past the late-night merchants who are still trading. After walking for about fifty minutes, we are almost at my hotel. I mention this to him, and he stops.

"Shall we go to your place for another drink, then?"

I consider his proposal. What does he expect? Does he mean just for a drink? Or more? For the first time here, I *really* miss the guidance of my Vixens Secret Handbook.

Mandatory Vixen Tests

This section outlines the tests you may set in your quest for hunting a suitable Mark. These examinations will help you to weed out the timewasters and enable you to choose the most appropriate Marks for vixens.

Quick Wit Test

While engaging in conversation, say something you think is witty, naughty, or humorous, then gauge how long he takes to come back with a sharp, funny reply.

Acceptable responses guide:

* Under five to ten seconds: Initial Pass
* Within ten to twenty seconds: Tentative Pass - retest
* Over thirty seconds: Undetermined result. Mark may be busy or distracted. Retest

Unacceptable responses:

Regardless of the time, if his reply is vulgar, inappropriate, not funny or witty, OR he did not understand your sense of humour - TEST FAILED!

FAIL= Delete from your contact list.

CHAPTER 8

The Kiss Test

There are hordes of staff everywhere in my resort. If I were to get in trouble, they are only a shout away. It's unfortunate that I must think that way, but self-preservation is a must. Without my Vixens' Secret Handbook, this is a harder decision to make. Oh, what the heck.

"Ok, sure! We can do that," I reply. "My hotel is only a couple of minutes further down this road. Are you going to be able to find your way back from here though? I don't want you to get lost!"

He laughed at my concern.

"Naah I'll be fine. At worst I'm sure a taxi can take me there – at least I know the address!"

I agree to his suggestion, then stop so abruptly that he bangs into me.

"What did you stop for, woman?"

"Well, you said you wanted to go to my hotel. This is it! I wasn't lying when I told you we were close!"

I gesture for him to follow me. We walk across the massive reception area and through tropical gardens to the pool.

"Wow, this place is amazing Arleia! Your resort is much nicer than the villa where we're staying. There are not many rooms here to share that huge pool either, that's gold!"

I remember him telling me there was a medium-sized communal pool at his villa complex. Servicing eight villas, with lots of family renters, meant the pool was always full of screaming kids. Since all his friends had hangovers each day, they weren't so keen to 'relax' by the pool.

I'm thankful I got lucky with this resort. Each day I've been around the massive pool it's been quiet. I doubt I've seen more than eight other people using it at once. A few times I had the entire pool to myself. It felt like my own private pool in paradise!

Swiping my card, we enter my room. I'm glad it's tidy. Prez flops down on my bed, relaxed. I pull my thoughts back to the present and offer him a drink. He'll have to agree to whatever I've got stashed in the minibar. There's not much choice. Duty-free vodka is it. I offer it straight, or with a mixer of coke or raspberry.

Setting our drinks carefully on the bedside table, I turn the TV onto a music channel and join Prez on the bed. He scoots over closer to me. My eyebrow rises in query, and I shoot him a measuring look.

Yes, he's cute. And our night thus far has been fun and interesting. Am I attracted to him? Yes. But do I want to take this any further? Indecision hovers in my mind. From his body language, I can see that kissing me is on his mind.

Oh, what the hell, hey! He's passed all my Vixen tests until now. No inappropriate endearments of 'Hun' or 'babe'. Emoticons are kept to a minimum when chatting online.

He is five foot eight; teetering on the deal-breaker side so that's perfect. His conversation is engaging, and I'm somewhat attracted to him. I might allow a trial kiss. Little does he know what goes on in my brain!

Mwaaahahaaahaaa! I laugh my Vixen chortle internally as I make my decision. Who needs the handbook anyway? I'm doing great by myself!

Our glasses clink together in a toast to our night so far. The vodka tastes extra strong in the small glass. The added courage of alcohol can be helpful in situations like this.

Although I've dated a lot of men in the past six months, I still get nervous. Not that you would notice. It's only a minor internal tremor. The more first dates I go on, the better I'm getting at beating my nerves.

My hand is enveloped by his, stopping my train of thought. His other hand strokes my thigh. I can tell what's coming next. We lock eyes. His head dips towards mine. I tilt my chin up to meet him. First a soft peck, then a meeting of lips. He gives me a longer peck.

I open my mouth, but he doesn't completely comply. Parted lips only half an inch wide is *not* the kiss I expected. His arm slides around my back to pull me closer. My breasts press against his chest. Our legs entwine. Fingers trace my lower lip before he cups my face. I'm drawn in.

His lips descend again. But he doesn't deepen the kiss. Another long kiss with barely parted lips. What the hell? My brain jumps out of fuzzy mode. What's this guy doing? No tongue? No movement? Hell no!

I'm thrust back to memories of a date a few months ago. I didn't listen to the Handbook, and it was a *disaster*! Please don't tell me I'm in the same situation again?

The last time I had an awful kiss I didn't speak up. Instead, I high tailed it away from the guy as fast as I could. Should I say something to Prez about his terrible kissing style ... or not?

I'm not the same woman I was six months ago. That girl was too polite to speak her mind. To say what she truly felt. She was worried about offending others with the truth. Not anymore!

Refusing to endure another kiss I push him back to arms-length away. He is surprised. Not aware of my thoughts, he comes in for another. My facial expression stops him.

"What?" asks the clueless Prez.

I sigh and get ready to deliver the bad news. He is strong enough to take it, I'm sure.

"Well, to be honest, that kiss was terrible. I was waiting for it to improve. But it didn't!"

His puzzled look tells me he thought his kissing technique was acceptable. I'm about to blow that misconception out of the water.

"Seriously, I don't mean to offend you! You're a great guy Prez! But your kissing technique needs some help."

I hold my breath and wait for his response. Emotions flicker across his face. Confusion, then comprehension. Acceptance, followed by a smile.

"Well, Miss Arleia! What advice would you give me then? I thought my kissing skills were fine!"

I'm relieved that he's taking this feedback well. His light-hearted response to my words tells me a lot about his character. He is open to change and improvement.

"Look, the best way to teach you is via a demonstration. If I agree to kiss you again, you have to follow my lead!"

I know he is intrigued. Doubt is still etched on his face, but he nods in agreement. He still honestly believes he's a good kisser! My smile is triumphant.

He sidles up closer to me. The air buzzes with anticipation. I lean in, kissing him slowly. Softly. First with my mouth closed. Then half-open. He follows my lead perfectly. My tongue darts into his mouth on the next kiss. Just the tip. It flicks over his lips, teasing. I encourage his tongue to meet mine. It does.

Moving my mouth slowly over his, my tongue delves deeper. He gathers me closer. Our lips press together harder, moving in unison. Both tongues venture further. Mouths open wider. Lips create a perfect seal for the private dance within.

He squeezes me tighter in approval while my fingers caress his face. The tip of my thumb traces his lower lip before I play-fully suck on it. A faint groan spirals up his throat. I start to pull back. He won't let me. I smile against his lips and retreat more forcefully.

"Now THAT was a kiss!"

Eyes glazed with a half-smile of wonder; his words make me laugh. I grin knowingly.

"You can't tell me that kiss was like the others! What do you think?"

His stunned look lingers.

"Holy shit, woman. Now I know what you mean. That kiss was awesome!"

"See! How much hotter was that!? Do you think you've been persuaded to the dark side?"

He shakes his head in disbelief. It's obvious he hasn't experienced an amazing kiss before. Women in his future will be forever grateful to me! I can see the glint of fire in his eyes. Before he makes a lunge across the bed at me, I spin around and bounce away.

"Aww! Where are you going, Miss?"

I laugh at his words, but the truth is, I'm tired. It's almost two in the morning now. My body needs sleep and Prez had his chance to bowl me over with charm and skill ... but he didn't! Apart from that, I've had enough togetherness for the evening. All I want is to kick him out and sprawl across my bed in an unconscious state. Alone.

I can tell he's hoping for more action. Not tonight, buddy! You don't possess a great kissing technique, so it's unlikely there are fantastic skills in other areas. It's like dancing. Anyone can learn to dance — but not everyone has a natural rhythm.

I *could* teach him other skills, but I can't be bothered. I prefer my men to have a natural rhythm when it comes to sex. Those that don't have it or haven't yet learnt it, I avoid. I'm past the age where teaching a new pup how to please a woman is fun!

My mouth opens wide, and I smother a yawn. Not so stifled that he misses the message that I'm tired. I stretch and sigh, just to drive home my point.

"Come back to bed, sexy!"

His attempt at convincing me to do so fails.

"I'm sorry Prez! It's been a long day. I'm almost dead on my feet now!"

He is crestfallen. He was hoping for a lot more than this tonight. Yes, it was an amazing kissing session, and he was a good student. Even those facts still can't entice me back to the bed. He can tell I'm serious and that his coercion isn't working. Resigned to the fact that I am not going to let him stay, he agrees.

"Yeah, I guess it's getting pretty late, hey. It's been a fun evening with you, Arleia. Thanks for the lesson too!"

He grins and winks at me broadly. I return the smile and walk towards the door. Taking the hint, he follows me.

"Damn, it's a shame you're heading home tomorrow afternoon! It would have been cool to see you again!" I manage to look regretful and yawn at the same time.

Smiling, he gathers me up for one last kiss. His new technique is perfect. I'm impressed and tell him so. With promises to catch up for a drink if I'm ever in Brisbane and vice versa, he heads towards the lobby.

The evening was lots of fun — but I still let out a huge sigh of relief once he's gone. What a night, I'm exhausted. And still horny. I strip naked and fall on the bed. Self-service is the answer tonight! In a matter of minutes, I am satisfied and asleep.

I drift straight to dreamland wondering who the next man is that I will meet, but I do wish I had my Handbook here!

Immediate Endearment Test

When a Mark addresses you in an overly familiar way before even meeting him, there is cause for concern. This shows a lack of respect and appreciation of you being a strong powerful woman. When he cannot be corrected in his endearment use, he will fail this test.

He is not worthy of a Vixen's attention.

Unacceptable terms of endearment:

- ✘ Honey/Hun
- ✘ Darling/Darl/Dear
- ✘ Baby/Babe
- ✘ Baby-cakes/doll/girl
- ✘ Hot chick
- ✘ Sexy tits
- ✘ Sweetie/Sweetie-pie/Sugar
- ✘ Cup-cake/Honeybun
- ✘ Pookie

Acceptable terms of endearment:

- ✔ Beautiful
- ✔ Sexy woman
- ✔ Temptress
- ✔ Vixen
- ✔ Gorgeous
- ✔ Additional acceptable descriptions:

- ✓ Sexy
- ✓ Enticing
- ✓ Delicious
- ✓ Desirable
- ✓ Mouth-watering
- ✓ Attractive
- ✓ Mysterious
- ✓ Tantalizing

When the potential Mark uses only approved endearments or descriptions acceptable to a Vixen in a respectful manner, proceed forward with the testing process... PASS.

If the prospective Mark uses the banned inappropriate endearments within the first ten lines of conversation in a familiar way you do not appreciate; and will not cease even after being given the basic acceptable guidelines of endearments... FAIL.

The result of sleazy endearments from strangers trying to get into your pants instead of getting to know you first, results in the immediate deletion and possible blocking of unsuitable Mark.

The Kiss Test

You have a Mark in mind who has progressed thus far through the Vixen testing process but be vigilant oh Vixen. Some start well, passing the first tests and conversing well enough to keep your attention. You may be lulled into thinking he is suitable to meet until the first kiss happens.

If it's a terrible kiss, you have two choices. Either pull out an exit strategy and escape — or teach him to kiss the way you like it! If you want to try option two, and he can follow your lead, then he may be worthy of a second meeting. If he can't follow your lead, switch to option one and end the date!

CHAPTER 9

Pink Elephant

Ah... another day in paradise! I stretch, open my eyes and giggle while reaching over for my phone to see who's messaged me. Woah! There's a lot of reading to be done here. Twelve new messages; sent from different men here in Bali. I'm not even including the five texts from home!

My three sexy regular guys have all made contact with me. Krystian has sent a suggestive photo of himself relaxing in his steaming outdoor spa entitled 'Wish you were here, Mistress Arleia'. Warmth towards him curls within.

Darz has sent a couple of casual, 'Hey sexy!" messages. But I know he's working away while I'm on holiday. With twelve-hour shifts at the mine, I rarely hear from him while he's there. Unless he's horny. Then he is great at sending me erotic suggestions on what we'll do on our next date. I love it!

As you know, Roshan has already instigated a naked video session. How many people have had a live erotic shower scene enacted before their eyes? I'm betting the general percentage is low.

Years ago, a friend of mine admitted to sexy video chats with her lover. At the time I was surprised because I hadn't considered this as an activity to engage in before. I was still within a long-term, monogamous relationship, and forgot that other people indulge in sex in person and video!

I focus my attention back on my contact list. Marco, the elusive Italian tops the list. He is back from Lombok Island. Finally! His next message deflates my bubble. His mates leave later today, so they all got smashed last night.

Typical boys! His last message was sent at three fifty-four am. There's no way this guy is up for a date today. I strike Marco off my list and continue. Maybe Reza is free tonight? We've chatted a bit. So far, he *seems* like an attractive guy whose English is comprehensive enough.

I've not dated a Persian guy before. He is young though at twenty-eight. What the hell. I'm on holiday. New experiences are valuable learning opportunities.

He's online now, so I say hello. An immediate response flashes back at me. We exchange holiday experiences so far then he asks me if I'm free later today. Hell yes! We arrange to meet at four o'clock.

A shiver of nervousness runs through me. No Vixen book. The two dates I've been on thus far have been ok. Only ok, not *fantastic*. I liked both guys. But the missing link is chemistry.

I console myself with breakfast. From sweetcorn soup to over-crispy bacon and poached eggs, I inhale the food. A chocolate croissant... then a banana pancake with vanilla ice cream and chocolate sauce. All complemented by fresh pineapple juice.

Now I wish I didn't miss my early morning walk today. I should have done that before chatting with those men! I need to remember to put *myself* first.

In need of walking off my feast, I stroll to the beach. Locals line the route in clusters touting their wares. From paintings to tattoos, sunglasses to the morning paper; everyone is here again vying for my attention and money.

How could I forget my bike ride today rather than walking? That's what happens when you are up too late with a date! I cross the walkway and head towards the glittering ocean.

My feet itch to sink into the warm sand. I slide my sandals off to paddle in the cool water. Surfers' heads bob between white-tipped waves. There are not many swimmers out yet. A few people walking and a couple of enthusiastic joggers are the only ones on the actual beach.

I love the beach, but I'd rather take a dip in the pool than the ocean here. It is so much more convenient with room service at hand, and the comfort of my room next door! Some days are so humid that I don't want to lie outside for long.

Right now, the sea breeze caresses my face. I draw in a deep breath. The smell of the salt lingers in my nostrils. The water is clear. The sand is pristine after its morning comb with a tractor which drags a large rake attachment behind it to remove sea debris and rubbish washed into the sea from various waterways.

If you weren't an early riser on holidays, you wouldn't know this happens. The authorities here want to keep tourists happy, and a trash-littered beach doesn't attract crowds!

Sweat is trickling down my back. The sun beats down higher in the sky as the cooler sea-breeze dies down. The heat tells me it's time to head back. I need a shower! Then a massage *and* pedicure. Perhaps a nap later before my date with Reza. Mwaaahaaahaahaa!

Four o'clock arrives in record time. Reza and I arranged to meet at a bar near the nightclub area in Legian. On the way, I walk past the memorial from the Bali bombings. A group of tourists mill around it.

A huge stone wall with names of the victims carved into it has a sombre feel amid the bustle of the streets. Some people stand in silence reading the victims' names. A few sit in the manicured garden surrounds in quiet contemplation. Others walk past oblivious to what they are passing.

Events like this lowers the earth's energy vibration. The memorial makes me imagine the difference in our world if more people were kind instead. One random act of kindness can have a ripple effect, as can a negative act. A simple smile from a stranger can make you feel happier and connected. So pick up that item that fell from the arthritic hands of a lady in front of you at the checkout. Or pay those few dollars short for the man desperately searching his pocket for more coins to pay for his groceries. Say hello to a stranger.

A simple act of kindness might change your life one day.

When I walk past this area there is a subdued feeling. I smile and greet an older couple sitting in the garden area who return my smile and wave which lifts my mood.

I spot our meeting place and enter. The humidity hanging in the still air makes me appreciate the oversized wooden fans above me. I arrive first. Great, I can choose the coolest place to sit and wait for him.

Right on the dot of four o'clock, Reza appears. Short dark hair, caramel skin, and white teeth flashing a smile; so far, it's a yes! He takes a moment to spot me, so I take in his baggy shorts, broad shoulders, and tank top. Do men wear anything else over here?

I wave in welcome as he weaves his way toward me. The bar is starting to fill up with cocktail hour here from four until six o'clock. He greets me enthusiastically with a hug and peck on the lips.

"Beautiful Arleia! How are you? I get you a drink. Yes?"

The compliment and wording he uses make me grin back. "I'm excellent thanks, Reza! A drink would be great, thank you!"

I've had enough time to read through the cocktail list and choose a White Russian. 'Sex on the Beach' cocktail is also a cocktail I want to sample, but I decide the name is too suggestive to ask for at this point. He might think I'm asking him a question, not ordering a drink. That would be awkward!

After a couple of cocktails and a reasonable conversation with Reza, I can feel the alcohol seeping through my veins. He's interesting and smart. Excellent English proficiency, although his sentences tell me it's not his first language. Reza's flirting and almost sitting on my lap, he's that close.

He leans in even closer. "I have eleven-inch cock baby. You like this?"

Glad of the alcohol buffer to absorb the shock, I mumble a positive reply. Who says that! And really, how many men own an eleven-inch penis? I've never seen one. He doesn't seem large enough to house such a big boy in his pants.

I admit I am intrigued. It's like the elusive white tiger, or should I say pink elephant? You've heard rumours of its existence. But you have never seen one for yourself! Does he really have such a beast hidden in his bushes?

The image of a white tiger leaping from his pants makes me giggle. A pink elephant trunk peeking out makes me snigger even more. But Reza thinks I'm laughing at something he said. Perhaps I'll chance a trial kiss first. Find out if it's worth going hunting in the jungle today. I order another drink. This time 'Sex on the Beach' slips out.

His return with our drinks is slow. The bar is by now hidden from view by patrons three deep taking advantage of the happy hour prices. I people-watch while waiting and notice how many attractive men there are. Yum! Note to self: Come back to this bar at happy hour again ... *alone!*

Three sips into my cocktail he kisses me. His overly wet lips press softly on mine. Then open wide like a fish. I can feel his saliva dribbling into my mouth, and desperately wish he would swallow.

Fleshy soft lips line an empty cave. A dormant tongue lies within. I try to break the kiss. He presses harder and draws me closer. Ugh! Will this kiss *never* end?!

I pull away from him more forcefully. Slobber lines my lips in a two-inch radius. I can barely disguise the disgust on my face. I have to do it. Grabbing a napkin, I swipe across my lips nose and chin to wipe off the dribble. Eww! My skin crawls as I grab my drink to wash his taste away.

That was revolting. Vixen exit strategy needed! There's no way I care about what animal he's hiding in his pants now. I can't endure another of those kisses. That was far worse than Prez's first inadequate attempt. Meanwhile, I'm almost vomiting and Reza's rubbing my thigh in triumph — he thinks he's onto a winner. Not with me buddy, that's for sure!

Trying for distance I suggest we go dance. The music's louder now, and the bar's atmosphere has revved up to club status as the sun sinks in the sky. He agrees and we head for the dance floor. I can't help myself. Pretending to watch my feet, I'm really staring at his crotch.

Surely his jungle bulge would be obvious when dancing. Hmm. There's something there. But eleven inches? I doubt it. It's possible he's a grower. But his tiger can stay hidden forever!

He dances closer, rubbing his crotch against my pelvis. Nope. If he truly owned eleven inches, I'd feel more than a twig. There may be something substantial there. But his slobbery kiss has put me off him completely.

"Hey baby, we can go private dance in my hotel room. What you think, mmm?"

Thankful I had already mentally planned my extraction from this slobbery disaster, I lay out my escape route.

"Ohhhh, I can't tonight Reza! I've booked a tour of the Sanur night markets with a friend. In fact, we are meeting at seven o'clock. Holy crap, it's after six-thirty now! I'm going to have to get my skates on or I will miss the bus from my hotel."

It takes a few seconds for my words to register. His face shows displeasure, then resignation. He gives it one last try.

"Baby! You will miss to see my eleven inches! Is much better than market... you no want to dance together?"

With false regret plastered across my face, I mostly evade one last short sloppy kiss before running for the street. Oh. My. *God*. A shudder of distaste runs through my body as I hail the first taxi in sight and slide in. My hotel is within walking distance, but I don't want to risk having him follow me.

I sink back into the air-conditioned comfort the taxi offers, as it whisks me back to the resort. Dammit! For the thousandth time, I wish I'd bought my Vixens Secret Handbook with me.

The book would have glowed red cautioning me. I wouldn't even have bothered to meet him then. Instead, I'd have deleted his chat and moved straight to the next possible Mark.

Dating without the help of my book is becoming peppered with average dates, terrible kisses, disappointment, or disaster dates!

Prearranged Exit Strategies

This is incredibly important, Vixens. The first meeting should ideally be able to be terminated within the first hour if it is not going well, but always in a polite and respectful manner.

Of course, you will not need to use your pre-arranged strategy at all, should you be having a fantastic time with your Mark! But for those times you need an escape it's an invaluable thing to put in place.

You never know when you will find yourself thinking "Holy crap, I've got to get away from this loser!" To leave the failing date without looking rude, make sure you have one of the following suggestions ready to go, so it doesn't seem like a lie to escape his vile company and save your precious time for something else more worthwhile.

* I need to babysit my niece/friend's child earlier than first expected
* I need to return to work for a meeting / to fix an unexpected problem
* My mother/Aunt/Granny just messaged me … I need to pick her up from the hospital earlier than I thought
* My friend's car broke down so I must go rescue her
* I must go bridesmaid dress shopping early as my friend's being a bridezilla
* I have another event to attend right now

Immediate extraction ideas (deployed in extreme cases of horror, revulsion, or boredom):

* Send a signal to a friend to call with an emergency that you need to leave immediately to help her
* Use kids (your own, relatives or a friend's
* child) as an excuse - vomiting, broken arm, out of control allergic reactions are perfect reasons to hightail your butt out of your date
* You suffer from sudden migraines and the coffee/alcohol/ icy water you drank must have brought one on, so you can't continue with the date

CHAPTER 10

Short Changed

After the slobbery date with Reza, I'm not so sure that I'm game to try another date here. I thought my 'dating international men' idea was inspired. But now I'm not feeling so confident. After all, it's not the man's nationality that counts. It's their individual personalities, communication skills, and general skill levels — especially their kissing skills!

I'm drawn from my musings by the taxi suddenly stopping. I get out but don't feel like going back to my room yet so walk a few hundred metres past my resort. A small gaily lit bar beckons from across the street. What the hell. I may as well add a cocktail or two to the ones already zinging around in my system.

Ordering a cosmopolitan, I find a cushioned wooden bar stool to perch on with my drink. I check my messages. There are three from Marco, the Italian. One message is from Amar, a Malaysian guy, and two from 'George the Greek'.

I can see Amar is online now. I'm not usually as attracted to

Asian men as to Caucasians, but Amar looks handsome in his pictures. I'll risk a conversation online and see where it leads me.

Arleia: Hi Amar! How's your day been?

Amar: Hello beautiful! It's been great thanks, how's yours?

Arleia: Excellent! I've been to the beach, had a massage, and lazed by the pool. What have you been up to?

Amar: My friends and I went to do some sightseeing here today. I have been to Bali before, but it's the first time for my friends here.

Hmm, he seems normal. I won't get my hopes up, though. Two normal messages don't always mean the conversation will go well. But it's a start.

Arleia: How many mates are you over here with?

Amar: There's me and three of my friends here. What about you? Who are you holidaying with?

Arleia: I've been to Bali several times with friends but this time I'm traveling alone.

Why do I feel like I need to explain? It's not like I don't have any friends. Maybe I still feel conspicuous. I guess most people do holiday with others, rather than alone.

Amar: Wow good on you for holidaying alone! Want to meet up later for a drink?

I wonder how much later he means since it's now seven-thirty. Unsure of whether I want to commit to drinks with him or not, I stall.

Arleia: Mmm, that might work... Depends on how tall you are! Haha.

Amar: Oh really... well I'm five-foot-five missy.

Arleia: Hmm that would make me taller than you by an inch!

I attach a couple of laughing face emojis to soften the blow. An inch taller is stretching my boundaries, but an inch shorter than me is shorter than I can cope with.

Arleia: True! So, what did you and your mates go to see today?

Luckily, he can't see my lip curled in distaste at his early assumption of bedding me. It really puts me off when a guy is too suggestive at the start of his first conversation with me. He may think it's a joke, but when I'm undecided about meeting a guy, it can tip the scales against them.

Amar: We did a few things... went to see a couple of temples. Tanah Lot temple was cool.

Arleia: Oh nice! I haven't been there yet... maybe I should check it out! What else did you do?

Amar: Well, after the temples we went to an orgy.

Wait. What?!! *An ORGY?* What the hell? I can't believe this dude has been at an orgy today. Who does that? Maybe it's more popular than I realise. My brain throws a million questions at me.

Where did the orgy take place? How many people took part? How do you organise this kind of gathering? What if the women or men there had a venereal infection? Were the women locals or tourists? Did the guys pay to go there? Does being naked in front of his friends not bother him?

These and more questions swirl around in my head. My questions are motivated by personal curiosity. Orgies are not something I'm eager to participate in.

As vixenly as I can be, I don't want to combine my men into

one big naked gathering and throw in a few other women for good measure. No. Not my scene.

I do know parties like these are held regularly around Sydney. Often by invite only. Single women and couples are welcome, but single men are often banned. There's a fee at the door, and everything is extremely discreet.

A girlfriend of a friend frequents these parties. She is well known and liked by the regular party guests. With a high sex drive, she's incredibly popular. It's not unusual for her to enjoy eight men in one night, and a couple of women too. Each to their own, I say!

I don't care that Amar indulged today, but I'm not interested now. Imagining crabs or worse nesting in his pubes is a major turn-off. There's no way I want to meet him now. But I do want some answers to the questions floating in my mind.

I find out that he was the one who organised the orgy. There were eight people there – four guys and four girls. They met in a villa hired for the occasion. The women were all local Balinese girls, and no, Amar did not have a problem being naked with his mates.

Before he invites me to the next one, I have to speak up. Letting him down gently I explain that orgies aren't for me at this point in time. Maybe never! I wish him a fantastic holiday and life and press the delete button.

I sigh loudly. My glass is empty, and I have wasted forty minutes chatting to someone I don't want to meet. Glancing around me, I realise the bar is a lot fuller than when I arrived. Should

I risk chatting to one of the hot guys here rather than hunting online?

Approaching a man in a bar isn't something I do often. If I find them attractive, a weird shyness attacks me and holds me prisoner. Approaching a hot guy is almost impossible without alcohol. However, if I'm not attracted to a man, it's easy to talk to him. I don't know why I behave like this. It's something I need to work on and grow my courage.

This is why men need to approach women. We like a go-getter! Confidence and bravery are attractive qualities. Women appreciate the courage displayed by approaching a stranger, risking possible rejection.

Sometimes it's easier to break the ice online, rather than in person. I may need another drink to gain courage. Glancing around the bar I survey the talent at hand. There are a couple of cuties, but I don't feel confident enough yet.

Another Cosmopolitan waits in my hand while I down a B-52 shot. Warmth spreads through my body instantly. That's more like it! Sipping on my other drink, I consider my options.

Two attractive men lean into each other near the bar perched on wooden bar stools. Is their friendliness alcohol-related, or are they gay? A cluster of loud Australian Bogans is to my far left. They gain instant dismissal from the possibility list in my head. Next to the Aussie boys, a gaggle of young girls twitter excitedly.

Three couples are dotted between the Bogans and girl-band at black-topped tables. A couple of local men sit near the bar's entrance. Four cute guys lounge in a relaxed manner to my right.

They are my best possibilities so far. Their table is not far away from me, so I strain to hear their conversation.

It's their accents I'm trying to catch. None of the men look or sound Australian, and they are certainly not locals. The noise from other patrons lowers long enough for me to pick up French then Eastern European accents.

I wonder if they are friends on holiday. And whether any of them are single? From where I'm sitting, each man appears attractive... I may be spoilt for choice! An oversized gulp of my drink results in a minor coughing fit. It's loud enough to draw the men's attention to me. *Shit.* Not quite what I had planned. I try to regain my composure.

Oh, God. One of them is getting up. Walking toward me! My heart beats faster in nervous anticipation. I'm praying that when I wiped the tears from coughing away, that I didn't ruin my makeup.

Maybe he's going to the bar. Nope. He skirts another table and makes a beeline for me. Do I look at him? Smile? Pretend I didn't see him there? Too late! Looking down I see muscular legs encased in jeans next to my thigh. I take a deep breath and glance upwards.

A handsome, smiling face greets my eyes. He introduces himself as Jakub and invites me to join them.

"A pretty lady like you... no drink alone! Join us for a holiday drink!"

Smiling, I agree. I'm relieved he's friendly and that I can understand his English. He takes my hand and scoops up my glass, leading me towards the other men.

Deep in conversation, they break it to turn towards me in greeting as Jakub procures another chair. Welcoming me warmly, they introduce themselves. Antoni and Jan are brothers from Poland, traveling together around Asia for six months.

Jakub is a friend of theirs who has joined the brothers for two weeks in Bali. I turn to greet the last guy at the table, Filipe. My heart skips a beat. Blood roars in my ears, I can't hear what he's saying to me. I ask him to repeat it.

"What is your name, princess?"

His sexy French accent caresses my skin. Hazel eyes twinkle and speak a secret language to me. An appreciative half-smile on his full lips, rough stubble on his face. Dark cropped hair with a muscled medium build. I am almost too stunned to reply. Our chemistry is instant.

"Oh! Uh, my name is Arleia. It's great to meet you, Filipe!"

"The pleasure is all mine, Princess. Can I buy you a drink? Maybe a different cocktail than before since it didn't agree with you?"

His veiled reference to my coughing fit makes my cheeks flame. Damn. I agree and ask him to surprise me. I'd do anything to have him away from me for a moment so I can snap out of Lala land. What's wrong with me? Yes, he is hot. So are the other three guys. But my eyes are drawn to him.

I chat with the other guys while Filipe heads to the bar. Antoni and Jan have four more months of their Asian adventure to look forward to, and excitedly share the highlights of their trip so far. Jakub wishes he could extend his time to join them in their travels. But I'm only half-listening, waiting for Filipe to return.

The hair on the back of my neck rises as I feel his approach. I turn my head to see if I'm right. We lock eyes as he slides into his seat next to me. Filipe places our drinks on the table without breaking eye contact. Blood rushes to my head and I take a deep breath, needing oxygen.

I can't remember the last time I felt such an instant connection. It's like everyone in the bar has faded from view. There are only the two of us. I swear his eyes are saying that he wants to devour every inch of me. *Completely weird.* I feel as though we are having a conversation with our eyes.

I shake my head as if to escape his mesmerising eyes and focus on my drink. The conversation flows easily around me, and I join the laughter when appropriate. Trying to regain my inner composure, I glance across at Filipe again.

His intense expression as he stares in my direction unnerves me. It's like he's looking inside me, to my soul. A faint, mysterious smile hovers around his lips as he studies me, and I wonder what he is thinking. Shifting uncomfortably in my chair, I rub at the sudden goose bumps on my arms and try to re-join the conversation.

Two girls nearby are eyeing off the smiling siblings. I silently will them to intervene and whisk the brothers and Jakub away. Just leave me the Frenchman. The boys are not too drunk to notice that something is happening between Filipe and me. They turn their attention to the girls vying for their attention.

Filipe moves closer to me, his thigh touching mine. I swallow nervously. Verbally he says nothing. But his eyes are speaking volumes. They say he wants me. *Now*. I can't look away. He has mesmerised me, and I'm falling deep into the abyss of his eyes.

I try to tip the world back in place.

"How long are you here for, Filipe?"

"Ahh, my Princess. I leave Bali tomorrow afternoon. Too soon — now I find you. I want to eat you, ma Cherie!"

I knew it! His eyes already said he wants to devour every inch of me. But he's leaving tomorrow? Shit. I finally find a sexy international man that I want to explore — and he's leaving. Goddammit! Disappointment courses through my veins.

"Are you heading back home to France then?"

"No, princess. I only stop here for holiday with my friends on the way to my new adventure. Next, I will go to Australia to work one year."

Australia? One year? My heart pounds in excitement. *Please* let it be New South Wales he's heading to. Knowing my recent luck, it will be the opposite side of the country!

"Do you have work already lined up in Australia, Filipe?"

"Yes! I work on a strawberry farm in Queensland first. Then I go to the boss's other farm to work near Sydney after this."

Near Sydney. We may meet again in Australia then. Stranger things have happened! Desire dances through my veins at the thought. He tells me he will be in Queensland for two months, before moving on to a farm in Leppington Valley. The valley is only just over an hour from my place on a good traffic day.

I tell him how close he will be to me and laugh at the coincidence.

"Princess is no coincidence in life. I come to Australia to meet you. We meet in Bali first. I like this!"

His words send a shiver through me. I also know there is no coincidence in life. Everything happens for a reason. Often the purpose is not clear at first. But spend some time pondering and the reason will emerge.

"It would be awesome to meet up with you in Australia too!"

I inhale to continue, but his mouth halts the words in my throat. His lips are firm, coaxing... Tantalizing to me. The tip of his tongue flicks over mine. Dancing, drawing me further in. His hand cups my neck, pulling me closer as we deepen the kiss.

Lost in our private world, all else fades into oblivion. Damn *this* man can kiss. Hallelujah! His lips exert the perfect pressure. Soft but not wet like Reza's. I sigh into the kiss. He gently catches my bottom lip with his teeth. Sucking for a moment, then draws me closer.

It feels like I'm being devoured by him. And I love it. For the first time, my body is in control, not my mind. God, I want all of him! I want his entire body, not just kisses. My mind stumbles over how this can happen.

I have no idea what is happening with the other patrons in the bar. He consumes me. I can't think of anything else with his lips on mine. My body aches to be naked, pressed against him. Woah! Danger alert! He hasn't passed all the requirements of the Vixens' handbook yet.

But right now, I don't care.

CHAPTER 11

French Fire

What to do? Filipe ends our kiss by nuzzling into my neck, then biting towards the back of my neck, sweeping my hair aside. Holy crap. I thought the kiss was amazing, but his teeth are grazing the exact spot on my neck that makes me throw caution to the wind. Tilting my head to the side, I allow him better access.

He sends shivers down my spine. It's not often I feel those. I feel like I'm a helpless damsel from two hundred years ago, offering her neck to a vampire. His rough stubbled cheek scratches my neck. Soft lips kissing, then another sharp bite. I sigh into it.

A growl erupts from his throat like an animal of prey. My body responds and I lean closer. The inconvenience of location and clothes vaguely annoys me. He pulls back and I feel empty.

"Princess finish your drink. We take this somewhere more private."

It was a statement, not a question. His complete expectation that there would be no disagreement is a turn-on. I love a he-man type display of confidence from a sexy man. Usually, I'm the outspoken opinionated one. But with this display of skill and rugged charm from Filipe, I feel more submissive. And I like it.

He glances around the bar to see where his friends are. Still engrossed in conversation with the same girls, they are busy. None of them will miss our presence.

"Wait here, Princess."

He slides off the chair and heads in their direction. I watch him, mesmerised. How many drinks have I had now? This is ridiculous! My body misses his closeness already. I silently will him to hurry back to me.

Jakub and the brothers look over at me all grinning, to call out their goodbyes. I wave back and call back across the room with a smile. They all know what's happening. It's of no concern to me. I see Filipe weaving his way back and I instantly forget about them.

The expression on his face has my heart skipping a beat. Intense concentration and focus. On me. His smooth movements appear more panther-like, his intent: to have me. Like a hunter approaches his prey. Walking with stealthy control, unsmiling. Silent.

I know everyone else in the bar has faded from view for him too. Only the two of us exist. Background noise swirls around us, unrecognised and unheard. My energy tingles in anticipation, jumping around. Wanting to escape my body and join his.

Filipe holds his hand out. I look up and place mine in his. The electricity between us crackles.

"Princess. Come now."

He draws me to my feet and leads me from the bar. A quick almost wordless discussion of whose place we were going to takes place. My resort is across the road. There is no question of whether anything will happen or not. The attraction is too great to resist.

We step into my room. The door has hardly shut behind us before I am in his arms. His mouth crushes mine. His arms gather me close and imprison me like steel bars. But I do not want to escape. My inner goddess is singing in delight. My tongue eagerly meets his to join the dance.

Brains are switched off. No words verbalised. Only our bodies are talking now, and what a conversation it is! His groin is pressed against my pelvis. My heart beats faster. His hardness grinds a sensual rhythm against me. Answering wetness trickles down my thigh.

Our clothes are an unwanted barrier. I wish they'd magically disappear. Sliding my hands underneath Filipe's shirt, I caress his muscled torso before pulling him even closer. He grunts in agreement, freeing a breast from the imprisonment of my bra.

Tearing his mouth from mine, he latches onto my breast. Suckling, and gently biting the hardened nipple. My head falls back in surrender. Shit that feels amazing. When a guy plays with my nipples it doesn't usually turn me on. But this time with Filipe it's different.

My top and bra mysteriously vanish, as does his t-shirt. His mouth recaptures mine in a crushing kiss. Our bare chests press together. One hand is cupping my face. The other encircles my waist in a possessive manner. I run my fingers through his hair as our tongues dance together erotically.

I'm almost impatient to be horizontal. To have his whole body pressed against mine, and feel him within me. I'm so aroused I can't think straight. I hope I am having the same effect on him. The hardness pressed against my belly says yes.

He guides me towards my bed without breaking our kiss, then tears his mouth away momentarily to slide my skirt down, along with my underwear. I gasp as his naked body presses the length of mine.

Filipe gently pushes me back onto the bed. He holds my hands above my head with one hand. The other hand explores my body. His mouth delights mine with another arousing kiss. My hips rise involuntarily, towards him.

The wandering hand has discovered my secret garden. It strokes across my thigh and slides deep into me. A gasp escapes me. He growls approvingly and rubs his thumb across my clit. Desire increases as he rhythmically strokes me back and forth. Not pressing too hard. The right pressure to drive me wild.

Holy shit, this Frenchman is amazing! It's not often that a guy can get this right the first time. They press too lightly, or in the wrong spot. Some move their fingers too quickly. Others press ridiculously hard and fast like they are trying to scrub an unwelcome stain off their thigh.

Not Filipe. His fingers are working magic. Slowly and sensually, he strokes at the perfect speed with just enough pressure to make me sigh delightedly. I can feel the crescendo building fast within me.

His fingers press against the perfect spot inside, eliciting a moan that's lost in his throat. Our tongues entwine fully, dancing faster. Mouths crushed together. Tongues and fingers blur the separation of our bodies.

His thumb caresses the swollen area while his fingers work their enchantment from within. I can't think. Only feel delirious pleasure. With a sudden rush of moisture, he takes me over the edge. I cry out against his mouth.

"Princess."

He caresses my thigh gently, instinctively knowing I'm too sensitive to be touched intimately for a minute. I'm vaguely aware of him kissing my neck, but my body is still convulsing with the aftershock of orgasm. A deep growl of approval erupts from his throat.

"Frenchy... Wow."

It's all I can come up with since my brain is so foggy. I'm having trouble articulating anything right now, and we are only at the start of exploring each other. He surprises me by sliding down my body to kiss the wet junction at the top of my thighs.

"Mmm, you are so wet, Princess. I love this!"

Had I not consumed so many cocktails tonight I might have been embarrassed at his words. Instead, I give him a saucy smile.

"Come back up here, Frenchy!"

I want to see his hardness. Pressed against me it felt sizable. But I haven't even seen or touched it properly yet! He slides his body suggestively back up along mine until his lips are close enough to plant a kiss. He flicks his tongue across my lips. I can taste the sweetness of myself in his mouth.

Reaching down I encircle him with my fingers and start stroking. I push him onto his back and prop myself up on an elbow. Now I can see him better. He's totally delicious all over; including his cock. So erect that the outer veins are ridged and pulsing beneath my fingers.

Leaning over, I lick the drop of moisture from its tip. This time it's him that groans. I trace my tongue upwards toward his nipples, capturing one in my teeth. Latching on, I suck on it gently while he allows my hands to explore his body.

My hair and breasts brush across his chest as I nuzzle my lips to his neck. My teeth graze lightly across his soft skin. Finding the sweet spot that I know drives men crazy, I bite down. He groans in desire. I smile against his neck and run my teeth across the area before biting him there again. He smells divine.

With a muffled growl he pulls me away and flips me onto my back. Staring intensely down at me, he takes care of protection and enters slowly. I can feel every inch of him filling me. Buried deep, he pauses. The pulsing within me feels amazing.

I can sense the control he's exerting. Our raged breaths mingle into a deep kiss. As he starts moving his hips in a slow circular motion against my pelvis, my hips join the erotic dance. He breaks our kiss to draw back and lock eyes, then plunges back in even deeper.

Our rhythm increases. Each time he drives deep he presses the exact place that arouses me the most. I can't think. I only concentrate on the immense pleasure we are creating. It's like I've lost my mind.

He withdraws and flips me over onto my knees. He teases

me. I frown in frustration, wanting him inside me. Now! My small moan of annoyance is cut short by him sliding his hard cock into me.

I gasp in pleasure. It feels like he's going to come through my stomach. I throw my head back in blind desire. Filipe gathers my hair in one hand. Wrapping it around his fingers he pulls hard as he drives into me again and again.

Wetness courses down my thighs. He slaps my arse hard with his free hand and I moan and buck against him. Guttural grunts tell me he's close to the edge. So am I. He slows for a minute trying to prolong the inevitable a little longer.

I don't want that. I want fast and hard right now. I'm teetering on the edge and want us to both topple over. *Right now*. I press back harder against him. He understands and pumps harder. Deeper... faster.

We are both panting. Sweat drips off my nose and trickles into my eyes. I feel the wave coming. It sweeps us both up into it, crashing around us. Our thighs quiver. His cock pulses deep within. A full-body shudder runs through me.

Collapsing together on the bed, our breathing is still ragged. Wiping sweat from my eyes; I blindly feel for his body next to mine. It's slick with sweat too. I feel like I've run a marathon. But far better!

The dryness in my throat forces me to roll off the bed in search of water. Getting him a glass too, I drip the cold water across his back as he lies spent. He jerks up in surprise. Seeing the glass in my hand, he gratefully accepts and downs it in a few gulps.

"Princess... You are wild, wild woman. I like this very much!"

I desperately need rehydration. Only after downing two glasses of water, can I reply.

"Mmm, Frenchy, you are like the hunter who devours his prey!"

Laughter erupts from his mouth. "When I saw you that's exactly what I wanted to do, Princess. Eat you!"

I knew it! I was sure I read that in his eyes at the bar, and I was right. At least I get *some* things right with men. Maybe not on this holiday so far, but with Filipe it felt so right. Damn. He could be dangerous for me.

"Come back to bed, Princess."

I didn't need to be asked twice. Frenchy leaves here tomorrow. Typical! I finally come across an awesome guy, but he'll be gone far too soon for my liking. I haven't had my fill of Filipe yet.

Entering his embrace, I entwine my body with his. I may only have tonight with this sexy Frenchman. There's no question. I will make the most of every second he's with me tonight.

The Natural Smell Test

Upon meeting your Mark for the first time, you need to conduct the Vixen smell test. We are all either attracted or repelled by each other's natural scent.

Why waste time with a guy if you are not attracted to the smell of his body, and cringe while holding your breath whenever he raises an armpit? If he is so drenched with his favourite cologne that hugging him makes your eyes water and you can taste the fumes on your tongue, you wonder what kind of odour he is trying to cover up!

This test involves hugging your Mark hello on purpose, ensuring your nose is well positioned into his neck to enable you to inhale a large dose of him to make an assessment. This is best done at the beginning, in case you gag at his stench and need to employ an immediate emergency exit strategy.

When enveloped in his hug, how does the smell of your date affect you?

Do you want to: A. Nuzzle your nose further into his neck or chest inhaling his scent more deeply, feeling like you want to eat him then and there because you can't get enough of how good his scent is to you?

Or do you want to: B. Vomit or hold your breath then run from the nostril-burning stench of stale sweat, strong spices, garlic, or the overpowering stench of cheap cologne?

Smell? What smell? C. Did you even notice your Marks' scent? If not, check again. Ensure you inhale deep enough each time as this is an important test. Should you still come up with nothing, you may be suffering from a cold or blocked nose and an impaired sense of smell.

If your answer is A: He has aced this test. There is nothing better than inhaling the aroma of a man you find delicious! PASS

If you answered B: Run now, Vixens! Put your escape plan into action and leave post-haste. His natural scent won't change so don't waste your time. Employ the sudden migraine or friend in trouble emergency action plan before you even order a drink, leave as fast as possible without being rude.

If your answer is C: You are either unwell or not paying enough attention. Shame on you, Vixen! Retest and determine whether he has potential or not.

CHAPTER 12

Recovery Day

Filipe left my room somewhere around six-thirty this morning. I think I only had a thirty-minute nap between our sex sessions. Last night now tops my list of most orgasms experienced in one night.

Hallelujah! Finally, I choose a man who could knock my socks off; a nice change from wanting to escape within an hour of meeting. I lie in bed drowsily daydreaming of Filipe. My muscles are so stiff this morning; I'm sore in places I'd forgotten existed!

I felt like an acrobat after all the positions I was in last night. Filipe was in control in the bedroom, which turned me on even more. I liked him telling me which way to turn, or how he placed my legs where he wanted. No hesitation. He was dominant and sexy as hell.

I roll over and groan. Oh god. It's lucky he isn't here any longer. I don't think I can have sex again for at least a week now! My body feels bruised and tender, but totally satisfied. The fantasies about last night are going to keep me going for weeks.

Glancing at the clock, I realise it's now past ten in the morning. My tummy churns uncomfortably.

I can hardly move, let alone get dressed. For the first time, I'm going to miss the buffet breakfast here. But I don't care. My upset stomach insists avoidance of food is advisable after so many cocktails last night.

Dozing until midday helps. After another couple of glasses of water and extra sleep, I feel more human. Filipe hung the 'Do not disturb' sign on the doorknob of my room when he left, so I could be undisturbed by the housekeepers.

Flicking through the television channels I come across an animated children's movie. If I'm going to laze in bed most of the day recovering, something light-hearted sounds perfect.

Before long, I'm hooked. It's after one o'clock now, and my stomach's rumbling in protest. I need something substantial. A grin spreads across my face. *Room service!*

Stretching across the bed, I reach for the menu. The pages are full of tempting local dishes, so I order an entrée and a main.

I couldn't resist Nasi Goreng with a side of satay chicken skewers with extra peanut sauce. Not that I need any more protein after last night! Mwaaahahahaaahahaa!

The vixen laugh escapes me, as my mind returns to Filipe. Thank God we were coherent enough to swap phone numbers before he left.

A knock on the door announcing the arrival of my feast.

Naked, I roll out of bed as fast as my aching body allows me to, and throw a beach dress on before opening the door.

A smiling waiter greets me and enters my room, setting the tray down on the edge of the bed. As soon as he leaves, I pounce on the tray. Lifting the lid, steam swirls out and the tantalising smell curls around me. Heaven! I bounce back on the bed, setting up my pillows as a back rest and table with the tray nestled on top. Now I'm set. I release the pause button for the movie and tuck in.

This is what I love about holidays — the decadence. There's no way this would ever happen at home. Even if I ordered a takeaway during the day it's not the same. I wouldn't be ordering from my bed; delivery would take way longer and my choices far more limited.

Speaking of choices, I realise I've had no thoughts of any other man but Filipe today. My phone flashes with ignored message alerts. The only ones I want to read are from him.

My hot Frenchman did send a couple of messages while packing. He's at the airport right now, so we text chat until he boards. I discover he will be in Queensland for nine weeks. This is too long to wait to see him again.

A weekend trip up the coast to see him would be feasible. I know he enjoyed last night as much as I did, and the chemistry is strong. But I still needed verbal confirmation in the harsh light of day that he feels the same when sober.

My stomach finally full, I sigh contentedly. Amazing sex, an entertaining movie, and now mouth-watering food. I can't think of anything except a two-hour-long massage to top off this indulgent day.

Since I'm being lazy, and my muscles are incredibly sore and tight, I reach for the phone. Like magic, my appointment is booked for thirty minutes from now. Boy, do I need a shower first though!

Three hours later I'm feeling less stiff and sore. The masseuse worked her magic, and my muscles feel relaxed. Lazing next to the pool is still all I can manage right now though. After scanning the same page of my book five times, I give up. The humidity has risen and the heat of the day shimmers around me.

Sweat trickling down my forehead forces a decision. I dive into the sparkling pool. No cold shock to the body here. Only delicious coolness caressing my sweaty limbs.

Floating on my back with my eyes shut, I block out the noise of the resort. Only the eerie underwater sounds penetrate my ears. It's almost like you are plunged into an alien world. Sounds are distorted, softer. The gurgling water surrounds my weightless body.

Every thought fades away; I am suspended in time. Absent from the world I inhabit. So relaxed, my limbs are as floppy as a ragdoll. Almost asleep, I drift enjoying the peacefulness of the water.

There's only a couple of days left of my holiday now, and I want to enjoy this pool before returning to reality. A vague feeling of guilt rises within. I realise I haven't answered any of my other texts yet today. I've been lazing about, daydreaming of Filipe. *All day*!

It's not that my regular men expect me to reply immediately while I'm on holiday. They don't. That's not what concerns me. The fact that I've spent all day mooning over one guy is not like me. I don't like it. Not one bit. I didn't even check for deal-breaking flaws!

I need to refocus on other guys. Earlier I was thinking that I'd not bother chatting to any other guys while I'm here. But I know I need to. Or memories of Filipe and I in bed will dominate the rest of my holiday.

A distraction is what I need. Maybe Deanna is free to meet for sunset drinks? I send her a message with my suggestion. She replies within a few minutes, and relief courses through me. I need to get my mind off this Frenchman!

Playful Vixen Essential - Deal Breaking Flaws

Each Mark *must* possess a Deal-Breaking Flaw. In play mode, a vixen does not want to accidentally fall for a Mark. To prevent this, a Vixen should choose a man who has at least two major flaws or reasons why you could not see yourself with him long-term.

Deal breakers are different values or beliefs that can break up relationships — and are different for everyone. What is perfectly acceptable to one woman is a hard *NO* for another. Be clear on what your deal breakers are, to avoid choosing the wrong men to meet.

Possible Deal Breaking Flaws (Two per Mark)

* Doesn't like children - Or is desperate for them.
* Smokes or does drugs - And you don>t.
* Likes music you hate - Like Country or heavy metal.
* Lives too far away - Or an area you'd never live.
* Family values - Can differ from yours for casual Marks.
* Excessively vain - Is longer in the bathroom than you.
* Obsessed with money - Attention is on money, not you.
* Cheap - You'd rather have a generous guy long-term
* Unemployed - To be relationship-worthy, must have a job.
* Snorer - Perfect if you don't spend the night, but not great in relationships.
* Untrustworthy - No trust equals no relationship.
* Poor grammar - A turn-off for all grammar Nazis.
* Lack of ambition - With no goals, there's no relationship.
* Excessive body hair - A tangly situation!
* Too short - Some women aren't attracted to shorter men.

Some deal breakers are not acceptable in ANY mode. Identify these traits early on and delete any Mark that shows signs of these traits.

'Delete Him' Deal Breakers:

* Hooked on their ex - We don't want to hear about your ex.
* Keeps you waiting - Doesn't value your time as precious.
* Lies - Once a liar, always a liar.
* Negative chatter - Vixens only want positive vibes.
* Bad breath - Proper dental hygiene is a must.
* Bad kisser - Often not known until the Vixen Kiss test.
* Lack of etiquette - No to dating cavemen.
* Suffering from low self-esteem. No thanks!
* Selfish - It's not all about you!
* Addicted - A waste of a Vixen's precious time.
* Broken - Men who need fixing are not a Vixens target.
* Boring texter -One-word answers equal deletion.
* Rude - Possible sign of underlying issues such as a bad temper.
* Toxic - Toxic people are not part of the Vixen world.
* Gross manners. If I see food while you are eating—adios!
* Talks too much (or too little). Conversation should flow.
* Poor hygiene - Proper grooming is essential.
* No car - We are not your free taxi.
* Know-it-all. No further explanation needed.
* Lack of humour - A vixen wants fun and laughter.
* Won't take "no" for an answer - No means no, dude.
* Anger issues - Hot tempers are a major turn-off.
* Unreliable - Wastes a Vixen's time by cancelling at the last minute.

CHAPTER 13

Double Disappointment

The sunset tonight streaks purples and pinks through the clouds across the whole sky. Deanna and I are lounging on massive beanbags, our toes dug into the sand. Two empty glasses are whisked away by the beach bar staff and replaced with full ones. We toast to our holiday, the sunset, and the beach before taking another sip.

"It doesn't get much better than this, hey Arleia! If only holidays could last forever!"

I laugh my agreement while pondering the thought. On holiday forever: can I imagine that concept? Would I eventually get bored and beg to go back to work? I doubt it. At this point, it's only a fantasy. I'm unlikely to find a multi-millionaire to marry, sadly.

My attention is drawn back to the present by the slurping noise of my straw against an empty glass.

"You're right Deanna. I'm not sure I *could* get sick of drinks on the beach at sunset... or indulgent massages in a luxury resort!"

We laugh together and gesture the cute local waiter over to order another round. Deanna fills me in on her fledgling business progress, I tell her about the jewellery makers I've met, and we share our holiday adventures.

Since Deanna's visited this island a ridiculous number of times, she's friends with several locals and ex-pats who live here full time. This makes it easy for her to travel alone, but not be lonely on holiday.

We chat comfortably until a sudden attack of the yawns makes me realise how tired I am. Operating on minimal sleep, my body is staging a protest. This is the first wave.

Deanna tries to convince me to join her at a nearby club, but I can't. I decline, regretful that I can't join her, but also elated within to get more sleep.

Tonight, I will be alone in bed. Hmm, probably for the best as my stiff muscles keep telling me! The resort isn't far from the casual beach bar, so I say farewell to Deanna and walk back. Back in my room, I'm in bed within five minutes.

Aaaah! My body thanks me, relaxing into the soft mattress. My eyes want to close immediately but I also want to see if I've had another message from Filipe yet. Nope. Nothing yet! I check the time and convert it from local to Queensland's time in my head.

I laugh to myself as I realise his plane hasn't even landed in Brisbane yet. It won't be far off, but I can't stay awake in hope of a possible message from him. His mesmerising eyes are the last vision I see before dropping into unconsciousness.

This morning I've awoken enough to miss seeing the hawkers along the beach path. Only two more days here. Gazing at the clear, smooth ocean I realise just how fast time has flown since I arrived.

I smile and twirl around, the sun warming my face as the breeze lifts my hair. It feels amazing to be alive! My fabulous mood couldn't have anything to do with the three messages from the French hottie I woke up to this morning ... could it?

Giving my head a shake, I focus on today. I can't spend the rest of my holiday mooning over a man thousands of kilometres away. When I get back to my room, I'm going to put some serious effort into meeting Marco, the Italian hunk... or Georgios the Greek god.

My three men at home are so much easier though. Can I be bothered? Dates with all my guys are comfortable and fun. It takes a lot more energy to meet new Marks.

On returning to my room, I check my phone, to see messages from Roshan, Darz, and Krystian. They must be missing me! There's nothing more from Frenchy yet though. It's still early, so I answer some messages before heading to the restaurant.

With time running out here, I can afford to be picky. Any guys with no personality are deleted. Poor English skills earn another automatic delete. Nice as Gabriel, my first French date was, our conversation didn't flow well.

Halfway through my chocolate croissant, Marco and

Georgios appear online. What a coincidence. I don't believe in coincidences, so I wonder what the message for me is.

I chat with both guys while finishing my breakfast. Marco's focus is on how sexy and cute I am. Boring! Georgios is regaling me with the touristy day trips he's been on while here. Neither is capturing my attention. A far cry from Frenchy.

Marco tries to coerce me into skyping with him by sending a picture of him in his underwear. Why video chat online? Why not just meet up for a drink? I'd much prefer a date in person. The more I chat to him, the more I wonder if he's even in Bali.

Yes, he said he was visiting Lombok Island and was busy with mates. But now I doubt every word he's uttered. Damn, I wish I had brought my Vixen book here. I'd know in an instant if he is full of bullshit and wasting my time.

I insist on meeting. He stalls and tries calling me on video chat. I'm not answering his call. If he really wants to meet me, he can see me in person. Marco attempts more sexual coercion but I'm unimpressed. The longer we talk, the more I become convinced that he's full of crap.

I set an ultimatum. Meet me this afternoon — or never. He spouts weak excuses, and my intuition tells me I'm right. He's lying. He's not even in Bali right now. Was he ever? I seriously doubt it.

I sneak another look at his profile. Now his location shows he is in Perth, Western Australia. Frowning in annoyance, I shoot off a harsh last message berating him for lying and wasting my time. He has the decency to apologise, but I doubt he means it.

I can't be bothered replying and hit the delete button instead. Another one bites the dust!

Georgios, the Greek, had better not be as disappointing as the Italian. His conversation is still holding my attention. He's funny, intelligent, and witty. Philosophy is an interest of his, and I find myself warming to our conversation, and to him.

He sends me a holiday snap of him visiting the Monkey Forest in Ubud today. At least this guy is in Bali... I think. Unless he's using a photo from a previous holiday in Bali! Oh my god, it's so hard to know whether these men are telling the truth — about anything!

We talk about meeting but he's hesitant to commit. The friends he's traveling with might have plans. Can he let me know later today? I agree. But I have a sneaking suspicion that something is not right. I can't put my finger on what's not right. It's just a gut feeling.

I spend my morning next to the pool. The mild thirty-one degrees brings super humidity today, and sweat's running through my scalp and between my breasts. A quick refreshing swim does help, but I need air conditioning now.

A facial, massage, and pedicure later at my favourite spa, and I'm in heaven. The girls here are well trained and professional. The spa is not the cheapest, but I'm pampered with superior service in a lush, comfortable setting.

Even before starting, a cold moist towel is offered to cool you. A free welcome drink is served at the comfortable couch in the open-air waiting room. Smartly uniformed girls with friendly faces beam greetings. Your feet are bathed, scrubbed, and moisturised before your massage starts.

It's the little details that make the difference. Here, fresh petals artistically arranged float in a copper bowl below the face cut-outs of each massage bed.

This is exactly what I needed after the disappointment of Marco. Feeling relaxed I head to the beach to watch the sunset before dinner. Georgios is chatting to me online while I sit with my toes buried in the sand. Something he says pricks my curiosity. What was that? I joke back in response, something about being married. He doesn't laugh back.

Georgios: Shit, I can't believe you picked that Arleia.

Umm... Hey? Picked what? I seriously have no idea what he means, but I pretend that I do.

Arleia: I'm a slippery one... Especially after that oily massage I just had!

Georgios: You're taking it well. I'm surprised.

Shit. What *is* he talking about? I reread our conversation, looking for clues. Wait. He's not talking about the married quip, is he? Does he mean that *he's* married? I play along a bit, but right now I'm confused.

Arleia: Well, nothing I can do about it.

Georgios: You're the coolest chick ever! I thought for sure when you found out that I'm married you would freak out at me.

AHA! I was right — the sneaky Greek has a wife. I frown in disappointment. A vixen has no time for married men. Dammit! I allowed another guy to waste my time today.

Looking harder at the situation, I reflect inwards. I'm pissed off. But I'm more annoyed with myself than with him. I forgot it's all about learning lessons and gaining clarity on what I want, and I realise that I'm not the expert dater I thought I was — without dating advice from the Handbook. Having to admit this annoys me.

That's it. I'm giving up on meeting any other men on this holiday. No one else would beat Filipe anyway. I've lost interest in Georgios. I need a cocktail or caffeine.

Something that can give me a kick up the arse for being so cocky thinking I was so great at finding suitable dates alone. I won't bother responding to the Greek charlatan. I delete him and turn my phone off.

Sighing, I head back to the resort and the comfort of my room. I'm in no mood to socialise. A movie while eating chocolates between handfuls of chips and a vodka mixer is the best 'pick me up' now. I'm going to concentrate on shopping and pampering myself for the last of my holiday. These international men can go to hell.

Flopping onto the bed with my snacks, I notice a show flashing frothy wedding dresses across the screen. I switch the channel immediately. I'm done with men, weddings, and poufy marshmallow dresses. A comedy adventure is more my scene at the moment. It's a closer reflection on my life recently.

CHAPTER 14

The Purple Glow

The plane lands at last. My neck is sore from sleeping in the wrong position and I'm crabby at having to return home. I line up with hundreds waiting to go through customs, willing the queue to magically reduce in front of me. Yawning, I gather my bags from the baggage carousel and head to the taxi stand outside. A cold wind forces a shiver through my body. Leaving Sydney airport in thin cotton pants and a tank-top that was perfectly suitable in Bali was a silly choice of outfit to arrive home in. My teeth chatter as I leave my suitcase to the taxi driver and slide into the back seat wrapping a thin jacket around me.

Now I remember why I prefer to miss some of our winter. After only two weeks in the sun, I've forgotten how chilly the wind can be at home. Fighting another yawn, I give the driver directions. The flight home was an all-nighter. I caught a few hours' sleep; but not enough.

I use the time in the cab to message each of my men. Krystian responds immediately. We have a conversation via text that results in us setting a spa date for tomorrow night. He'd better have his outdoor heater cranked up and ready or I'll be too cold to get out. I've missed his spa. Oh, and Krystian.

Mwaaahahahaaaa!

Darz is still away for work, but we have set a tentative date for next weekend. I'll have almost forgotten about my holiday by then. No. I won't think negatively! I have a couple of days left of holidays plus the weekend before I'm back to work. As if I could forget my holiday after Filipe anyway.

After dropping my bags at the door, I collapse across my bed with my warm fluffy robe thrown over the top of my summery clothes. My body aches for sleep. Another glass of water, then I will snuggle under the covers with my electric blanket on high. It's a stark contrast to the light sheet I had over me in Bali.

I must have zonked out faster than I realised. One second, I was thinking how warm I was. The next second the afternoon sun is fading. My stomach growls so I call for Asian home delivery from the cosiness of my bed, pretending I'm still in Bali.

This forces me to get up immediately to shower and dress warmly before the doorbell chimes. My mind wanders back to my holiday as I eat. Wait. The book! Mid-chew I jump up from the couch and run to my bedroom, heedless of the noodles splashing sauce on my chin. There it is! It's been safely tucked away in my bottom drawer. Carefully protected, wrapped in a velvet cloth.

I bring it out to flick through while eating. A purplish colour flickers around the books' edge. What is that? I know the book glows golden if a Mark is approved. It also flashes red in warning if there's a disaster date looming.

But purple? That's never happened before. I try to recall the words of the mysterious gypsy who *insisted* I was the books' rightful owner. I thought she was crazy, but now I know she's not.

Since I started following the guidance of this book, I've had some amazing dates. That's how I ended up with three casual boyfriends who are all ok with me dating other men!

There are not many women brave enough to be completely honest and open when dating multiple people. Nor brave men. The idea of dating several men goes against the traditional view of society. If you are a man and you date multiple women, you are hailed as a hero among peers — as having achieved the greatness all men strive for, becoming a bachelor legend.

Society is not so accepting of women who openly date several men, however. And it sucks that people judge women with negative labels and feel falsely superior about it.

It is past time that these antiquated thought patterns are squashed. As long as all parties are open, honest and the dating or sex proposal and protection is acceptable to both people, what's the harm?

Another flicker of purple catches my eye. A response to the question of what the purple glow means is answered by my intuition. *Change.* Is that right? What did the gypsy tell me a purple glow means? I need to figure this out! Impatiently, I finish my food and dash to wash my sticky hands first. I don't want to get saucy fingerprints all over the pages!

Finally! I leaf through the book slowly. What, if anything, is different? I read the first section, Successful Selection of a Mark. The first 'S' has a purple tinge so maybe something's changed here.

Essential Criteria for Mark Selection:

* Hot, sexy, and single
* Treats women well and with respect
* Playful nature with a naughty sense of
* humour
* High level of emotional intelligence
* Quick-witted with a curious mind
* Interested in exploring fantasy play
* Outside of your social circle
* Willingness to be ensnared
* Likes to have fun
* Skilled at communicating in your native language

There it is! The difference I've been looking for. I've read this book often enough to know it well. That last point about communicating in my native language — *did not exist before my holiday in Bali.*

I swear. I've never seen that sentence before.

A chill runs down my spine. My mind conjures up the image of the dark-haired gypsy stranger. I should have listened closer. The undeniable truth sits here in front of me. The book has changed. By itself! When did this extra point appear? Can the book know what I'm doing as I do it — even when I'm thousands of kilometres away from it?

I scoff at the thought. It probably has a hidden micro-chip thing somewhere inside. LED lights? A new thought occurs.

Does the handbook update information via Bluetooth through my Fitbit watch or something?

Magic is hard to believe in. So are miracles. Yet they happen every day. Whether we acknowledge them, or not! Our inner light accepts this truth, but our human minds fight against the unbelievable.

My mind is struggling to believe my eyes as I flick through further. More 'purple glow residue' catches my attention. This time it's in the Vixen's testing section. I scroll down the page.

I pass the quick wit, acronym, and endearment tests. A mood quiz, emoticon, and smell test. The six regular tests are the same. I count them to make certain. Wait a minute. I must be still tired. There are now *seven* tests! Number '2G' was not on this page before I went to Bali! But there it is. Plain as day on the page in front of me! I rub my eyes in disbelief.

I read the new words over again. 'Matching words and actions test'. What had happened to prompt the book to add this for me? It only takes a second to figure out who this new rule connects to. Marco!

His words and actions definitely didn't match. He *wasn't* in Bali although he insisted that he was and wouldn't meet me. I was almost one hundred percent sure that he was full of shit before. Now I *know* he is a liar. Why else would the book have added this Vixen test to 'suggest meeting as quickly as possible'?

I read on.

'Record the guys' excuses. If the potential Mark keeps coming up with reasons he can't meet; it's three strikes and you're out. Assume he's not genuine. This type of man is a 'time-wasting ghost.' He loses the opportunity to meet you.

Delete and block!

Wow. Well, that describes Marco to a tee. He *was* a time-wasting ghost! Just out of reach. You know he exists because you've interacted... but it seems impossible to meet him in person.

He did send me a personalised video to say hi, so I've had proof of his existence. Marco looked the same as his pictures in the video, so I didn't question whether his photos were fakes or not.

The problem was his ability to have me believe he was in Bali too. He's researched Bali enough to know about tourist day trips, nearby island names and gained local knowledge via the internet: or he's been there before.

But he certainly wasn't in Bali when I was. Without the book, I couldn't have been sure though. His lie was well thought out. I have no idea why anyone would do that though.

Men are wired so differently to women! I'm relieved I didn't waste any more time on him. If I'd had my handbook with me, I would have had no time for him. Oh well... you live and learn. I'm going to have to take the book everywhere from now on. And take its dating advice more seriously in the future.

CHAPTER 15

Spa Date

Krystian busts through his front door before I can get out of the car. Wearing a huge grin, he opens my car door and almost drags me out into his huge bear hug.

"Miss Arleia! So good to see you! How was Bali? Was it fun? Did you meet any men there? Tell me everything! Come in, come in!!"

Overwhelmed by the questions being fired at me, I'm unable to respond. Not because I'm struck dumb or anything. He still has my face crushed against his chest, so I actually can't speak! I pull away and gasp for air.

"It was great thanks... but let me get in the door first and catch my breath after you squeezed all the air out of me!"

He laughs with me and ushers me inside. He offers me a variety of drinks, food, or even drugs... anything I want. Krystian's sensual kisses, eagerness to please, and ability to make me feel welcome and important to him is why I like him so much.

I settle for a glass of champagne and tell him to bring the chips outside. He'd better have that heater fired up! Krystian doesn't disappoint. A cosy glow of warmth greets me. Steam rises from the bubbling spa, inviting me in. Blinds border two sides of the spa, creating privacy and cutting out the cold wind.

The leafy garden bordering his patio displays new plants and creates a jungle feel. He has been busy since I've been away. Perched on the edge of the outdoor lounge, I admire his handiwork.

"Your garden is looking amazing Krystian! These extra pots and waterfall give it a tropical feel. If I sit closer to the heater, I can pretend I'm in Bali again!"

He laughs, delighted that I noticed. It must have taken a lot of hard physical work to get this much done since I saw him last month. We chat about the garden, then talk turns to my holiday adventures.

I'm completely honest with Krystian. He is non-judgemental and open-minded with a similar sense of humour to me. I start to regale him with tales of my holiday dating efforts, but he stops me in laughter after I tell him about my date with Gabriel.

"I love your stories woman! Why don't you jump in the spa, while I will refill our drinks? You can relax in the water. I'll be back to hear more!"

Agreeing, I slip my woollen jacket and clothes off. A black, lacy camisole and matching pants are today's 'spa wear'. I slide into the spa as fast as I can.

There are a few reasons for this course of action. Firstly, it's damn cold outside. I need the warmth of the water caressing my skin, not the cold wind! I sink in deeper. Welcome heat infuses my body.

I'm also feeling a tad self-conscious. The daily feasting on irresistible buffet breakfasts has taken its toll. I almost died when the scales this morning told me I'm three kilograms heavier than before my holiday. Shit. Those sneaky buggers creep up on you!

I'd rather hide the extra holiday tummy roll from Krystian. Until I work it off again. Maybe I should push those chips further away from me. I know he wouldn't notice or care. But I do. It affects my confidence if I'm feeling bloated or heavier than usual.

He returns from the kitchen with fresh drinks and refills the chip bowl. Oh well. Tomorrow, my diet starts! Smiling my thanks, I sip the champagne. The cold bubbles rising up my nose are a stark contrast to the warm bubbles that surround me.

Krystian reappears holding two massive beach towels and places them within reach. I am impressed. With a splash, he joins me. Reaching across me for his drink, he's distracted by my breasts bouncing in the bubbling water. I'm glad it's my breasts that have his attention, not my stomach.

We clink our glasses together in a toast, and he directs the conversation back to my holiday. By the time I finish telling him about all my disappointing online dating efforts, he's in tears of laughter.

"You should have taken the orgy guy up on his date offer, Arleia! It might have been an eye-opening date. He'd have invited all his mates too for a gangbang!" He teased.

I smack him in the arm.

"Stop it! He would not! Plus, he was too short for me. You know how I hate a guy to be shorter than me!

"As he said, height doesn't matter when you're horizontal! Plus, you may have liked a few Malaysian guys giving you their undivided attention!"

Laughing, I punch him in the arm again for teasing me. But internally I consider the thought.

What would it be like to be with several guys at once? My brain can't produce the answer. I don't know. How would I feel with multiple hands-on my body? With mouths kissing me everywhere simultaneously, while different appendages vie for my attention?

Would that experience be arousing or degrading? Fun, or plain awkward? Do you all do a group hug and high-five each other at the end? How do you practice safe sex with so many distractions?

What location would be safe, comfortable, and neutral enough for this to take place? How would that experience be for each guy? Do they get off on watching their friends with a girl, or do they just like watching other naked men?

My head spins with unanswered questions. I ask Krystian if he's had any experiences with multiple partners. He replies by nodding and laughing. Pressing further, I demand examples.

To my surprise, he's indulged a few times. Not in orgies, only a few threesomes and the occasional foursome. He tells me about himself and two girlfriends in the spa a few months ago. I'm impressed he's able to do this. It could have turned ugly if the girls got into a cat fight over him!

As much as he is entertained by my stories, the same goes for me with his. I'm fascinated by the outlandish sex tales he shares with me. There are more crazy women out there than I expected!

We share a lot of raw honesty between us, and that's what grows our friendship. Neither of us is afraid to speak our minds. We never judge each other. No masks are needed; we don't need to play any roles other than the sexual ones we decide on.

It's rare to find another human that will be completely honest with you. But Krystian and I have a strong bond of friendship that will outlast our sexual attraction. I'm just as happy talking to him as having sex with him.

Occasionally we have shared nothing more than great conversation and a few kisses and hugs. But still, we both enjoy each other's company immensely. On most dates, however, we do fool around.

Tonight, I want to tell him about Filipe. Not wanting to make him sound too amazing (lest Krystian's male pride be dented) I relay our meeting in the bar. The hunters' eyes wanted to devour me. My decision to take him to my room, and the amazing sex that lasted all night.

He's intrigued. Krystian's never seen me this excited about any guy.

"Have you heard from him since? Are you going to see him again? Where does he live? Has he been to Australia? Ohh, I'm excited for you Miss Arleia!"

The enthusiastic bombardment of questions makes me laugh.

"Yes, I've heard from him. He's moved to Australia for a

year-long working holiday. He's in Queensland now for a couple of months, then moving to New South Wales.

And before you ask; working on a strawberry farm, then he's moving here to work on another farm. So yes, I might see him again!"

He teases me about the Frenchman, but I don't care. His words hit the target. I want to see this guy again. I hope Filipe feels the same way. He's sent me a couple of messages, but he has started straight into twelve-hour workdays, which is taking some getting used to.

I don't think he's lying. The thought of returning to work on Monday is depressing me, and I only work eight hours! But the experience with Marco has left me doubting my internal truth-o-meter.

Although it's embarrassing, I tell Krystian about Marco too. How the Italian duped me into thinking he was in Bali too and kept pressuring me to video chat in a sexual way. Loser!

Krystian asks for his profile name, telling me he knows a lot of people in Europe... and Italy. Men who could find this idiot! Make him sorry for his lowlife actions.

I laugh at Krystian's macho response. So protective! I appreciate his caring soul, indignant that I could have been hurt. I reassure him there's no need. Plus, I already deleted him. There's no point in stirring the pot. It's a waste of energy.

Talking about Filipe has aroused me. The alcohol, spa, and Krystian swirl together. He leans forward and pulls me closer to straddle him, kissing me. I can feel his hardness pressing against the crotch of my pants. An answering throb of desire flows through me.

Mouths locked; he reaches between us to sweep aside the barrier to what he wants. Cupping my buttocks, he pulls me closer, driving himself deeper inside. My arms encircle his neck. His head dips down to latch onto a wet nipple.

Water swooshes around us. We are surrounded by hot bubbling liquid, matching our erotic motions. My eyes are closed. Filipe is in my head... my hot fantasy man. Thoughts of him arouse me instantly.

I daydream about Filipe watching, then joining in. One hard cock sliding in and out of my mouth, touching the back of my throat, while the other drives hard into my core bringing me closer to the edge. I can feel a gush of natural wetness spill from me.

Krystian groans. He's close. After that sexy vision in my mind, I am too. I urge him on... faster, harder! Lips smashed together as we spiral out of control.

We reach release together, both grunting in satisfaction. The frenzied water calms as we part, sinking in deeper.

As my heartbeat subsides, I wonder who was in Krystian's head. I know Filipe was in mine... but who did Krystian think about? Me or someone else?

CHAPTER 16

Orange Glow

Getting back into my regular work mode is a drag. I keep having visions of the resort pool, or being pampered with massages and room service. Slouching further down into my chair, I quickly look up flight prices to Bali on sale. As my eyes glaze over at the beachy tropical images, I pull myself together with a quick mental slap.

No! Arleia you can't go on another holiday yet! I silently admonish myself, and return to my work screen with determination, knowing there is a lot of work to do and that I'm wasting time. But a piece of me inside wonders what else I would need to get the online jewellery business started so that I *could* go on holidays more often?

With eyes glued to the computer screen all afternoon, I forge ahead. I am so focused on getting caught up that I forgot my phone had chimed at me from in my desk earlier. Completing the last task for the day, I sigh and slide my chair away from the desk. Pushing my shoulders back, I stretch out in the limited space I have, hearing a satisfying click from my back.

My attention wanders for a moment from my back to Bali massages, until another ping from my phone draws me back to the present. Sliding the phone from my drawer, I take a quick glance hoping to see Filipe's name. I slump back into my chair. Nope. No message from him today yet.

I tell myself that he is working long hours or doesn't always have his phone, but is that true or am I just making excuses for him? Is he still interested or has the memory of me dimmed?

Uh oh! An unfamiliar wave is washing over me. I haven't felt insecure in quite a while, so it catches me by surprise. No other man has had this effect on me before. I wish that I had taken the book to Bali to see what the handbook's opinion of him is.

Too late now, he's not even in the same state. But I could visit there for a weekend. It's not that far a flight – close enough, even just for an overnight stay! My body hums in anticipation as the idea takes hold in my brain. Filipe said he is working six days a week at the moment, but surely he would be happy to see me for a night, wouldn't he?

Uncomfortable with this fear of the unknown, I mentally give myself a slap. Stop being ridiculous, girl! Speaking sternly to myself, I know what I need to do. My regular guys are not providing enough distraction, so I need to go searching for more Marks to engage with and erase the mesmerising French man in my mind or go crazy. I grab my bag with a sigh and head towards home.

With nothing planned for tonight, I will revisit the

supermarket of lust and find some new men to distract me from Frenchy! After heating a tin of soup from the meagre offerings in my cupboard, I realise where I *should* be shopping is the grocery store, not online — but I ignore that thought.

Flopping on the couch, I drag my laptop from the coffee table and perch it on my knees. I realise how long it has been since I seriously searched online here. Too long! My fingers fly across the screen, cutting out the unsuitable men and whittling my choices down without too much thought until something catches my eye.

Another French man! Hmm, maybe I should see what he's like. Are all Frenchmen fantastic in bed and do they all smell as delicious as Filipe? I hit the accept chat button and say hello. Kasmir is enthusiastic and complimentary, which boosts my mood. Maybe I should meet him?

Throwing caution to the wind, I agree to meet him the next afternoon straight from work. I'm surprised at my brazenness at agreeing to this impulsive date and spend a moment high fiving myself, until another thought fills me with dread.

Shit. Bloody hell, damn idiot ... hopeless Vixen, shit aaaaarrrgh!! WHY. Why did I not even have a moment of thought of consulting the secret handbook? Hanging my head, I let out a yell of frustration. Rookie mistake. A mistake that may cost me!

Jumping up from the couch I race into my bedroom to retrieve the book from my bedside table. I can see a faint glow fading from it — but I can't quite make out the colour. Was it gold for a great date, or red for a disaster date? Or something else?

How can I find out? I don't want to go on another disaster date tomorrow with Kasmir. I wrack my brain to come up with an answer. What if I asked the book? No! Don't be stupid. That woman from the psychic fair didn't say anything about *talking* to the book, did she?

Feeling silly, I stare intently at the book, silently willing it to answer me in some way. Fear of the unknown curls around me. I guess that either no*thing* will happen — or *something* will happen. Either way, I may as well give this a try.

"Vixen's Secret Handbook! Reveal to me the answer. What is your opinion on my date tomorrow with Kasmir?"

I draw in my breath and hold it, waiting. My eyes are locked on the book, willing it to reveal to me the knowledge I have asked for. Nothing is happening. I drop my shoulders; I was silly to think this would work.

Just as I start to turn away, I see the book give a slight shudder from the corner of my eye. Spinning back around I stare at it. A faint glow is appearing, growing stronger. But wait, what colour is it? Not red or gold, the glow strengthens in colour to emerge as a vibrant burnt orange glow.

Stepping back in surprise, I stumble and catch myself. Orange? A new colour! Well, what the hell does that mean? Staring in wonder at the book, I notice the orange flash brighter before fading away. I heave a big sigh and try to make sense of the confusion inside. Not red. Not gold. *Orange.*

Clearing my mind, I try to take myself back to the day this book came into my life. What did the gypsy woman say? I should have paid her words more attention.

Tomorrow's date with Kasmir will have to remain a mystery until then. Unless I cancel it and don't go. The temptation to cancel it is strong, but I need to know what orange means. How can I find this out if I don't go on this date and see what happens?

No, I won't cancel. I have an exit strategy ready if needed — how bad can it be? At least the book didn't glow red — the colour of a disaster date! Packing up the laptop I head to bed.

A disturbed sleep filled with flashing lights through a darkened building awakens me at two-thirty. It takes my mind and body another forty-five minutes to sink back into a dreamless sleep.

CHAPTER 17

Bakery Bungle

Finishing up work as quickly as possible, I run for the elevator to snag it before dozens of office workers on each floor congregate in the halls waiting for the already full lifts to pass. Since I'm about to meet Kasmir, I'd rather not run late or hurry the two long uphill blocks to the designated cafe. I don't want to arrive all sweaty and dishevelled.

Sliding into the lift, I squash myself against the ten people already in there, with the same idea as me, escape! Entering the street, a blast of cold air greets me. The last dregs of winter are determined to hang around and hold up the arrival of spring.

With my coat pulled tightly around me to cut out the chill, I start at a brisk pace up the sloping street. My watch tells me I have plenty of time, but weaving through the throng of people on the sidewalk, slows my progress.

Ten minutes later, the inviting glow of the café's lights beckons me inside. I glance around the interior, searching for a man sitting alone. Great, he's not here yet! I order a Vienna chocolate and walk over to a free booth to wait for Kasmir. The red vinyl seat squeaks as I slide along the bench. I wonder how old the wilting flower is in the tiny glass vase on the table.

Just as my hot drink arrives, I finish reading messages from Krystian, Darz, and Roshan. Darz is due back from working at the mine in a couple of days, and I am keen to see him when he returns. Roshan is now away on holiday in Western Australia, so I will have to wait a little longer to see him.

I take a sip of my drink and look up as the café's doorbell rings. A slim, dark-haired man walks in, hitting the backpack dangling from his shoulder against the glass door. Glancing around the café, he runs his fingers through his shoulder-length hair. His eyes alight on me, he smiles and walks towards my booth.

"Arleia? Hi, I'm Kasmir!"

His words hang in the air a moment before I respond.

"Hi, Kasmir! Nice to meet you — have a seat!"

He gestures to my drink and asks me if I'd like anything else. Assuring him that I am fine, he walks across to the counter to place an order. This gives me more time to check him out without him seeing me!

His build is slighter than I prefer, but he does have a nice smile. Swept back from his face, his hair reminds me of an unkept seventies style. Baggy jeans held up with a belt poke out below an open striped shirt and a white t-shirt. Nothing about him screams French to me except his accent, and he is a vastly different-looking Frenchman to Filipe.

Returning to our table, Kasmir slides into the shiny red

bench seat across from me and enquires about my day. After five minutes of boring small talk, I struggle not to yawn. It seems his main passion is cooking, and his interest in discussing recipes confounds me.

Two months into his two-year study visa, Kasmir reveals that he has seen nothing of Sydney yet, and has only been concentrating on his course. If I were in a new country, I would not be able to wait to get out and explore!

Surely, he has gone on one ferry ride across the harbour to take in the spectacular harbour views. No! Not even once. It's like this guy has no sense of adventure, and no interests other than cooking. Kasmir reads my face and on some level realises he has lost my attention.

Reaching for his bag, he releases the zip. My attention returns to idly wonder why a guy would bring a backpack along on a date. Unusual! His hand searches around in there for a minute until he grabs hold of what he is searching for.

A grin breaks across his face as he slowly starts to slide something out of the bag.

"This I make for you beautiful!" The look of pride on his face as he pulls a plastic container from the depths of his bag, makes me stifle a giggle. It was as if he was going to show me his newborn baby! I lean forward, curious as to what may be inside.

Flicking the lid open in a 'ta-da' gesture, he showcases the interior with a hand sweep. I peer inside and still wonder what it is. Staring back at me is a round icing-less baked cake of some sort. I can see flecks of something in it, and the textured top is different from that of a normal cake. It reminds me more of a round banana bread loaf.

I suddenly realise all is silent, and Kasmir is watching me with an expectant look in his eyes. Oh shit. A guy has baked me a cake from scratch — this is a first! Unsure of what it is, I try to be diplomatic.

"Wow! Did you make that for me? From scratch? That's amazing, thank you!"

His chest puffs out as he smiles and gives me a look of modesty, which sends a cold shiver down my spine. I still don't know what the hell it is that he has just given to me, nevertheless, I don't want to be rude

My ignorance doesn't last long. Kasmir is eager to list every ingredient he used in the cake! It feels like I'm being brainwashed with a bizarre carrot cake recipe of almond flour and powdered egg substitutes. My eyes glaze over in hypnotised with boredom as he drones on about the cooking process of the hard rock-like lump in front of us.

I can't take his container home with me. That will almost certainly end in me having to return it to him, and quite frankly that's not going to happen.

My mind searches for an answer. Maybe I've got a disposable shopping bag in my handbag that I could use to slip it into? My hand sneaks in to search for a folded bag while Kasmir warms to his culinary crusade with a list of his favourite items to bake.

Heaving a sigh of boredom that I can barely disguise, I decide this date must fast come to an end. Flipping the shopping bag from my purse, I declare out loud that I have the solution. This stops him mid-sentence.

"What?"

His look of confusion almost makes me laugh. He has been so engrossed in his love of baking that I genuinely think he forgot I was there.

"This bag! The perfect solution to carry your delicious-looking cake home in. I don't want to take your container from you!"

He still looks a bit confused.

"But I thought you might like to try some while you're here."

I stop myself from giving him an eye roll and play nice. Trying a piece of the cake won't take a minute, and he's obviously eager to see if I like it.

"Oh of course! Sorry I didn't realise you meant me to eat a slice *now*."

My eyes search the table for something to cut the cake with but come up empty.

"Oh look, don't worry about it, there's no knife here, and I don't want to ruin it! I'll just take it with me as it is."

His look of determination tells me that's not going to happen, as he dips his fingers into the box and breaks off a large chunk. Holding it out towards me, he gestures for me to take it. I have no choice. Oh God, I hope it's not laced with drugs or something!

My hand reaches out to grasp the crumbly mess. There's no way out of this. I'm going to have to take a bite. With his eyes trained on me and the chunk of cake, I lift it to my mouth and take a bite. Flavourless crumbs congeal together with saliva as my mouth becomes as dry as the Simpson desert.

Nodding my head in approval, I try to swallow the tasteless mound and reach for a glass of water to wash it down with. He waits across the table impatiently, leaning forward to read my face for a reaction. Smiling, I take another swig of water to return my mouth to normal.

"Wow! That was an interesting texture for carrot cake. And you say you adapted the original recipe? Amazing!"

I can't tell him the truth. It would be too mean of me to shoot his cooking creation down in flames. Flicking open the bag with my free hand, I gesture towards it.

"Actually, I might just put the rest of this piece in here to enjoy with another cuppa later tonight. I think it really needs a hot drink accompaniment to enjoy the taste to its fullest!"

Reaching over the table, I lift the rest of the bland slab out of his container and slide it into the bag.

"Perfect! Thanks so much for bringing me such a thoughtful gift, I appreciate it!"

I can tell he's disappointed that I didn't clamour for a second piece, but my acting skills have their limits! I swing the cake laden bag into my own, thankful that it fits inside. The vibe I'm getting from him is that he is totally clueless that I am bored stiff. There's no point in correcting him — better to leave and not waste more of our time.

Sliding out of my seat I thank him again. As he makes to slide out of the booth he almost bumps into my chin. A quick step backward removes me from the collision zone as he awkwardly reaches across to hug me goodbye.

Smiling a false smile that hurts my cheeks, I make use of my exit strategy of dinner plans with friends, and high tail it out of the café as quickly as my feet can take me. After a minute or two of walking at a brisk pace towards where my car is parked, I glance behind me. Seeing no sign of him, I breathe a sigh of relief.

Wow. That was the most *boring* conversation I've ever endured. Reaching my car, I slip into the drivers' seat and sling my bag onto the seat next to me. It thuds against the passenger door with the weight of his crumbly gift inside. Laughing, I set off for home, glad I was able to escape quickly.

Safely home, I retrieve the gift and flip the cake onto the kitchen countertop. What am I going to do with this? It stares back at me accusingly. As if it knows there's a fast track towards the bin in its immediate future — there's no way I'm going to eat the rest of this unappealing hunk of home cooking.

I step on the metal bin lever to pop open the lid. Feeling guilty for a second, I hesitate — the teachings of my childhood of not wasting food echo around my brain for a moment before I toss the offending bakery item in the bin. When I hear it hit the bottom with a resounding thud, I know this is the right decision as I offer up a sincere apology to its creator.

Heaving a sigh of relief, I wander into my bedroom. An eerie orange glow fills the room, emanating from the handbook. Shit, that's right! The new orange glow. What does it mean? I think back to the date I've just had with Kasmir. How would I best describe it? In one word, boring! Each minute felt like an hour. An orange glow must mean that I should beware of the most boring date ever ahead.

Shrugging, I feel a sense of relief wash over me. At least now I know what the orange light means. It was a better outcome than the red glow of a disaster date, but still a waste of my time. After tonight's escapade, I don't feel like another potentially boring conversation with anyone else right now.

Making up a plate of nibbles, I pour a glass of wine and find my favourite Netflix documentary series on the television. Sinking into the couch I press play for the next episode. To my disgust, it's about baking methods in ancient times. No thanks, I've experienced enough baking for today!

CHAPTER 18

Blue Hue

After the most boring date *ever*, I need to see one of my regulars! Darz should be due home now, so maybe a date with him will elevate my mood. A few messages later, our next date is organised. I haven't seen him since before I went away, so I'm definitely overdue a little Darz magic!

My phone pings, announcing another message. Expecting Darz, I glance down, and my heart skips a beat. Frenchy. Memories of the night with Filipe in Bali flood my mind. I *must* go and see this man again, and soon!

I suggest my idea of me flying up to visit him for a weekend and wait for his answer with bated breath.

'Princess. You come here for me? In Queensland? Yes!'

A grin spreads across my face as I read his words, and my stomach has a swirly feel going on inside. Ignoring it, I reply. Fifteen minutes later an overnight visit is organised, and my flights are booked for two weeks from now. The only thing left to be reserved is a hotel room for the night. I can't stay with him as he shares a place with several other guys that he works with, and after our last sexy interlude, we will need some private space.

Mwaaahahahaaahahaa!

It feels good to let out that laugh. I haven't been feeling too vixenish since my last date of boredom.

Over the coming weeks, I will keep distracting myself from thinking about seeing Filipe by going on even more dates with my regular guys. Perhaps I'll try another newbie or two. My Vixen's handbook must be consulted more often since I'm obviously not as skilled at choosing men as I thought I was!

The arrival of the weekend heralds not only my date with Darz but also an opportunity for man shopping online. This time I'm putting the handbook right next to my laptop and watching it like a hawk.

Early morning sun streams through my window to beckon me outside. I indulge in a mindfulness walking meditation to the nearby park. Breathing in the fresh air, my chest rises and falls rhythmically. Being present in the moment is amazing for growing your inner light — and mine obviously needs some serious attention.

I flick the thoughts of my boring date with Kasmir, to concentrate on listening to the birds. The laugh of a kookaburra merges with the warble of magpies. Rushing water across stones in the creek adds to the echoes of their song.

Stopping, I stretch my arms to the sky. Thankful for this sun-kissed morning, and the journey of adventure my new life as a vixen has taken me on. My confidence has grown immensely since I started the voyage into the unknown. Even with a few disaster dates, I have learnt so much!

Reenergized from my meditation and the uplifting energy from nature, I feel lighter. With my extra energy I head to the gym — something I have been avoiding since returning, but my body is feeling those extra few kilos I brought back from Bali.

Self-care sorted for the morning I move onto my next task, shopping online! Since the day is promising a slice of warmth, I set myself up outside with my laptop, handbook, and banana smoothie on the patio table.

Since I started the day off healthily, I'm determined to continue! Stepping towards my chair I come to a halt. My Goddess cards! How could I have forgotten them too? This attraction to Frenchy has addled my brain. It's like I've been walking around in a fog since I met him.

I stride to the buffet and pull them out of the drawer. Today I'm going to keep the good energy vibe happening with a card reading for myself before I start! The Handbook gives me great dating advice, but my cards help me with life journey guidance.

Seated back outside, I shuffle the cards. Silently willing a card to jump from the pack with a message for me, I focus on the question 'What do I need to know today?'

A card jumps from the pack, flipping itself over to reveal the answer. I read it and giggle at the first line of advice.

Lakshmi

Bright Future

'Stop worrying. Everything is going to be fine.
This is a kind universe, and everyone within it is working

in your favour. There are no tests, blocks, or obstacles in your way, except your own projections of fear into your future. Take a moment and hush your mind, quietening it from worries and fears. Feel me brush your brow with a new energy of faith, hope, and optimism. These energies fuel your exciting present time, as well as all future moments.

Why would you wish darkness upon yourself when light shines all around you? Step into this brightness by lightening your thoughts and feelings. You must stop worrying, as this anxiety squelches the goodness that seeks to find you!

Clear your heart of fear and replace those energies with ones that will serve you instead. Refuse to think of anything except your bright today and tomorrow, and I promise you that it shall be so.'

I know in my heart these words are true. This morning in the park I felt it. A peaceful feeling washes over me. I *want* to be open to the goodness that seeks to find me!

I remember the spanking session I had with Darz only a couple of months ago. Something odd happened then too. My eyes looked different in the mirror, and I felt that strange surge of power.

The next morning, I dismissed the event as fanciful musings. The colour of my eyes looked back to normal, and I wondered if I had dreamt the golden flecks of change. When I think back to my negative mindset around men when I started this journey. Being cheated on rocked my world and forced change upon me.

But with the adventures of vixen life, I have come to

understand myself and men better. My inner light has grown, and I am not the same person that I was six months ago.

This realisation stops my thoughts in their tracks. It's true. I have changed immensely, and my power has grown. I have been so distracted with dating that I haven't really thought about how much I've grown.

A grin spreads across my face as I high-five myself, then pat my left shoulder.

"Good on you Arleia! Well done girl!!"

This day has been full of discovery already, and I haven't even made it online yet.

Mwaaahahahaaahahaa!

Settling in for a couple of hours of perusing the online menu of guys, I stretch skyward before starting. There are always more contact requests on here than I can keep up with. I haven't ever sent a man a contact request once yet! Maybe that's because I am always too busy sorting through offers rather than hunting myself.

Twenty-two deletes later, I have narrowed the field down to a few possibilities. As soon as I add the Latino-looking guy to my list, he shows up as being online. Mere seconds later a message from him flashes across the screen.

Latinlover69: Hello beautiful! What a smile ☺

ATrixenVixen: Hello yourself! Thanks!

Latinlover69: Did you fall from the sky? Because you look like an angel x

Oh boy. This one has some smooth lines going on already.

I wonder whether there is more to him. Since he's the only one online right now, I may as well find out!

ATrixenVixen: What have you been up to today?

Latinlover69: I'm working all day today ... I work for myself in the telecommunications industry and occasionally work a Saturday. But chatting with you will be a pleasant interlude to my day!

Holy crap a guy who answered in a paragraph rather than a sentence! This is most unusual. The fact that he used the word interlude surprised me too. He's a far cry from the 'Hey babe' guys who are usually online!

We continue our chat, and I discover we have a few things in common. Maybe I might like to meet this one. William lives about fifteen minutes away from here in a nice suburb, works for himself, and loves to travel.

After he passes a couple of vixen tests, I'm feeling *fairly* confident that it will be worth my time to meet this guy! I wonder what he smells like.

Latinlover69: How about we meet for a coffee next week? There's a great café I know of near your area – I'll send you the address if you like?

Oh, why the hell not hey. After all, I'm on the hunt for international Marks, and he fits the profile perfectly. I agree immediately, prepare to give a victorious Vixen laugh ... and freeze.

Dread fills my chest as the book beside me shudders. Oh shit. Oh no, what is happening? Instead of high-fiving myself, I feel fear wash over me. Gradually a blue light appears from the book. Pulsing in a kaleidoscope of blues, my eyes are glued to it. Oh no! What does this mean? I've never seen this blue light before, and I don't like it! Already dealing with the new addition of orange, I'm not sure what to make of this message.

Hurrying back inside, I reach for the vodka. A healthy splash, mixed with orange juice, qualifies as an acceptable late morning beverage. What have I just agreed to, and what could the blue mean? Could William be gay? Bisexual? Have some major personality flaws? My mind races with possibilities but I have no clue yet as to what this colour might signal.

I guess I will find out in the coming week when I meet him for a coffee. Oh God, I hope I can figure out what the blue means on this first date! The thought of cancelling crosses my mind, but I'm too curious to do that now. I need to know what the blue glow means, and the only way to do this is to meet Mr. Latino Lover next week.

CHAPTER 19

Fluffy Cuffs

Finally, it is time to see Darz again! Sometimes our work schedules don't mesh well with him working away — it's ages since we saw each other. He's coming over this afternoon, and I have a surprise in store for him.

Since he has always been keen to try different things in the bedroom, I found some fluffy handcuffs at a market stall in Bali which made me think of him. Thank God I didn't get my suitcase searched on the way back through customs!

I think it will be fun to play with them today if he is open to the idea. In my mind, it's him that is wearing them, not me. Sliding my feet into low-heeled sandals, I adjust my long-sleeved jersey dress and hope that my toes don't get cold. Although the sun has been trying lately, spring is still sluggish to arrive.

The afternoon sun peeks through my blinds as I slouch on the couch waiting. Another ten minutes pass, and a sliver of annoyance curls up my spine. Darz is now almost twenty minutes late.

A smile spreads across my face. What if I were to 'punish' him for being late? What could I do? Think Vixen, think! It's no punishment to be cuffed and have me play with him — I doubt he would think that's punishment in the slightest.

A loud knocking at the door pulls me from my musing and I rush to the door, then set my face into an annoyed look before I open it.

"I'm so sorry I'm late Arleia! The traffic was..."

Halting mid-sentence, Darz finally notices my expression. The single raised eyebrow is enough to have him realise something is going on.

"I'm so sorry too, that you have wasted my time. You know there's a punishment that comes with being late, don't you?"

He ducks his head to hide his grin of amusement, before rearranging his face into a contrite expression. I almost get lost in his brown puppy dog eyes before I can pull myself back into the game.

"I apologise, Mistress Vixen! Allow me to fall to your knees and kiss your feet in a gesture of remorse and apology."

Dropping to his knees, he lifts one sandaled foot to kiss lavishly, and then the other. It's killing me not to laugh but I don't want to break character now I've started this. Schooling my face into a stern look, I continue.

"To the bedroom! Right now!"

Pushing him along the hallway I gesture for him to enter.

"Clothes off and lie down on the bed on your back!"

Tossing his shirt to the ground, he then shimmies out of his jeans. Shooting me an enquiring look, I nod at him.

"Yes, I want everything off!"

Hooking his thumbs into his underwear, he slowly slides them down his thighs, then kicks them free of his ankles. They are airborne for a second, before hooking themselves on the doorknob, and swaying for a second. The urge to laugh out loud is too strong. A giggle erupts from me before I can squash it and return to character.

"On your back I said!"

Darz complies with a grin, flopping onto the bed with a bounce then rolls onto his back. Reaching into the bedside drawers, I retrieve the fluffy cuffs and twirl them around on my finger. Now what the hell am I going to do? I should have thought more about how this was going to play out before he got here.

"Hands together above your head!"

Keeping my face schooled in a stern look, I reach for his hands and snap the cuffs around his wrists. I don't want to do them up too tightly and hurt him, but the fake fur should protect his skin and not cause any harm. A brilliant idea starts forming in my mind.

Grabbing a silk scarf from my collection, I wind it around the cuffs, then tie the scarf to the headboard of my bed. Pulling the scarf tightly, I make sure I double knot it, to be sure he can't escape.

I lean over and give him a long, leisurely kiss on the lips. I can tell he's loving this game so far, but he might change his mind with what I have in store for him! The thought that I should have dropped in at the supermarket beforehand has been swirling in my head. Why not do it now?

Moving lower, I rake my fingers down his chest, raining light kisses along the path my fingers have taken. Encircling his girth, I stroke slowly a couple of times and kiss the tip of his head. A few strokes of his shaft then a lick of the wet tip of his cock before I move downward.

Darz moans. I smile a wicked grin against his left thigh as I kiss the toned muscles there and move across to his right leg. Dragging my nails down his thighs I move further down. Kissing knees, shins, and finally his big toes.

I know he is aroused — that is obvious. But instead of turning the heat up, I've decided to let him cool down for a while.

"Your punishment is about to begin! You wasted my precious time. So now I will leave you here for the exact number of minutes you were late today. I will be going out to do a spot of shopping while you wait!"

The expressions crossing his face right now are priceless! Confusion, then arousal. Desire flashes in his eyes as he speaks.

"I'm so sorry Mistress Vixen. You are right. I deserve this punishment and more!"

I turn abruptly towards the door before he can see the grin spreading across my face. Without replying I stride down the hallway, grab my purse, and slam the front door behind me.

As soon as I am in the soundproof zone of my car, I almost wet myself laughing. His face was so funny to watch when I told him I was leaving. I wonder what he's thinking right now. Wiping the tears from my eyes so I can see to drive, I head to the closest shop.

Five minutes have passed since I left him. Shit, I better not be too long — what if he needs to go to the bathroom or something? That thought has me laughing out loud which draws the attention of two customers nearby. Yes, that's right shoppers; I'm a strange vixen who ties men to her bed and laughs to herself when alone in public ... deal with it!

As I walk down the aisles, I can't believe I left Darz tied up on my bed to come shopping. A giggle bubbles from my lips as I twirl the basket and add some chips and nuts, even though I've already got a couple of hot nuts waiting at home for me.

Mwaaahaaahaahaa!

I finalise my purchases and hurry back to the car. Twenty minutes have passed and I'm eager to get back home and make sure he is okay. I drop the groceries on the kitchen bench and hurry to the bedroom. With a sigh of relief, I see that Darz is still where I left him.

"Is it clear to you now that you must never waste a Vixen's time?"

"Yesssss Mistress! I await your command."

Slowly sliding my underwear down from under my dress, I kick them away and step closer to him. Hey, wait a second! Those knots in the scarf don't look the same. What happened while I was gone? My eyes narrow in suspicion.

"Did you dare to move while I was away?"

Darz erupts into laughter at my question.

"Shit, sorry Arleia, I really needed to go to the bathroom. Thank God I was able to untie the scarf and go. You're not really that good at tying knots, you know!"

Oh, shit indeed. That could have been messy! The thought

did cross my mind while I was out, but I dismissed it. I was only gone for about twenty minutes, but sometimes bladders can't wait. I will have to remember this if I ever leave another man tied up alone in my house.

Mwaaahahahaaahahaa!

"Oh my God, you know I did have a fleeting thought of that ... sorry Darz! At least we know I will have to learn how to tie knots much better for next time!"

Both of us laughing, I kneel on the bed and straddle him. Rubbing myself along him a couple of times quietens the laughter as I lean forward and kiss him deeply. His hands are still tied. Even though he has tied the scarf back up to the bed head, I'm sure he can pull free if he wants to. But for now, he chooses not to.

Reaching between my thighs I take hold of his hardness, slide on protection, and guide it in like a homing beacon. We both sigh, motionless for a moment. I rock my hips backward and forwards slightly. Sitting upright I run my nails down his chest, causing him to shudder.

"Untie me Arleia! I want to touch you."

I reach for the offending scarf which falls away easily.

"So cheeky! You made me think you were still tied to the bed!"

I slap him playfully across his cheek and he laughs. His hands finally free, he curls one around the back of my neck and draws me closer to him. Our open mouths lock, tongues dancing together, as I resume rocking gently back and forward until he growls in frustration and neatly flips us both over.

Driving in deeper he groans. Hips raising to meet him, I urge him to continue. Sweat glistens on our skin. Tension building, I can only focus on the sensations crowding my mind and body.

Slick bodies move together as we both get closer. Pinning my hands to the bed he leans forward to capture my lips. I'm almost there, I can feel it. His tongue dancing in my mouth makes the rushing noise in my ears grows louder.

A shudder and guttural groan from Darz pushes me over the edge with him. Feeling him pulsate inside me makes me shiver. I am lost in the sensations washing over me.

It takes a few minutes for me to return to earth and realise that I have a hot sweaty man plastered across my body, almost suffocating me! I push feebly at Darz, completely drained of energy and speech. He understands my unspoken request to move and flips over onto his back beside me.

"Holy crap I need a shower! Not only do I have my own sweat to deal with, but you dripped your sweat onto me too then you know!"

The bed shakes as Darz silently laughs at my statement beside me.

"Well, it was you that made me so hot Miss Vixen, so you can hardly blame me! Come on, let's jump into the shower — I promise to wash your back for you!"

"Aww, only my back?"

Pushing my lower lip out I give him a look that tells him I want more. Grinning, he rolls off the bed and hauls me up against his chest. His flaccid dick twitches against my thigh. I slap his round peachy butt cheek and laugh as I push him back towards the bathroom. Someone to lather me up all over in the shower to finish off this interesting afternoon is exactly what I need right now, as was round two in the shower!

Hours later, I stare at the golden glow of the handbook beside me. Where did this book come from? How old is it? Who created it? How did it become enchanted or magical?

I haven't yet told my closest girlfriends the truth about the book. It might freak them out too much — they already think I'm weird enough! I told them about the stranger giving it to me at the psychic fair, but not the magical instructions bit.

They think it's a Vixen's Secret Handbook — a simple guide to dating that is like any other book. How do I explain to them what the book can really do and what all the glowing colours from it mean, when I don't have the answers myself?

My sleep is fitful and full of dreams that night. When I awaken in the morning the last wisp of my dream lingers around me, with the impression of a mysterious stranger laughing at me.

CHAPTER 20

Blue Puzzle

An uneasy feeling lurks in the back of my mind today. I can't quite put my finger on what it's trying to tell me, though. I know it's not related to the date I just had with Darz — oh my God, that was so much fun! When I told Lulu about it earlier this morning, she laughed so hard that she fell off her seat.

Once recovered, she demanded to see the cuffs next time we catch up. I class Lulu as another vixen type on the prowl for fun too, so I feel comfortable confiding more details about my dates to her than I usually divulge to friends.

Some women I know who have never tried online dating for fun and adventure worry about me. There's no need to be concerned just because of *their* fear of the unknown. Sure, I had no idea what I was doing at first — but by stepping out of my comfort zone regularly, I feel more confident now than I ever have before in my life!

By breaking free of my old belief patterns and trying

something new, I am embracing change and increasing my bravery. Because fear of the unknown is strong, not many people choose to instigate change or force themselves out of their comfort zones.

Although I have only been in the dating arena for a short time, I can feel the difference within me — with my old beliefs changing to new ones. I've grown, become less judgemental, learned to value myself and my time more, and have strengthened my boundaries.

This is not what I expected at the start of my journey. I'm starting to realise how much I love this astonishing new feeling of confidence!

A couple of years ago I thought about starting an online business, but I let fear stop me then. Safer to stay with what you know, were the inner whisperings of fear back then. When I listen for the same whispers now, they are gone.

I have made a start with some contacts in Bali so I will follow through and explore my options. Since I love holidaying in Bali, I am sure to go for another vacation there again soon.

The future vision washes over me. Regular buying trips combined with relaxing by the pool with massages would be something I'd like to create in my future business.

I've already created so many new dating adventures, why limit myself with creation? I could apply my newfound confidence to the business world and build a new side-line that would be fun and include my love of travel.

A shiver of excitement washes through me. A vixen can do anything she puts her mind to, I decide. But since I can't afford another Bali trip again yet, I need to shelve the idea for now. I can start with photographing the jewellery I bought on my recent trip and start on a website.

My phone buzzes beside me, pulling me back into the present. It's Darz thanking me for the fun date. No sooner do I finish reading his message when my phone vibrates again. Frenchy! All thoughts of Darz vanish. 'Can't wait to see you, Princess'. Tapping out a reply I end it with a smiley face with love-heart eyes. Oh no! When did I last send love-heart anything?

A third message comes through from William. How is it that I either get several texts at once or none?! I open his message to find the address and time of our coffee date tomorrow.

Still unsure what this meeting will bring with the advent of the new blue glow of the book around him, I flick him a text back agreeing to his proposal. I'm never going to find out what the blue light means if I don't go on this date, and I want to meet this guy before I head to Queensland!

Arriving at the café a couple of minutes late, I stop to catch my breath. The afternoon sun streams through the big glass windows making it easy for me to anonymously spot my date. The café is about half full of couples and small groups of people chattering over the clink of china amid the aroma of coffee beans.

Metal chairs surround square tables with fresh carnations adorning each table. William's back is angled towards where I'm standing, so I'm in the perfect spot to check him out sight unseen. The Brazilian bug-eye date from a few months ago pops into my head. Surely, I can't be unfortunate enough to have that happen again? I wrack my brain for the image of William's face before entering.

Phew! He did send me a picture of his whole face. I don't want to make that rookie mistake a second time. Taking a deep breath, I mutter the vixen laugh softly under my breath for a confidence boost and step inside the café.

Tantalizing smells waft around me as I walk over to where William is seated. Mmm, there's no way I'm missing out on one of those delectable bakery items while I'm here!

"Hi, William?"

The man turns his head at the mention of his name.

"Arleia? Great to meet you! Have a seat!"

He stands as he greets me, giving me a quick hug before settling back into his seat. An empty coffee cup sits in front of him along with his phone. Once seated I study William. He looks almost the same as his pictures online, which is a good start. His smile is friendly and engaging, giving me a good vibe.

"Can I get you a drink, Arleia? And what about something to eat? Those cakes in the display out the front look amazing!"

I'm thankful it's not just me who's salivating over the smells around us.

"Yes, that would be excellent, thanks. I might go for a hot chocolate and whatever cake you think looks the most delicious!"

"Ooh, that's daring of you! Are you sure you wouldn't like to choose something yourself?"

"I trust your judgement. However, if you fail to deliver the tastiest on offer, you will lose a brownie point before we even start!"

He laughs and sets off for the counter to order for us. I can't help watching him leave and checking out his butt. The rounded cheeks fill out his work pants nicely. I nod my approval — so far, so good!

What could be wrong with him that the book glows blue? There's no sign of any physical problem — he's quite attractive with dark wavy hair and olive-toned skin. He was articulate in greeting, is being thoughtful and seems pleasant.

William returns with a buzzer to collect the order when it's ready and throws me a smile.

"I hope I have chosen correctly Arleia. I can't have you desert the date just because of an ill-chosen dessert!"

He sniggers over his little joke, and I smile. At least he has a sense of humour.

"Well, if you have chosen wrongly the wrath of a vixen will be upon you!" I tease back.

"Hmm... A vixen upon me? I don't think that sounds like a punishment at all!"

"Very smooth, I'll have to give you that! What did you order for me anyway?"

"It's a surprise, Miss Impatient! You'll have to wait until it arrives."

He grins a saucy grin to take the sting from his words as he launches into asking me about myself. With a condensed version of my past delivered, I am just about to ask him more about himself when the buzzer on the table starts vibrating and dances across the table.

"Just a second and I'll go grab our order, Arleia!"

Nodding my head in agreement, I check out his butt again. Why does this dude make my book glow blue? So far, he's chatty, interesting, and cute. Maybe he bought a coffee flavoured dessert for me? That might earn a scowl of disapproval!

William makes two trips to our table. First to deposit our hot drinks, then with the long-awaited desserts. I check out the offering as he deposits it in front of me with a flourish. German apple cheesecake smiles up at me and makes my mouth water.

"Did I make the right choice of dessert for Madame?"

His teasing tone makes me smile.

"Yes, an extremely lucky one. You can keep your brownie point this time!"

He gestures to his choice and only then do I notice a big fat chocolate-filled brownie sitting in front of him. I laugh and slide it towards me.

"Oh, nooo miss! You're not having them both!"

He raps me across the knuckles with the cake fork to make me let go of his treat and slides it protectively towards him.

"Maybe we can strike up an exchange agreement for the desserts?"

I consider his proposal. As much as I love German apple cheesecake, the brownie with steaming chocolate oozing from its centre has my attention too.

"Deal!" I declare with a flourish of my cake fork. We call a dessert truce and divide up the treats. I can't decide which one I like most, *and* I'm enjoying this date and conversation.

William tells me more about his telecommunications busi-ness, the fact that he has two sisters and a brother, who have produced a total of nine nephews and nieces. The family beach house on the south coast, his trips overseas, and his love of the beach.

The more he talks, the more puzzled I am. What the hell does the blue light mean? I can't pick out any reason yet why the book would give anything but the golden glow. When I get home, I'm checking the colour again.

We end the date with a hug and peck on the lips. William wants to see me again. I can't think of any reason to say no. The date and company were enjoyable — something I'd like to repeat, so I agree. I don't have much time free before I head to see Frenchy again, so I let him know the date I leave.

Since he spends most weekends at his family beach house, the fact that I will be away on a weekend doesn't matter. William suggests another catch-up at the end of the week before I go away, and I agree. This will stop me from thinking too much of Filipe until then, which is a good thing. I don't want to become too emotionally caught up in Frenchy!

Arriving home, I race for the book. Will it have changed its tune? An answering blue glow tells me no. I'm still no further in figuring out what that colour means than before I went on the date with William. Perhaps a second date will give me a hint?

CHAPTER 21

Latino Lover

After a week of messages from all my men, I have been sufficiently distracted from the sexy Frenchman who's been filling my mind. Plus, I have the second date with William later today which will distract me for a few more hours until I fly to the Sunshine Coast in Queensland tomorrow morning.

I'm more excited about seeing Frenchy again than about a second date with William, but I need the distraction of a date with someone else right now.

We are meeting at the Park Royal hotel near Darling Harbour for dinner, then enjoy a stroll along the harbour to soak in the sights. Hurrying to get ready after work, I chew on my lip while perusing the closet. Selecting a figure-hugging black dress that ends below the knee, I pair it with ankle boots and a colourful scarf.

Now, what will I choose to wear underneath? The clinginess of the dress calls for reinforcement underneath to smooth the rolls of fat under my dress, so I think about my options. A corset? No, the boning will show through the dress. I'd rather not have a guy know what's underneath unless I choose for him to know. Fossicking around in my lingerie drawer, I find the perfect solution.

A sheer, black, fitted chemise that has a secret suck-my-tummy-in panel! That will give me a better silhouette. I glance at the time to see it slipping away as I squeeze into the complicated lingerie, and fix the criss-cross straps into place.

A quick check in the mirror makes me smile. I don't know if I will let William in on the secrets under my dress — but I feel more confident and sexier wearing beautiful lingerie. With a last brush through the straight blonde hair falling across my shoulders, I touch up my lips with glossy red lipstick. Dropping it into my handbag, I run for the door.

I'm catching a train into the city because parking is a nightmare near Darling Harbour. Getting off the train at Town Hall, I walk downhill towards the Park Royal. I'm looking forward to the evening, but Frenchy is on my mind. I shake my head as if to dislodge thoughts of him from my brain and take a deep breath. William, here I come!

As I step into the lobby, my eyes search for the bistro section. I haven't eaten in this hotel before, so have no idea which direction to turn. Sensing my hesitation, the doorman asks me if I need any help. With a smile and wishes for a good evening, he points me in the right direction.

Standing at the 'Please wait to be seated' announcement on a fancy gold-lettered sign, I look around to see if I can spot him from here. My attention is drawn back to the podium where a haughty-faced young waitress has appeared.

"Do you have a reservation, Madame?"

Madame? Geez, that makes me feel old. I know she's trying to be polite, but she could have chosen the younger sounding 'miss' instead! Her stunning face wears a slight frown as if she disapproves of me. With her dark hair slicked back from her face into a tight bun, she reminds me of a prim schoolteacher scolding a student.

"Yes, I have a reservation thank you. For two, under the name of ..."

I falter and stop mid-sentence. Damn. What if William has booked this using his last name? I don't know what that is! Bloody hell, I hope to God he's used his first name. I clear my throat and a hesitant 'William' emerges with a question mark at the end, as if I am not at all sure whether such a booking exists.

"Ah yes, no problem at all, Madame. Your companion, Mr. William, is already here. Follow me and I will escort you to his table."

Mister William? Is that his *last* name? Looking down her nose at me, she spins and takes off through the tables before I can ask her. Rounding the corner, I spot William in a corner booth and smile. He looks handsome with most of his dark waves slicked back, while a couple escaped curling down his forehead. His crisply ironed patterned white shirt teamed with charcoal pants that are stretched across his thighs is a welcome sight. Frenchy who?

My Latino date is looking hot tonight. With a big grin, he

leaps from the table and envelopes me in a warm hug. A quick peck on the lips becomes something more as he holds me tight against him.

"That was an enthusiastic hello, I must say!"

Sliding into place next to him in the corner booth feels cosy. At the café we were further apart, but this time I'm close enough to smell him. I did catch a pleasant whiff on the first date with that initial quick hug, but it was difficult to perform the Vixen smell test properly with such a short hug.

Drawing in more air deeply, I breathe in his scent. Damn. He smells delicious. I'm not sure which aftershave he is wearing, but he smells almost good enough to eat. I'm trying not to let him notice what I'm doing, so I engage him with a question as a distraction as I lean down and scratch my ankle to get a better whiff.

Mmmmm yes, I am impressed with his scent. It was difficult to tell when we were in that café on our first date. There were so many delectable aromas wafting in the air that day!

As I sit back in my seat properly, the thick white tablecloth brushes against my knees. I notice how secluded the position of this booth is. The ornate white cut-out metal screen across the top of the bench behind us also adds privacy here. Convenient. I must remember that for future dates.

Mwaaahahahahaaahahaa!

The waitress returns with our wine, and I'm surprised to see William has ordered a bottle rather than a glass each. That's fine with me — I'm not driving home, so a few wines are not an issue tonight. Chatting easily, the first bottle of wine disappears before our main course arrives. With a wave of his hand, William indicates to the waitress to bring another bottle of the same.

The meal is delicious, but I'm slightly distracted by the puzzle of the book's blue glow. He's been a perfect gentleman so far, so I'm still clueless. Interrupting my internal musings, William slides his fingers across my thigh to gain my attention.

"Where are you baby? I want all your attention right here, right now."

His fingers coax my head to turn to him as his face approaches me. This time I know what's about to happen, and I need it to. I have already performed the smell test, now I need to test his kissing skills. If he's terrible, then could the blue mean 'worst kisser ever'?

Latino lover draws me closer as his soft lips press against mine. Gently coaxing them apart, he teases my lower lip with the tip of his tongue. Pressing harder, his arm encircles my waist and pulls me closer. My fingers stroke his cheek, and he flicks a cheeky tongue across the tip of the one closest to his mouth. Smiling against his lips, I surrender to the kiss.

A soft growl reverberates in his chest as he deepens our connection. Hooking my knee over his thigh he slides his hand higher along my thigh. I grin against his lips and slap it away with my free hand. He laughs in protest.

"Hey, I was enjoying that!"

"I bet you were! Well, actually I know you were!"

"You know it, baby, that was a great kiss!"

I must agree, it was indeed a ten out of ten kiss. I might go as far as saying it was a toe-curling kiss! Damn, that means still I have no clue on the blue glow — but he did call me baby, which I *hate*. He waves the waitress over for the bill and she nods.

"Yes, Mister William, it will be taken care of."

That was odd. Maybe he already gave them his credit card earlier? Finishing our dinner, we take a stroll down along the water. Throngs of people are out taking advantage of the mild evening. Restaurants are filled to the brim with people, the hum of chatter reaching us from several meters away. We had barely started our walk when William turns to me, grabbing my hand to slow me to a stop. I turn to face him with my favourite eyebrow raised.

"Arleia, I know it's a nice evening out, but I have a suggestion."

"What do you want to suggest?"

"Well, I didn't want to mention it earlier, but I actually have a room at the Park Royal for the night. It was part of an incentive from one of the companies that I do work for. That's why I chose the restaurant for dinner there. I hope you don't mind that I didn't tell you earlier!"

A hotel room, hey? I'm surprised he agreed to the walk and didn't just suggest we go straight there. I stare at the reflection of the lights shimmering on the water. Yes, the evening is pleasant tonight, but would it be nicer to have this Latino lover wrapped around me horizontally? Noticing my hesitation, he sweetens the deal.

"I have a full mini bar with snacks up there, and we could order something from the dessert menu later and have room service deliver it."

The final offer of dessert via room service clinches it for me.

"You have a full mini bar? And we can order dessert?"

I want to be clear before I agree to be swayed by the treats on offer. He throws back his head in laughter.

"Wow, you really are serious about your desserts!"

His teasing draws a grin from me, and I turn abruptly on my heel back towards the Park Royal.

"Well, are you coming then? These desserts had better be out of this world!"

Ducking his head with a smile, he links his arm with mine and we head back to the hotel. He inserts his key card reader inside the lift, pressing floor thirteen. I hope that's not an unlucky number for me tonight! He again waves the card at his door and opens the door, with a gesture to enter. I can't help but be impressed as I step into the suite.

CHAPTER 22

Hotel Hottie

The bistro on the ground floor had a mediocre view of a small, manicured garden outside, but the city from this vantage point looks incredible. Glistening water is lit by hundreds of twinkling lights as it laps at the harbour edge. Mini people milling around watching a busker with a guitar below, but I can't hear what he's singing.

I turn from the window, taking notice of the room properly for the first time. With a high ceiling, separate lounge suite with a carved wooden coffee table, and small dining area, this room feels larger than any regular hotel room — and more opulent. More like a studio apartment size.

William walks to the carved wooden slatted cupboard and opens it to reveal the mini bar Squatting next to the fridge, he lists the choices. The vodka in there will work for me.

He pours our drinks and gestures towards the couch with a smile, which is angled to soak up the unique view. I sink into the comfortable pillowy lounge, and my dress blends with the dark suede cushions.

While we sit in comfortable silence appreciating the view, his fingers trace patterns up and down my thigh. Although I'm outwardly ignoring his fingers, I am highly aware of every circle they make. Reaching the edge of my dress, they swirl around innocently pushing my dress further up my thigh with every pass.

"So uhm, how did you score such an amazing suite through work, William?"

"I supply the company with up-to-date telecommunications systems for all their locations. This suite is part of the contract."

He shrugs as if to say that it's not important and wiggles his fingers further up my thigh. Pulling me closer, he nuzzles into my neck, grazing his teeth against me in the spot that really turns me on. How did he know where to find that? Is there a homing beacon alert flashing on my neck, or is he great at reading body language?

My head drops to the side automatically to allow better access for his teeth on my neck. I sweep the rest of my hair out of the way, and he murmurs his appreciation against my neck and bites down harder. It's like he's injecting a drug of desire into me. I can feel resistance melt away as the drug spreads through my system.

My knees drop apart and my back arches towards him as he bites harder on my neck and slips his hand further up my skirt to my dampened lingerie. The grunt of approval near my ear relaxes my free knee further. Reaching his hand around to cup my butt cheek, he smoothly slides my body further down the couch to a horizontal position.

The conscious part of my brain, which has not yet fully succumbed to desire applauds the smooth shift. Maybe this Latino lover has some moves I've not seen before. I like the sound of that! Lifting my knee so my foot is placed on the coffee table, he tickles the back of my thigh. He reaches my ass and cups a cheek firmly before his thumb deliberately presses against the mesh of lace at my crotch. Pressing harder there makes me gasp. He captures my mouth mid-gasp, invading it with his tongue.

Sensations wash through me. I lift my hips slightly from the couch in invitation. Understanding, he pushes his fingers across the edge of my black lacy underwear to slowly dive into the warmth below. An involuntary moan escapes my lips and travels down his throat.

Cupping my neck with strong fingers, he finishes the steamy lip-lock to trace light kisses down my throat. My dress slides off my shoulder easily as he works his way towards my breast. He pauses for a moment. I can feel his hot breath caress me through the lace.

With a rumble of appreciation, he draws the material aside with his teeth and draws my hardened nipple into his mouth. A tiny conscious part of my mind chants 'don't bite too hard' until his gentle sucking soothes it.

His hardness presses against my thigh. In the grips of desire clear thinking flies out the window. My body answers the rhythm of his fingers. I am drawn into the rising spiral of desire.

Unbuttoning his pants, I slip my hand inside. Rock hardness greets my fingers through his underwear. I frown at the fabric in my way.

Understanding my intention, he lifts his hips. His free hand slides his pants and underwear to his knees as he leans heavily against me for a moment. My hand still in place, he comes to rest against my palm. I can feel the blood pulsing beneath my fingers as I encircle him.

Even though he is rock hard, his dick is a bit smaller than I like, to be honest. It also seems to have a distinct curve to it, which draws my interest. Perhaps the angle of entry will feel different? I urge him on with my hips, his fingers releasing more tendrils of desire within.

Cool air swirls around me for a moment. William has completely withdrawn to kick free the restricting clothes around his knees. With my eyes closed, I sense rather than see him slide on protection. His lips return to mine in an instant.

His fingers are at the centre of my radiating heat. I gasp as I feel him gently probing before sliding all the way in. He moans against my mouth.

"Fuck yeah, Arleia. You feel amazing!"

I can only blink in response as he sets a slow deliberate pace. Each time he slides in deeper, the bend of his cock pushes against the exact right place to release a flood of wetness. Panting now, I urge him to go faster. Deeper. My fingers dig into his arse cheeks. My hips are rising at a more frantic pace. Sweat trickles down my neck.

His lips recapture mine briefly before he pushes my head to

the side to scrape his teeth against my neck. I cry out. Encouraged, he bites harder as he deepens his stroke, sucking hard on my neck as I gasp and sob for release.

The surge is coming. Crying out against his lips, my orgasm crashes through me. Wave after wave causes shudders to ripple through my body. His deep groans of satisfaction fill the air moments after mine.

Sinking back against the lounge cushions I readjust my dress. Well, at least I won't be losing any clothing here tonight since none came off! William excuses himself to wash up in the bathroom, while I laze a moment longer.

I need to stand up to readjust my knickers into place! Begrudgingly I stand and reach up my skirt to adjust them and stop in surprise. Oh crap. There's a massive wet spot on the back of my dress! Bloody hell, I can't get back on the train with a dripping dress as well as smelling like sex.

Walking back into the room, William wants to know why I'm standing awkwardly.

"Well, I seem to have a slight problem. You found the water faucet button or something, and the back of my dress is all wet!"

Howling with laughter, he reaches for the visibly wet material to feel for himself.

"Babe, that's awesome! I love it when a chick gets really wet like that!"

Heated flames of embarrassment lick up my neck. Damn you, fair skin! I always feel uncomfortable when guys talk about things like this, so I ignore his comment.

"Do you mind if I use the bathroom? Do you know if there's a hair drier in there or an extra towel?"

I draw his attention back to what's important — getting my dress dried!

"Oh yeah, sorry babe, of course you can! Yes, there probably is a drier in there, just check the cupboards under the basin."

Nodding my thanks, I make a hasty retreat into the glossy white bathroom. Once the door is closed, I twist and lift the back edge to sniff the fabric. Damn! The material does smell strongly of sex. I can't dry the smell into my dress. What if people on the train notice?

I quickly slip the dress over my head. With a plug in the basin, I squirt some hand soap into the filling bowl. After assessing the offending area, I carefully dunk it in and out of the water, giving the material a squeeze to encourage the scent to disappear. A few dunks should do it!

I wring the water out and run the spot under fresh water. Squeezing as much moisture out as I can first, I retrieve the drier and flick the switch to high speed and heat. The shrill whine of the drier fills the bathroom as I wave it across the damp spot willing it to dry faster.

The feeble power of the hotel drier will work for this small section of material. Imagine having to dry an entire dress with it, it would take an entire day! I shimmy back into the dress. What the hell? I can still smell the aroma of sex. The realisation that it's my knickers makes me laugh.

No time for washing and drying them too now, I want to leave as soon as possible. I slide them to the floor and fold them into my hand. The side pocket of my handbag is where they will have to travel home tonight. I'm going home commando style!

Returning to the lounge where William is sprawled half-dressed, I make my excuses. He knows I'm heading to Queensland tomorrow morning, so he won't be surprised that I have to leave. Shooting him a smile, I sweep my bag up from the floor and sling it over my shoulder while discreetly tucking my underwear into the unzipped pocket.

"Thanks for the fun evening William! If I'm going to make my flight tomorrow, I'm going to have to head home."

"No problem babe, it was great! Do you want me to walk you to the train station?"

"Naaah, I will be fine thanks! It's not that late!"

He gets up from the couch to envelop me in a tight hug. With a couple of kisses as a farewell and promises to catch up again I slip out the door. Heading for the train station I sniff deeply to see if the smell from my underwear escapes my bag. Nope! Phew, I really don't want strangers looking at me weirdly on the train!

I make it home before midnight and strip off to collapse on the bed. A faint blue glow lights the room. Oh no! Did I notice any further indication of what this blue glow might mean? I wrack my brain but come up with nothing. Too tired to care, I sink into sleep. It's going to be a big weekend and I need all the rest I can get tonight.

CHAPTER 23

Sunshine Surf

The dawn light peeks through my window as I groan and turn over. Wait. Frenchy today! My eyes fly open wide at the thought and I'm out of bed before I realise that I'm awake. Damn, I wish I had packed my case yesterday instead of leaving it to the last minute.

Pulling the suitcase from the top of my closet, I flip it onto the bed. Still wiping sleep from my eyes, I sigh loudly. What the hell am I going to pack? The weather in Queensland will be warmer than here in Sydney, so I won't need too many warm clothes. In fact, there's a good chance I will be naked a lot of the time while I'm there, so maybe I don't need to pack many clothes?

Mwaaahahahaaaahahaa!

I giggle to myself while I toss in an assortment of clothes and lingerie. Since I'm only going for an overnight trip there's no point in filling the suitcase to the brim, but I want a couple of outfit choices. Collecting my toiletry bag from the bathroom, I sling it in the top of the case. That should do for the packing!

Showered, dressed, and ready for another adventure, I set off towards the airport in a taxi. My flight leaves late morning and will arrive at the Sunshine Coast early afternoon. Filipe is working today until three, so my plan is to grab a late lunch somewhere, then head to the apartment we have booked for tonight.

The flight is smooth and fast. Arriving on time, we are hustled off the plane and directed to the baggage pick-up area. My bag is almost the last to appear, but I'm not in a hurry. There's still a couple of hours until Frenchy will be free, so I taxi into nearby Mudjimba to find a café.

Dropping me off at the Esplanade seems like a good idea since it's beach front and there are a lot of food choices along this stretch. Paying the taxi guy, I grab my bag and stroll down the street. I didn't think of lugging my case with me along the road — I'm glad it's only small!

I spot a likely lunch contender and select an outside table, so I can look across to see the beach while I eat. It's not practical to go for a walk along the grainy shore dragging my bag, so this is the closest I will get to the beach for now. Breathing in the salty smell of the sea, I grin. There's almost nowhere else I'd rather be at this moment than this exact spot.

After ordering, I swivel my chair to watch the small waves crash against the white sand. When I close my eyes, the sound of the sea is louder. Shrill cries from sea gulls echo through the palm trees as the noise of nearby traffic fades.

A meditative daydream takes over. Sounds seem muffled and

distorted, except for the ocean crashing onto the beach. Peace flows through me as I relax. I breathe deeply, inhaling the holiday feel of the salty air and release the tension in my shoulders that I hadn't realised was there. Ahh, this is the life!

Wait. What? Is someone talking to me? My impromptu ocean meditation ends abruptly. A waiter has arrived with my food and is addressing me.

"Madame? Hello madame, this is your order? Yes? Number sixty-nine?"

My eyes flash open to see a handsome face scrunched into an enquiring look, from only two feet away. I straighten immediately in my chair and nod.

"Oh! Sorry ... Uhm, I was just soaking up the sun and ocean. Erm yes, that is my order, I think. What did you say you have again?"

He confirms my order and leaves me in peace to stare at the scene before me. Wow, I am hungrier than I thought! I almost inhale my meal, then sigh in happiness.

The studio apartment we have booked for the night is super close, so at least I won't have to drag my case far. It's almost time to check in now, so I will head over there.

Thanking the waiter as I leave, I wander slowly past a bustling shopping precinct and turn onto the hotel's road. My outfit clings to me. Bloody hell. I had forgotten about humidity since I was in Bali. I wipe at the beads of sweat trickling down my forehead. A quick shower before Filipe gets to the apartment is needed!

. Checking in at a small reception desk, I take the lift to the fourth-floor apartment. A moment after stepping inside the door, a sigh escapes me. The chilly air of the airconditioned room cools me down by at least ten degrees. This is more like it!

Eager to look around, I poke my head into the bathroom near the entryway. A double-headed roomy shower encased in white marble greets me. The double sinks in the vanity are also bordered by sparkling marble, with a large spotlight-edged rectangle mirror.

Cute! Where is the light switch for those? I flip a switch and the room is filled with dazzling light. Hell no! I won't be turning these on when I am naked in front of him, I can see every imperfection already. Not so cute after all. I snap them off and wander into the main living area.

My eyes are drawn to the king-size bed that dominates the space. Fluffy white pillows begging to be messed up, atop a white spread. Extra plump throw cushions adorn the bed in muted silvery grey tones, matching the slate-grey two-seater couch. I flop face-first onto the mattress to test its firmness. A three-bounce softness result. Perfect.

Mwaaahahahaaahahaa!

I scramble off the bed and lift my suitcase onto a chair. I have just over an hour free before Frenchy arrives, and I want to be fully prepared by the time he gets here. Plucking my toiletry bag from my case, I head for the bathroom.

Cool water cascades over my heated body and makes me sigh with satisfaction. The shower alcove is so spacious that four people would fit in here. I giggle at the thought. Perhaps just two people in here will be plenty this weekend! Snapping off the water I quickly dry myself and risk a glance in the mirror. With the regular bathroom light on I don't look too bad.

Should I tempt fate and turn those spotlights on again, just to have a look? Before I can think about it, I flick them on. Just as I suspected — these lights are worse than any changing room in every clothing store I know of!

I return to my suitcase to decide on my outfit. Sexy but cool is the requirement for this climate. A black and red lace bra and matching underwear is my choice to start. I fish around for the colourful printed sundress that I threw in the bag.

As I slip the dress over my head, I think about the lights in fitting rooms. It can't only be me who hates looking in the mirrors there? On a normal shopping day, I usually feel good about how I look, until entering the dreaded cubicle.

I then immediately find two pimples on my face that didn't exist before I left home. Then I spot an inch-long black hair protruding from my chin— which I've been in public with *all morning*. All before I even try anything on!

Snapping back to the present, the balcony calls. I step out the sliding doors to check out the view. Ocean waves glisten in the sun between two other buildings in front of ours. At least there's still a sea view. The humid warmth of the air caresses my skin. I'd better go back inside before I need another shower!

Exploring further I discover a mini bar fridge hidden in one of the kitchenette cupboards, but it's empty. Damn! Why didn't I think to stop at that shop I walked past to grab a few supplies? My foot kicks the fridge door closed more forcefully than I intend. Come on brain, what doesn't involve me having to leave the apartment?

Home delivery! A few stabs of my index finger online and hey presto — a selection of nibbles, wine, and soft drinks are ordered.

I feel like I've achieved a lot in a short time, so I laze on the couch and check my watch. Three o'clock ... woohoo! Filipe should be here shortly. I send him a short message to let him know I've checked in already. A moment later my phone pings with his reply.

'I finish work, Princess. I come now to you. '

My heart does a little skip in excitement. I haven't seen Frenchy since I was in Bali quite a few weeks ago. We have been messaging each other sporadically, but he works long hours — so we have only spoken on the phone twice since then.

How far are the fields that he works in, from here? I wrack my brain to recall what he said. It might be about a twenty-min-ute drive to here, so the food and alcohol may arrive around the same time. Well, that shoots down any idea of greeting him at the door in lingerie. What if it was a delivery guy there and not Filipe? How embarrassing that would be!

With nothing to drink, I feel even thirstier. Sucking on a mint from my handbag helps slightly but I'm wishing my order would arrive. Another ten minutes of waiting passes. Just as I decide I'm going to have to drink water straight from the tap, there's a knock at the door.

Yes! I skip over and fling it open. To my surprise, not one but two young delivery guys are standing there. One from the bottle shop, and the other from the small grocery store around the corner. They look at each other awkwardly, then back at me.

"Grocery delivery for Arleia?"

The second guy finds his voice and I nod my reply.

"Yes, thanks ... and are you from the bottle shop?

I address the second dude holding a cooler bag, hopefully with my wine inside.

"Yes ma'am!"

"Ok cool, can you guys come in and put the orders over there. I can't carry them both at once!"

They follow me in and deposit the goods where I indicate. The grocery guy is silent and shy, but the bottle shop dude is much braver.

"Having a party here tonight? Looks like you're well-stocked now!"

His flirtatious smile and wink make me laugh. I can't help having a bit of fun with him and adopt a sultry tone.

"Yes, I am in fact ... a private party for two."

Redness stains his cheeks as he realises, he is out of his depth.

"Oh, err ... well enjoy your evening ma'am!"

This parting greeting is delivered in haste, as he almost trips over his feet backing out the door after the grocery boy. A giggle erupts from me at his hasty retreat. You're too inexperienced to play with a vixen, young man.

Mwaaahahahaaahahaa!

CHAPTER 24

Frenchy Fun

Fully hydrated, I lie across the bed flicking between TV channels with the remote while I wait. I can't concentrate on anything except for the shiver of nervous excitement vibrating through my body. I hope he's as good in bed as I remember!

A noise at the door brings my senses to full alert. Is that him? More muffled sounds at the door and the click of a key card confirms it. Filipe has arrived! I jump up from the bed and smooth my palms over my dress. You never know how a weekend with a virtual stranger will go, and I feel bubbles of nervousness erupting in my stomach as he enters the apartment.

"Princess!! I am come to you!"

With this grand announcement, he drops his bag and sweeps me into a bone-crushing hug. Although he has come straight from work and is in dire need of a shower — I'm still attracted to his natural scent. After a long and passionate kiss, I can finally speak.

"Frenchy ... still as sexy as ever! I can't believe we are together again after Bali. How do you like Queensland?"

My hands have a mind of their own as they slide down to grasp hold of his butt cheeks and squeeze.

"I like, Princess, I like. Is different from my country but is good."

His hands encircle my waist, and his strong arms lift me off my feet to twirl me around, laughing.

"Best thing of Australia, you mon chéri! Mmm, so delicious, I remember. Wait, Princess. I shower. Then we eat?"

I murmur my agreement and reluctantly let him go. He's right, though. With dirt streaks across his skin, he really does need a shower first! Raiding the now fully stocked fridge, I mix myself a drink and head back outside to sit on the balcony.

A cool sea breeze greets me as the glass slider opens with a woosh. Heaven! I feel like I'm on another beach holiday as I breathe in the fresh salty gusts. My mind returns to our night in Bali together. Did we talk much there? I'm fairly sure I'd had quite a few cocktails by then. I can't really remember!

Was it all about sex or did we click personality-wise too? I struggle to remember, because my most vivid memories of that night are not about our conversations. What are his expectations of this weekend? Why am I just thinking of this now? Why don't I consult the ... Oh shit!

"Noooooooooo!"

What the hell's wrong with me? Why wouldn't it have been the number one bloody thing to pack in my suitcase? My chest heaves with a massive sigh, and I stomp my feet against the blue tiles of the balcony.

"Idiot! How is this possible? The most important thing you needed to bring on this trip, and you forgot it! Arrrgghhh!!"

Berating myself out loud, I can't believe I forgot to pack the secret handbook. As you know, I didn't take it to Bali, so I don't know what its opinion of Filipe really is. Our last hours spent together were certainly anything but boring, so I can rule out orange for Filipe.

Now what? Uneasiness prickles down the back of my spine. My original plan was to bring the book and secretly check its glowing advice when Filipe is asleep. Oh, man. Sometimes I can be my own worst enemy!

Wait, I need to alter my mindset. There's nothing I can do about forgetting to bring the handbook, so why worry about it? That will only set a negative vibe for the weekend, and I want to enjoy my time with Filipe.

With a final chest-heaving sigh, I let the harmful self-talk go and feel the tension fall from my shoulders. The air rushes through my lips and into the universe, removing the negative energy and thoughts from within.

I'm not worried about this weekend with Frenchy. I know we connect on some level, but I haven't got a clue where this might go. The sexual pull towards him is strong. This makes me feel uneasy — I haven't been this attracted to any guy in ages. I need to keep my defences up until I can get both him and the handbook aligned to know what's really happening here.

His eyes that night in Bali were so mesmerising. I remember

the look of hunger in them and shiver. The memories of that night swirl in my head. I squirm in my chair. What am I doing? Why am I outside alone when there's a delicious man soaping himself naked in the shower?

This thought pulls me sharply back to the present and I leap out of the metal chair, almost overturning it. Why am I not taking advantage of every moment I'm here? Downing the remainder of my drink I step inside and listen for the shower. It's still running, but I can't hear the exhaust fan — perfect!

I hurry to the bathroom door. Slipping my dress over my head, I toss it on the bed and take a deep breath. Am I really doing this? For an extra confidence boost to remind me that I'm a strong awesome woman, I let out my vixen laugh then pull open the door. Steam clouds greet me as I quickly close the door.

"Princess! You come to wash my back, yes?"

A giggle erupts from my throat. Wash your back? I'll be doing more than that!

"You are taking so long, I thought you might have drowned in there! I was coming to your rescue with a towel, Frenchy!"

By my tone, it's obvious this is *not* why I am here.

"Ahh, you tease me, Princess! Come here. Too long I am wait for you."

Swinging open the shower door, we lock eyes. The teasing twinkle is replaced by a flare of raw desire as he realises what I am wearing. Muttering something in French his hand snakes behind my neck and draws my face roughly towards his parted wet lips. I sigh into his mouth as small droplets of water rain across my forehead and shoulders.

He wants to draw me further into the shower alcove. I want this too, but I don't want to get my lingerie wet. Pushing against his chest, I free myself long enough to unsnap my bra and shimmy out of my underwear before stepping towards him, wearing only a saucy smile.

Steam swirls around us as our bodies meet in an embrace. Hot water cascades in rivers between us, and around our joined bodies. Droplets of water frame long dark lashes as he looks into my eyes. Bottomless pools of hunger unsatisfied. I'm captivated by his eyes drinking me in.

An answering fierceness echoes within me, and we move together. Soap sliding over each other's bodies. Hand's dancing and teasing while we both explore with our hands as our mouths again lock together.

The combination of the water, soap-slickened bodies, and kisses create a parallel world of touch through the mist. The tiled shower ledge is the perfect place to put my foot to change the angle of entry. As the throbbing heat of his cock penetrates, my hands brace against the cool tiles. Desire whirls around us. Our tongues embrace and invade each other's mouths. The thrusting motion of his cock presses my back hard against the cool tiles. Heated bodies slide together faster. He bends to capture a watery nipple between his teeth as he cups my arse and pulls me toward him, pushing his hard cock in even deeper.

Motionless for a moment, his dick pulsating within, time stands still. A sudden movement elicits a cry from my throat as he quickens the pace, sliding his stiff rod into my heated, quivering core. Harder. Faster. I urge him on, my fingers digging into his arse cheek encouraging him to sink in even deeper as our bodies slam together.

He groans and I know he's getting close. So am I. His grunts of desire turn me on and send me spiralling over the edge. Succumbing to the blissful waves of orgasm, my last conscious thought is that this could be the longest shower in history.

Colours of the sunset streak across the sky by the time I am redressed for dinner later. Thankful for the endless hot water supply here, I feel cleaner than I ever imagined possible! Filipe calls for me to join him outside with fresh drinks and a cheese platter.

"Princess! So good woman. You think of everything and bring me food. Thank god or I die of hunger after this workout!"

His words cause an eruption of laughter from me as I join him on the balcony. We clink our glasses and take a sip. The percentage of vodka in my drink makes my eyes water. I slice off some cheese and pair it with a cracker to ease the burning in my throat.

"You want we go out for dinner, Princess?"

I nod in agreement.

"What food you like? We can find, I think. Or maybe you just like eat French food all night baby?"

We both laugh at his joke, knowing he is only half-joking. I consider that option for a moment. Even though I'm only here for one night, I don't want to spend the whole twenty-four hours away cooped up in an apartment, delicious as Filipe is!

"Nah, let's go out for dinner Frenchy. The evening has cooled down now and I saw lots of enticing eateries nearby earlier. We can go for a wander and see what catches our fancy!"

"Princess, it is you who caught me, I think this. Sexy woman! But we walk soon to find restaurant. Maybe next to beach, yes?"

I agree and we sit chatting awhile longer. His English is worse than I remember, but we did spend most of our time together *not* talking! Having to slow my sentences down a bit is taking some concentration, but at least we can communicate.

Balmy is the first word that pops into my head as we walk along the shore front. A huge full moon is rising over the ocean, adding to the enchantment of the evening. The clink of glass drifts across the road from the restaurants. My stomach growls in appreciation of the aromas carried over by the gentle breeze.

"What sort of food do you feel like Frenchy?"

"We cross the street now, Princess. We will find."

The first café we come to is Mexican. Exchanging glances, we continue past the doors. A few more steps away is an Asian fusion restaurant. With numerous Asians eating there, we decide the food is probably authentic. However, the restaurant is filled with young families with crying children, so we keep walking.

Eighties music blasts out of a hotel nearby, with a cover band belting out lyrics while patrons yell to be heard. Nope! That's not for us either. With a protesting growl, my tummy tells me I'd better find something soon. Then I spot the perfect place.

Nestled between two apartment buildings is a small quirky café. Brightly coloured sheer drapes edge large windows, show-casing cosy wooden tables and booths with richly polished benches. The layout looks to be designed to enhance each table's privacy. Perfect! I point it out to Filipe, and he nods his agreement.

Candlelight greets us with a flicker of flames atop the small round table. Our knees touch as we chat comfortably while waiting for our food to arrive. It looks delicious! Filipe laughs at my tummy's loud growl of anticipation.

"Princess. You so hungry! I think we lucky to find this place. If no, you so hungry you start eating me!"

I stab him not so gently with my cutlery before starting to devour my food.

"Ahh Frenchy, you are my dessert!"

Filipe reaches over and pinches my butt cheek then slides my chair closer. Leaning closer, he sweeps my hair back. But instead of the whisper I expect, he grazes his teeth across my neck to kiss my jawline and capture my lips. The taste of his wine-stained mouth adds taste to the sensations. A shiver of anticipation tingles along my spine. If this afternoon was the warmup session, I can't wait for the main event!

Filipe unfolds several notes from his wallet, tucking the money into the leather payment sleeve. Grabbing my hand, he leads me out the door. It's only a few minutes' walk to our apartment from here, but right now that feels too far.

We round the final corner, Frenchy in front of me. A darkened shop alcove gives me a naughty idea. Just after he walks past, I yank him backward and push him into the nook. Plastering my body against him I press my lips to his while running my fingers through his dark hair.

A moan of desire rumbles in his throat. We are partially

hidden from view, but any stray strollers could spot us. Grabbing my arse, he grinds his hips into me, so I can feel the extent of my impromptu public display of affection has on him. I smile against his lips and whisper.

"Let's go sexy man ... I want to see you naked!"

No more encouragement is needed. Filipe grabs my hand and almost drags me back to the apartment. Once inside, he pushes me up against the wall.

"So naughty, Princess. I like this! Come. We make more music together."

Needing no further encouragement, I pull his shirt over his head. Filipe's smooth, bare chest glows in the moonlight.

CHAPTER 25

French Fantasy

Flattening my hands against his torso, I push him so that he falls onto the bed. Joining him with a bounce, my laughter soon fades at his masculine growl. He pins me to the bed with his body and feasts on my lips before his hot breath tickles my shoulder as he moves down my body.

His fingers slide across my slick hot centre before slipping inside me, while my breast captures his mouth's attention. My back arches and I pull his head even closer to my chest as my nipple hardens to a rosy peak as he sucks harder.

I feel frustrated that I can't reach to touch him. Somehow, he knows. Filipe curves his body closer to me so that I feel his hardness press against my thigh. I reach down to stroke the rigid shaft. He growls in response and presses his fingers hard against the internal button that drives me crazy. My hips jerk in response. I feel his smile against my breast.

The throbbing tip my fingers are stroking is wet, and I circle the wetness around the rim, eliciting a moan from Filipe. With a growl he recaptures my lips briefly before flipping me over, slapping me on my butt cheeks.

While firmly holding my hips still, he slowly slides his full length in as deep as possible making me gasp. I want to move my hips, but he won't allow me to, yet. I want him faster, harder! Now! But he holds me still and slowly moves in and out.

Restricting my movement increases my need, and just when I think I can't take this torture another second, he slams into me hard, over and over again, now allowing me to push back against him, our bodies moving together in a heated frenzy. The spiral is building. I reach between my legs to flick my clit in rhythm with our sweat-slickened bodies. He encourages me, leaning forward to whisper in my ear and I tip over the edge. A guttural groan fills the air moments later, and I can feel him twitching inside me as his orgasm takes over.

Upon awakening the next morning though, it feels like I've been run over by a truck. Protesting muscles scream at me to stop moving after a simple stretch. My knees feel sore. It takes me a moment to get my bearings in the unfamiliar bed. A soft snore rumbles near my right ear.

The previous night floods back to my mind and I giggle. No wonder my knees are hurting. I flip the sheet off and raise my left leg in the air to check out my knee. A red angry square patch of skin stares accusingly back at me. I hope the other skirt I bought is long enough to cover this for my flight home later today!

Not wanting to wake Filipe, I close my eyes and revisit the night. A first satisfying session left us both thirsty about ten-o-clock. Wrapped in sheets, we stood on the balcony chatting together while we rehydrated. But it wasn't long before a twitch against my thigh told me he was ready for round two.

Ohh, *that* must have been when those carpet burns occurred. Mwaaahahaahaaahahaaa!

We both crashed out early last night. It couldn't have been much past midnight. I thought we'd be awake almost all night like we were in Bali. But now I think of it, that was an unreal expectation.

Filipe had to work yesterday before meeting with me, so of course, he was knackered. Add three sex-filled workouts on top of a day's work on the farm, it is no wonder he's still passed out. The snoring next to my ear increases with a snort then dies away.

I should have realised this earlier and reduced my expectations — he must have been so tired. Not only that but for him yesterday was the end of a six-day work week. Instead of being annoyed that we fell asleep so early, I should be thankful he had enough energy for me at all!

My limbs feel stiff, but a hot shower will soon fix that. There might be time for a day session or two before we check out at twelve. I slowly ease myself up from the mattress trying not to wake him, while my body groans in protest. Last night's clothes are strewn across the floor. A soft laugh escapes me as I gather what I need from my suitcase and head towards the bathroom.

Twenty minutes later, I feel like a new woman. Soothing heat from the water has revved up my sluggish, stiff start. I wonder if Frenchy is awake yet. Slipping quickly into my clothes, I check the length of my purple fringed skirt against my knees.

Just long enough to hide the raw patches! I lift a foot and rest it on the vanity to get a better look at reddened skin and groan. Ouch, that was still too much movement after last night. The raw patches look angry. What do I use to ease carpet burn? I don't want to ask a pharmacist — how embarrassing!

I bet Filipe doesn't have carpet burns on his knees. Something in the back of my mind from last night jumps out at me. He did kneel for a while, but that's because I was doing something for him. Did he return the favour? No!

Now I'm trying to remember. Did he head southwards on me when we were playing in Bali, or not? The memory is hazy. Bloody hell! I should have written it all down immediately in my vixen spreadsheet the day after! Alcohol-tinged memories are not exactly accurate.

Don't get me wrong, sex with him has been hot and steamy so far. But I do prefer men who love to go down on a woman, and happily instigate oral sex often. Decision made. I'm writing everything I can remember about Frenchy in my spreadsheet as soon as I get home tonight.

I must admit, we did struggle with some conversation. But I think it's more a translation thing than a communication problem. Between thoughts, I boil the kettle. With a steaming tea in hand, I head towards the terrace. Frenchy stirs and rolls over with a grunt, falling back into a gentle rhythmic snore.

I carefully slide the glass door shut as I step outside. I don't want to disturb him yet. He obviously needs more sleep after yesterday! Sunshine and blue sky greet me. Glistening water laps quietly at the shore, and the fresh breeze is no more than a whisper around my bare shoulders.

I breathe deeply. Who would have imagined a year ago that I'd be here soaking up the Queensland sunshine, while a hunky French man snores in my bed? Half of me wants to go back inside and ravish him. The other half is just delighted at the sunny morning. Ahh a holiday dilemma!

The strong attraction I first felt in Bali for Filipe is still present. What's wrong with me? The tight control I usually exert around any sappy, romantic feeling disappears around him. I've never flown anywhere just to meet a guy before. Bubbles of panic rise in my throat, but I squash them back down.

Stay calm. Breathe. When you get home, consult the book. Then you'll know. There's nothing more you can do now, but to enjoy the time you still have here, Arleia!

My short internal pep talk works wonders. I drain my tea and head inside determined to entice Filipe's eyes open. It doesn't take long to rouse him from slumber and for him to pull me down on top of him, with one hand. Rubbing his eyelids with his other hand he yawns.

"Ma Magnifique fille. Yes, come! How is my Princess this morning?"

Still sleepy, he rubs the tips of our noses together before brushing his lips against mine. His breath is sweet enough to go in for a longer kiss. Realising that I'm dressed, he makes a sound of protest, indicating that I am wearing too many clothes for his liking.

I re-join him in the bed, and a couple of hours fly by in a haze of sexual desire and mutual satisfaction. Finally, we come up for air, exhausted.

"Bloody hell ... that was amazing, Frenchy!"

I can see his chest rise and fall next to me rapidly, as his body struggles to adjust.

"Princess. Oh my God. You are wild woman. You know this, yes?"

Peals of laughter erupt from deep within. Yes, I do know this. That's what vixens are. Wild, strong, and confident women in search of adventure and fun. Displaying bravery by stepping out of their comfort zone into the unknown. Feeling the fear and saying 'Fuck it! I'm taking a leap of faith anyway'.

I'm so far from my comfort zone I don't even know where it is anymore. But I don't want to. I like this expansion of consciousness and new connections. The creation of new adventures and a new reality. My self-confidence is growing continuously, I'm becoming braver than I have ever been before in my life.

Filipe gives my butt cheek a playful slap, which pulls me back to him.

"Princess. We must hurry. Look the time already! So sad ... we have no time for this!"

I know he's right as I glance at the clock. Eleven twenty-two already! Damn, I do need to move my butt out of bed right now. In a flurry of activity, we both somehow manage to get showered, dressed, and packed up with two minutes to spare before checkout.

Returning to our favourite café for a quick lunch before my flight home, we take advantage of our last hour together. Sultry kisses are sprinkled between bites of food as my flight time draws ever closer.

After promises to see each other again and a passionate hug, I board the plane. Distress wells up in a throaty lump threatening to choke me. What the hell is wrong with me? I need to get my head back into the dating game and distract myself from the attraction I have to this man.

The Sydney Opera House shimmers in the sunlight as the plane descends towards the airport, while miniature cars line the Harbour Bridge.

My taxi driver deposits me at my doorstep with a wave, and I hurry to unlock my door. It feels like forever since I left. Far longer than just for an overnight stay. Dragging my case to the bedroom, I drop it on the floor and make a beeline for the handbook.

Retrieving the book from my drawer I unfold the velvet cloth it is wrapped in. With the book in my hands, I close my eyes. Please give me guidance on Filipe! My silent internal plea reverberates around my head. Nervous to see if the book responds, I open my eyes.

A tiny white spark shoots from the secret handbook. What the hell? I wait in silence, holding my breath. More small white sparks fly from the pages, with an ominous crimson glow increasing as the twinkling sparks pop around me.

Shit! A red glow of warning coupled with white sparks. A cry of frustration at still not having the clear answer I seek escapes me. I know the red is a disaster date warning, but what does that mean paired with white sparks?

Arrrghh!! Why does this book have to be so mysterious?

CHAPTER 26

Holiday Hangover

Mid-week already after my trip away, and the effort to respond to the several text messages from my Marks this evening is arduous. Although I do want to see Krystian, Roshan, and Darz again soon, I'm still tired from my weekend on the Sunshine Coast. Work has been busier than usual too, depleting any extra energy for dating.

The mystery about the three unknown colours weighs heavily on me. The orange, then blue, and now the red with white sparks has my mind spinning. I need to see my Latino lover again to uncover what the blue means. I am fairly certain that the orange signifies a boring date. But I'd rather not experience another dreary date with him to confirm my theory!

Should I just date my regulars? At least I know what to expect from them — and they have been approved of by the book with a golden glow of acceptance. But they are the known, and I am drawn to the unknown!

The idea of dating many different nationalities to see which I prefer most is still appealing. Even though, after meeting with three Frenchmen, I've discovered that men from France differ wildly from one another.

Frenchie's Gabriel, Filipe, and Kasmir are all so different, so my theory so far is wrong! What if I try to find another Polish guy like Krystian, or a Sri Lankan man like Roshan? Sydney is a multicultural city after all — there are a plethora of international men on my doorstep.

Setting myself up on the couch with my laptop on my knees, I venture forth. As usual, there are stacks of contact requests from hopeful men to go through, but this time I am specifically hunting a Polish or Sri Lankan male.

Aha! This guy looks promising — he has mocha skin with a dazzling smile. What nationality is this dude? I check his profile for race first. Yes! Another Sri Lankan hottie to add to my list.

I glance across at the handbook perched on the edge of my coffee table. It remains silent. Pressing the accept chat button, I shoot off a quick message saying hi.

Another ping from the laptop lets me know one of my contacts has just come online. In an instant, a message from William flashes onto my screen.

LatinoLover: Hello beautiful! How was your weekend away?

Punching out a reply, I press send. Another chime sounds. I expect it to be William, but I see that the prospective new Mark I've just added is now online and writing me a message. I flex my fingers and stretch my arms skywards, to prepare for two conversations at once.

PJ0669: Hi I'm PJ. How are you today?

Well, that was a boring first message, but first messages often are! I manage to shoot back a polite reply before checking William's next message.

LatinoLover: That was such a fun night we had hey! When might you be free for a repeat?

ATrixenVixen: Yes, I had a good time, thanks! I was a bit slow to get ready for my flight the next day though haha. How soon are you thinking to catch up again?

LatinoLover: Tonight? Hahahahaaa ... just kidding!

ATrixenVixen: Thank God! It's been a busy week and I need to reenergize lol

LatinoLover: Hey short notice, but I have a suggestion.

ATrixenVixen: Oh really? And what might that be?

Another message from PJ distracts me from William.

PJ0669: You have the most gorgeous smile! Nice profile and I love your pictures too, beautiful. What are you looking for on here Hun?

I read the message with a smile until I get to the last word — 'Hun'. Man, I hate being called that. Or Darling. Even worse is being called 'Dear'. That term of endearment should be reserved for women in their eighties or nineties, not a sexy vixen who's just breaking into her forties!

PJ, I'm sorry to say but you've just made a blunder. No 'Huns' allowed in the vixen world! Before I reply I check out his private pictures. Holy Mother of ... this guy is the size of a giant gladiator! My eyes pop out of my head almost as much as his biceps are bulging through his shirt.

This dude looks like a serious beefcake — the type I might like to barbecue on all sides.

Mwaaahahahaaahahaa!

Forgetting William for a moment, I feast my eyes on the deliciousness of PJ's image. His thighs strain against skin-tight black jeans. Broad shoulders and a strong chest with hard pebbled nipples are clearly visible through his white dress shirt.

I need a cold drink and a fan. It sure got hot in here fast! Fanning my face will have to do. I can't drag my eyes away from the screen to get a drink yet. A dazzling white smile. A handsome face with a shaved head and diamond twinkling from his ear complete this mountain of brownie goodness.

ATrixenVixen: Thanks for the compliments ... I appreciate it! But I must tell you that I hate to be called Hun. Beautiful, or gorgeous vixen gets the tick of approval, however! Haha

PJ0669: Oh, shit sorry, you're right. A goddess such as yourself is far beyond just a Hun LOL

I like that he has a sense of humour and that he took my

admonishment so well. Maybe I will add him to my *must meet* list! Within a few minutes of chatting, I discover that he is a personal trainer, who grew up in Sri Lanka, but has been living in Sydney for the past eight years.

After swapping numbers, we agree to catch up soon. Conveniently for me, he's off to the gym now — so I can get back to my conversation with William!

ATrixenVixen: Sorry for my slow response ... I was distracted by a phone call! What was your suggestion?

LatinoLover: All good Arleia! I'm wondering can you get any time free on Friday during the day?

Friday? I wonder what he has in mind. It's possible that I could ask for this Friday off.

ATrixenVixen: I am supposed to work, but I might be able to get the day off if it's for a good enough reason! Why do you ask?

LatinoLover: I have a work-free day on Friday because I'm attending a seminar on Thursday night in Manly.

ATrixenVixen: Okkk ... so what does that have to do with me and Friday?

LatinoLover: Patience Miss Vixen! It will be a late finish there with the guys, so I've booked a room for the night in the hotel where the seminar is being held. Want to join me in Manly for the day on Friday? Sorry for the short notice.

I consider his proposal. It's tempting! Do I like him enough to take the day off? Regardless, having one less day of work this week is appealing. Before I can give him an answer, I need to check with my manager Corrine.

ATrixenVixen: Mmm … sounds fun. Leave it with me for a minute, and I'll check to see if I can get the day off!

I decide that calling her would bring me a faster result. Corrine and I are friends out of work, so I know she won't mind me calling now. She answers after the first ring.

"Arleia! What's going on, girl? You never ring me on a Wednesday night!"

I laugh at her words. It was true, we saw each other most days at work so usually there was no need to call each other after hours.

"I have a favour to ask you! Would it be ok to use my toil time and take this Friday off? I need to recuperate and catch up on things here after being away."

Skirting around the truth, I don't tell her why I really want the time off. As close a friend as she is, she disapproves of my constant dating. It's easier not to tell her about most of my dates, but I did tell her about Filipe. That was bad enough!

Corrine was horrified that I'd met Filipe at a bar and took him back to my hotel room. I endured a twenty-minute lecture about not dating so many men, and keeping myself safe. Not something I want a repeat of.

I love her dearly, but since she met the love of her life at the tender age of twenty, she doesn't understand how different the dating game is now. Never having had her heart broken, or being disappointed by several men, Corrine struggles to understand this new world of meeting guys online.

"Sure, thing let me check the work schedule. Hang on a sec, Arleia!"

Loud rustling emanates from my phone's speaker as she looks for this week's calendar. I wait patiently for her ... and hope that William is too! Finally, she returns.

"Sorry about that! Hallie left her homework all over the table on top of my things, so I couldn't find it!"

Corrine huffs into the phone making me laugh. I knew her bluster was for show — she was thrilled that Hallie was doing her homework instead of watching TV. I can tell she's distracted, so I prompt her to return to answering my question.

"Oh sorry, yes! Yes, that is fine for you to take this Friday off, no one else has put in for time off that day. Lucky for you! Well, I will see you tomorrow at work anyway. Have a good night — Hallie, clean up this mess! Sorry Arleia, it's chaos around here. Talk to you tomorrow!"

I end the call and sit quietly for a moment, appreciating the silence. No pandemonium here! I love my solitude and my own space. I'm not sure how I would cope with so many noises, animals, and people around me after work each night. Oops, time to get back to William!

ATrixenVixen: It must be your lucky day. Friday off for me has been approved!

LatinoLover: Wow that's excellent, can't wait to see you again gorgeous ;) I will text you the address of the hotel babe.

Babe? Have I not explained previously to William about this endearment? My enthusiasm cools a fraction as my eyes fall on the handbook's bright blue glow.

"Oh shit! You're right!"

I say aloud addressing the book. I still don't know much about William. I'm not even sure where he lives. The mysterious blue light winks, taunting me. If I don't meet Latino Lover again, how will I discover what it means? I can't help but feel wary.

Another thought enters my mind. I forgot to check the book when PJ was online. Sighing with frustration I snap the laptop closed and head to bed. When will I learn?

Recognition of Supermarket Duds

Types of men in the supermarket of lust are varied. Some are past their sell-by date, some appear delicious but taste horrid, while others are so boring it's preferable to starve. Here are a few of the types of men to watch out for and avoid whenever possible:

* Cream Puff Man - Looks delicious, but empty inside - no conversation, relies on his good looks alone
* Sweet Pie Man - Likes to divide himself up and share a piece of himself with every girl he meets
* Glazed Donut Boy - Delicious and satisfying but gone too fast before you get a good taste
* Mud Cake Man - Appears tasty but will weigh you down after eating
* Chocolate Chip Brownie Dude - Dark skinned dessert hiding a secret inside that's not always delicious
* Frosting Laden Cup Cake Boy - too sickly sweet on the outside, covering a boring stale lump underneath
* Fruity Tart Man - A little bit of craziness to top off a sugary sweet flirt
* Kitchener Bun Boy - A sugary bun on the outside, with a creamy interior and a speck of jam, that squirts cream when bitten too hard
* Sponge Roll Man - A quick roll with him and you are covered with cream and jammed out the door
* Gingerbread House Man - Promises sweet treats to lure you to his house prematurely
* Banana Bread Boy - A little plain and not too sweet while hiding a nutty surprise
* Meringue Man - Incredibly sweet and looks beautiful, but is

hollowly empty inside
* Lamington Man - Covered in brown muck and always leaves a trail of mess behind him

CHAPTER 27

A Shocking Twist

This morning, I find myself wrapped in my sheets like an Egyptian mummy after unsettling dreams last night. All I remember are shadowy figures and a feeling of unease. I know it is related to William, but that's all.

Thoughts of him seep into my head. Come to think of it, something is a bit odd. This is the second time we will be meeting in a hotel. While I love meeting in a safe neutral place, hotel rooms are not usually on the vixen-approved list. Our café meeting was short, and the café's location was a bit secluded. Or was that just romantic?

The William puzzle remains in the back of my mind for the rest of the day. Something is off, but I can't put my finger on it yet. I brush Corrine and her enquiries as to what I will do on Friday aside with a vague 'catch up on house stuff' response. There's no way I'm telling her about my Latino lover, she'd have a fit!

Lulu will have to be informed though. I need to tell someone

I trust where I'm going and with whom, just in case something unforeseen happens. Safety first when dating is the rule, and I don't want to break that rule.

Mwaaahaaahaahaa!

Friday arrives with a sprinkling of sun peeping through my blind. We're meeting at nine-thirty, so I'll miss most of the heavy morning traffic on the drive to Manly. The last time I was there was on my date with Sean, who I've nicknamed 'Dreads' because of his dark, long dreadlocked hair.

Wow, that was right out of my comfort zone! I went to a café to meet Sean several months ago, and although he was nice, his fetish preferences are unfamiliar and slightly scary. He's made the effort to keep in touch with me since, but I don't know if I'm brave enough yet to take him up on his Dom/Sub offer.

Twenty-two degrees and mainly sunny is the forecast today so I dress for spring but add a jacket to take just in case. At least then I can adjust depending on the weather. Once I'm on my way, I call Lulu.

"Well, helloooo Miss Vixen! What are you doing calling me on a Friday morning? Aren't you at work today?

"Hahaha, I have the day off. I dared not mention to Corrine that I'm heading out on a date this morning!"

"Who with? Darz? Roshan? Krystian? A new Mark? What are you up to? How was last weekend with Frenchy?"

I laugh at her barrage of questions. I'm glad I called to catch her up on what's been happening. Filling her in on my previous weekend with Filipe first, I then move on to today's escapade and the blue light mystery.

"What do you think it means, Arleia? I reckon you're right, there's something fishy about this Latino lover of yours. Keep yourself safe, girl, and give me a call if you have any problems!"

We finish the call with a promise to catch up soon, and I turn my full attention back to the road. The traffic is still heavy but I'm almost there. A refreshing ocean breeze greets me as I turn onto the esplanade. Smelling the salty air takes me back to my weekend with Filipe.

In less than two months he will be moving to New South Wales. Another farm that his current boss owns is located around an hour southwest of Sydney, and he'll be working there for six months. Although still a long way away from my place, it's more accessible than traveling interstate.

I spot a car reversing out of a park just ahead of me. Perfect! I'm only a couple of blocks away from where I'm meeting William, so this might be as close as I can get on a busy Friday morning in Manly. Scooting into the park I do a final check in the mirror.

Raking my fingers through my hair, I fix the windswept look. After a swipe of pink gloss across my lips, I take a few deep breaths. The mystery of the blue glow needs to be solved today.

The sparkling water lapping at golden sand catches my attention as I walk towards the hotel. With a deep breath, I turn into the doorway and head across the foyer. A small café is attached to the front, and I can see William seated in a chair with his back to me.

A feeling of mischief overcomes me. I tiptoe quietly towards him, so he doesn't hear me approach. Slapping my hands onto his shoulders, I demand to know what he's up to in a loud, gruff voice.

Jumping out of his chair in a frightened panic, he knocks it flying. Fear splashes across his face followed by a scowl. I'm laughing so hard tears are forming and I can hardly squeeze any words of apology out.

"Shit, sorry William! I didn't mean to scare you that much. I just saw you from behind and couldn't resist!"

His glare tells me he doesn't see the funny side yet. Ohh. Maybe I shouldn't have done that?

"You nearly gave me a heart attack, Arleia! Not cool. Bloody hell!"

I'm taken aback by his response. Yeah ok, maybe I shouldn't have scared him, but my mischievous sense of humour didn't stop to consider that. His brows are still knitted together in a frown. Geez, let it go alright, I said I was sorry!

He calms down and shoots me a forced grin. Relieved, I allowed him to take my hand and pull me along behind him. William's room is only on the first floor, so we take the stairs. Before we ascend the wide gleaming wooden staircase, I can't help teasing him.

"Are you sure you don't want a piggy-back ride up the stairs?"

He gives me another glare. I am puzzled. I thought he had a better sense of humour than that. I slap the rounded orbs of his butt cheeks as we reach the landing and earn a smile.

"This way, vixen!"

He produces a key at the third door we come to, and swings the door wide open, gesturing for me to enter first. Furnished in a beachy theme of pale blue and white, the room has a cheery feel to it. The pale blue walls effortlessly match today's sky, and the bed is made up with an ocean of sea-green textured pillows as well as matching material throw across the bottom of white cotton sheets.

Large, clear glass windows frame the ocean scene that demands your attention. However, William ignores it and sprawls across the bed on his back with a bounce, messing up the perfectly placed pillows.

I can tell he's waiting for me, so I drag my gaze away from the window and sit on the edge of the bed next to him. With a hand across his forehead, I shake my head.

"You are definitely in need of something. You're feeling too hot, we better loosen this shirt before you catch on fire!"

Unbuttoning his shirt, I indicate that he needs to sit up so I can remove it entirely. I lean down to brush my lips against his. Slowly nibbling on his lip, I coax his mouth open. I can tell he's resisting the urge to pull me down hard against him.

Another minute of feathery kisses and teasing flicks of my tongue and he's had enough. Groaning he pulls my head closer and deepens the kiss. I respond with a sigh.

Linking my fingers through his, I lift his arms above his head. With our mouths still locked together, I press his hands into the pillows. My favourite moonstone ring on my right finger squashes uncomfortably against my fingers.

I break our kiss to examine my fingers. Wait, what's that? A glint of gold sparkles next to my silver ring. I look closer. A thick band of gold circles the ring finger of his *left* hand. You have got to be kidding me. He's *married*?!

Pulling away I straighten my spine. William is lounging on the bed, with his eyes closed. I have to confront him. Bloody hell, this must be what the book was trying to tell me! I think of when a blue light is used. Police, ambulance, and fire warnings. The pieces of the puzzle are all falling into place.

No wonder he wants to meet me in a hotel. What I *thought* was romantic, is really a ruse to hide what he has been doing. Being unfaithful to his significant other. A nauseous feeling washes over me.

Any attraction to this man has flown out the window. Leaping up from the bed, I back away from him. Finally, he realises something is wrong and opens his eyes.

"What the fuck, William! Are you married?!!"

The expression on his face tells me all I need to know. Guilt glints in his eyes as he combs his black locks from his forehead and tries to form a reply that doesn't damn him to hell. Twisting the offending ring, he attempts to hide it from view.

"Arleia, I was going to tell you! I'm sorry! Things haven't been great between my wife and me lately, we don't even sleep in the same room anymore! I guess I was just looking to see what else is out there."

At least he has the decency to hang his head in shame. I don't believe his confession for a moment; he's just trying to make himself look less of a bastard. If I had known he was married from the start, I'd never have agreed to meet him even once. Grabbing my bag, I turn to face the lying arsehole.

"I'm not interested in your explanation. All I know is that you're married, and you are a liar! I pity your poor wife — you're a shitty excuse for a husband! Don't call me again and do me a favour, lose my number!"

Slamming the door on his feeble protests I almost run down the stairs. I don't want him to follow me, or hear any more weak excuses. Crossing the road to where I parked the car, I get in and lock the door behind me. Idiot!! I'm not sure who I'm berating. William, or myself?

I sigh in disappointment. My sneaky daytime date turned out nothing as I imagined. That's it, I'm over men for the day! The need to vent is strong, so I wonder what Lulu is up to today.

Punching out her number, I wait for her to answer.

"Arleia! Is everything okay? What happened? I thought you were on your date this morning?"

"Yeah, I was. Long story. I'm okay thanks, but I do need a girly catch-up with you. What are you up to today?"

"I'm out now but will be home in an hour. Come by, I've got a full bottle of vodka there with our names on it if we need it!"

I'm thankful for the distraction she offers. Stopping to buy a raspberry mixer and nibbles, I head towards her place. Thank God I have a friend who understands the world of vixen dating!

Forbidden Marks:

Vixens are not to set their sights upon any man who is married whether they are happily married or not

Never pursue men already in a monogamous relationship

No vixen shall meet with a Mark whom she knows is seeing a sister vixen, unless the vixens previously agree on terms

Marks who say they are in an open relationship, but their partner is not in agreement or have no knowledge of their 'open' relationship status

Failure to adhere to these rules can incur extreme misery and persecution from wronged women.

Vixens are of light and wish to avoid negative drama in their lives. **Knowingly entering into vixen play with an attached man of any kind is forbidden.**

CHAPTER 28

Solving Sparkles

Even with my side detour to the shops, I beat Lulu to her place. Waiting for her in the car, my mind returns to William. What an arse! A ring is something I do check for. He must have removed it for both the café and dinner dates. I'm sure I would have seen the band on his left hand if it were there.

Lulu arrives at her house about ten minutes after me. She waves while pulling into the driveway, so I smile in greeting and push William from my mind.

The imposing two-story house is surrounded by an impeccably manicured garden. White roses nod in the breeze lined up along the edges of squares of lush green grass. I follow the paved path bordered by the flowers to Lulu's front door and enter.

The foyer's high ceiling towers over the curved wooden staircase leading to the second floor. Ignoring that route, I head through the lounge towards the kitchen. Lulu's muffled voice greets me from the pantry.

"Arleia! Shall I grab the gin as well as the vodka? Something tells me we might need both!"

Laughing, I tell her we will start with the vodka first.

"Tell me what you've been up to today, then I'll let you know what happened on my date this morning!"

"Damn, I bet your date was far more interesting than my day so far, girl! I got up early, went to the gym then got my nails redone. From there I popped past the shops and was just called into my chiropractor's appointment when you called me. So quite boring really. Come on, grab your drink and we'll head outside — it's too nice a day to sit inside!"

She notices I have some snacks and gestures for me to head out with our drinks, while she finds a bowl for the chips. The shaded patio is protected by a forest-like vertical garden along one side which makes you feel like you are in the jungle, rather than Sydney suburbia. Palm trees lined along the patio adding to the tropical feel of the backyard.

Setting the glasses on the glass-topped wicker table, I lounge back into the cushioned seats with a sigh. Lulu follows a minute later and sits across from me. I slide her drink across and suggest a cheer.

"Here's to Fridays off!"

She laughs and we both take a drink. The refreshing liquid flows down my throat sending liquor zinging through my veins. A couple of sips on an empty stomach magnifies the effect. For a few minutes, I avoid talking about my disaster date, until Lulu forces the issue.

"Come on, I'm dying to know. What happened with your date this morning?!"

I take another sip before stuffing a chip in my mouth to give me more time to think of how I want to answer. Do I choose the mindset of victor or victim? My feelings are still so raw. I haven't processed the negative emotions I still feel at the realisation of him being married.

I can choose to focus on this aspect, or on the fact that I confronted and ditched him, running as soon as I realised that he was married. According to the handbook and my own morals, I do not date married guys. I am glad I called him on his bad behaviour and left immediately.

The book's blue glow equals the guy being married or engaged. I know I am right about this — there is nothing obviously wrong with Latino Lover; except for the fact that he is married!

"Earth to Arleia!! Are you going to answer my question or stay locked in those thoughts I can see flashing across your face?"

"Oh shit, sorry Lulu! So, my date. I will give you the short version! We met at Manly, chatted for a bit then went to his room and started fooling around. He was lying on the bed, we were kissing."

"Damn don't go into too much bedroom detail woman, that will make me wish I had a date lined up for tonight then!"

Giggling, I continue my explanation.

"So, I'm leaning over kissing him on the bed. I linked my fingers with his and my ring got uncomfortably squashed, that's when I noticed a gold wedding band on his finger! That was what was pressing against my moonstone band."

I watch her face as she digests the bombshell I've just shared. Pivoting from laughter to anger, Lulu shakes her head.

"You've got to be kidding me, what a low-life dirt bag! Fucking liar!! Did you slap him across the face? Oh my God, what did you do then?"

"I was not impressed as you can imagine! I jumped up off the bed and confronted him with it. He tried to weasel out of it with lame excuses which were just total bullshit. I wasn't going to stay to hear any more of his justifications, so I grabbed my bag and high-tailed it out of there!"

"Bloody hell Arleia, good on you! I'm proud of you for getting out of that situation and for confronting that liar. His poor wife — makes you feel for her, hey. Wait, ok so that's what happened on the date. What was the revelation you just had?"

Lulu is the only one of my friends I've confided in about the Vixen's Secret Handbook so far. It's hard to explain a magical book to friends who already think I'm a bit crazy for dating so many men. But they haven't had their hearts broken recently. If they had, they might understand my need for fun and adventure right now.

As I tell her about the latest development with the blue glow related to William, Lulu's eyes widen.

"Shit, I think you are right Arleia. Blue has to mean the guy is married! If there was nothing else that you noticed about William on those dates that rang alarm bells, then this must be right."

I agree with her. No other explanation makes sense. I think back to earlier when I surprised him, and his over-the-top reaction. He probably thought he had been caught out by a friend or his wife. His angry response makes more sense now.

My mind replays our other dates as the pieces of the puzzle all fall into place. I did have a small niggle of unease a couple of times, but I thought I was imagining things. Now I know I should have listened to that inner warning system.

She refreshes our drinks and tears open the spicy capsicum dip. After downing one vodka, a second one is needed after that revelation. I take her lead and eat something to counteract the alcohol weighing down my limbs.

This is the first time we have caught up since I returned from my trip away, so although I have told her about the Frenchy in Bali episode, she hasn't heard about my Queensland trip to see Filipe, or the new colour lingering around the book when I returned.

I fill her in on my time in the Sunshine Coast with him, ending with the book glowing with the red and white sparks. Lulu's eyes bulge in disbelief.

"Wait, what? Another colour? But didn't you say red meant disaster date ahead?"

"Yeah, I did, that's when it's just a plain red glow. But I've never seen it glow red with white sparks before, Lulu. I don't know what that means! Obviously, if it's paired with red there's some type of warning there. But I've not felt any danger signs with Filipe yet. We have had a great time together so far, so I don't understand."

"Hey Arleia, what if the white sparks mean sexual chemistry?

You know, like sparks flying when your eyes meet. What do you think?"

I ponder her idea for a moment. She might have something there. The sparks between Filipe and myself are hot. Even now, when I remember the first moment that I saw him, with his animal eyes wanting to devour me, I still feel shivers of desire curl in my stomach.

"Bloody hell, yes! Good on you, Sherlock — I think you've cracked the sparkling mystery!"

We toast the new discovery in laughter. I really do think she's onto something here. The sparks would perfectly explain this animal attraction Filipe and I share. But what is the warning part about?

Catching up on Lulu's life I discover her dating expeditions lately have been disappointing. With a sharp-edged blonde bob, animated personality, and rocking body, I can't believe she has any problem getting a date. She informs me this is not the case!

One guy stood her up last week, and another acted like he was related to an octopus. She couldn't wait to escape his grasp. Yet another took her to his office and spun her around like a naked lazy Susan on the boardroom table.

Three drinks later we are howling in laughter at her disaster dates. I'm feeling much better about the William fiasco of this morning now — there's nothing like a deep belly laugh with a close friend to put life into perspective. With our laughter dying, Lulu suddenly has a sober thought.

"I wish I had a secret handbook to help me too. I really suck at this dating game right now!"

I wonder whether the book could help her too, or if it will only glow for me. The gypsy-like woman who gave it to me didn't say anything about that. She did, however, tell me that I was the book's owner, but can I ask it to help my friends too?

The idea swirls around in my head. If the strange woman hadn't disappeared so quickly, I might have had more of the answers I seek around the book!

CHAPTER 29

Orange Illumination

After a long overdue catch-up on the weekend with Roshan, PJ, the other Sri Lankan guy I've been planning to meet, comes to mind. We have chatted briefly since our original conversation but haven't been online at the same time recently.

The middle of the week has arrived, and tonight I plan to spend time online in the hope that we can reconnect. The idea of dating two guys originating from the same place to compare them is still appealing. My French men experiment wasn't a failure. Will it be the same with Sri Lankan men?

Seated on my couch, I place the handbook to my right, and my goddess cards to my left on the coffee table. There is no chance I'm ignoring either of these tools tonight! I need fair warning with any dude I talk to — so I know whether to immediately delete them or continue chatting.

Opening the box, I withdraw the large gold-edged cards and start to shuffle. I clear my mind, asking for a card to jump out at me for guidance on what it is that I need to know right now. Hardly a second passes before my request is granted. Flipping from the pack, a card lands face down on the keyboard of my laptop.

Aeracura

You are just getting started, so have patience with yourself and the process, and do not give up.

In many ways, you are like a flower bud who is ripe and ready to open and grow. Don't try to rush this process, as it's part of your beautiful path. Enjoy learning new knowledge and skills. Take your time to gather new ideas. Soon enough you'll get the unmistakable signal that it's time to put your learning into action. Have patience. Keep the faith.

My brows knit together as I read. That's a bit cryptic at the end! An unmistakable signal? What could that be? And which knowledge is the card talking about? With a sigh, I acknowledge that the first part of the message is right. I *have* only been on this dating adventure for a matter of mere months. But so much has happened that it feels like far longer.

Patience is not a great strength of mine either, and I wish I knew where this journey is taking me. I didn't enjoy the discovery about my lying Latino lover ... but I guess the Aeracura card is right. Don't rush the process, be patient and keep the faith!

The handbook lies innocently on the coffee table staring at me, waiting for me to log online. With PJ in mind, I enter the supermarket of lust. The stars must be aligned, because a mere thirty seconds after I have logged on, the green light appears next to PJ's name, broadcasting his presence.

A grin of delight breaks across my face. Thank you, goddesses, and thank you universe! I can see the pencil icon moving on the screen as he writes me a greeting.

PJ0669: Hello beautiful lady! How's your week been?

ATrixenVixen: It's been excellent thanks PJ! What have you been up to?

PJ0669: I've had lots of extra training sessions in the last couple of weeks, so I haven't had much time online.

Ahh, that explains why I haven't seen him on here recently. At least he's not ghosting me! We chat about mundane subjects until he gets to the point and asks me when I'm free. Bingo, about time! I'm eager to test my theory and meet him.

ATrixenVixen: Well, I'm free tomorrow night, do you want to meet up for a drink then?

Who would have thought I could become so bold just a short time ago? I agree with the goddess card's message — life certainly is a process and a journey! PJ is free, so we have already agreed to meet up tomorrow evening before I remember to check what's happening with the book.

Instead of the golden glow I was expecting, it's pulsing orange. A sigh of annoyance escapes me. Even when I have the bloody handbook right next to me, I still manage to forget to check it. Well, at least it isn't blue or red, that would be worse!

Heading to meet PJ the following night, I now have low expectations. After the orange glow with Kasmir and my assumption that orange equals boring, there's no point in expecting too much from the evening ahead. My eyes connected to his biceps rather than his brain, so that's probably not a good sign.

We are meeting at an Indian-themed cocktail bar ten minutes from my place. I won't travel too far for this orange glow rated date. I park my car in the car park behind the bar and enter through double glass sliding doors. Two seven-foot elephants with raised trunks on both sides of the doors greet me as I walk in.

A shiny, polished metal bar to my left is framed with hundreds of colourful bottles filled with alcohol. High-backed silver barstools line the bar with only three occupants seated there. Another couple lounge in plump, black leather armchairs arranged around a small table, sipping multicoloured drinks in tall glasses.

A wall of glass doors fully opens out onto a beer garden area featuring Hindu statues. With multilevel wooden platforms dotted between lush greenery in tall planter boxes, this secluded garden seating space has an intimate feel. I check to see if I can spot PJ between the plants, but there's no one here.

I turn back to the bar and order a drink before choosing a table away from the bar's occupants and the couple. The garden bit will work, so I position myself facing towards the door so I can see when PJ arrives. I focus on my breathing, taking deep slow breaths as I inhale my surroundings.

Rushing water draws my attention to a small, natural-looking rock waterfall peeping through leafy green fronds. Incense smoke curls past me, the scent filling my nostrils. I relax back into the wooden bench seat to wait.

Glancing at my watch, I smooth the teal material back down over my black leggings and reach for my glass.

Just as I'm about to check the time, I see him. Six feet of pure bulging muscle strolls in the door. He hasn't seen me yet, so I take advantage and stare. A pale purple shirt barely restrains his hulk-like muscles and thick neck. Denim jeans tightly hug his enormous quads falling freer around his calves and ankles.

Holy crapoly, this guy is *built*! PJ saunters towards the bar to scan the area. He spots me in a second. With a grin he strides towards me, his shaved head glowing above his handsome face. Well hello mister orange-glow, what will this evening bring?

I stand to greet him for a brief hug before he sits down. Staring at his straining shirt buttons, I'm surprised that one of them doesn't just give up and ping off, shooting me in the eye! Exchanging greetings, he asks me if I'd like another drink.

Hell yes. This means I now get to check out his rounded arse sculpted to perfection by thousands of squats in the gym. I dip my head to wipe at the corners of my mouth in case I've drooled by accident. My fingers itch to feel the hardness of those biceps beneath his shirt. I'm surprised he can find a dress shirt that fits his arm girth!

PJ returns with our drinks and slides into his seat. I find

myself wanting to ask about how hard it must be to buy shirts, and whether I can please touch his muscles. Resisting the urge, I ask if he's been to this bar before.

"Yes, but only once before. They've done up this garden area since I was here last, the new layout with the plants is cool."

"It's the first time I've been here, so I didn't realise how nice it was! I might have to put it on my list of places to revisit in the future."

We ease into conversation. So far, although, not incredibly entertaining yet, he seems nice and does answer each question I ask him. He's certainly not as boring as Kasmir was, so now I'm a bit confused. Maybe the orange glow doesn't mean a boring date like I thought? I know the night is young, but I don't have the same vibe as on my cake-bearing Frenchman date.

His arm muscles flex across the table at me each time he picks up his glass. I'm dying to feel the hardness and size of his bicep ... I don't know why I'm so obsessed. The words gurgle around my throat as I try to stop them from breaking free. Too late!

"PJ, there's something I want to ask you."

"Sure thing, Arleia, what is it?"

Think of something else to ask, anything else! My mind tries to come up with another question but returns a blank.

"Do you mind if I touch your biceps?"

The rosy stain creeps up my neck to fan into my cheeks. Trust me to blurt that out! He laughs and nods.

"Uh, okay if you want to! I've worked hard on these rocks, baby."

I laugh and slide closer so I can reach his arm as he does a full flex of the massive muscle. My fingers try to curl around his bicep, but they don't get far. The hardness beneath my fingers is the size of a boulder. Roshan has got a sexy gym-honed body, but PJ's size takes muscles to a whole new level.

Since my mouth has started me down this track, I may as well keep going. I want to know whether he can buy regular off-the-rack shirts or not.

"Wow, those really are some rock-hard massive biceps there, PJ! How do you get shirts that fit your arm size?"

His arm flexes a little tighter straining the material across the bulge further before answering me.

"I get every shirt custom made. You're right, regular size shirts don't fit my arms, shoulders, or neck without swimming everywhere else! I have a favourite tailor who has my measurements on file."

Another thought pops into my head. If his muscles are this abnormally large, then what does that mean for his penis? Even if he is sizeable, it would have to look small against the rest of his bulk.

Now this is all I can think about. I need to sneak a look somehow. I know some guys are 'growers not showers', but with a guy this size, you would hope to see *something* in the crotch area! Somehow, I stumble out a coherent reply to his tailor's revelation.

How can I get a better look? Aha! If I offer to buy us another drink, I could ask him to get them for us so I can get a better look. Arleia, you're a vixen genius! I suggest my idea and hand him a twenty, flashing him a cheeky smile. As his attention is on getting up and turning towards the bar, the perfect opportunity to stare at close range appears.

I'm shocked to see an almost flat zippered area facing me. Where the hell is it? He turns from me just as I lean forward to get a second look. Dammit! I'll have to wait until he returns and watch him walk back. Puzzled, I angle myself further around so I can see better.

Surely, I'd be able to see more than a tiny bump if his jeans were hiding anything of substance beneath the denim barrier. Roshan is not that big a guy, but I can certainly see a decent bulge in his pants when he's dressed!

I notice PJ turn with our drinks in hand and stare hard. Even as he draws nearer, I still can't see anything pushing against the front of his pants. The front of his jeans has barely a wrinkle! Adjusting my eyes to his as he arrives back to the table, I smile and thank him.

We chat for a few minutes, but I'm not really listening. The question of his dick size is still at the forefront of my mind. I need to delve deeper to see if I can figure this mystery out. Directing the conversation to his personal training, I ask how long it's been his passion.

"Twelve years now, Arleia, and I love it! It's not uncommon for me to spend two hours in the gym on training for myself, aside from working with clients too. I've always loved working out and started going regularly when I was seventeen. I wanted to grow muscles to impress the girls back then!"

We laugh together at his admission. Two hours on your own

body plus training others every day? Bloody hell, that's a lot of working out, no wonder he's the size of an ox!

"Do you take supplements, drink protein shakes, and eat six meals of grilled chicken each day too?"

He laughs at my question.

"Yes, to all of that and I weigh my food as well. I also do meal preparation for the week ahead. It takes dedication!"

"I bet it does! But I know of some guys who work out a lot and eat right, but their muscles are nowhere near as massive as yours! Is it a genetics thing? Are your family all like you?"

He leans in closer to me as if to share a secret.

"The difference is steroids, babe. You can't get this big without them!"

Ohhhh. The penny drops and the lolly rolls out of the machine. No wonder he looks gumball size! Steroids have been proven to have a shrinking effect on the size of a guy's penis. Shit. Well, I don't need to spend more time with this guy.

Outwardly I nod, but internally I'm hunting for the best exit strategy to use so I can get the hell out of here. I finish my drink in record time and set the stage with a yawn only half covered by my hand.

Interrupting his daily gym workout monologue, I start with an apology.

"Look I'm so sorry PJ, but I have to go into work early tomorrow morning to finish off some reports. I have to call it a night so I can get to bed early enough not to curse the alarm clock in the morning!"

I smile to soften my words, but the cold fact is that I'm

leaving. Now. As I finish talking, I slide towards the edge of the seat to stand.

"Oh, ok Arleia! No worries, shall I walk you out to the car?"

God no, that will only prolong this date and possibly put me in the awkward situation of having to fend off a goodnight kiss!

He rises, so I give him a hug goodbye, declining his gallant offer, even though he smells nice.

"I'll be fine, but thanks so much for offering! You stay here and finish your drink — I'm just parked outside the doors, so I'll be okay!"

Before he can insist, I extract myself from his arms and skip down the step off the wooden platform. Waving to him with a smile as I exit through the elephant-framed door, I step out of his sight. Phew! A perfect exit strategy.

I hurry to get in my car just in case he decides to follow. I'm glad I discovered the reason for the only small muscle on his body, but I'm still disappointed. On my drive home I mull over the orange glow mystery, comparing dates.

PJ wasn't that boring; it is his apparent lack of penis size that was disappointing. Kasmir was boring, and his cake was rock hard, but I don't think hard cakes and biceps are the commonalities here. I recall my date with Frenchman number two. I was so disappointed that he was totally unappealing compared to Filipe.

Wait, that's it! The common thread tying these two dates together is *disappointment*. I think I've solved the orange glow mystery! Both dates really were disappointments and neither lived up to my expectations. Dammit!

CHAPTER 30

Comfort Zone

After my dating experiences of the past couple of weeks, I only want to see my regulars. Self-love is my focus for this whole weekend. I need a dip in Krystian's spa, and Darz owes me a back massage after his escape artist trick. Shooting off a few quick messages, I slot in meeting times for both guys this weekend.

Friday night I'm visiting Krystian. He is working on Saturday morning, so that will ensure that it's not a late night. Darz is scheduled for Saturday afternoon, so I can have a sleep-in, go to the gym and spend some time meditating in the morning. I need time to think about what I've learnt from my dating experiences so far.

As I head towards Krystian's house, I'm excited at the thought of sliding into that steamy jetted water. Today it reached twenty-five degrees, the perfect weather for a relaxing dip!

After a tight hug in greeting, Krystian waves me in and leads me through his lounge to the patio area outside.

"Jump straight in the spa, Miss Arleia, and I will bring you a drink!"

Heading towards the spa, I drop my towel and handbag close enough to reach as I undress and slip naked into the frothing water. He returns from the kitchen with our drinks in hand, sliding the glass door closed behind him with his foot.

Krystian places the drinks within reach and slides down beside me into the spa with a splash. Picking up his drink, he raises it in a toast.

"To you, gorgeous vixen!"

I smile while clinking my glass against his before taking a sip. He has made the effort to buy my favourite wine, and I appreciate the taste as the cold bubbles tickle my nose. I lower my shoulders under the water and sigh. This is the life! Being served drinks in a spa is the perfect end to my week and start to my weekend.

"Tell me everything! I want to know everything, Miss Arleia! What's been happening?"

I laugh at his enthusiasm, so I start filling him in on my recent dating escapades, while we relax in the churning water. I fill him in on the lying Latino, mini muscle fiasco, and the boring cake bearer. He is laughing so hard he almost goes under.

"Bloody hell, Arleia. You have been having some crazy dates! And that William guy? What a prick! Just say the word if you want me to go and rough him up a bit for you!"

I laugh at his response and assure him there is no need to go after William. Karma will get him in the end, I think! I continue to fill him in on what's happening with Frenchy, who will be moving closer soon for work.

"You really like this French dude, hey? Are you going to see him when he moves here?"

"Yeah, hopefully. But he doesn't fit my criteria of safe dating with those wild animal eyes of his! I'm tired of dating men who disappoint, Krystian. Maybe I need to date some guys who are willing to fulfil my every command; like I'm their Queen!"

This elicits a thoughtful expression on Krystian's face. I wait patiently for him to speak, wondering what he has come up with.

"What if you did go searching specifically for slaves, Arleia? You told me before about your date with Sean so that was a start. Didn't you tell me that you had been contacted by a couple of guys who wanted to be your slave too? They could sexually satisfy you like a Queen, then clean your house as well!"

I'd forgotten about them. I've had two requests from guys looking for a mistress to serve, but I just laughed and deleted them. Maybe I shouldn't have been so hasty. I have no idea what a mistress does really. I can tell Krystian is warming to his new idea by his enthusiastic clap splashing water across my face.

"I know what you can do, Arleia, make up a second profile on the dating site. A mistress profile! Yeah, I'm a genius — that's exactly what you should do!"

I waver. My answer should be a flat-out no, so why am I considering this ridiculous suggestion? Seeing that I'm seriously contemplating his idea, he continues with his vision.

"You wouldn't have to put a picture up of your face on there or anything, Arleia. We could take a picture of a leather boot and whip or something and use that as your profile picture. I can help you make up the written bit, it will be fun!"

"Don't get too carried away, Krystian! I don't even know what a mistress does. I'm fairly sure a guy who wants to be a slave to a chick will figure out fast that I have no idea what I'm doing!"

"Yeah, but you could learn, it will be fun! I know you like reading, so why not read up on what being a mistress involves. Especially while you are in the casual dating mode. Wouldn't you like a choice of guys to massage your feet, serve you drinks, and pleasure you whenever you wanted them to?"

I must admit the picture he's painting in my head is appealing. What woman wouldn't like those things? But if that's all there is to it, then why aren't there more mistresses out there? I hate to admit it, but Krystian's right. Some further research is needed before I can seriously consider his idea.

Long after I arrive home, Krystian's words swirl around in my head. Do I have the courage to try something as crazy as setting up a mistress profile with the intention of gathering slaves? I don't have the answer to this question, but it's something I will think about — especially if I keep having dud dates like the last few!

Perhaps I need a refresher on the criteria of Marks, so I can increase my dating success in the future. Drawing my handbook out of my bedside table, I flick to the guidelines section. There seems to be a few points there I had forgotten about when choosing men in Bali to meet for a date. The 'Interest in exploring fantasy play' line jumps out at me. Does that mean like a 'mistress' in a dominant and submissive agreement? Or just getting your date to pretend he is the pizza delivery guy, or a handyman coming to fix your pipes?

Mwaaahaaahaahaa!

My thoughts return to Krystian's idea. What do people who engage in this type of relationship do with each other? There is a giant blank hole in my mind — apart from a vague idea that it involves pain and pleasure and black latex, whips, and restraints; I really don't know. As I drift off to sleep, I decide I need to learn more. No surprise that my dreams are haunted by black leather outfits and the sharp crack of whips as I toss and turn restlessly all night.

Successful Selection of a Mark

Vixens target men who are unsuitable for long-term relationships only. Henceforth men deemed suitable for Vixen play are known as 'Marks'.

Essential Criteria for Mark Selection:

* Hot, sexy, and single
* Treats women well and with respect
* Playful nature with a naughty sense of humour
* High level of emotional intelligence*
* Quick-witted with a curious mind
* Interested in exploring fantasy play
* Out of your social circle
* Willingness to be ensnared
* Likes to have fun*
* Skilled at communicating in your native language

*Note: You may think emotional intelligence would not be needed and that fun is a given, but remember Vixens are smart, playful, and mystical – dumb men are far too easy to access and will not be able to hold your attention or appreciate your vixenly ways.

Optional Criteria Suggestions for Mark Selection:

* Broadminded and open to new things
* Meets your age requirement: five to fifteen years younger than you; or 10 years older – personal choice
* Possesses a member worthy of your attention
* Attractive face and body
* Meets the minimum height requirement determined by you

CHAPTER 31

Self-Love

Sleeping in later than I intended, I stretch to shake off the lingering remains of my dreams. I remember my plan of a gym visit first thing today and groan. No, that's not the attitude to have this morning, young lady!

I sigh at the admonishment and swing my legs out of bed. Thank God I was organised before heading to Krystian's last night and already laid out my gym outfit for today on top of the dresser. I pull on my black leggings and slide my t-shirt over my head. If I dress immediately after waking, I am still in automatic sleepwalk mode.

I'm ready and out the door before I have time to think. Otherwise, I could talk myself out of going! The gym is only five minutes' drive from my place, so by the time I arrive I feel more awake.

Workout complete, I head home for a shower to freshen up and continue my self-love weekend with an hour-long meditation. Standing under the cascade of warm water, I reflect on my dating journey to discover my inner light and power so far. I have grown a lot, but I feel like there is still so much to learn about myself before I could ever contemplate looking for my forever guy.

Once dressed, I decide that the outdoors is the place for my meditation today. Picking up my cards and round brass singing bowl along with its mini embroidered gold pillow, I bring them outside to the patio area with me and flop down on the padded grey sun lounger.

Sitting up straight, I cross my legs and balance the bowl and cushion on the lounger in front of me. To help clear my mind of thought, I chime the wooden mallet against the side three times. The mallet slowly circles the top of the bowl, magnifying the chimes into a melodious hum around me.

The notes vibrate through the air, increasing in sound and strength. The energy of the waves pulsates around me. I close my eyes, still slowly circling the mallet around the edge. Noise transforms into a throbbing melody of the universe as I breathe deeply and clear my mind.

My inner strength increases as I draw in the energy of the universe, replenishing my supply until I am recharged. With a last deep breath whooshing from my lips, I open my eyes and squint against the blinding sunshine glinting off a window.

It occurs to me to ask what it is that I need to know now in my journey forward. I start shuffling the cards with this question in mind. After a few minutes, my request is granted as a card flies from the pack:

Oonagh

There is no need to hurry or force things to happen. Every-thing is occurring in perfect timing.

Don't worry about your purpose or your goals. Make no sudden moves. Slow, steady progress is best right now. Ease into your new life instead of rushing it. Do your new work as a part-time venture to begin with, while slowly exiting your career.

Wow. Don't rush into my new life. I guess that puts the brakes on Krystian's mistress idea for now, but the card didn't tell me to abandon the idea. Interesting! My online jewellery business plan fits in with the new career advice.

Seeking confirmation, I shuffle the cards again, asking for more clarity. Granting my request, another card falls from the pack.

Ostara - Fertility

It is the perfect time for you to start new projects, access new ideas, and give birth to new conditions. Springtime is any time when the light increases within your mind and entire system. Fuel yourself with positive intentions, nutritious foods which will increase your energy.

Feel more energized and powerful as you spruce up your inner and outer worlds. Then capitalise on this increased vigour by starting a new project that really makes your heart sing with excitement!

Your new idea or venture will be successful. It's an opportune time to make life changes.

I grin while reading the words aloud. Well, if that isn't confirmation, I don't know what is! Encouraged I visualise a new career working for myself, with lots of jewellery buying trips to Bali. Hey, I'm liking the sound of this!

Before I get too carried away with my imagined new life, I'd better check the time. Holy crap, another hour has flown past in the blink of an eye. It's lucky I had a shower as soon as I got back from the gym, or I'd be running late for Darz.

He's arriving in just over an hour from now, so I had better get ready for my visitor. I manage to get everything done in record time. I'm constantly surprised at how much faster I can clean up the house with the pressure of an impending visitor.

With easy access for a massage in mind, I choose my clothes carefully. Darz is likely to get oil on my clothes, so something that's black, stretchy, and easily washable will be the best choice. I select a black butt-hugging ribbed knee-length skirt and pair it with a loose off the shoulder multicoloured t-shirt. Now underwear. Maybe I won't wear any.

Mwaaahahaahaaahahaaa!

The naughty thought spreads an evil grin across my face as I decide to go the commando option. He will love that! It also prevents him from dripping oil over my satin and lace lingerie. The tight, stretchy skirt pulls me in at the waist while following the curve of my butt down to hug my thighs. The loose t-shirt covers my rounded hips and falls in flattering folds across my tummy.

With ten minutes spare, I locate the massage oil hiding in the back of the bathroom cabinet. I want no excuses from Darz as to why he can't spend the next hour massaging my back and shoulders! I sit a large beach towel with the oil onto the coffee table in readiness for my guest.

Since he's not known for punctuality, I crack open a can of vodka and orange to pour into a glass of ice. The chill against my fingers feels refreshing as I carry it to the sun lounger to wait. I position a small wicker cube for my drink next to the lounger before sinking onto the cushioned seat.

Halfway through my drink, Darz arrives. Walking towards my front door, he shouts out a loud greeting. I call out in reply and tell him to come around through the side gate since I'm feeling too lazy to get up now. The clink of the gate's latch tells me he heard my response, and moments later his smiling face appears around the corner.

"Well, look at you beautiful! Lazing like a queen on her lounger ... no don't get up! I'll come over there to pay my respects to her ladyship."

Kneeling next to me, he takes my hand and kisses the back of it regally. Then he drops all pretence of propriety by licking the inner part of my wrist.

"Naughty boy! Off with his head!!"

He clutches his chest as if mortally wounded and falls to the ground with a thud. The impact sounds heavy, so I jump in alarm.

"Are you okay Darz? Shit, it sounded like you hit the pavers hard then!"

He grins up at me, pleased at my concern.

"Mistress Vixen, all is well; I am tougher than I look, your Majesty!"

Maybe he did hit his head a bit too hard then? I can't help but run a hand of concern over his head looking for a bump, but I find nothing.

"See, I told you! I'm fine woman, all I need is a drink. Geez, luckily I brought my own, since you've been a terrible hostess so far and didn't even get up from your chair to answer the door!"

I laugh, knowing it's the truth, but roll my eyes at him anyway.

"Yeah yeah, whatever! What can I serve you, my prince?"

I bat my eyelashes furiously at him to emphasise my servitude, flicking a strand of fair hair from my face. He jumps up with a growl grabs me around the waist and spins us around. As our twirl slows, he lowers his face to capture my lips in a light kiss. I nip at his lip, and he grins, deepening the kiss.

Damn, he's a sensual kisser. My body temperature has risen at least two degrees since the start of this kiss. I'd better break free before we are both naked on the sun lounger. He owes me a massage first!

I seize the chance to pull away when his arms loosen around me. Taking his hand, I lead him towards the kitchen with a grin, asking him what he wants to drink. He gestures to his beer and asks for a stubbie holder to keep it cool. Yes, that's right, your beer will be getting warm while you massage me without something to keep it cool in!

Darz pulls the other sun lounge across closer to share our makeshift drinks table.

"Oh shit, I forgot to get the oil and the towel while I was inside. Can you go get them for me, please? They are both sitting on the coffee table."

"Oil and towel?"

His quizzical look has me cracking up in laughter.

"What, did I forget to mention the back massage that you're giving me today Darz? Since you were late *and* escaped your bonds when I specifically told you to stay put, there's a price to pay."

Comprehension dawns across his handsome features and his eyes light up with a flash of desire.

"Ahh, yes you did forget to mention that my vixen queen. But I am at your service to massage wherever you choose milady!"

Since it's so sunny, a risqué outside massage is ideal. My patio is quite secluded from the neighbours right here, so it's not like anyone else but Darz will see my bare back. I suggest that we lay the sun lounger flat and cover the cushioned cover with the beach towel.

He sets the area up as instructed, then heads inside to procure a comfortable cushion for my head. Trying to drink from a glass whilst lying down won't work, so I order him back inside to get me a straw for my vodka.

This is kind of nice, really. Ordering a guy around who will do anything you ask. Well, the benefits of ordering him around are what I really like. I grin when I remember he doesn't know I'm having a commando day today.

Standing at the foot of the towel-covered chair, I wait while he positions the pillow and drops the straw into my drink. He turns to face me with a flourish.

"It is ready, my queen. Lie down on your stomach and I will send you to heaven with my magic fingers!"

A giggle bubbles from my lips. Raising my hands above my head, I allow him to strip the t-shirt over my head. A cool breeze flutters around my bare breasts as I lower my arms. His look of surprise is priceless as he drops the forgotten t-shirt to the ground and cups my breasts to kiss them both.

"Mmm, an unexpected bonus I must say, milady. Perhaps if you enjoy your back massage, you could be open to me massaging more?"

I grin in encouragement as I lie face down, resting my arms in a bent position to rest my forehead on. The snap of the lid opening sends a shiver of anticipation down my spine. His calloused hands brush lightly over my back in a caress before I feel cool drops of oil peppering along my back. Warm hands slide across my back and begin to gently knead with the perfect pressure. A sigh escapes me as I sink further into the lounger in relaxation. His fingers feel magical as they glide across my shoulders and down my spine. Circling, kneading, moulding me into mush.

His fingers graze the sides of my breasts, causing a leap of longing lower in my abdomen. Thumbs tracing down my sides hook into my skirt and slide it down to bare my butt cheeks to the sun. He murmurs in appreciation of my lack of underwear.

Sliding his hands slowly lower, he circles his hands around my butt cheeks, kneading them gently before sliding a finger along the crack between. My hips start to lift of their own accord every time he slides his fingers closer to the spot that is becoming more sensitive with each pass.

Woah! This is turning out to be like one of those Bali massages with a happy ending that I've heard so much about. I grin, and allow Darz's hands to travel lower to where no more lubrication is needed.

Dipping his fingers into my wetness he growls his approval. One hand slowly kneads my oily bare cheek, while the other works its magic within.

I slide my thighs apart slightly to give him better access. He spreads my cheeks and licks me from my pussy to my butt crack and slips a second finger inside as he circles my swollen clit with his thumb. I moan my appreciation against the cushion.

His other hand spreads my cheeks and I shudder in surprise as his tongue circles my arsehole. His thumb traces the path of his tongue, and I feel extra oil drip between my cheeks as he slowly slides it into my arse.

Pleasure washes through me. His fingers delve deeper, pressing against the internal spot that makes me even wetter. His other thumb flicks faster over my clit, as my hips buck against his exploring fingers. Small panting moans fill the air. He growls and lifts my hips even higher. His fingers are everywhere, I can't think, only feel.

It's building fast. Overtaking me. His fingers thrust inside my pussy and arse deeply again and send me over the edge. An explosive release shudders through me as I muffle my scream into the pillow.

I can't move. Waves of pleasure still wash over me. My limbs are turned to mush, and it takes a few minutes to return to earth before moving.

Darz is laying back on the other chair stroking his rock-hard cock. Eyes closed; he moans with pleasure. I wrap a towel around me and watch. A murmur of approval from me sees his dick jump in response so he squeezes the tip harder and slides his fingers along the shaft even faster.

It's so sexy watching a guy stroke himself and cum. I take note of how he strokes himself, so I can mirror that when I pleasure him.

Watching him is making my pussy throb. I want to sit on that magnificent cock and have it deep within me to feel the spasms of his orgasm when he comes. His groans tell me he's getting closer, so I move. Dropping the towel, I roll off the lounge to straddle him, poised above his throbbing cock for a second as he releases his shaft to grab my hips and drives his hard cock deep inside. I gasp and match his rhythm as he strokes my clit then slams into me harder. My breasts jiggle faster as our pace increases. I know he's close. With a bellow, he drives hard within. His cock pulsing with release deep within me. The feeling of his orgasm throbbing within me sends me into a second release. He pulls me down to kiss me and slaps my bare butt.

"I think we both need a shower, my saucy Vixen. But I need a few moments to recover!"

I laughingly agree and head inside to wash off all the oil. A satisfied giggle escapes me as I prepare for my second shower of the day. I spot the golden glow of approval emanating from the handbook and laugh out loud.

As the steaming water cascades over my shoulders, Sean pops into my mind. The one date I had a few months ago with Sean, aka Dreads, scared me a bit, so I haven't repeated the experience yet. I'm attracted to him, but fear of the unknown has stopped me from exploring his offer to play as his mistress.

I feel the pull of fascination towards this unknown world. What does it feel like to command a man to do your bidding? To brandish a whip and have that power given over to you? I honestly don't know. I'm going to need an in-depth discussion with Lulu about this unknown direction and give Krystian's mistress profile idea more serious consideration.

CHAPTER 32

Girls Night

On the way to meet Lulu for a desperately needed catch-up, I feel excited. Not because I'm meeting Lulu, though I love her to bits. The excitement is around Frenchy moving to New South Wales this weekend! We have arranged to meet up this Saturday. I haven't seen him for several weeks now, and our communication has been sporadic because of his long workdays.

I arrive at my destination — the same Indian-themed bar I met PJ in. Lulu hasn't been there since the renovations either and was keen to see it. Walking through the elephant framed doorway brings the date with PJ to mind again and makes me shudder. At least I found out what the orange glow meant for sure that night!

Lulu is standing at the bar. Looking over her shoulder, she spots me approaching and emits a squeal of delight.

"Arleia! Oh my God, this bar is sooo cute, I love it! Great idea to meet here babe. Love the Hindu statues and water feature too. We should organise a group girls' night out here sometime."

We hug in greeting and I agree. The only thing tarnishing this place is the memory of my date, but since it wasn't a total disaster, I can live with coming here again without a negative attachment to this place. After we order, Lulu leads me to almost the exact same spot where I sat with PJ. I've already filled her in on my date with PJ, so she laughs when I tell her.

"Let's try for a 'better than disappointing date' with me then, Arleia!"

Giggling, we clink our glasses together in agreement. I encourage her to share her dating news first, since I know she has been on a couple that I've not heard about yet.

She starts with her date with a hot Croatian guy who seemed nice in the beginning but kept cancelling at the last minute. Upon finally meeting, she realised he could never love anyone else as much as himself. Her entire ninety-minute date was filled with a monologue of his achievements and career path.

"Thank God I took your advice and used an exit strategy to get the hell away from him, Arleia! The only problem was that it took me that long to try and cut into his non-stop speech. I think he was shocked that I wanted to leave and not hear more about his self-proclaimed fabulousness!"

"Bloody hell, that sounds as bad as some of my dates have been. But the fact that he's Croatian really blows my theory of it being possible that one nationality is more attractive than others. Darz is Croatian and he's such a great guy!"

"Yeah, I'm finding that too on my dating journey. It's not where a sexy looking man was born that makes him attractive, it's his individual personality, conversation, and energy that either attracts or repels you."

"So true! Hey, we should all go out for a drink together one night so you can meet Darz. What do you think?"

Lulu has heard all my stories about Darz — even the one where I tied him to the bed then went out shopping, which I've only shared with her, and you! So, don't go blabbing about this to your friends — I'm trusting you to keep the vixen sisterhood code.

"Sounds great! Yeah, it will be fun to finally meet him. Do you think he will be up for meeting me too?"

"Yeah, he would love it! I'll check when he is back in town and organise a night out for us."

I laugh at the thought of how excited Darz will be at the idea, then fill her in on our latest adventure. But that's not what I want her advice on, and neither is Filipe. Before I can mention him, she asks when the French man is moving closer.

"This weekend! Woohoo, I'm so excited to see him!"

I tell her of our plans to meet on Saturday at a rustic cabin located just over an hour and a half southwest, near the farm where Filipe will be working. We only have one night together, as he starts at the new place at six on Monday morning.

But since he will now be under two hour's drive away, it's possible to see him more often. Shit, that's what I want to talk to Lulu about too — the mistress profile idea of Krystian's! We've gone over the handbook's red glow with sparks meaning for Frenchy, but did I tell her about the guys I deleted with the odd request to be my slave?

Her eyes widen as I tell her of these men's wishes to be a slave, and Krystian's excitement about creating a mistress profile for fun. Lulu's mouth drops open for a moment before she can respond.

"Wait, what?!! Guys want to be your slave. What does that mean? What do they do? What would you have to do? Is this common? Shit, I think I need another drink before I hear more about this!"

I laugh and agree as she heads to the bar. My thoughts mirrored hers when I was first presented with the idea. I've never known of any woman yet who's had a slave. What if it's not really something that happens, and those guys were just weirdos asking to be a slave to someone? But Sean seemed normal, intelligent, trustworthy, and generally a nice bloke, and I've done a bit of research.

We discuss my previous date with him, and his nickname of Dreads with his matted rope-like hair. I've kept in contact with him intermittently over the past few months, but only had one date. I'm still hesitant to meet him and take him up on his offer. More research is needed before I can decide whether to step further out of my comfort zone to try something this foreign to me.

Step out of my comfort zone? Bloody hell, that would be a gigantic leap, not a mere step! I share this thought with Lulu, who cracks up laughing and ends with a snort.

"I bet these guys were just pulling your leg, Arleia. I've heard of this dominatrix mistress stuff of course, but I don't think many men would be into it. We have been on so many dates between us. Wouldn't we have heard more about this slave stuff by now?"

"I honestly don't know. I've seen it in movies and documentaries, but I don't think it's commonplace. You've read my profile Lulu; did you notice anything I've written in there that implies I'd want a slave?"

She giggles at the thought.

"No! Nothing. Weird hey. Maybe you should do what Krystian suggests. I doubt you'll get any more than a couple of chat requests anyway."

I can tell she's warming to the idea by the gleam in her eye.

"Wait, you wouldn't post a picture on this profile with your face, would you Arleia?"

"No way! I probably won't even chat to anyone either. I'm curious now, to find out how many guys are into this stuff. Krystian advised taking a picture with a leather boot with a whip next to it which is perfect. I'm thinking of it more as a research project, that's all."

Lulu snorts loudly, drawing the attention of a couple of patrons nearby. She gives them a wave and a smile before directing her attention back to our conversation.

"Oh, you have to meet one potential slave guy! Just *one*, Arleia. That would be hilarious! Do it for me, come on!"

"Keep your voice down, girl! I don't want the whole world hearing this conversation!"

In lowered voices, we discuss the idea. I'd rather not meet a new guy for this though. A second date with Sean is the safest way to test out this foreign concept since he seems to know a lot about the world of domination and submission. Darz is also a good option since he liked the butt-slapping playdate.

After another hour of discussing dating adventures and men, we part with a hug and promises for another vixen catch up soon.

Driving home, my thoughts centre on Filipe. Excitement at seeing him is tinged with concern. I get that there's a warning of some kind, but it's still not clear what the handbook is trying to tell me.

Our dates have been far from disastrous, which red usually indicates. So, I'm confused. Could I be at risk of losing my heart to this delicious French morsel of a man? Is that what the book's trying to tell me?

All I can do is to go on another date with Filipe and see what transpires. I need to know what this is before I get completely caught in his web by accident. That's *not* what I want to have happen.

CHAPTER 33

Blue Discoveries

It's the night before driving down to meet with Filipe, and I'm feeling antsy. My bag is packed for tomorrow with everything I could possibly need.

Housework is complete and plants watered. I didn't plan anything tonight, because I thought I'd be too busy, but today I've outdone myself and am ready way earlier than expected.

Pacing the living room, I look for something out of place to do. I see nothing, except the blinking light of my laptop on the dining room table. No! I ignore it and flop on the couch. Stabbing the remote towards the television, I fluff the blue cushion behind me and start flicking. Once I've gone through the entire list of channels twice without finding anything I want to watch, I punch the off button.

I heave a huge sigh and fall onto my back to stare at the ceiling. The mysterious glow relating to Filipe is weighing heavily on my mind. Dammit, I need a distraction! Sitting up, I scoop my goddess cards from the coffee table in front of me. Maybe I need to do a reading for myself about this weekend to see if I can gain any insight before I go.

The cards feel warm in my hands as I shuffle. Willing my guides or angels or whoever it is that helps me in times of need to give me some helpful guidance. Two cards fly from the deck. Uh oh. Does this question need *two* messages?

Kali – Endings and Beginnings

The old must be released so that the new can enter. The coming changes are for the best. Keep your thoughts positive, as they're immensely powerful. What appears to be a loss is really the beginning of a happy new phase. Let the past go — it's time to move on.

Uhm, what does that mean? I'm not expecting any coming changes or losses. What is going to happen this weekend? I chew my bottom lip; not knowing what to make of that message. Damn, I hope the next card is clearer!

Brigit – Don't Back Down

Stand up for what you believe is right. First, be quite clear about your intentions. If you're unclear, confusion will lessen your power and force. Like a candle in the dark, be clear and bright in what is acceptable to you in this situation. Be assertive. Don't worry about what others think. Speak your truth, put your foot down and stick to your opinions.

Arrrgh! I toss the card back onto the table and sigh. This

message is getting muddier by the second! I need to see if I can make any sense of this.

Change is coming, be clear in your intentions and opinions and speak your truth — during whatever it is that's about to happen. Well, that's clearer, but still not encouraging. A cold shiver of fear prickles across my shoulders. Oh no, now I *really* need some serious distractions.

I jump up from the couch and snap open the laptop on the table. Flicking it on, I race to my bedroom for the handbook, then pour myself a healthy dose of Baileys on ice. Now, let's get some distraction happening to keep my mind off the weekend I was looking forward to earlier!

Unsettled, I delete seven requests before I come across one that may be ok. I glance at the handbook beside me for guidance. It responds with an orange glow. Hell no. *Delete.* No more disappointing dates for me thanks! Nine more deletes before I spy another possible Mark.

Pietro is Italian, thirty-two, and looks quite handsome with his chiselled jawline and dark, swept-back hair. His profile states that he loves to travel, meet new people, and hang out with his friends. Not very inspiring, but at least there are no red flags there yet. I accept his request and realise he is online right now.

Italiano001: Ciao Bella! Such a gorgeous smile, I am in love already beautiful woman.

ATrixenVixen: Hello to you too, and thanks for the compliment. But surely no one can fall in love that fast ... although I'm not surprised. Haha!

Italiano001: Already I am smitten, Bella! I will shower you with flowers, but they will pale against your beauty. I am Pietro, please tell me your name gorgeous!

I look down at the book for an answer and it doesn't disappoint. Blue seeps from between its' pages like an emergency services blue-light warning. Is this dude *married*? I re-read his profile but see no clues there. He's written 'single' in relationship status, but that can't be true. I need to know if I'm right about the blue glow meaning, so I'm going to keep him chatting to see if I can find out!

I discover that he's an engineer on a six-month holiday here in Australia. He gives me no helpful information until he drops his last name Aha! Now I can google search his name and see what I can find out.

It doesn't take long until I discover what I'm searching for — his Facebook page. Scanning down his profile page I find his relationship status. Engaged!

Several pictures are visible of him and his fiancée in his profile. It looks like they were taken in Italy before he came here for a final fling. Convenient for him to forget about her as soon as he lands in Australia!

Wait, this means the blue glow from the Vixen's Secret Handbook does *not* mean married. It flashes blue when the man is in *any* kind of committed relationship. Woohoo, finally I'm sure blue equals attached!

No longer needing to talk to him, I hit the delete button and Pietro's conversation disappears. With a sigh, I flip the laptop closed and head to bed. Pietro's lies have left a bad taste in my mouth, and I'm already apprehensive about this weekend after the goddess card messages of warning. I fall into a restless sleep, not knowing what lies ahead.

Vixen Success Tools

The first important tool a Vixen must use is her *brain*.

Make smart decisions about which Marks you add. Ensure they have at least two deal-breakers, but also that they possess the minimum requirement of positive traits you desire.

The second crucial tool Vixens need to use is *intuition*.

Learn to trust your instincts when it comes to men. When something does not feel right, or you get a 'gut instinct' about someone, trust it.

If you feel like there is something negative about him, trust that you are right and move on. There are plenty of other men to fish for in the online ocean of adventure!

CHAPTER 34

French Fail

Opening my eyes to a bright sunny Saturday morning lifts my mood. Last night's discovery about Pietro, confirmation of the blue glow's true meaning, as well as the mysterious message from the cards had me feeling flat.

Running out of the house with my overnight bag, I check the handbook, and goddess cards are packed. I may need them! With a piece of toast held firmly between my teeth, I throw my things onto the seat next to me and slam the car door.

A quick stop off for a belly-warming drink and I'm on my way south-west towards the historic miners' cottage we have rented for the night. I'm glad I left early this morning. I thought the drive would take me about an hour and a half — but the GPS says two hours.

Filipe flew into Sydney at midnight last night. He was catching a ride out to the farm from the airport with other co-workers. His plan was to sleep, unpack then meet me at the cabin at twelve.

With only one wrong turn on my trip down, I turn into the narrow lane leading to our accommodation early.   Surrounded by an overgrown cottage garden filled with multicoloured spring blossoms, the square stone structure has a long porch attached to the front. Dropping my case at the heavy wooden door, I search for the hidden key under the pink pot plant on the veranda as instructed. Aha, there it is!

Turning the brass key in the lock, I can't wait to see it inside. The door swings open, and I gasp. Gleaming wooden floors reach out to creamy coloured walls decorated with colourful garden prints. A tall ceiling with wooden beams makes the cosy space seem larger. Spotting a tiled fireplace, I grin at the basket of logs placed beside the plump butter-yellow couch. Who doesn't love a good fire?

I pass through the rustic style kitchen to deposit my case in the bedroom. Wow, a four-poster king-size bed with netted drapes! Dropping my case, I run forward and jump, bouncing in the centre of the huge bed. Fluffy crimson cushions tickle my nose as they fall forward from the force. I sigh happily.

The whole bedroom is done out in romantic reds with a hint of dusky rose on the walls. An adjoining bathroom looks recently updated, but with a cool textured grey stone wall in the shower alcove, that feels modern but rustic.

With a sigh, I roll off the bed. Filipe will be here soon! I hurry to explore the rest of the cottage before he arrives. Opening every cupboard and drawer as I go, I make my way outside on the large wooden deck. There's an inbuilt six-person spa steaming at one end of the patio, with a hooded barbecue and blue wicker outdoor chairs lined with buttercup cushions near the entrance to the lounge.

Surrounded by lush greenery in full spring flowers, there are no other houses in sight. Perfect! The slamming of a car door announces an arrival. I run back inside to greet him.

Filipe's face lights up as soon as I swing open the door, and he crushes me to his chest, peppering my face with kisses.

"Princess! It has been too long! Many nights I wait. I miss you!"

His lips swoop to claim mine in a thorough greeting before he releases me to swing the heavy door closed behind him. Kicking his bag aside, he advances with a growl.

"You have an appointment with me in the bedroom woman! Lead the way!"

With a laugh, he wraps his hands around my waist from behind and pushes me forward. I lead him into the bedroom, where he lets loose a bark of delight at the sight of the netted four-poster bed.

"We have a royal red romantic sexy bed for you here Princess ... mon Dieu!"

"Very fitting, don't you think, Frenchy?"

Too busy removing his clothes to answer, he recaptures my mouth to silence it, and pushes me back onto the bed. His knee forces my thighs apart as he leans forward to kiss me again.

His hand swoops between them to press his palm firmly against the damp material. A growl rumbles in his throat as our tongues dance together. He pulls the offending garment to the side, to access the wetness his fingers seek.

I reach down for his hard cock, encircling it, stroking my fingers along it as it stiffens further and veins strain along his shaft. It's been too long. I want him now.

He responds to my nails digging into his bare arse and repositions himself. Motionless for a second, the wet tip of his cock touching my lips, he plunges in.

I cry out a groan of satisfaction before his rhythm captures me, and I'm lost to the sensations flowing through my body.

Two hours later I am weary but delighted. Wrapping a towel around my naked body, I head towards the spa.

Filipe is passed out across the bed snoring lightly, and I don't have the heart to wake him yet. Draping the towel over a nearby chair outside, I step naked into the warmth. The water embraces me, steam swirling across the deck. Strong jets pummel my back and thighs.

Damn, I should have brought a drink out here with me! The hypnotic bubbling keeps me in the spa for another fifteen minutes before thirst wins out. With a sigh, I lift myself from the water and wrap myself back in the towel. Conscious of dripping water everywhere, I step gingerly in the house towards the kitchen.

The fridge has an assortment of cold drinks inside, so I pour an orange juice, and add a decent slug of vodka to it. As I tread carefully back across the wet floor, I hear Filipe talking from the bedroom. He must have woken up to answer his phone. Not wanting to disturb him, I continue towards the deck until I hear something that makes me freeze.

"Oui, I arrive at the new farm yesterday, Mon Frere. Oui, oui!

I see the blonde woman now. She is attractive, no? She will make good wife. Then I stay in this country!"

Uhm, *what*? A good wife?!! I sneak out the door backward and slide into the spa, my head spinning at what I've just overheard. This must be what the secret handbook was trying to warn me about! I know there is this raw animal attraction thing going on between us, but never did I suspect he was looking for a suitable candidate to marry to stay here.

A million thoughts whirl around in my mind. I should have taken my handbook to Bali and listened to my brain instead of my body. What was that warning from the cards last night again? Change is coming, speak my truth and stick to my opinions. The old will be replaced with the new. Well, maybe Filipe has just become the 'old' on his way out to make room for the new!

The soothing jets on my back help combat the tension caused by his unexpected confession. I definitely don't want a husband! Especially one who just wants to stay in the country by marrying whoever says yes first.

I sigh heavily and drop my head. Recently, I congratulated myself on so much growth. It feels like I just slid downwards on a snake in the dating game of Snakes and Ladders.

What will I do? Confront him with what I heard — or stay silent? Pretend nothing's wrong and stay here overnight, or leave now? I realise that Filipe looking for a wife to stay here *must* be the reason for the red warning glow accompanying the white sparks for chemistry. The question is, what am I going to do about it?

With no sign of Filipe joining me yet, I've got time to think this through. I will be a wife to no one unless I choose to do it — for reasons of love, not lust or citizenship. If that is what he's after, then there's no point in seeing him again. Unsure as to my next move, my gut churns uncomfortably.

This place is so gorgeous, I don't want to miss out on a weekend away in the country — or on the fresh bacon and eggs in the fridge waiting for my breakfast tomorrow. But can I keep my mouth shut long enough to enjoy the rest of the day with Filipe, and not let on that something is wrong?

Hell yeah! I'm a vixen and I should bloody well remember it! Damn straight, I'm not running home when there's a fully stocked fridge, a spa, and dinner being delivered to us here in an hour's time. Besides, I've already paid for half of this getaway package upfront.

I hear the shower running over the noise of the spa jets and make my decision. I will confront him with what I know tomorrow after breakfast but play nice until then. The least he can do is pleasure me a few more times before I hit him with what I overheard!

Brushing the damp hair from my face, I realise my fingers have come to resemble prunes. A sign that it's time to get out of my relaxing frothy retreat and re-join Filipe inside the cottage. Squeezing the excess water from my hair, I re-wrap my soggy towel around me and shiver with cold. Running for the bathroom, I smack Frenchy's bare arse cheek as I pass him shaving in the mirror of the granite-topped vanity.

"Cheeky woman! Have you been lazing in the spa?"

"I sure have! It was amazing, mister Snore-a-lot!"

"Wait Princess, what this means?"

I laugh, shrug, and shake my head at his innocent protest as I duck under the warming shower spray. As soon as I close the glass door, the steam veils him from view. In the cocoon of mist, the soothing water cascades over me, washing away any doubt about my decision. The negative energy held in my body joins the water and drains away from me.

Once dressed, I re-join Frenchy on the couch where he is slouched wearing faded ripped jeans and a white t-shirt, watching soccer on the television. My stomach swirls in desire. Goddammit, why is this man so damn attractive to me? He smiles and hooks his arm around my neck to bring me closer for a kiss.

A knock on the door interrupts us. Filipe curses under his breath in French before regretfully leaving the couch to answer the door. The aroma of Chinese food fills the room. He must have called through the order while I was in the bathroom.

I make space on the coffee table for him to set it out before getting drinks, plates, and cutlery from the kitchen. My stomach growls loudly in anticipation as I return to the couch, making Filipe laugh.

"So hungry, Princess! Eat baby, but first, we toast. To this country, I love this! And to you, beautiful woman!"

I smile and incline my head, but don't respond verbally. Clinking my glass against his I take a sip, whereas Filipe empties his whole glass in one gulp. I'm finding it hard to push his words to the unknown caller out of my mind.

"Princess, I will get the bottle, yes?"

He jumps up from the couch to retrieve the bottle from the

fridge as I dish up the most delicious-smelling food onto my plate. When Filipe returns from the kitchen to refill his glass, I am already on my third mouthful and my tummy is sighing in delight.

After downing another wine while dishing up his food, he finishes the bottle and starts on the next after a few mouthfuls of food. The soccer has him hypnotized, and his food seems forgotten as Filipe pours another wine. If he doesn't stop soon there will be no chance of a bedroom performance from him tonight!

Hmm, that could be to my advantage in a way. He will have to focus solely on pleasuring me if he happens to suffer drinker's droop. I don't want him to get too drunk though, or the likelihood of him passing out early is too high. I'd have to do the pleasuring myself then.

Mwaaahaaahaahaa!

CHAPTER 35

Spiral Upwards

By the time I've finished eating, Filipe is halfway through the second bottle and has forgotten all about the existence of his meal. Refilling my glass before the wine disappears, I ponder my next move. I will tidy up, then suggest a spa session to extract him from the television screen. Leaving him to watch the soccer for now, I clean up the plates and put any remaining food in the fridge.

As I am stacking the plates in the dishwasher, Lulu comes to mind. She will be shocked when I tell her the real meaning of the red warning glow from the book that we've been discussing! The clink of glass from the lounge room alerts me to the fact that I'd better hurry up before he's so smashed that he can't perform.

"Hey, sexy Frenchman, why don't we go for an after-dinner spa? It was so relaxing in there earlier! Plus, you've had a massive week with work and moving — we may as well take advantage and jump in while we're here."

He leans forward and grabs my hand, pulling me down on top of him on the couch for a quick kiss before he replies.

"Mmm yes Princess, we play in the spa together!"

"Wait, I will get us some towels to take out with us. Do you want another drink to have in the spa?"

At his nod, I push myself up off him and head to the kitchen with a grin. I pour us both vodkas to take outside — but make his only half as strong as mine. Stepping onto the deck, I place both drinks in reach near the spa, taking note of which is mine. There is no sign of Filipe yet, I will have to go back in to drag him away from the hypnotic effect of the big screen.

Returning to the lounge, I spot my unfinished wine. I down it first before I attempt to persuade Frenchy to come outside to the deck area with me. Light teasing kisses help to draw him off the couch, but I turn away with a laugh when he reaches for me.

"Catch me in the spa, Frenchy!"

I tease him as I run towards the door, stripping my dress off to reveal no underwear underneath. Yes, I did pack a pile of sexy lingerie — but after what I heard I don't feel like putting in that much effort. With the revelation of my naked body backlit by the glow of underwater spa lights, he stumbles out the door after me as I step into the bubbling water with a sigh and reach for my vodka.

After shedding his clothes, he falls into the water — a sign of the wine consumed so far. I smile to myself and point out his drink. After a few minutes of relaxing in the spa, he moves closer. Our bodies entwine as we kiss, surrounded by rising steam and the sound of churning water.

I whisper my idea to him, and he grins his approval against my ear. I've suggested he go down on me since I can't remember him doing that yet. Breaking our kiss to raise myself out of the water, I sit on the edge of the spa and lean back against the padded spa cover.

Dropping my knees apart, I invite him to explore. Filipe kneads my inner thighs. Sliding his hands towards the junction, he licks me like a cat. A tentative tongue in the wrong place doesn't bode well for the fireworks I'm hoping for.

I shift my hips closer to the edge to give him better access. His fingers stroke the sensitive skin following the path of his tongue, but I can tell he is distracted by the soccer. This hasn't managed to get my motor started yet.

Another two deep swigs of my vodka and I'm glad I have the double strength one. With all his skill in the bedroom and his wild animal-desire eyes, I missed his lack of enthusiasm for this task. A roar from the television distracts him and his head turns towards the sound.

You know what? Just go, Filipe! I know you're dying to watch the rest of the game!"

The words have barely left my lips before he abandons the task at hand and launches himself out of the spa sloshing water all over the deck. Grabbing a towel, he does a quick swipe over his body before dropping it to run inside.

"Princess, you're the best!"

I slide back into the spa and realise I am grateful he left. He did manage to oil the pistons if not start the motor, so I might as well complete the job myself.

A few minutes later I'm feeling far more satisfied. Sinking deeper into the warmth swirling around me, I think back to the Goddess cards' message.

I don't want to marry someone to help them stay in Australia, and I won't be swayed on this. The change coming is to strike Filipe off my list of Marks, and I'll speak my truth tomorrow when he's sobered enough to hear it! Maybe I should get my cards now for final confirmation before our confrontation tomorrow? Yes! I slip out of the spa and wrap the towel around me to sneak through to the bedroom. Filipe is too engrossed in soccer to notice. I make it back to the spa but am careful to keep my hands dry.

I shuffle carefully holding the cards over the edge to avoid a soggy disaster. Stopping, I flip the top card over and read the inscription.

Rhiannon – Sorceress

You are a magical being who can manifest your clear intentions into reality. Recapture your personal power by simply stepping outside. Allow the light of the sun, the moon, and the stars to stir ancient memories that may be dormant.

Recall the times of your magical abilities, then put them to use for good. Awaken one and all to the magic that is life itself. You are the one who can help with this mission.

I'm not feeling like a magical being right now. Unsure of what this card is trying to tell me that relates to the situation right now,

I push the words from my mind and sink lower into the churning water.

When the jets suddenly shut off, silence fills the air. The faint drone of soccer fans cheering is muted with the closed door. Dropping my head back to rest against the spa, I gaze at the full moon rising just over the darkened treetops. My moonstone ring glimmers in its light as if to recharge itself.

I'm tired of these lying males — my time is too precious to waste! I do need to create a change. Maybe I'll stick to my regular guys and just add a slave or two. A shiver runs down my spine at the thought, but I can't tell if it's fear of the unknown or excitement. Perhaps a bit of both.

A faint hum fills the air. It reminds me of my singing bowl, but I can't place where it's coming from. The vibration surrounds me, filling the air as it intensifies. What is going on? I didn't consume *that* much alcohol tonight! I wiggle my fingers in my ears, as if to dislodge the noise filling them. Instead, it increases.

Moonlight shimmers across the steaming still water, bouncing off the surface. Hang on, now I can see actual tiny sparks of light in the air. They twirl in front of my face in a mesmerising dance, before combining into a sparkling river of energy. The glittering stream moves to circle around me faster and faster through the mist.

I look again to the stars, my mouth wide open in shock as the spiral of light rises to swirl above me. Suddenly, the sparks gather in intensity, whooshing into me through my open lips. Energy zings around the inside of my body. A prickling sensation fills my fingers as they start to glow.

Holy shit, what is happening? I imagine the tingly energy shooting out of my fingertips to leave my body. But instead, white light streams out of them. I clench my fists quickly in shock and the flow of illumination halts. The tingling sensation of this energy passing through my body is making me feel lighter.

My shoulders tremble with an involuntary shudder. All else is forgotten; I am caught up in this mysterious internal light energy vortex. Could this have anything to do with the handbook? Seriously, my life was boringly normal before I started on this journey of adventure; I've never had anything like this happen before!

First, there was those strange golden flecks that appeared in my eyes after a session with Darz a few months ago, before Bali. Now this weird energy thing! I am not frightened, as it feels amazing. But what does it mean?

The zinging feeling inside slowly fades as I watch the moon rise higher. Sinking further into the steaming water, I realise I still have my fists clenched beneath the surface. Dare I open them? The underwater spa lights are off. If anything glows when I stretch my fingers out again, I'll see it!

Peering into the darkened water, I take a deep breath and uncurl my hands. Tiny beams of white light wink at me from the depths. I didn't imagine it! Could this be a permanent glow? I laugh as I imagine new career paths as a magician or a tour guide through dark caves. Imagine if anyone saw this, they would lock me away somewhere and study me for years.

This glowing energy must be connected to my secret hand-book somehow. There's no other explanation. Opening and closing my hands makes the tiny beams appear; then disappear. I don't think the light will be visible during the day — but does this mean I can't go out anywhere at night ever again?

Lifting my hands from the water, the minuscule lights pierce the darkness. I study my fingers closely. That's odd! I've been in the spa for quite a while now, and my fingertips have no signs of the usual shrivelled prune effect. The energy must have affected the cells of my body somehow.

The weird feeling in my body is subsiding, but the white light remains. Well, the handbook did say to shine your inner light out into the world, but I didn't think this is what it meant!

A wave of tiredness crashes over me. With the inadvertent revelation of Filipe's plans to marry me coupled with this weird-ass moonlit spa experience, it has been quite a night. I step out of the spa and wrap the damp towel around my now shivering body. Tiptoeing inside, I see Filipe sprawled across the couch.

His chest is rising and falling rhythmically in sleep. With his mouth open, a faint snore resonates from his throat. Since I am less than thrilled with Frenchy right now, I'm leaving him on the sofa. Picking up a blanket off the back of the couch, I drape it over him in case he gets a chill by morning. But I'm heading to that massive plush four-poster for my 'princess sleep' alone!

I lean over him for a moment. Filipe's long black lashes brush his cheeks in sleep. Relaxed, his features look more boyish and less attractive to me. I reach out a glowing finger to brush a lock of dark hair from his face — but when I touch his skin, an electric zap repels it away. Shit!

Frenchy stirs, pulls the blanket up, and sighs before the

rhythmic movement of his chest resumes. I tiptoe away from him carefully before turning towards the bedroom. Laying naked amongst the plump red pillows, I sigh. This is not how I had imagined this weekend to go at all!

CHAPTER 36

Sparkling Boundaries

At six am sharp, my eyes pop open. The unfamiliar scarlet surroundings throw me for a moment before I remember where I am. Sinking back into the plush pillow, I am thankful for my dreamless sleep. Enough is happening in my waking hours! I can still feel the unfamiliar tingle of change within from last night.

Leaping from the bed with more enthusiasm than usual, I head for the bathroom. The silence inside the cottage tells me Filipe is still in dreamland — so if I'm lucky I'll be dressed and packed before he wakes up. With water streaming over me, I examine my hands. There seems to be nothing unusual about my fingers today.

Dressing quickly in the bathroom, I wipe the mist from the mirror and study myself. Again, golden flecks dance in my eyes as they did all those weeks ago after the spanking date with Darz. I am sure they weren't visible before last night! So now I've got golden eye flecks and white light fingertips. Holy crap, what's next?

I revoke that thought from the universe immediately. I have already learnt to be careful not to ask the wrong questions. If I only ask what is next without being specific, then the universe will show me. The same as when you have a couple of things go askew, and you ask, 'What else can possibly go wrong?!"

Oh man, that is the worst question *ever* to ask. The energies of the universe will grant you your request — and helpfully show you what else *can* go amiss!

The amazing thing is though if you ask the right questions, the universe can deliver spectacular opportunities and results. Like when I became suddenly single and asked for guidance on how to create a new, adventurous life filled with new experiences. Through meditation, when I listened for the answer, I was guided to the Vixen's Secret Handbook.

Ever since then, I must admit, life certainly has been a journey of new escapades and encounters. Yeah, yeah, I know. Not all my dates have been successful. But I have gained so much confidence and learnt an awful lot on this journey so far. This 'inner light shining through' thing was my intention, but I didn't for one second think it could be literal.

I need to check again. Plunging the bathroom into darkness, I ball my fists for a moment before stretching my fingers skywards. Thin pinpoints of light dance on the ceiling. Shit, they still glow! I clench and open my hands several times, which gives the bathroom a disco ball feel. I giggle at the ridiculousness of the situation. Maybe the light will fade as the hours' pass? There's nothing I can think of to stop it!

Relieved that this new affliction is much less noticeable in the daylight, I head into the bedroom to pack. Silence still surrounds the cottage, with only the chirps of birds outside filling the air. My stomach grumbles a protest and I realise it's now past eight. Almost time to see if Filipe has awoken — and get some bacon sizzling!

I gather the ingredients to make scrambled eggs before frying up the bacon. Filipe is still asleep on the couch, but I have no intention of waking him yet. A confrontation over breakfast is more appealing than on an empty stomach! While whisking the eggs with a fork, I turn on the hotplate ready for the frying pan.

As soon as I droop the first piece into the hot pan a loud sizzle fills the air. Working with two frying pans, the scrambled eggs and bacon cook simultaneously. The crackle of the bacon is so loud I don't hear Filipe come up behind me until his arms wrap around my waist.

"Princess! I'm so sorry I fall asleep on sofa last night. You cook breakfast! Mmmm, I like this!"

Frenchy leans forward over my shoulder to take in the aroma better when his face turns pale. He runs for the bathroom, and I can hear alcohol-induced retching from behind the closed door. I can't help but laugh as I press the toaster lever down and set the table.

After I have set out our breakfast feast on the table paired with steaming mugs, Filipe appears. Still looking a little paler than usual, he grins as he pulls out the chair across from me.

Inhaling his coffee before taking a tentative sip, brings some colour back into his cheeks.

"Do you feel better after that quick bathroom trip?"

I can't help teasing him, since I feel completely fabulous this morning. Piling my plate with crispy rashers and fluffy golden eggs on top of my toast, I wait for his answer. Several swigs of coffee later, he responds with a sigh.

"Oh my God Princess, I need this coffee! Yes, I am better. I drink too much last night!"

"How's your head feeling this morning?"

He answers with a groan and rubs his temples. Munching away happily with my stomach celebrating, I am relieved I didn't overindulge. Filipe swishes his coffee mug around to stir the remainder before draining it. Looking brighter, he reaches out for the hot cooked breakfast to fill his plate. Once his mouth is full, I decide to hit him head-on with what I overheard.

The surprise reflected in his eyes tells me all I need to know. It's true. Time to speak *my* truth! I reprimand him for not being open and honest with me from the start. Even with a strong attraction from the start, you cannot build any relationship on a lie. He tries to persuade me otherwise, but I know the facts.

The confidence gained through my vixen adventures has strengthened my boundaries. I won't put up with any dishonesty. Frenchy swallows his food and tries to explain how great it would be if he could remain here, and that I wouldn't have to stay married to him for all that long. Laughing, I shake my head.

"There's no way I would marry you, Filipe! Number one, I don't want a husband. Number two, If I ever do want one, I will get hitched for love, nothing else. It's been fun, but you really need to look elsewhere for a wife."

He can tell I will not be swayed, even as he teasingly offers the benefit of nightly pleasures. After last night's attempt, I think I'll pass. I want a man who can satisfy me in all ways, not just a couple — even if he has the most hypnotic, lustful eyes.

Kissing him goodbye is bittersweet. The pull of attraction towards him still resides within, but it has dimmed with the new revelations. We really did have some fun times, but this path is not what I want. He pulls me tighter into his embrace. I'm reluctant to end this adventure with Filipe, but I know this is the right action for me to take. The old must be swept out to make way for the new.

With a last wave and beep of the horn, I ease down the dirt driveway towards the highway. As soon as I turn onto the solid bitumen, my shoulders relax. The confrontation with Filipe caused inner tension that I need to shake off on the way home.

While driving home I need to calm this feeling of 'dis-ease' within. Consciously engaging in deep breathing techniques and focusing on the lush greenery of the countryside helps ease my inner tension. By the time I reach the edge of suburbia I feel much better. Being such a handsome French man, Filipe is sure to find a woman to agree to his proposal — just not me!

But what is it that I *do* want? Really, I was too vague about my intention to date men of different nationalities to find which ones I prefer. I need to be mindful of exactly what I put out to the universe in the future.

Krystian, Darz and Roshan are all great. It is a shame that I can't say the same for the rest of the men I've been on dates with. Filipe called me his princess but didn't treat me like one. I think I'd like a taste of being adored and served.

As I mull over the paths forward, Krystian's suggestion of a mistress profile pops into my head again. Can I be brave enough to investigate this unfamiliar world? To learn of what happens when men choose to be compliant slaves, willing to do the bidding of a mistress? What would I need to do?

Fear of the unknown mixed with excitement washes over me. Being served refreshments and having someone spoil me with foot rubs and massages — then clean my house and leave *does* have a certain appeal.

Mwaaahahaahaaahahaaa!

The next time I see Krystian I am going to create a dominatrix mistress profile as he suggested. Maybe I could contact Sean again and arrange another date to grill him on exactly what happens in this kind of casual relationship.

I don't know if this mistress thing is for me or not, but it can't hurt to learn more about it, right?

In the boot of my car, the Vixen's Secret Handbook trembles in my bag. An iridescent lime green glow grows stronger until it fully surrounds the book. Bright flashes of light flicker like purple tongues of fire from the pages. But in mere minutes, the flames are doused and the green afterglow fades. Any evidence of what just happened has vanished.

It lies innocently waiting for me. Anticipating the time when I will need it, once again.

embers. "You're one of Bartholomew's pieces. He gets desperate, it seems, in his dotage."

The clockwork goat nodded and its jaw dropped open, and it spoke in a tinny voice that hummed like a plucked string on a viola. "My master sends greetings, Lord Magus of the Smokestack. He wishes peace between you, and I have come as he bid me as an offer of goodwill."

The Smokestack Magus studied the goat through hooded eyelids. "Bartholomew may be aging," he said, "but he remains ever wily. What assurances do I have that it is safe to entertain your presence?"

"You have entertained giants, and ghosts, and unicorns. What need have you to fear a simple construct like me? My master wishes peace, to reach an accord between you. I come bearing his knowledge, his research, and his friendship."

"There are stories about a horse," the Magus said, "which was offered in friendship and caused the downfall of an empire."

"That there is," the clockwork goat said. "I am not a horse."

"You are not," said the Smokestack Magus, "but this matter requires contemplation. I will retire for a day to ponder the mystery you represent. Knock again tomorrow, and I will consider your request again."

And so the Magus left and the clockwork goat waited another day, drawing curious eyes from the men of Moloch Alley who crept closer and closer as shadows grew long. The goat did not move, and at the thirteenth hour of the fifth day the goat knocked once more and waited until the Smokestack Magus returned, stepping through his copper doorway with flames roaring at his heels. He smoked his pipe and stood over the goat, puffing gently as he regarded it with a frown and quizzical eyes.

"I have researched," he said, "and considered, and pondered the mysteries of your creation. A goat? Why that? What purpose is there in this form when all the beasts and birds of nature are at Bartholomew's disposal? Why a goat, of all things? If you are possessed of all his knowledge, tell me this so that I may consider your offer in the spirit with which it is made."

"There are stories," the goat said, "of goats serving as a sacrifice, carrying the sins of a tribe into the desert. There are stories of goats providing succor to gods, providing them with abundant nourishment to ensure they grew up strong. Perhaps my master intended both, perhaps he did not. Perhaps I am both, a symbol of past sins and succor for your future friendship. Perhaps I am not."

"Perhaps?" asked the Smokestack Magus. He puffed upon his pipe, sending black smoke into the air.

"I know all that my master knew, but I do not think with his thoughts. I can tell you what he has learned, but not what he plans to do with such knowledge."

"A good answer, but not a comforting one," the Magus said. "This requires contemplation. Knock again tomorrow, when I have pondered your offer further."

And another day wore on and the clockwork goat waited patiently, his ticking filling the silent seconds between the moans and groans of the factories. And again the men of Moloch Alley grew closer, close enough to study the mechanical beast and see their grubby faces in the sheen of the goat's silver carapace. They whispered to one another, afraid, falling back when dawn grew close, and the clockwork goat waited and knocked on the door, and when the Magus returned once more the denizens of the alley were hidden in the shadows.

"I remain conflicted," the Magus said. "For your offer is tempting, too tempting by half. I have warred with

Bartholomew for a century now, competing with him for the favor of the Crown and the merchants. I have been driven by that contest, that need to best him in the eyes of others and become the greatest of the magi. I know he once felt as I do, that he was driven to his success by our rivalry. So I ask you, good goat, why he wishes to make peace between the two of us now?"

"Perhaps he sees greater discoveries made by combining your intellects, with two thoughts achieving what one mind cannot," the clockwork goat said "Perhaps he wishes to study in peace, for its own sake, rather than focusing his work on the necessity of building favor with men and women of influence. Perhaps he concedes defeat in your contest, and sends me as a concession of your superior brilliance."

"You do not know?" the Magus said. "You cannot tell me why he sent you?"

"I know all that he knew, but I do not know his thoughts."

"Then again I am conflicted, and you must await another day for my answer."

Then the Smokestack Magus disappeared in a swirl of smoke, slamming his door behind him with a thump like an engine's piston. Once again the clockwork goat waited, silent on the doorstep, but this time the denizens of Moloch Alley crept forth, peering and prodding the silver chassis of the construct.

"If you know all that a magi knows, then you have the secret of their magic," one of the denizens said. He was a tall man, reedy, with eyes that looked like they'd been stolen from a ferret and shined up until they gleamed with cunning and guile. "Would you tell us, if we asked it? Could you tell me the great magi's secrets?"

"I know all that my master knew, all the formulas, the

theories, and the science," the goat said. "I know all my master knew, but I could not tell you his thoughts."

"Then tell us," the ferret-eyed man said, for he had intelligence enough to seize on an opportunity when it was presented to him. "We would soak up what you know, and use it to improve our lot."

And so the clockwork goat recited the formulas and the theories and the science, night after night as he stood there waiting on the Magus' steps. Every day the denizens of the alley would scatter when the Smokestack Magus emerged to ask his questions, holding their breath while they waited for the Magus' decision to delay a day longer. Every night the denizens of Moloch Alley learned more, until they had mastered many secrets and became magi themselves. They learned the magic of the cog, and of steam and coal. They learned the power of the furnace and spread it through the city like a plague of rats, driven by the dangerous combination of avarice and knowledge that has marked all the great magi.

Unden became a place of wonders, a place where science and magic prospered, though with so many magi spread across the boroughs the Smokestack Magus found it hard to maintain favor amongst the nobles and merchants of the court. He grew poorer and weaker, and the copper door tarnished as he lacked the power to keep it whole. Moloch Alley remained a place where ne'er-do-wells went, but now they were men who had heard tales of the clockwork goat, canny brigands and greedy gamblers who wished to know all the goat knew. They learned on the doorstep of the Smokestack Magus' home, but he had not the sense to open his door and see where his competition came from.

And so things continued, and so things went, until one day, three years after the goat first arrived, the Smokestack

Magus opened the door and invited it inside. "It is decided," the Magus said. "I accept your master's offer. You will teach me all you know, and I shall use it to best this upstart magi in my city."

And so the clockwork goat told him, and so the Smokestack Magus learned, though the knowledge availed him little with so many others who now possessed it. He recognized the plans and the inventions that the other magi used, the sciences and the experiments with which they impressed the Crown. "It was you!" he cried, preparing to strike the goat. "You have brought this blight of learned men to my fair city. It was you who taught them the mysteries that have robbed me of my wealth."

"It was," the goat said. "For that is how I was created. I will answer those who ask and tell them all I knew. If you had but allowed me in, those who lived in the alley would not have interrogated me for my secrets."

Then the Smokestack Magus did strike the goat several times, denting the silver chassis and breaking the delicate gears. He destroyed the creature and melted the parts, scattering the cooling ingots across the four corners of the globe. But this destruction did nothing to improve the Smokestack Magus' standing at the court, and his door corroded and warped until it could not open, and even now there are stories about the ghost of Moloch Alley, a creature of soot and sorrow that seeks to absorb all a man knows with a touch of its grubby claw.

But that, perhaps, is a story best kept for another time.

THE BIRDCAGE HEART

1.

She likes watching him dress. He likes to be watched, so he goes through the motions: yesterday's underwear; Levis, left leg following the right; the belt threaded through the loops, tugged tight and fastened; yesterday's black socks; the crimson sneakers, the laces, the left foot before the right. The shirts always last, always the struggle.

"No undershirt," she says. "Leave it off today."

He hesitates, the black shirt stretched between his forearms. "It's cold out."

"No shirt." She stands up, stretching. His sparrows chirp in response, adjusting their footing on the ledge in the cage. She takes a step towards him, predatory, like a cat. "Leave your buttons open. For me. Until you leave, at least."

She closes on him, reaches for him. One hand on his arm, holding it free of the buttons. Another on his chest, moving from flesh to golden bars, tracing the outline of the cage door. The sparrows flutter their wings against her fingertips, panicked and trapped, unable to flee. She likes that, the control. She likes the way the birds move within him when she presses herself against his chest. "Please, Nathaniel, for me."

He leaves the shirt unbuttoned. The sparrows chirp, and she's content.

And it is cold out, without the undershirt. Not freezing, but damp and chilly and uncomfortable as he walks to work, drawing stares from his fellow pedestrians when they hear the sparrows fidget beneath the straight line of his shirt-buttons. Cold enough that he wants to run home and tell her, as if his being right would matter. As if anything he says ever really fits into her world view. There are three of them in the relationship, her and him and the birds in his chest, but there is never a moment where the majority rules.

He goes to work, he puts in the hours. He eats lunch in the park, feeding crumbs to the shivering birds. He tells himself that it isn't always bad, that there are times when he loves her more than he can say.

And the sparrows sing as he makes his way home, urging him to fly south before winter curls its grip around them.

It hasn't always been sparrows. There are days when he feels like every bird has left its mark on him, a reminder of the time they spent in the hollows of his chest. The crows left him bleak. The peacocks left him a dandy, resplendent in suits of silk and velvet. The doves left him unafraid of romance, opening him to a sweetness he thought himself incapable of. So many birds have passed through him, have sung soft trills from the cage inside his ribs, and their memories remain long after their departure.

He likes the sparrows because they were his first bird, a birthday present from his father who never seemed entirely sure what to make of his son's condition. The sparrows come loaded with memory: waking up to find his father kneeling beside the bed, two small birds ready to be delivered into the cage that was finally large enough to contain its own life. The birds chirped an agreeable song in the centre of his shallow chest. "They're Sparrows," his father said, "dependable birds. Treat them well and they'll keep you safe."

And he lay in bed, shivering, unsure of what had happened. The short hops and twitching wings in his chest unfamiliar, so strange, but somehow right. Complete. Real. "Thank you," he said, and his father nodded. There were tears forming in the corner of his father's eyes.

That was the morning of his sixth birthday. The two of them never spoke of it afterwards.

The sparrows remind him of this, the silence and the gift; of the first time he was permitted to fill the cage of his heart.

The cage isn't normal. He knows that. People ask all the time, demanding stories and explanations. He's never sure how to handle that, has never had an explanation that makes sense to him, but he muddles through as best he can. "Airports are a pain," he says, "I always have to plan ahead for the security check, and the birds get freaked out once we're flying."

It's a good line, it gets a laugh. Humor satisfies their curiosity in a way the truth does not. Not like that time when he was sixteen, lying in bed with his first girlfriend.

She put her fingertips on the cage and studied the birds, and she asked "what happens if I open it? What happens if I let them go?"

"Nothing," he said, "they fly away. It's just a cage, you know?"

It changed her feelings for him, when she heard it. It seemed she didn't know at all.

There are times when she's almost sweet, and that helps him endure the rest. "If I were a bird I'd live in there," she says, stroking the bars with the soft edge of her finger. "I'd crawl into your heart and live there, safe and comfortable, and I'd let you keep watch over me for all the days of my life."

The sparrows in his chest flutter at the suggestion, wings brushing against his ribs. It occurs to him, suddenly, that he's never wanted anything more than this, to hold her in his chest and keep her safe.

"Marry me," he says.

"Sure." Her voice low, her fingertips soft, the birds in his chest lulled into slumber.

"I'm not kidding," he says. "I want you to marry me."

She opens the cage door and reaches in, fingertip stroking a sparrow's head. Nobody has done this, not in all the years he's caged birds in his chest. It's an unfamiliar sensation, intense and vaguely unpleasant. He gasps and the birds flutter against the invading fingers, the tickle of feather on skin causing giggles to fill the small bedroom of her flat.

"Yes," she says. "Of course, yes."

She says it so naturally, like there could ever be another answer that would satisfy either of them.

2.

Sometimes she wears a gold scarf with tassels, bright and profoundly ugly. It is the only splash of color in her somber wardrobe, her clothes normally styled from cloth possessing the black sheen of raven feather and the powdery grey of owl down.

He watches her in the park, walking towards the coffee vender, scarf fluttering in the breeze. It entrances him, the gold and the tassels, the stark contrast with her dark wardrobe and pale skin. Gold like the bars of his birdcage heart, a little connection between her and him.

"It's so pretty," she said once. Then, "I wonder what its worth. If we got into trouble, could we sell it? Just clip a bar free and drop down to the local jeweler, sell it on the sly with no one the wiser?"

"That'd probably hurt," he said, although he doesn't know for sure. He's careful with the birdcage, unsure of what happens if the bars are damaged. The first lesson his father taught him was be careful of your heart.

"If we were starving," she said, "if we were on the run and needed money...."

"I think its tin," he said. "The gold's just a veneer. It's all pretty ordinary and cheap underneath"

"Oh," she said, and smiled. "So much for that plan. Best we stay out of trouble, then."

The tassels dance, caught on the breeze. He feels he could watch them forever.

They're walking to the video store when she asks the inevitable question. "Does it have to be sparrows?"

"No," he says, "It could be anything. I just like the sparrows. They're familiar. I understand them."

"Good," she says, and smiles at him. He's seen such smiles before. "You don't mind if we experiment then? Give you a spot of color?"

He likes pleasing her. She likes to be pleased. He raises a smile to mask his true response as he tells her, "Sure."

"Good," she says. "Good. Leave it with me. I'll try and think of something."

He dreads the possibility of a lovebird. To delve into such cliché seems abhorrent and unnecessary. Also on the list of unfortunate choices: nightingales; budgerigars; parrots in all shades of the rainbow. All have been inflicted upon him in the past, and none have been satisfactory.

They rent three movies—*Evita*, *Tango and Cash*, *Once Upon a Time in China*—and walk home in comfortable silence. Later, while she sleeps, he sits in the dark lounge room and studies the photocopied covers in the DVD cases. The birds in his chest stir, a momentary fidget before returning to sleep.

This is who we are, he thinks. *This is what we've become.*

He sets the sparrows free in preparation for her gift, standing at the window with the cage door slid open. The wind whistles against his chest, pushing through the bars and filling the hollow spaces within, cool and uncomfortable against the exposed bones of his ribs. The sparrows fly off, bobbing against the breeze, angling up and up and away, their wings fluttering against the air as they rise. The morning air is cold, the bright sunlight doing nothing to warm the bare skin.

He makes a list of birds he's willing to cage, should the opportunity arise: the emu; the myna; the dodo; the swan. The larger birds are uncomfortable, hard to fit within the cage's confines, but there are times when discomfort takes a back stead to novelty, and there are very few species that have not resided in his chest at one point or another.

He wonders if he should mention this, decides he should not. It would hurt her, to hear this, now that he's given her permission to make a change. She wants to deliver something new, to give him some bird that exists between the two of them.

He buttons his shirt, covering the empty cage, and practices the face he will make when she delivers something expected and ordinary.

She says, "I've brought you a surprise, Nathaniel," and smiles like the words were unexpected. His breath catches, a facsimile of surprise. She's the only one who calls him Nathaniel, refusing to abbreviate his name. This doesn't comfort him the way it once did. The words seem to echo inside his empty chest.

She hands him a pair of robins, red-breasted and bold of song.

He has tried robins before. They're brave birds, unafraid, aggressive defenders of their territory. "Thank you," he says, "they're beautiful."

She smiles. He smiles.

In less than a month she tells him to replace the robins, driven to distraction by his untoward acts of jealousy.

For a moment he hopes they're done, that the experiment

with the robins is enough to dissuade her, but it appears he's not that lucky. In the spring she gives him geese and his temper grows foul. She laughs about it, often, after the geese are removed. He suspects they were only given to him so she could make puns about his behavior.

In the summer she gives him ravens, unsure of what will happen. He leaves the cage door open and lets them escape, tells her it's an accident when she asks what happened.

In autumn he's given vultures. It ends far better than either of them expects,

By winter it's become an addiction. She keeps bringing him birds, an endless aviary of ornithological specimens, and he keeps accepting them, bird after bird, just to keep her smiling. Their house becomes home to a mismatched flock of birds. The neighbors complain about the smell.

"We're going to build an aviary," she says, "a place for them to feel at home, after you've set them free." And the next day there are workmen, a construction crew and an ornithologist consulting and long lengths of curved rib bone that arrive on the back of trucks. He doesn't particularly want an aviary, but it proceeds without him. He refuses to speculate on the nature of the ribs, the where and why of their arrival.

"It has to be bone," she tells him. "We want them to feel at home, and it wouldn't be authentic without them, yeah?"

He misses his sparrows. He doesn't say this aloud. He misses his sparrows so much his heart aches.

3.

He killed his first sparrows, though he doesn't like to think about it. He went to sleep without covering the front of the cage, and woke screaming from the pain as the birds inside him died. They were his to look after, and he failed them. He was only seven, but he feels the shame acutely. Still feels it when he loses things, when the world changes around him and he should have noticed.

Since then, he's refused to name any of the birds he keeps. Since then, he's cared without getting too close.

It takes three years to complete the aviary, the vast structure dominating the top floor of their house. He learns the name of the workmen who arrive every morning, hammering and sawing in the early hours. He learns to fill his heart with the bird of her choice, coordinating their features with his suits and ties and t-shirts. He learns to pretend, to be happy, to forget who he used to be. He learns to hold his tongue when she names the birds and treats them like pets, disappearing into the aviary for hours at a time.

He's not the man she married anymore. They're both aware of that.

She leaves him with the house, the aviary, with three hundred and fifty-eight birds that have all spent time in the hollow cage of his chest. She leaves him the scarf, black with gold tassels, and he loops it over the curtain rail so the loose threads dance in the breeze and the faint remaining smell of her seeps through the house on the morning air. He goes through the motions: coffee, two sugars; a bowl of fruit-loops, humming a short jingle half-remembered from his childhood; showering; shaving; dressing for the day.

There are one hundred and seventy-seven types of bird in the aviary, the result of her mania for collecting mated pairs of every breed she tried. None of them fill the hollows left by her absence.

He rings his father and breaks the news. They move on to the weather, then back again, the conversation following an erratic flight path.

"The birds," his father says, the notion coming to him suddenly. "My god, Nate, all those birds. How are you handling things?"

He hasn't been to the aviary in three days. He doesn't wish to see the birds. The birds are so small, so delicate and weak. He doesn't wish to see them, to take them in, to be like them. "They're fine," he says, "the birds are taken care of."

That's what he does, him and his birdcage. They take care of things, they cope and they secure.

He's owed some leave, and he takes it. Doesn't go anywhere, just stays home and broods.

She liked to watch him dress. He thinks of this as be pulls on underwear and considers the last pair of pressed, pristine jeans sitting in his wardrobe. He pulls on an undershirt, keeps the cage of his heart secure and warm.

It's time, he thinks, to go upstairs.

The aviary curves around him, the bars of white bone

curving against the walls, and it occurs to him for the first time that something great and terrible died to cage these birds for him. He lies on the grimy floorboards, down amid the bird shit, and he watches the former occupants of his heart flitting between the covered branches: jackdaws and parrots and lovebirds, the macaw with its brilliant feathers, the wide wings of the own as it stretched and yawned from a lowest perch. A hundred birds, a thousand, all of them cawing and cackling and trilling in the morning air. Angry geese hiss at him from the space behind the ottoman.

We built this, he thinks. *The two of us built this place for them.*

The birds sing, an avian cacophony. *There is comfort in that,* he thinks. Silence, now, would break him, would remind him of his failure.

He closes his eyes and breathes, savoring the sulfurous tang of bird dung in the air. The floor is hard and uncomfortable. His jeans are getting dirty and he no longer needs to care.

Tomorrow he will go out and purchase two sparrows. That will give him twenty-four hours to start coming up with names.

ON THE CLIFFS, BY THE SEA

It's a small town, little more than a village. Small and cold and built on the sea cliffs, caught between the grey waters and cloud-soaked sky. Home to those born of the salt and the foam, a broad-shouldered breed with protuberant features and wide, generous mouths. Folk accustomed to the ocean and its dangers, who make their out on the waves, navigating paths between the reefs and treacherous rocks. Their fishing boats leave the shore before dawn, returning home at dusk. Those who stay behind fret and pray and walk the widow's walk, unwilling to rest until their loved ones come back safe.

On Sunday, day of rest, the whole town gathers in the local church and their baritone voices join together in a faithful chorus.

They do not sing to a lone god, not as you or I would know him. Their hymns go out to Kraken Queens and Kings of the Abyss, to things that rest uneasy in the murky depths. Their canticles are lullabies for things best kept sleeping, lest the world prove to be more alien than expected.

And on the days when the songs do not soothe them, when the Kings and Queens are restless and the waves pile against the rocky cliffs as though intending to push all the world into the sea, the folk give over their church to darker forms of worship, and sate the royal hunger with blood and ritual.

It's not a place to stop, this town. They have no love for tourists. Lucky travelers are hurried on, motivated by the dour expressions of the locals, or the terse reception their visit receives at the Mobil station just outside of town.

The unlucky ones venture into the township proper, seeking food at the small café on Dowser Road where they serve a weak, milky form of coffee, or lodgings in the quiet motel on Bleak Street that rarely sees long-term business.

Wise outsiders, if forced to stay overnight, do not venture out after dark.

The sea is restless, on this day. There is no mistaking the tumultuous waves, nor the dour sky where the storm front gathers and prepares to whip the coast.

And he doesn't look like much, the Stranger who arrives amid these sour omens. No more trouble than any other stray traveller who has found their way to the cliffs.

He is long and lithe as an oboe reed, this Stranger; fingers built for music and his smile built to charm. His Volvo stalls just three hundred meters from the Mobil, the engine growling and spluttering into death, and if he's bothered by the monosyllabic response his troubles receive at the gas station, he shows it not a whit. The Stranger pays for a mechanic to bring his vehicle in for repairs, walks the last kilometer into town with a pack on his shoulder and a guitar case in hand. Takes lodging at the motel, announcing his intention to stay for a week.

The hotelier nods and hands him keys.

Not long after, the whispers and phone calls begin.

There are precious few places to eat, so inevitably the Stranger arrives at the small cafe. He sits at a corner table, guitar case at his feet, and watches the quiet row of houses on the north side of Dowser Street. "Quiet kind of day," he says, just making conversation, and the gentleman who waits on the customers can do nothing but nod in agreement

He is older, this gentleman, this purveyor of bad coffee. Steel-haired and in possession of a slight limp. A fisherman in his youth, he knows what it means when the sea is all a-churn, knows what it means when the hymns are insufficient.

The Stranger drinks his coffee. Sups on a meal of stiff bread and seafood broth, salty and thick with the ocean's bounty, good enough to serve as a consolation for the poor coffee and begrudging service. He orders another bowl and another beverage, for after, and this time his coffee served with a soporific crushed into the steaming mug.

They are not cruel, the people of this town. Pragmatic, yes, and prone to secrets. Hardened to the necessity of spilling of blood when needed. What cruelty they exhibit is inherited from their place in the world, from the demands of the Kraken Queens and the Kings of the Abyss. The cruelty that comes naturally when living by the cliffs and watching the moods of the sea.

The Stranger eats with gusto, says, "You know, this is damn fine chow, mate."

Says, "I gotta say, I never knew this place existed. It's kinda pretty, when you see it up close."

Says, "You fellas aren't much for conversation round here, right?"

And there is no response to any comment, not unless

you count the delivery of a hastily scrawled bill and the frown from the gentlemen behind the counter who is puzzled that his soporific is not yet affecting his chosen target.

The Stranger finishes his meal and collects his guitar case before paying. He walks the full length of Dowser Street until he finds rocky cliffs and the rickety wooden stairs leading down to the docks and the beach. He stands at the edge, hair whipped across his face by the wind, his free hand seeking out the warm pockets of his jacket. He closes his eyes and breathes the air, tastes the salt and the damp and the smell of gutted fish.

He hears them coming, notes the scuff of boots on concrete. They are big men, dark-eyed and dour, muscles toned by a lifetime hauling nets. The first carries a stout cudgel, slapping it into his open palm. The second merely approaches, thick fingers splayed as though ready to wring The Stranger's neck. They make no secret of their intentions.

The Stranger does not run, but he does put down his guitar case. He ducks the cudgel, disables the armed attacker with a strike to the wrist and another to the throat. When the second fisherman grabs him, the Stranger breaks his grip and applies a knee to the nethers, follows it with a kick that leaves the bigger man stunned.

When they are found, a half-hour after their failed assault, both fishermen are unconscious. There is no sign of the Stranger or his guitar case. There is no sign of the cudgel they wished to use against him.

The sea churns. There are storm-clouds on the horizon. Twice they have failed, but the Queens of the

Kraken still demand blood. The Kings of the Abyss are hungry for a sacrifice.

The local Constable appears at the scene of the attack, takes in all the details while a crowd of locals gathers. He's a stout man, the Constable, and his shaved head is covered in scars and lumps, the legacy of keeping peace in quiet town where no outsider shows.

It doesn't take long to surmise what's happened, nor what needs to be done.

The men gather together, searching in twos or threes. They arm themselves with knives and clubs, with the hooks used to gather nets into their boats. They search the yards and the houses, the idle lanes and the quiet allies, the lonely hills that surround them, keep them isolated from the world. When they finish their patrols, finding nothing, they report their failure to the Constable, who spreads the word to the hotelier and the limping waiter at the cafe, and to the mayor, who also serves as the town pastor, leading its people in holy chorus.

They cannot find the Stranger, and this bodes ill.

The hotelier breaks into the Stranger's rooms, searches the lonely rucksack left sitting on the bed. Discovers three sweaters, some underwear, a handful of shirts. A tattered paperback about angels and demons in Toronto. A photograph in a silver frame, a woman who, perhaps, shares the Stranger's appearance. A sister, perhaps? A cousin? The hotelier frowns at the photograph, lingers on it. Tries to recall if she's passed through, on some other storm wracked evening.

But there have been so many faces.

There have been so many storms.

Theories are spread via telephone and whispered talk,

a thread of fear running through. What magic there is in worship and song, what magic there is in blood, these are not things understood by others. They are secrets, known only here, and they rely on the discretion of everyone involved.

The Constable keeps everyone searching. For two days they scour the streets and the fields outside of town, the beaches at the bottom of the cliffs and caves where the waves have worn away the stone. All the patrols are armed. Some do not return at the appointed time, and when the their paths are followed and their tracks can be discerned, they are found, defeated, their weapons missing, eyes closed. Some are merely injured, left to the bliss of unconsciousness.

Others, in time, are killed. Their throats slit. Their necks snapped. Noses bludgeoned, cheekbones broken, faces battered to pulp.

At least, the Constable tells his men, the Stranger hasn't fled. At least there's still a chance to contain him and keep their secrets from spilling out.

This thought comforts no-one, least of all the grieving widows.

That night, the sea grows wild. Waves pound upon the shore like a sledge hammers stone, eager to crack the earth and see what falls from the ruin.

The hotelier is found dead, seated in his easy chair. The guitar case is found in the empty cafe, loaded with explosives that detonate when it is opened. Only the limping waiter escapes the inferno, staggering into the rain-soaked night, and there he is assaulted and left bleeding in the streets, the knee of his good leg shattered and his piteous cries whipped away by the wind.

The Constable is called, forced to brave the weather. He surveys the burning building, makes his notes, throws glances at the squalls forming out beyond the docks. Townsfolk gather to put out the blaze, but the work is hard and dangerous.

They are searching for the Stranger, still, even now, men going forth in numbers as if that will afford some measure of safety. The storms make that perilous, even if the Stranger were not there to complicate matters. Men will slip and fall on treacherous paths, made worse by the driving rain. They will be struck from behind by flying debris, caught on the powerful winds.

The Queens of the Kraken are growing restless, and all the town knows what that means. They will not be placated by song this Sunday, nor the many Sundays that follow. They must spill blood, and spill it in quantity, for there is no other option to keep the them all safe.

The Constable turns up his collar and heads up the main street, knocks on the front door of the Mayor's lonely residence.

There is no answer, no sounds from within the house. It is late, but the Mayor is surely still awake. There is no other choice in an emergency such as this, and the lights still burn against the storm from the upper floors of the dwelling. The Constable knocks again, and shouts the man's name. When, once more, there is no response, he draws his pistol and tests the door, his breathe catching in his throat when the handle twists and the door swings open.

There is no-one in town who does not lock their doors, this night.

The Constable eases his bulk up the stairs, quiet as a burglar. He does not bother announcing himself, or calling out once he enters. He turns each corner, gun at the ready, expecting some kind of trouble, and in the master bedroom he finds it.

The Mayor is not a little man, and there is no mistaking the stillness of his great and unmoving bulk, facedown on the rug with his forehead smashed to pulp, the blood-smeared cudgel left beside him now that the job is done. The Constable kneels and checks for a pulse, is unsurprised when he finds nothing.

He rises and turns, taking in the entire room, waiting to be attacked.

"Did he give the order?" the Stranger says, and the Constable starts, executing a clumsy turn that ends with his gun pointed at the open window. The Stranger loiters there, peers through his fringe. The long, delicate fingers are smeared with blood.

The Constable watches the Stranger. The Stranger watches the barrel of the gun.

You don't understand, the Constable tells him. What we do is necessary. We did not prolong her agony, or tan her hide for later use. We did these things, once, for we did not know any better. For the world was smaller and secrets easily hidden, but we adapt as all things adapt, and we are not what we were.

There is no change in the Stranger's expression. He lifts his head to meet the Constable's eyes, reads the intent in the officer's gaze. The Stranger is moving by the time the gun fires, twisting free of the bullet's path.

He crosses the room, ducks and weaves. Takes the Constable's wrist and breaks his hand, kicking the gun beneath the opulent bed.

The Constable backs away and the Stranger follows, a predator cornering prey.

"Five years," the Stranger says, "five years since you took her."

He kicks the Constable in the stomach, and the Constable doubles over. A finger is snapped at the end of his arm. Pain, such pain, wracks his body.

"I've seen your church," the Stranger says, applying his knee to the Constable's ribs. "I know what happened when you took her there."

And he says even more, but the Constable is folded like a paper doll, folded on a crease of agony that runs through his stomach. Perhaps a rib is broken. Perhaps it is not. He doesn't hear what the Stranger says, not with the hurt inside him. Not with the cold wind rattling against the windows.

Even here, in the lonely house, the Constable can hear the angry rumble of the waves.

He wants to tell the Stranger that his sister's death was necessary, that placating the Queens of the Kraken is a duty. Should the Queens of the Kraken wake, should they rise and gather up their husbands, calling them from the Abyss, then others will rise with them. The Kings of the Abyss will bring even darker things, the myriad children of deepest ocean. Formless and protean and altogether dangerous, an enemy that will devour the land and eliminate all life.

He wants to say this, but knows he cannot, for the Stranger is in no mood to heed such warnings.

And so the Constable straightens, and is hit for his trouble, a punch beneath the ribs that makes the agony beat against his chest like a second heart.

"Necessary," the Constable gasps. He follows it with: "The Queens..."

The Stranger punches him one last time, strikes him against the temple. The Constable falls, vision swimming, but he falls towards the bed. Towards the pistol that skittered beneath the fringe of the duvet, just visible from his vantage point when his head strikes the hardwood floor.

They understand sacrifice, in this town. The know what it is to endure boundless pain.

There are only four feet between the Constable and his weapon. No distance at all, if he needs to crawl it, although the Stranger will fight him every step of the way.

The wind howls. The Queens stir, in their slumber, deep beneath the waves.

The Constable forces himself to action. His broken hand aches with every motion, his shoulder offers him both support and agony. The Stranger is on him, kicking, bludgeoning. The Constable ignores him, even as he feels bones shatter and break.

He reaches for the gun and the Stranger stomps on the extended hand. The Constable howls like a wounded beast.

"In case you haven't noticed," the Stranger says, "I don't give two shits about your Queens."

He walks across the room and collects the fallen gun. Turns back towards the Constable, a grin on his lips.

"Bang," the Stranger says, then he points the weapon.

They raise them cold, in that part of the world. They understand sacrifice.

The Constable lifts his eyes to the heavens. "Ah," he says, little more than a whisper. "Ah."

He received a foot to the ribs for his troubles. The crease of pain inside him colonizes other areas. A rib is broken, the Constable thinks. Probably more than one.

He coughs and there is blood. He breathes and the air tastes wet and coppery.

"Ai," he whispers, searching for the words of his prayer. "Ai—"

A gunshot has the final word. The Constable's lips cease moving.

It's a small town, little more than a village. Small and cold and built on the sea cliffs, caught between the grey waters and cloud-soaked sky. It doesn't take long for the ocean to claim the hillside, to pull down the fringe of stone from the top and send parts of the village tumbling into sea. Few of the local fisherman leave, believing their sacrifice may be deemed worthy, even if they are not of innocent blood.

They are fearless men, born of the salt and the foam, and their bulbous faces and broad, generous mouths are not seen again in the aftermath of the storm.

On Sunday, the day of rest, the remaining folk gather in the local church and sing in their deep, rich baritone voices, hoping against hope that their faith will stop the apocalypse.

As he strides away, the Stranger looks towards the waves, churning and wild with the oncoming storm, and he expends a single, idle thought on how much blood is necessary. How much will it take to calm the Queens and keep their Kings a-slumber.

But then, he doesn't believe. And those who do not believe are dangerous.

That which is sleeping will not stay a-slumber. You know that. We all know that. We hear it in our cradles, take it with us to the grave.

And so, tonight, we sing.

And tomorrow, we do what we must.

BRIAR DAY

I asked Jay what he was doing when the thorns came, because that's what people do when they get together on Briar Day. He sighed and rolled his eyes at me. "I thought we weren't going to talk about it."

We weren't. We'd run into each other at an seminar for the ANZ, one of those pre-arranged accidents we set up around this time of year. He'd picked the bar on Elizabeth Street because it showed no interest in the day, a quiet place hiding behind a narrow flight of stairs and fading sign. The kind of place people went to drink, not party or reminisce.

That had been four hours ago, and now it was getting late. I should have been home with Annie and we both knew it. Jay looked ready to tell me so, so I said: "Come on. Four years we've been doing this. You've never been curious, ever?"

Jay sighed again. He signalled the waitress in cherry-red Docs, put in an order for another round of drinks. She smiled and I smiled back, gave her a twenty to cover our order. Jay scowled at me, drummed his fingers on the table.

He knew me well enough to figure this wasn't going to go away. "You first," he said. "If we're going to do this, we do it right. What were you doing?"

"I was at work," I said. "Three days in the bank, eating breath mints and watching the vines put pressure on the glass doors. They cracked after a few hours, gave way before the first day was up. We had to put down the security grill, just to hold them off."

"Bad place to be," Jay said.

"There were worse," I said.

"Did anyone try to get out?"

"Sure," I said. "A couple of customers made a run for it, but they mostly got cut to shit by the thorns. I sat tight. Allergies, you know? I was fucked the moment the briars grew."

"Huh," Jay said. The waitress arrived with our beers, putting the heavy steins on the table along with my change. I took a long slug from mine, but Jay just held his with both hands. "What about the dragon?" he said.

"We heard it," I said, "but it was just roaring and the sound of wings; I had no idea what caused the ruckus until everything was taken care of."

Jay's face tightened, his mouth a thin line. He wanted to put this off, sidestep the story for another year, but he was out of questions and my time in the Briars didn't amount to much. That's the reason I catch up with Jay every year, go through the ritual of pretending we didn't care. He never made me feel like I missed some great, defining experience the way other people did.

People don't get it, me being so close to the action and seeing nothing. It was like I'd lived through Kennedy's shooting, in an apartment on Elm Street, Dallas, in November of sixty-three, and the only thing I'd noticed was a bit of a crowd that day.

Still, I'd brought it up, and I wanted to see it through. Nothing to do but plough forward, bait Jay into talking.

"So," I said. "How about you?"

Jay stared into his beer. "We do this once," he said, and he tipped the stein to one side. Watched the beer slosh around before putting it on the table.

"Just once," I said. "Okay."

Jay took a deep breath.

"You never met Caroline," he said. "That's probably why we're still friends. I had people, friends, stop talking to me because of her. No real reason, just picking sides. The usual shit that happens when people stop living together and relationship turn ugly. And me and Caroline, man, we fucked things up, and the briar's made it uglier."

He stopped and closed his eyes. Took another drink. "Maybe that's not a good way to start it. Let's try this," he said. "I was baking."

I blinked. "Baking?"

He nodded. "Butterscotch cookies, probably. I do that when I'm upset. They smell good, and I eat when I'm pissed off or sad. Safer to bake than buy a whole pack, that sort of thing. And let's be clear: I was bad, back then. The whole thing with Caroline had fucked me up good. I wasn't going to work that day, hadn't gone to work for a week or more. I baked and I cried and I wanted to punch the walls. Kept trying to make sense of how I'd fucked up, assumed it was me 'cause who else would it be?"

"Alright," I said. "You were baking."

He nodded. "So I'm pulling a track of cookies out of the oven when it hits neck of the woods. First thing I notice is the kitchen going dark, shadows on the windows and stray rays of sunlight creeping through the foliage. No warning, just like, wham, all of a sudden, there it was: thorns longer than your finger and those weird blood-rose flowers that were bigger than your head. The only things I could see from my kitchen were vines and the top of the street lights.

"None of this is special, I know that. It's the same shit everyone blabs about: thorns, flowers, freaking out. Nothing special at all, but it felt like it should have been. I went through all the stages they talked about: disbelief, rationalising, calming down and accepting that it was actually happening. For a few hours I wasn't thinking about Caroline or the mess we'd made of things, 'cause the world had taken a sharp right turn into the realm of what-the-fuck, you know?

"And that's when my phone rang.

"I knew who it was, before I picked up. Even back then, on the old land-lines, before every call came with ID and a warning. I knew it was Caroline because she'd been calling, and every time I answered I just felt like shit.

"I didn't want to be that guy, you know? Just another asshole who cut the woman he dated out of his life because it was over, yeah? And I told myself Caroline was the kind of girl who'd keep ringing until I gave in. She wasn't one for reading between the lines when I didn't answer.

"So I answered and Caroline was still in the rationalizing phase, all 'I can see all these giant fricken' thorn bushes out my window. It's not just me, yeah? You can see them too?'

"'It's not just you,' I told her. I was laying in bed, speaking on the cordless. I can remember playing with this red pillowcase I had, picking at the stray threads. Caroline didn't say anything after I reassured her, and I wasn't really in the mood to be speaking, so I just sat there listening to the phone line crackle and the soft scratch of thorns embracing the house.

"This was how our phone calls went, ever since I

moved out. She called, we said two words to each other, and then the silence set in. Her not saying what she really wanted, me not saying what I truly felt. So I told her, 'Caroline, I gotta go, yeah?' And I still felt weird, calling her that, because we'd spent three years relying on pet names. All that stupid stuff you pick up, once the relationship starts. She wasn't Caroline to me, she was Kitten or Babe or Love. Calling her Caroline felt like an ending, and we were both shit at ending things.

"'I'm sorry,' she told me. 'I shouldn't have called. It's just…'

"She didn't finish that thought. I don't know if I wanted her to finish it. I told her that I understood, that everything was cool. I told her I'd call later and got the fuck off the phone. Then one of those flowers bloomed, right next to the window, and I felt like a bastard without knowing why. I crashed out on the bed, not really thinking about the thorns anything, just wanting to drink and break stuff. If the thorns hadn't been there, I would have gone out and got hammered.

"Instead, I hated myself for an hour, right up until I heard the dragon for the first time."

Jay's face disappeared behind the beer stein, doing his best to drain it. Jay didn't drink heavily, any other day, but he always got drunk on Briar Day. I nursed my own drink, feeling awkward in the silence. "I thought the briars weren't that bad, out your way?"

"Maybe they weren't, but some people's standards." Jay wiped the beer foam from his cheek. "The dragon still came close. It flew over the house and I heard the wings, that noise like the echo of a slap across the face. That freaked me out more than the thorns did."

The bar crowd had grown thicker as he talked, a steady buzz of conversation building up around us. All those wrinkled old people hunched over their drinks and talking. It was too hot in our booth by then, far too hot for comfort. Jay's eyes were red, bloodshot. He should have been calling it a night. I should've been calling Annie, letting her know I was coming home late. Just to be polite, you know? That's what you do when you're dating.

Jay blinked a few times, found something to focus on just behind my shoulder and struggled to keep his eyes there. "I tuned into the news, just like everyone else," he said. "I mean, what else did you do in an emergency back then, before twitter fed you details as it all happened? I sat through that anchorman with a perfect helmet of hair telling us that the suburbs were swamped, that there'd been sightings of a dragon in the city centre, that there were reports of the dragon kidnapping a maiden and holding her to ransom. They even called her that on the news: the maiden. You could tell he didn't want to be saying it, but someone was making him go through with it. I guess once you accept the city is overrun with giant thorns, everything else becomes credible, so you start covering all the bases.

"He did a good job, the anchor, given the circumstances. Refused to be rattled by anything. They trotted out specialists to tell us what they thought was going on, then cut back to footage of the city getting choked to death by plants. You could hear the steady whine of the rotor over the reporter's commentary.

"The phone rang during the sports report. I muted the sound and picked it up. Didn't even bother saying hello. And there was Caroline on the other end, asking if that was it. Wanting to know what good the news was if that's all they had to offer.

"'What more do you want?' I asked her.

"'Explanations,' Caroline said. 'Direction. Some idea about when it'll end.'

"I was all, 'It's not like they have any answers, is it?'

"'It's the news,' Caroline said. 'They should have answers. That's why we watch.'

"'You don't watch the news.'

"'I did today.'

"'Once,' I said. 'Just once, this year. I'm not sure you've got grounds for a complaint.'

"Caroline laughed. I laughed. It felt like old times. Sometimes that happened, when she called, and it hurt. The sports report switched over to the weather; sunny with a strong chance of thorns and rain. Caroline wasn't saying anything. I wasn't saying anything. We remembered we weren't together anymore.

"'So,' I said.

"'Yeah,' she said.

"The phone line crackled.

"'I don't have any answers either,' I said.

"'Yeah, sorry,' Caroline said. 'It's just…'

"'Yeah, it's just,' I said. It was always *just* back then, and I kept letting that work. I fidgeted, tapping out a rhythm on the coffee table with my toe. I don't know what Caroline was doing on her end of the phone, but I'm willing to bet she was crying.

"'Look, I'm just irritable,'' I told her. 'You know how I get when I'm inside for too long.'

"'Yeah, I know' Caroline said. Her voice was hard to hear, like she was whispering through a keyhole after locking herself in the bathroom.

"She hung up. I hung up. I left the news on mute and listened to the thorns grinding against the windows, trying to get in.''

"You want another round?''

I jumped. There was a waitress looming over our table, thick eye shadow like two slices of orange peel beneath the line of her manicured eyebrows. She picked up my empty glass and added it to the pile on her tray. I looked at Jay; he shrugged.

"Sure," I said. "Why the hell not?"

"You got any plans for later?" she asked. "Couple-a young guys like you, surely you're heading for a party somewhere?"

Jay rolled his eyes.

"Probably not," I said. "We're just after a quiet one, you know? A chance to sit back and reflect."

"Fair enough," she said. "Happy Briar Day."

The waitress took my money and headed for the bar. Jay sneered at her back. "Fuck it," he said. "This was a bad idea."

"One waitress," I said. "It's not a big deal."

"You started this." Jay jabbed a finger in my direction. "You know you started this, yeah?"

"Fine," I said. "Fuck it, it's my fault."

"It is." He started patting down his pockets, searching for his cigarettes. "Has Annie called yet?"

"No," I said, and maybe it was true. I didn't check my phone, didn't see the need. Annie would be there when I got home, or she'd be out doing her own thing.

I fished a pack out of my jacket and slid it across the table. Jay lit up without pressing the issue, content to let everything drop.

I was the one who started it again. "We were probably the first people to hear the dragon, down in the bank."

"Bullshit." Jay adjusted his glasses, fixed me with a glare.

"No bullshit. I was awake a lot of the time, 'cause the flowers were doing a number on me. Even with the antihistamines, I just kept sneezing, yeah? So I was awake a lot, miserable, nothing to do but listen when everyone else was sleeping. And I heard this rumble, the kind you feel in your gut, like the moment one of those big rigs goes past you on the highway."

"The dragon." Jay waved his cigarette, a curt gesture dismissing the whole damn thing. "Everyone goes on about the dragon, but the only person it hurt was that dick with the sword. You know what frightened me? The flowers."

"Yeah," I said. "They sucked."

"They did more than suck." Jay hunched of the table. "I hated the way they burst open, all quick and soft. That soft pop throwing all the pollen in the air, big enough that you could see it on the breeze. Being stuck there, thinking, 'well, there's another thorn bush. Nothing I can do about it, and we're all going to die.'"

His eyes were frightening, wild as hell. I took a deep breath, tried to placate him. "Yeah," I said. "The flowers. I dream about them sometimes."

The waitress brought our drinks over. Jay looked at his like it was hiding something dangerous, swaying in his seat. "I tried to go to work," he said. "That second day I got up and got ready like it was no big deal. I rolled out of bed and I showered, drank the last of the coffee and made a note to pick up more on my shopping list. I don't know what I thought was going to happen when I was done. The house was still wrapped up tight, the windows blocked by thorns and vines. I couldn't even see the streetlights anymore. There was no hot water either; I was on solar in that place and I figure the thorns had grown over the panels. I cut myself while I was shaving and I ironed a shirt while I was still half-asleep. I turned the radio on while I was having a shower and the Morning Crew was making jokes about the dragon, the knight, and that girl, the maiden, who they'd found hiding on the roof with the dragon around three in the morning. I turned it off again when I was dressed. All I really wanted at that point was some music.

"I got as far as the front door before I realized there was no way of leaving the house. I spent the rest of the morning on the couch, eating cracked fragments of butterscotch cookies, flicking through the news channels until I figured out what was going on. They had footage of the dragon in flight by then. It was a big, dark fucker, that dragon; black as an evil glass of cola. You could see it on every channel. The dragon and the attempts to get decent footage of the blond girl it captured—"

Jay clicked his fingers, searching for the name.

"Diana Crowther?" I said.

Jay nodded. "Yeah," he said. "Her. I watched them trying to coax her out from underneath that satellite dish. I remember how weird it was, in this day and age, that suddenly there were dragons and kidnapped maidens on the TV. They were just starting to get the first real shots of that Crowther girl out in the open on the roof, the camera zooming in from a helicopter a couple of kilometers out from ground zero. Grainy details, a little pixilated, but you could see her yelling for help and crying. I got pissed off watching that, thinking about all those people who needed help, people trapped in their homes, hurt or dying, and this bitch was getting the focus because she'd been kidnapped by a dragon.

"Then they cut to the first footage of the knight.

"He looked like something off the cover of a romance novel. He had one of those square jaws with a dimple and the kind of long flowing hair that most guys can't manage because they forget little things like washing it every day. He was harder to believe in than the dragon, somehow. The dragon looked real, for all that it was a big lizard with wings. The knight looked like he was an illustration given life, slicing his way through the briars, making a beeline for the city. And it wasn't even like Diana Crowther was a princess, not when you saw her up close like that. She was just a pretty girl with blond hair and business suit, maybe twenty-three years old, who happened to be trapped on a roof by a dragon.

"The news reporters avoided words like *knight* at first. They just called him an *unidentified citizen*. We'd all been watching him go at it for two straight days before they got with the program and started using the term we'd all been thinking. I mean, he was good looking, he had a sword, and he wore about thirty kilograms of solid steel for protection. That means he's a knight, no matter how you cut it. I think the anchorman was jealous of all that hair.

"Eventually they got bored with following him and taking long-range shots of the dragon, so we had the specialists trotted out to deliver the same messages as the night before.

"The phone rang. This time I counted to three before I answered it.

"'I can't go to work,' Caroline said.

"'There's a lot of that going around.'

"'I got dressed and fed the fish and went to open the front door, then I remembered.'

"'Yeah,' I said, and the conversation stalled.

"'I'm sorry,' Caroline said. 'I know you'd prefer it if I didn't call.'

"'It's okay,' I said. 'Today's a weird kind of day.'

"'Did you hear the roaring last night?' she said. I told her about the dragon.

"'A dragon?' she said. She didn't sound convinced.

"'According to the news,' I told her. Then I gave her everything I remembered about the theories and the dragon and the knight. I searched the cushions for the remote. I flipped through channels until I found some cartoons.

"'Wow,' Caroline said. 'I figured it was a lion or something.'

"'Why would there have been a lion roaming the streets?' I said.

"'I don't know,' she said. 'There was a roar. Lion's roar. Why wouldn't it be a lion?'

"'Because it's the middle of Brisbane city,' I said. 'Did it just get bored and go looking for a decent club?'

"She told me to shut up. That I was being an asshole.

"I felt like being an asshole, so I said: 'Maybe it was just searching for a late-night cappuccino?' And I remember being proud of that one, thought it was fucking brilliant.

"'It might have escaped from a zoo,' Caroline said.

"'Of course,' I said. 'Happens all the tie. Lions duck out before curfew, get locked out and forget there's a key under the flower pot.'

"Caroline told me to forget it," Jay said. I cleared my throat, interrupting him.

"Brisbane doesn't have a zoo," I said. "Not one that keeps lions, anyway."

"Like it fucking matters," Jay said. "I was being a dick, she started to find it funny. Like the old days, when I amused her instead of hurting every time we talked. She laughed at me, and I started laughing, and it felt so damn good. Like it was possible to forget about the thorns, or believe everything would be okay in the end.

"Then Caroline said, 'I miss you.'"

Jay shook his head. "The laughter stopped. I let the line go quiet for a bit. I think she surprised herself with that one. The silence panicked me and I said something about the dragon, plunging on as though I hadn't heard her. I tried making a joke about dragons having weird virgin fetishes, but it didn't really work. In the end I shut up and closed my eyes, counting under my breath. I didn't trust myself to plug the silence. Then we made our excuses, hung up. And afterwards all I could think about was that once upon a time I'd been good at making Caroline laugh."

My phone buzzed in my pocket. I took it out and flipped it open, checking the number.

"Annie?" Jay said. I nodded. The message asked me what time I thought I'd get home.

"Should you be going?" Jay said. I shook my head. Annie and I had met at the bank, a couple of weeks after the briars were gone. Lots of people got together after all that happened, patching things up with former partners or falling hard for someone new, but whatever made us cling to each other was starting to wear off. I had plenty of friends who had separated over the last year. It made you think about what you had, and what it was really worth.

"Why are you still here?" Jay said. He drained the last of his beer out of its stein. "It's getting late. She'll worry. She'll worry and you'll fuck things up."

"Finish your story," I told him. Jay's head rolled back a little as he focused his eyes in my direction.

"You're a stupid fucker, you know that?" Jay said "Fine, fuck it, the rest of the story.

"It ends like this: on the third day, at six in the morning, I get another phone call. Caroline again, all in a panic, telling me to turn on the TV and tune into the news on Channel Nine. She stayed on the phone until I found it, waiting until she could hear the fight through the receiver. And there it was, the Knight squaring off against the dragon. Sword versus scale for the fate of Diana Crowther.

"You can't really imagine what it's like, seeing that live

with your ex crying in your ear. Seeing it without knowing what's going to happen, thinking the dragon's going down because that's what knights and dragons do. The knight kills the dragon and saves the girl; happily ever after. But it didn't go like that, and I was sitting there with Caroline falling apart on the other end of the phone, and all I could do was say fuck over and over until the word started to go soft and I needed something worse to express my feelings.

"The camera zoomed in on the girl on the edge of the roof, watching it all go down. She wasn't screaming, wasn't crying, just standing there all pale and calm. Like she still thought someone was going to come rescue her. Caroline was crying on the other end of the phone and I couldn't really handle it anymore. I hung up and had a shower, trying to wake up. I leant against the tiles, letting the cold water wash over me. I pushed my face into the shower head and pretended I wasn't crying.

"And when I got out I made breakfast like nothing had happened. I ate toast, let the phone ring a couple of times before I got fed up and unplugged it from the wall. I went back to bed and closed my eyes, pretending that I could go back to sleep. I thought of the girl on the building, guarded by the dragon, waiting for someone to save her. Someone had to, sooner or later.

"For a moment, just a couple of minutes, I wondered if maybe it could be me. I started rummaging through the house, found myself a jacket, something thick and heavy to help fend off the thorns. I searched the kitchen for a big knife, something that could hack its way through the arm-thick strands of the vine. And I got as far as the front door before I changed my mind. I put my ear to the wood and listened to the thorns, the quiet scritch-scritch of barbed fronds desperate to break inside. Then I went back into the lounge room and plugged the phone in. It wasn't long before it rang.

"'He died,' Caroline said. 'Oh my god, it killed him.'

"'Yeah,' I said. 'It did.'

"'But the girl,' Caroline said. 'The dragon? All the thorns around the city?'

"'They're problems,' I said. 'Someone will fix them. I mean, fuck it, that's why we have scientists and armies, yeah? She doesn't need some random guy with a shiny sword, she needs a SWAT team and the fire brigade.'

"Then I hung the phone up and cut the cord, hacked through it with a knife. I didn't turn on the news until the thorns went away a couple of days later and everyone started walking around like something special had happened. I didn't replace my phone for a week, didn't answer it for three or four. And there was no more *it's just* with Caroline after that. No more conversations, no more phone calls. We were people who sued to date, that's it."

Jay opened his mouth to say something else, then he stopped and looked away across the bar. His knuckles were white as he lifted the beer stein. He drank everything that remained in one long gulp.

I've seen the footage of that fight. They replayed it from time to time, especially now the documentaries have started and everyone wants to remember. It's always the same thing: the knight is slicing his way towards the tower, the dragon sees him and swoops down. No-one had gotten close to that tower with the dragon there, so the news was all over it. You saw shaky close-ups of each burning breath and sword stroke from a dozen angles, played out on every network. You saw that moment when the dragon catches him, picking that blonde-haired knight up in one claw. You saw the blood as his head was squeezed off, twisted between two claws.

And that close-up on Diana Crowther, watching all this from the top of the building, her face pale and her eyes full of tears. She was an average-looking girl, but that shot made her look beautiful. She instantly became the kind of girl you fall in love with. She was something more, something special, and I fell for her every time they interviewed her on the television.

"Fuck," I said. "Aren't you a charmer."

"It's not like I'm proud of the way it went down." Jay stole another cigarette and lit it. "I'm not a knight, you know. I write computer code for a living. I work with a laptop. I drink beer on the weekends. I wasn't saving anyone, and I was tired of holding onto the idea that I could."

The fireworks started in the town square. We could hear the soft pops over the buzz of the bar. Jay turned towards the noise and closed his eyes. Somewhere out there, in the centre of the celebrations, Diana Crowther would be giving a speech or smiling for the cameras. They might even be shooting her hiding under that famous satellite dish, miming her fear of a dragon that's been dead for four years. The waitress came and took our empty steins away. We didn't order anything else. Jay nodded towards the sound of the fireworks.

"That's what I imagined those flowers sounded like when they bloomed," he said. "Just like that, but softer."

I nodded. Jay shook his head and stood up. He'd looked better. "I gotta piss," he said. "You should go home."

"Annie's not a worrier," I said. "I can stop off and buy her flowers or something on the way home. She'll forgive me."

"It's not about worry," Jay said. "Hell, sometimes it's got nothing to do with flowers. Call her and go home, you stupid fucker." He shook his head and lurched away from the table, heading towards the men's room. Maybe he was pissing. Maybe not. The sound of the fireworks ended and Jay still hadn't come back from the bathroom. As I left I called Annie, punching the numbers on my phone with a clumsy thumb. She answered on the fourth ring, her voice sleepy. "I coming home soon," I said. "I love you, okay?"

She said she loved me too, the words exchanged in our regular routine. A quick conversation, easy as hell; neither of us had to feel a damn thing.

L'ESPRIT DE L'ESCALIER

Rat opens the double doors and the stairwell smells of baking, the air thick with dull warmth and the smell of yeasty dough. He wrinkles his long nose and wonders if it will be like this for the entire way down, or if the doughy stink will gradually transform itself into the aroma of fresh-baked. He hopes not. Rat worked in a bakery one summer, and he hasn't enjoyed the smell of bread since. It reminds him of the finger burns and the thick coats of lard painted into hot bread trays to keep the dough from sticking as it cooked.

He flexes his fingers. The big backpack is so heavy it's cutting off the circulation to his arms, so he has to remember to keep his fingers moving.

Someone has bolted a sign to the mahogany balustrade, warning people not to throw coins or pebbles down the centre of the stairwell. The guidebook says this is for the safety of fellow climbers. Every year someone is struck on the head when they're 130 flights below, and there's no chance of getting help in time when you're that far down.

There's another sign that warns people not to jump. Rat's guidebook says this isn't, in fact, the warning to the habitually stupid that it appears to be on the surface. Originally it was posted as a warning to the suicides that come to contemplate the twisting drop of the stairwell's core. It is easy to assume the stairwell has an end because that's what stairwells do, but the fact that no-one has ever reached the bottom leaves the question open. No-one ever thinks of stairwells as being bottomless, not even the people who stand on top of big buildings like the Empire State where the ground is a distant and hazy memory over 1,800 steps below. There's a hierarchy to such things determining what truly can go on forever. Wells? Yes. Pits? Yes. Trenches in the seabed where giant squid may live? Sure. But stairwells? No. Never. Hence there's a sign, a warning, to make the suicides rethink before leaping.

Rat isn't thinking about jumping over the railing. He turns around and looks at the first step. It's a foot high and four feet wide, a lump of grey marble that's cracked and covered with a random assortment of tags and graffiti. Rat looks at some of the things people have written and snorts. It's easy to write graffiti on the first step; it's the lower ones that require commitment. He wonders how far he'll need to descend before he reaches virgin territory.

The guidebook says that the lowest step anyone has reached is 120,828 steps down. People have probably gone lower, but they haven't come back. It's assumed that the suicides make it to the bottom.

If there is one.

If they were lucky.

The stairwell requires a lot of assumptions. The guidebook tells you to get used to that.

Rat figures the guy that hit the low-point 120,828 steps down probably had better things on his mind than leaving graffiti. He shrugs off the backpack and starts searching for his sharpie. It's a big backpack full of cunning pockets and hidey-holes for passports. The sharpie is in one of the cunning pockets Rat never uses, right next to the outer pocket that contains the plastic baggie filled with Marlo's ashes.

The smell of the uncapped sharpie is soothing. Its mentholated tang cuts through the yeasty heat. Rat chews on the cap for a few minutes, thinking, then leans over and writes *But I love you* on a blank patch of the first step. His handwriting is awkward, full of childish loops and a tendency to curve without the benefit of a ruled line.

Rat wishes he had something better to write; *But I love you* seems trite, and it probably didn't need to be said. He'd lost arguments with it before, with Marlo and others. He could have skipped the first step and used the first 500 to think of something better. He could have used the time to think of something poetic and elegant.

"No," he says, and his voice echoes down the stairwell. "No poetry."

Poetry would defeat the object. Just because something is trite, possibly even expected, doesn't make it any less true. He hasn't spent the last month preparing just so he could sacrifice truth for elegance. Marlo deserves better than that. So does he.

Rat puts the lid back on the sharpie and returns it to the backpack. He snaps everything shut and makes sure it's secure, twice. He's only packed three sharpies. It wouldn't do to lose them; he may need all of them before his descent is done.

He pulls the backpack onto his shoulders again, sagging with the weight. His hands are slippery. The air's not that hot; the guidebook says it'll get hotter, but Rat sweats easily. He spent a whole week planning ways he can stay hydrated. One hand rests against the railing, holding him steady. Rat places his left foot on the next step and lowers himself down.

"Two," he says, thumb hitting the click-counter at his belt. He keeps clicking away as the descent begins in earnest. "Three, four, five, six..."

The guidebook is small enough to fit in Rat's pocket, but he keeps it tucked into the backpack. Just in case.

They found the guidebook together, Rat and Marlo. It was hiding in the bottom of a used book bin, out the front of a Salvation Army store. Marlo found it; Rat has never been a big reader. The guidebook is the only book he's ever read all the way through. It's the only book he's ever attempted to read more than once.

"Check it out," Marlo said. "A book about the Endless Stairwell."

"What?" Rat said.

"The Stairwell. You know about the Stairwell, right?"

Rat shook his head. He'd never heard of the Stairwell before Marlo found the guidebook. That wasn't unusual. Rat rarely knew about the things Marlo knew about. Marlo was smart. Rat was smart, too, but he didn't think on his feet. Marlo said his talent lay in cunning, and Rat was okay with that.

"We should go one day," Marlo said. "Promise me we'll go."

Rat didn't promise. He thought an endless stairwell sounded stupid.

Rat meets six young couples coming up the stairs, all before he reaches step 500. The couples are young and giddy, with young men dressed with understated elegance. They are men dressed in casual clothes that are meant to look impressive. One of the couples has a camera.

Another couple, the second-last couple Rat passes, looks dour. They stand on separate sides of the steps, maximizing the space between them. Rat is forced to cut between, muttering an "excuse me" between clicks of his click-counter.

Rat's surprised by the number of couples he passes, but he shouldn't be. The guidebook says that step 657 is a popular place to propose, a landmark right up there with Niagara Falls and New Year's Eve fireworks.

When he reaches step 500, Rat uncaps a sharpie and thinks about the dour couple, unhappy in their long climb back to the surface. He leans over the step and writes *That would have been us, I think, if only things had gone differently*. He stands up and looks at his scrawl. Better, but still not great. Rat wonders if this really needs to be said.

"Five hundred and one," he says, "Five hundred and two."

He descends. There are no more couples. He has a smooth run between step 500 and step 657.

The romance step; the step where proposals happen. The guidebook gushes about its ambiance.

Rat schedules a rest stop on step 658. He drinks his water and looks up the stairwell, trying to work out what makes the step just above him so special. The step smells of old prophylactics. When Rat peers over the banister, he can see used condoms stuck to the side of the stairs. The stink mingles with the dough smell, turning Rat's stomach. There's nothing special here; grey marble with a worn patch on the centre; endless graffiti that links two sets of initials with a crude heart around the outside and the number "4" between the names.

Rat digs Marlo out of the backpack, cradles the plastic against his cheek.

"Will you marry me," he says. "You should say yes, you know. It's traditional to say yes when you love the person who asks you."

The baggie says nothing. It's cool against his cheek, but he feels cold talking to it.

It's hard to have a conversation with Marlo these days. Somehow, it just doesn't seem right.

Rat digs the ring out of a pocket in his jeans. There's only one diamond, small and flawed. It should have been better. Rat was going to propose to Marlo outside a cinema after a really good film, but the moment slipped away before he got the chance. He puts the ring on the romance step, the proposing step, right in the corner where step meets wall. Its yellow band is pale, hard to see against the darkness and the marble's whorls.

"Last chance, babe. You should have said something if you wanted the ring." Rat takes a long sip of water and shoulders the pack. "Six hundred and fifty-nine..."

At step 1,000 he writes out the lyrics to a Leonard Cohen song and underlines the refrain. He stops 500 steps later and writes out the number of times he thinks Marlo faked orgasm during their time together. He stares at the number, unsure of its accuracy, then adds a question mark. At 2,000 steps he admits in writing that Marlo was right, that he did sometimes fantasize about dating her sister.

There is a plaque on step 2,109. It tells Rat that he's climbed the length of the Sears tower. Rat doesn't look at the plaque; he knows what it says because he's read the guidebook.

He stops again at step 2,500. He writes: *I wish you were here. I'd like to kiss you right now.*

Rat stops when he reaches step 3,000. According the guidebook, most people turn before they reach step 3,000. A lot of people lie about reaching it. Rat takes out a sharpie and writes: *I wasn't sure if I would cry for you, but it appears that I can.*

It's a lie; Rat hasn't cried yet. Rat isn't a crier, not really.

He stops and camps on step 5,418. He drinks water and pecks at trail mix for dinner, saving the substantial fare in his pack for further down. Nights are cold on the Stair; the guidebook has warned him of this. He unpacks a green sleeping bag and nestles against his pack, using it as a pillow. He listens to the wind echo as it slides down the stairwell.

A Rastafarian is there when Rat wakes up, lounging against the balustrade while Rat struggles to open his eyes. Rat looks up, noting the long line of the Rastafarian's body, the black dreadlocks that brush against the marble step.

"Your hair must weigh a lot," Rat says. The Rastafarian grins, and his teeth are a flash of white amid his face. Marlo dated a Rastafarian once. She used to tell Rat stories about kissing him, letting her hands get lost in the tangled chords of his hair.

"It's light," she said. "So much lighter than you'd expect hair like that to be."

Rat wonders whether it was this Rastafarian. It seems unlikely, but so does an endless stairwell. Rat is prepared to embrace the unlikely at present.

"Good morning," the Rastafarian says. He has an

English accent, upper crust. Rat keeps waiting for him to say "Mon", but he doesn't. The silence seems awkward.

"Hi," Rat says. He sits up, still wrapped in the sleeping bag. "Sorry, am I in your way?"

"Not at all," the Rastafarian says. "Maybe you were, once, but I've adapted, yes?"

The Rastafarian drops into a crouch, his face filling Rat's vision.

"Up or down?" the Rastafarian says.

"Down," Rat says.

"How far?" the Rastafarian says.

"As far as I can," Rat says. "Then a few steps further, just for good luck."

"Brave," the Rastafarian says.

"Maybe," Rat says. "Maybe I'm just stupid."

The Rastafarian grins again. His dreadlocks are pooled around, spreading over step 6,417. He looks at the backpack that Rat's been using as a pillow.

"Big pack," the Rastafarian says. "You're prepared, so you aren't stupid. Foolish, maybe, but not stupid."

The Rastafarian looks at Rat, his brown eyes so dark they look like giant pupils. Rat squirms.

"So," Rat says. "Up or down?"

"Both," the Rastafarian says. "Neither. Depends on my mood."

"You're a strange man," Rat says. The Rastafarian nods, dreadlocks sliding across the marble. He stands up and offers Rat a hand.

"Come on," the Rastafarian says. "Big day ahead."

Rat nods. He lets the Rastafarian lift him onto his feet. He folds the sleeping bag and stows it in the backpack while the Rastafarian watches. It's hot again, the air thick with yeast, but the Rastafarian smells like hair-oil and cinnamon.

The Rastafarian ascends. Rat descends. Both of them have their hands on the mahogany banister. Rat can hear the Rastafarian's hair swishing against the marble as the Rastafarian walks away.

Step 6,500: *I never wanted to hear about your exes.*

Marlo loved her Rasta boyfriend because he scored her free weed. She'd told Rat as much when she was explaining her ex-boyfriends. The revelation made Rat feel inadequate. He'd never scored Marlo weed, free or otherwise. The only greenery he'd given her was a potted plant, and that died on her windowsill after three weeks of neglect.

Step 7,000: *I loved you. I didn't love you. I can't really remember anymore.*

Rat stops for lunch. It isn't much; a cheese sandwich on rye bread, slightly squashed after two days in the pack. It tastes great. A day-and-a-half over, and Rat is already sick of trail mix. The cheese is waxy, a little flavorless, but it hits the spot. He wasn't supposed to eat it today, but the stairwell is hotter now, and the cheese wasn't traveling well.

He sips water from a flask. It's tepid. He digs through the pack and pulls out the guidebook, looking for the pink post-it tag that marks Rat's notes for the second day.

The guidebook says that this is the toughest part, the second day of descent. It's the part where most people start to think about turning around, heading back up to the surface in order to escape the heat. A day-and-a-half of climbing means you've lost sight of the top of the stairs.

Rat stands up and leans over the balustrade. He looks down. He looks up. The guidebook is right—both directions look the same. He knows the top is up there, somewhere, but he can't see it.

Rat checks the clicker. He has covered 8,369 steps. He could turn around now if he wanted. No-one would really know. It's not like he told anyone his plans. It's not like he should be ashamed. He's already eaten the sandwich he was saving for the third day. Most people turn around on the second day of climbing. Rat has always been good at giving up.

He can't think of anything to write on step 8,500. He sits on the marble, chin in his hands, staring at Marlo's ashes. Eventually he uncaps the sharpie and writes *Happy birthday*. It doesn't really work. Rat crosses it out. Then he writes *Happy Birthday Happy Birthday Happy Birthday*.

Marlo always said that repeating something thrice meant you didn't really mean it.

The world's second-longest stair is in Switzerland, dug into the side of a mountain. Rat knows this because the guidebook told him, and because someone has put a plaque on the appropriate step. The world's second-longest stair has 11,674 steps.

Rat stops to read the plaque this time, trying to feel like he's accomplished something.

He doesn't. He just feels sore. His legs are burning

He stops for the night on step 11,700. He writes *I'm sorry. I did love you* on the marble because he's too tired to think of anything better. He sets up his sleeping bag and uses it to cover the declaration. He tosses and turns all night, bothered by the heat. The yeasty smell gets worse at night. It makes Rat's nose twitch.

. . .

Marlo was going out with one of Rat's friends. He probably shouldn't have slept with her that first time, even after she said she'd broken up with the other guy. Rat wasn't always called Rat, but he'd earned himself the name and it suited him too well to go away.

On step 12,073 he sees his first suicide. The body whistles past, not even screaming anymore. Rat's surprised by the way the arms and legs twist, struggling against the fall.

On step 50,500 he writes *There were many expressions you used that drove me crazy. I still think of killing someone every time I hear the words "done and dusted" in conversation. Nothing is ever done. Nothing is ever dusted.*

He is on his second sharpie. He killed the first after forgetting to replace the cap while writing on step 15,000.

He runs out of sandwiches on the fourth day of climbing, but there's plenty of trail mix and tins of beans. The plan was to descend until he ran out of things to say. Rat never bothered thinking about how he'd ascend once the task was done.

On step 120,000 he writes *Fuck cancer*. He crosses this out and writes *It wasn't my fault*. Deep down, he believes neither of these things, despite the fact that he should. The doctors were wrong; it wasn't the cancer that killed her.

The heat turns slick and humid 300 steps later. His rubber soles squeak against the moisture coating the ancient marble.

. . .

At step 120,828 he pauses and pulls the guidebook out of his backpack. He flicks through the worn pages, looking at the detailed notes he's scrawled into the margins. Pauses on the photograph of the step he's reached. The point of no return, the deepest step anyone's reached and still returned to the surface. He's followed the guidebook's advice when it comes to supplies. His pack is lighter now, easier to handle, but he could still return.

Rat tosses the book over the balustrade. He looks up the stairwell, then down. Sweat streams across his forehead, soaks through his T-shirt. Rat's been wearing the same outfit for days. He's pretty sure he smells.

"Hello?" he says, and his voice echoes across the stairwell. His throat is dry, so he drinks some water. More than he should, regardless of his decision. Rat figures he can extend his supply a little this far down, assuming he's willing to lick condensation off the stairs.

He pulls Marlo out of his pack and holds her in both hands. Better to do it now, regardless of the decision. This is where they were headed when they'd first planned to come here. Too many things could go wrong once he moved into uncharted territory.

"We made it, babe," Rat says. His thumbnail punctures the plastic and sets the ashes free. The cloud disperses across the empty space, descends on the breeze. Slow-moving, delicate, waiting for the next suicide to free-fall through its mass. Even in death Marlo is beautiful. Rat misses her more than anything.

He sits down on step 120,829 and grieves, shedding tears for the first time.

Step 121,500: *We were never meant to be happy. I'm no longer sure that matters.*

On step 200,000 Rat commits an act of poetry. He chooses to keep descending. Poetry bothers him less this far down the stairwell.

Rat knows three things to be true. The first is this: he will run out of food and water before he runs out of things to say. Two: what goes down need not emerge at the surface. Three: there will be no ending. The ending lies above, at the first step, in the life he'd live if he walked away. Endings are destinations and the Stair has but one, found only by backtracking and returning to the beginning.

The heat gets worse as he hits the lower depths. The balustrade is hot enough to redden his palms. Rat sheds clothing, equipment, leaves his sleeping bag on a step. The sharpies leak in his pockets, bleeding ink across his thighs.

ON THE ARRIVAL OF THE PADDLE-STEAMER ON THE DOCKS OF V—

Our tiny hotel room is boiling, even now, but heat doesn't bother Patrick and he sleeps, shirtless, with the thin sheet coiled round him like a loving serpent. It's a trick for him, nodding off. He cultivates a talent for sleep, adores the act of dozing off like it's a second lover. He says it keeps him young, and perhaps it does, for people are always surprised to learn Patrick's real age.

I've started smoking again, since it no longer matters. Patrick copes with things through slumber, while I survey the world, my exhalations accompanied by the splash of river meeting dock. The river is the life-blood of V—, they tell you that in all the flyers.

My free hand teases the fraying hem of the Mickey Mouse t-shirt we picked up in Anaheim back in the days when Patrick wasn't quite so fussy about which magic kingdom he got to visit. My fight-induced insomnia means I'm awake to hear the small boats punting their way across the river, their owners making soft cries, like whippoorwills, too-whit-too-woo, to warn their fellows on the opposite shore. No one wants to get knifed in the dark, after all, or pushed in and left to drown.

The cries of the boatmen are subtle and faint. Patrick hears nothing, curled up on the lumpy mattress, eyes closed and smile beatific, short brown hair stuck to his head like a halo. Slumbering. Dreaming. Patrick in boxers, his chest waxed-smooth.

He's the pretty one in our relationship. Always has been.

The Mickey Mouse shirt is vaguely absurd on me, barely covering the middle-aged spread of my stomach, but it amuses Patrick to see me wear it and there are days, even now, when that's all that matters. It is four in the morning and I feel another fart forming, another in a long night of uncomfortable flatulence. My bowels hate it here; they hate the heat and the food and the unfamiliar spices. The humidity and the stink that make it feel like you're breathing your own piss.

Patrick whispers and turns over, reaching out for the space I no longer occupy. Part of me hopes, in vain, that my absence will wake him.

We've come to V— because Patrick wants to be kidnapped by faeries, and this is one of the few remaining places where such things are possible. The fey come to the docks every seven years and select pretty, foolish boys to leave the world behind. Seven boys disappear, going to the land of the fey. We do not know what happens then, but Patrick is sure that it's better than staying here. He's sure the boys are treated like kings, that they can laugh and folderol and remain pretty forever. He's sure it's a place where there are no doctors, no x-rays with black spots that are little more than grainy patterns on the film. A place where I don't tell stories to our friends that begin with the phrase, "It's like looking at very deadly, unmovable specks of dust…"

Patrick doesn't like it when I call young men boys, not even in the early days when the pronounced difference in our ages weighed heavily on my mind. Yet he accepts the title with pleasure, preening at its use, the moment we have a discussion about the fey and their desires.

Patrick is very pretty, and he is definitely foolish, and the face he presents to the world is fresh and soft as cream that's yet to go sour. Yet I am sitting in this hotel room, farting, par-broiled in the fetid heat. I am not the pretty one or the young one and never have been, but there is no doubt I'm a bigger fool than Patrick will ever be.

The man who runs the hotel says his name is Yuri. He's vast of chest and hook-nosed and pretends to be a Russian immigrant, one of the many who came to V— three decades ago, searching for the treasures of the Steamer-folk in the aftermath of the war. Yuri sits behind the hotel desk and watches the news on a portable television, the travesties of the world replayed via the magic of CNN. Yuri doesn't look at us when we pass through the lobby, doesn't acknowledge Patrick's friendly greeting or comments about the shoddy reception. When we showed up he looked us over and said, "You two are…Australian?" and the way he said it left little doubt about what he was really asking when we walked in, hand in hand.

And still Patrick said, "Sure, of course we are," because Patrick doesn't pick up on subtext.

The hotelier doesn't like us, that much is obvious, but Patrick refuses to be deterred and starts asking questions about the Steamer. It's the first thing since we checked in three days ago that draws Yuri's attention away from the television. He looks at Patrick, and at me, and he spits on the ochre tiled floor.

"The Steamer's gold," he says. "Gold and silver and ancient oak, but you will not notice this beneath the lights, yes? It is beautiful, very beautiful, and when you look at it —" He stops speaking and thumps his chest. The noise makes me jump. "—it will hit you right there," he says, "like a spear of ice to the heart, yes?" He nods, satisfied, and crosses his arms. "That is what the Steamer is like. Just like that, and nothing like it."

"That doesn't make any sense," Patrick says, but Yuri has lost interest in the conversation. He shrugs and turns his back to us. Black hair pokes past the collar-line of his wife-beater, curled and thick as wire.

Patrick looks to me, as if I have an answer. I do not, so I shrug, and Patrick just nods like he's learnt something important. Like everyone thinks the arrival of the Steamer and the people who come to see it are a blessing to the city of V—.

Talking to Yuri has made Patrick petulant, so I let him choose the café where we eat breakfast. We walk up a narrow flight of stairs and sit on the terrace, looking down the long street filled with cyclists and porters and beggars clustered around the alleyways. The café has glass tabletops that are damp with morning condensation, the droplets of water still touched with the brown of the river. There are streaks of dirt on the red tile floor. The café was recommended by a friend of Patrick's back in Brisbane. I wonder if we too will recommend it once the distance of hindsight banishes the horror of eating there, or if I will recommend it alone, as part of the tragic story of Patrick's disappearance while holidaying overseas.

I order toast and nibble it. Patrick eats with an appetite, consuming experience as much as flavor. He cracks the shell of a boiled egg and dusts it with paprika, biting the fleshy mass in half with a satisfied grin. He speaks with his mouth full. Usually that doesn't bother me. Usually. He says: "Do you think they'll come tonight?"

And I, irritated, snap back: "How the fuck should I know?"

Patrick nods and says I have a fair point. He refuses to be drawn into an argument this morning, after the vehemence of the previous night.

Later, when we're walking through one of the street bazaars, I drift close to him and say, "I'm sick of curry. Let's go find ourselves a McDonalds," and Patrick just nods and starts jabbering to one of the locals, getting directions so I can have a cheeseburger and a thick shake that doesn't threaten the state of my bowels. It's always this way when we travel. Patrick speaks the language and I do not. Patrick wants to go native and I want to find a nice hotel. I was hoping for an argument when I brought up the golden arches, but all I got was a ten-dollar burger and disgruntled memories of home.

I don't acknowledge the existence of faeries and never felt the need too. I refuse to clap, even, during pantomime plays, content to let Tinker Bell waste away. Patrick is more than willing to make up for my deficiencies, believing in everything twice as hard just to make up for my cynicism. I prefer to think of it as dealing with reality, but he insists that it's cynicism and will not accept any substitute phrases to make it sound better than it is.

There are days he seems so much younger than I, days when I feel so much older.

I sleep no better on the third night. The flatulence is worse and there's no sign of the Steamer on the river. Before V— we spent a month in the back rooms of London pubs, looking for the cracks in the city where you could steal away to somewhere magical. Before London we prowled the canals of Venice, hoping there were secrets in the water. Before Venice, well, I no longer remember correctly. Anaheim, maybe? Looking for the secret door in the dark hollows of Space Mountain? Patrick hears stories and we go looking, the search keeping us together so long as there's momentum that can be maintained. He denies he's too old for such things, despite celebrating his thirty-first birthday just months before our departure. There's a part of me that doesn't have the heart to deny him, and so we've hit the magic kingdom time and time again.

There will be no more trips. This is the last of them. There are no more cities left, if the fey do not appear in V —. We have visited them all, all the places they come, and there is never a shortage of pretty fools willing to go along with the fey. When we walk the docks in the mornings, searching for signs the faeries have come, all we see are the hopeful, the pretty, vacant faces that seem more familiar with every city.

The routine of the search is simple. There are usually five days before Patrick gives in to despair. The sixth day will be the least pleasant of all our unpleasant days in V—.

There are parts of V— that retain their beauty, but the docks aren't one of them. We peruse them in the afternoons, indulging Patrick's anxiety, but I tire of dilapidated buildings and the creak of ancient boats long before he does. I'm forced to coax Patrick away with the promise of a museum, a local building dedicated to the faeries and their thrice-yearly visits. It's small and well-kept and filled with photographs and portraits. Patrick spends an hour studying the images, comparing himself with those identifying the Taken. "I think my nose is quite similar to that one," he says, and "he had terrible teeth. I didn't know you could have bad teeth and still be picked."

Mostly he looks for patterns, some commonality that suggests why they were chosen. Mostly he looks for hope. I sit on a bench in the centre of the room, beneath the overhead fan turning a lazy circle, and I'm grateful for the distraction and the reprieve it affords me from Patrick's inevitable tantrum. There are thousands of pieces in the collection, walls filled with several centuries of the faeries' chosen passengers, and it keeps Patrick busy for some time.

I feel like I should have a plan for when the fey say Patrick's name. I do not. I do *not*. It nags at me like a plantar wart, a niggling spike of pain in the thick callus of the heel.

The man who runs the museum sports a perfectly groomed mustache, the two short lengths of carefully styled hair, each waxed to a fine point. His hair is thinning a little, but he's one of the few natives of V— who sports a perfect mouth full of teeth when he smiles.

"Your friend is very enthusiastic," he says.

"It's one of his virtues." I shuffle sideways on the bench, making enough room for him to sit. "He wants—"

"To leave with the faerie." His wrinkles are very pronounced when he smiles. "You learn to recognize them, after a while. There's something about the way they approach things, a particular kind of look in the eye."

"Any way of telling who's going to get chosen?"

The caretaker shakes his head. "Only why they're doing it. Some do it for the adventure, some because they need magic. People like your friend, they do it to run away."

"Yeah? From what?"

"Take your pick: depressions, family, cancer. The fey never take the truly ill."

"Lucky for Patrick, then."

"He's not sick?"

"Not him."

The caretaker studies me for a long time. "But you?"

"No." I fold my arms. "Not yet, but probably one day. I've got plaque on the brain. Early warning signs."

He nods. "And yet you're not the one trying to get out."

There is no easy answer to this.

"I'm not Patrick," I tell the curator. "We deal in different ways, I guess."

I try to whisper, to keep my voice low. There is a scuffle of feet behind us, and Patrick slouches across my shoulder. "This place is awesome," he says. "You should give them some pictures of me when I'm gone."

"Assuming that happens," I say.

"It's going to happen," Patrick says, leaning over to kiss me.

On night five Patrick sleeps with an arm thrown across his face, shielding his eyes from the naked bulb after I refused to turn it out. The light throws a square on the night-dark water, my silhouette wavering with the rise and fall of the waves. The air is still and the night is cool. A single snowflake falls from the empty sky and rests against my cheek. I press my fingers against it and it melts, leaving a damp spot like a tear. The heat eases, the snowfall begins in earnest, and the soft chug of the Steamer drowns out the calls of the boatmen and their punts.

When I see it I feel ashamed of sitting beside the window, wearing my sweat-stained t-shirt with the fraying hem and faded picture of Wolverine. I feel ashamed of the gas that builds up in my intestines, ready to seep through my tightly clenched buttocks. I feel ashamed of my teeth, my hair, and my unclipped nails.

And it occurs to me that Yuri is right, when he talks about the light and the silver. The Paddle-Steamer of faerie is beautiful. It's a ship designed to cleave the heart in two. There is no need for the faerie to kidnap children anymore. Tourists will throw themselves at the Steamer-folk of their own accord.

It's this that Patrick has come for, this ship and the chance to disappear on its decks, dissolving into the frigid air in a place where snow should not exist. He is hungry for secrets and a place that is not home.

I am here for Patrick, and it shames me that I hope the faeries will not take him. So I sit at the balcony and watch the snow fall. I watch the Steamer chug past, its bells chiming through the night as the temperature drops.

There are goosebumps on Patrick's bare arm and chest. He mews softly, confused by the sudden cold, and a part of him wakes and blinks in my direction. "Is it?" he asks, voice still thick with sleep, and I nod towards the river.

"Yes," I tell him, "the faeries are here." And the look on his face is blissful. It is bliss I've never known how to give him.

Patrick wakes completely, buoyed by a jolt of adrenaline. He joins me by the window and slips an arm around my neck, holds me as the Steamer disappears around the bend.

Afterwards, despite the cold, I shed my shirt and allow him to drag me to bed.

When I wake up, hours later, there's a faerie on the balcony, small and neat and sallow of skin, watching us through segmented eyes that seem terrible and dark in the morning sunlight. We were hoping for one of the greater fey, the tall and elegant children of the night, lithe and sinuous and glorious as the morning sun. The creature who sits on the cast-iron balcony rail is the color of mud and locusts, its fragile wings beating softly as it maintains its precarious balance.

I get up and attempt to shoo it away, motioning with my hands. The faerie simply grins, showing off two sharp teeth that jut from the top of its mouth. It holds out a slip of paper the color of ivory, offering it to me like a gift.

I'm too old for such things. I'm far to old for faeries.

And so I close the curtains and return to bed. Patrick snuffles happily as I wrap my arms around him. The faerie watches us through a crack in the curtains, content to wait and deliver its invitation when the opportunity presents itself, but Patrick sleeps soundly through the night and it cannot be waiting there when the dawn comes.

In the morning we go down to the dock and stand at the fence, watching the ice form around the prow of the moored ships. The Paddle-Steamer towers over the crude boats of the V— river, mirror-bright and beautiful even in the daylight. Dark clouds loom over the city, disgorging snow, and yet the docks are packed with tourists, men and women who have come to V— exclusively for this moment.

That night the faerie returns to our window, invitation in hand. I close the blinds and go downstairs, pretending to search for ice.

Yuri sits behind his counter and watches the news on

CNN. He drinks coffee from a mug the size of my head, preferring it black. He wears a grubby white singlet and faded jeans and a perpetual scowl. He seems to prefer it when I emerge without Patrick at my arm, although there is no overt sign of this, simply a feeling I get when he meets my gaze. Yuri sports a short mustache that's dark and short and neatly clipped. As if his pride, what remains of it, is bound up in his facial hair.

"The ship, she has arrived?" he says, eyes not leaving the screen.

"Yes," I say. The question seems to demand no more than that. Yuri nods once and lights a cigarette, rolling the paper tube between his fingers.

"You've been chosen?"

"Maybe."

"You've been chosen." He exhales like a contented dragon, eyes flicking towards my face. "They always pick one from this hotel, nine time out of ten, yes? It is their way, it is why you chose to stay here. You have done your research, you and your friend. I know when people have researched."

"Yes, I suppose we did."

Yuri taps the side of his nose, then points a finger in my direction. "Their presence breaks things apart," he says. "It is their purpose."

The lobby of the hotel is very, very still. I can hear the quick puff of Yuri's breathing, the steady lap of the water in the river outside the window. There are chunks of ice in the river now, we saw them just before sunset. Dust motes dance in the daylight, as does Yuri's smoke. They swirl and eddy and dissipate, leaving behind nothing but a sour smell that scrapes against the back of the nose.

"There's something on the balcony," I say. "I'd like to know how to make it go away."

"Accept the invitation." Yuri grins around his cigarette. "Give it to your friend and allow them both to leave."

"I don't think that's how it works," I say.

"Da," Yuri says, "but it's worth a try."

I shake my head. "Too old," I tell him. "Twenty years ago, maybe, but it's not for me. Not now."

He finishes his cigarette and stubs it into the ashtray. The butt sits there, bent in half, smoking, still smoking in the aftermath. There are tanks on the television, tanks and rows of young men, walking side by side in the desert. It's unnaturally cold in the lobby. Winter has come to V—, as it does for seven days every seven years.

"You should go," Yuri says. "Leave your friend. Go. Is bound to be better there, on the other side. Maybe they don't have wars there? Maybe you'll be, how you say, safe?"

"I really don't think that's how it works," I say, and Yuri laughs along with me. We are comrades for but a moment, and then his face grows sour. If there are any good memories of the fey within him, I suspect they are hidden deep and rarely unearthed for public consumption.

Patrick dresses in the cool of the morning. He wears jeans for the first time since we arrived and the heat became untenable, and I'm grateful, at least, for the change in his ensemble. I have always favored Patrick in jeans. His knees are horrible to look at, scarred and knobby, better off hidden. He pulls a t-shirt over his chest and looks at me. He says, "You're sure they didn't come," with enough force to convince me that perhaps he knows who visited us, and I shake my head and tell him, "No, no one came," with as much truth as I can muster.

We go to the restaurant for breakfast and eat warm slices of toast with melted butter.

"We should talk about the plaque," I say, spreading butter over my toast, like the plaque is an ordinary thing to mention over breakfast. Patrick flinches, looking away, eyes turning towards the river, and I tell myself it doesn't hurt to see him react like that. "If this doesn't work," I say, "if they elect not to take you, we should talk about what's going to happen. We should plan, don't you think?"

"I planned," Patrick says.

"We talked about it. That's not the same as planning."

Patrick puts down his knife and bunches his fist. He does it every time I mention the plaque, every time the topic of the future comes up. "You said you were okay with this."

"And I am."

Patrick's eyes accuse me of being a liar.

"We're out of cities, Pat," I tell him. "If you don't get chosen here, where do we go?"

He bites his bottom lip a moment. "Then I'll get chosen here. There's seven spots."

"Seven spots, sure, but there's hundreds here. That's a long way from definite."

"I'm not them." Patrick shakes his head, clearing his thoughts, and the fist pressed against the tabletop goes loose when he's done. "If it doesn't happen," he says, "and that's just if, then we'd have to talk, I guess. I set up accounts. I made sure you'd be taken care of. I'm just not sure, you know, that I can…"

Patrick closes his eyes.

"It's okay to be afraid," I say.

"I'm not afraid." He rolls his head back and breathes deeply. The air smells of burning bread and morning snow and a heady mixture of spices, paprika and cardamom and a sharp peppery spice I can't quite place. Patrick exhales and forces himself to look me in the eye.

"I know about the invitation," he says.

"I don't—"

"I took it for you, when you went downstairs. His face contorts, screwing up like he's trying to swallow something bitter. "I want you to go, I think. It'd be better if you went."

He looks at me. I look at him. Neither of us prepared for this conversation, not in all the times we imagined what would happen. It was always Patrick going, always me staying behind.

"I'm to old to live forever," I say.

"We don't know that you will."

"I want to stay," I say. "I want to take whatever comes. I want to be with you."

"That's not what I want," Patrick says. Slowly, cautiously, he begins to cry.

"I don't want to say goodbye," I tell him.

"I do," he says. "Now, while it's still easy." Tears glisten on his cheek. "While it still means something to both of us."

We return to the hotel, neither of us willing to speak. Patrick bolts for our room, slamming the door behind him. I wait in the lobby, meeting Yuri's questioning gaze.

"So, he knows," Yuri says, and it isn't really a question.

"Yes, I suppose he does."

"You could use a drink," Yuri says, and once more the question is lacking. I slump against his counter and nod, offering no resistance as he unearths the vodka and two small glasses from the bottom drawer. He turns down the sound on CNN and pours a generous measure, his coal-bright eyes watching me until I've drained the entire glass.

"Another," he says, "for luck."

And then, "Another, for Anastasia."

I drink. He drinks. There's no explanation offered as to who Anastasia is, nor why we'd need to drink to her. I do not ask for one. It seems unseemly.

"What do you think happens," I say. "To the ones who get taken, I mean. The ones who go on the Steamer ship."

Yuri considers that for a moment, his mustache twirling in careful thought. "I think they are eaten," he says. "Cut apart for meat."

I snort vodka through my nose and it burns, making it difficult to breathe. I splutter and gasp for air, trying to compose myself. "Eaten?"

"It's a theory," Yuri says. "One of many that have been expressed by those who have passed through my hotel."

"What do you know?" I try to give him a knowing stare, but I don't have the assurance to interrogate with my eyes. The best I can manage is an awkward squint. "Seven years the fey have recruited from your place, surely it's not a coincidence."

"I know it is hard, being the one left behind." Yuri holds up his glass in salute. "They do not take the lonely, only those who are loved. They only take when it would hurt, one way or another. It is better if they eat the ones they take. There is less chance of hoping they would return, less pain, da, when you think of them?"

"Da," I say, trying the word out for size. It feels better than saying yes. More strident. More defined. "Da, I suppose so."

Yuri knocks back his drink in a single motion. I force myself to do the same.

"You are older, da? Older than your friend?"

I hold my up glass, wait for him to pour. "Twelve years," I tell him, "more or less."

Yuri sucks air through his teeth. "That makes it harder," he says. "Being the older one. It makes people think they need to be sensible." He pours another healthy shot, nods in satisfaction when I reach for it. "Do not be sensible, this time around. This decision, it should be selfish, da?"

He pours himself a drink and closes his eyes. For a moment I find myself wondering if Yuri is close to tears.

On the ninth night I sneak out of the hotel, stealing away while Patrick sleeps, the invitation tucked into my jacket pocket. The streets are quiet and oddly slippery, the ancient cobbles covered in a thin layer of slushy snow, but the steady chime of the Steamer's bells and music keep me moving forward. There are people on the docks. Spectators, hopefuls, locals who still come down here to fish, regardless of the spectacle or the ice-filled waters. I shuffle past them all, heading for the pier, where I show my invitation to the guards who unlock the gate and let me approach the dormant ship.

There are faeries on the deck. Green-skinned and black-skinned and those with skin the color of a burnished apple. Some bear wings, like moths or butterflies, but only the smallest of them flies. They dance and revel to the discordant music, and in the heart of the throng I see six other men, mortal and fair-skinned and pretty as a new day's sunrise, men eager to be carried away to whatever winterland the fey inhabit when they're not sailing their Steamer down the frost-ridden river.

I climb up the gangplank and find my path blocked, an enormous goat-headed faerie giving me a sharp-toothed smile. He holds out his palm and bleats, demanding my invitation, and it's only once I present the ivory-colored card that he stands aside to let me board, indicating the party with a sweep of his broad hand.

The music of the fey is the stuff of nightmares, every note filled with terrible beauty.

"I'm not coming aboard," I say, although I have to shout to be heard amid the cacophony. The hircine creature cocks his ear, signaling for me to repeat myself. "I'm not coming," I shout. "This isn't what I want. I've come to make a deal instead." I look towards the bacchanal and say, cautiously, "Is anyone here in charge?"

Goat's Head almost kills itself laughing. Several of its fellows join in, filling the air with riotous titters, and the laughter spreads like a ripple in a stream. One of the fey steps forward, thin-faced but mostly human, its lips and tongue built to do more than bleat. The music dies away, replaced by a cold and eerie silence, a winter-morning silence designed to freeze all tongues.

"What one knows," the faerie says, "we all know. You may…negotiate…if you wish."

They are looking at me, all the fey, and my glance flits from face to face, meeting eyes that resemble insects and sharks and cats and birds, every creature imaginable except those of a human, and when I swallow there's a lump in my throat.

"I got your invitation," I say, "and truly, I'm very flattered, but I don't want to come with you. I don't want to be part of your entourage."

The goat-fey and the fair-faced fey exchange a smile. "You are dying," one says, as if it's the only argument that's needed.

"Not yet."

"You will," it says, "and it will not be easy. We're here to spare you that."

"Thank you," I say, "but I don't care. I don't need this to be easy. That's not the point. It's not my pain that I'm worried about."

There's a picture of Patrick in my jacket pocket. I don't know if the faeries can even see it, if their vision is limited like cats and dogs, but I produce it and hand it over, showing them Patrick's face. "He's not sick," I tell them, "but he wants to go. He's the one who needs to escape all this. He's the one who needs to be somewhere that isn't around me."

"Too old," the fey says.

"I'm older."

"In years," the fey says. "We have other measures. He will grieve far longer than you."

"He wants to go," I repeat. "I do not. I'll give him my place."

"We do not trade," the faerie says. "We do not accept one in place of the other."

They step forward, the fair one and the goat-headed one and a handful of winged pixies beside, and I step back down the gangplank. I loop one leg over the guide rope, letting myself lean towards the freezing water. "You can't make me go," I say. "I'll drown myself first."

The fair one smiles. "That's been tried before."

"I'll fight back."

"Not for long."

"I'll weep," I say. "For as long as you need me to, to make taking Patrick worthwhile. I'll do all the weeping you need."

"You cannot," the fair one says. "You're destined to forget. To do otherwise would be cruel."

I look the faerie in the eye. There is something there, a light, maybe. Staring at it terrifies me.

"What does it take?" I say. "Just tell me what you need to give Patrick my place in your damn boat?"

The rumble of the faerie crowd is like the tinkling of tiny bells. Beside them I'm a creature of mud and flesh, a pudgy man with a rotting brain and intestines full of gas.

The goat-headed faerie produces a silver needle. He waves the point of a needle before my eyes, threatening as a knife blade. "If you want to stay," he says, "then we need to ensure you survive. We need to ensure you remember, long after your Patrick has gone away."

"Fine," I say.

"You'll linger," the faerie says. "We cannot heal you, but we can extend your life. We can sew your Patrick's presence into your mind's eye, hold it there as other things fall away. The memory of him will not fade, it will simply sour and rot. It will be worse, much worse, than coming with us on the morning tide."

The needle jabs closer and I blink, but do not shy away. "Fine," I say, "if that's what it takes."

"If you're sure," the faerie says, and I nod.

And the faerie plunges the needle into my eye.

The first time Patrick and I met, I knew he'd end up breaking my heart. That's the nature of pledging yourself to the young and pretty, knowing that in the end you'll be the one left alone. I resisted the idea of dating him, of moving in, of binding myself. He was only twenty-three and I knew better, so much better, than getting involved.

"I don't want that," I said, explaining the decision to friends. "The way these things end, it's never good for the older guy."

For a long time Patrick proved me wrong. He pursued me. Charmed me. Enticed me into his bed. He was glorious in every way and even I doubted my convictions as years tumbled by.

I give Patrick his invitation and he doesn't ask how it arrived. He simply looks at me, with my bloodshot eyes and frost-bitten fingers, and nods. He picks a single bag, a rucksack I gave him on our first anniversary, and begins to pack. I sit on the bed and watch him, each movement and article of clothing sinking into my memory with perfect clarity.

After a few minutes he pauses and says, "I wish you'd reconsider," with enough force to convince me that perhaps he does, but there is no chance of that happening so he loses very little in saying so. It pisses me off to hear him, and it pisses me off that I'm pissed. I will not forget this moment, I will always remember the little irritations.

Patrick says, "I'm going to miss you."

And I say, "Fuck off. You really aren't."

Patrick chooses not to piss me off any further by pretending this isn't true. It is the nature of all such stories. One person wants to run away to the new world, one person stays behind and remembers what's been lost. In the end, both of us are cowards, too locked into the parts we've played to step out and be something else.

He selects a jacket and a scarf and a battered old fedora we bought in the local thrift store six or seven cities ago. He arranges himself, checks the image in the cracked mirror in the bathroom. Finally he declares himself ready to leave, and I walk him down to the docks where the Steamer is waiting.

It's still dark out, despite the morning hour. There's no

hesitation once we arrive. Patrick walks up the gangplank, a backpack slung over one shoulder, his face shining in the cold morning air. There are faces in the portals along the Steamer, smooth and pale as ice, yellow and green eyes watching the procession of young men. It's hard to stare at anything through the glare of the boat. Everything is illuminated. Everything shines with the luster of diamonds and silver and aluminum foil.

He doesn't say goodbye this time. I do not wish him ill because of it.

I'm still on the docks when the Steamer departs. The sun sets and the engines start and the Steamer's lights spill over the water, picking up speed as it hits the open water. The city is dark by the time it finally disappears, slipping behind a bend in the river. I blow on my hands, rubbing them together. It's cold there, on the docks, so close to the Steamer's mooring. That won't last, now the faeries are gone. Soon it will be too warm for my jacket.

The snow melts while I walk back to the motel, turning into slush before evaporating in the warming air. The streets of V— remain silent, although behind the curtains and slat-covered windows there are still lights burning. I think about Patrick and the bag full of gear sitting on his side of the bed, debating whether to take it home when I depart.

Yuri mans the desk when I arrive at the hotel. He uncaps a bottle of vodka and places two glasses, each barely larger than a thimble, on the greasy ledger where he records arrivals. His eyes have a red, washed-out kind of look as he pours the first glass. "Drink," he says, "it will help."

"I'm not looking for help," I tell him. "Help disagrees with me."

Yuri blinks his wet eyes and rubs his hooked nose, giving me a wan smile. "More than this?" he says, waving a hand at my face. "It disagrees more than this?"

I open my mouth to say something, but I know he's right. The faerie curse feels like someone's tied strings to every internal organ and pulled them tight together, bunching them around my swollen intestines and the uncomfortable bubble of memory that resides there. "No," I say, "I guess you're right," and I accept the first drink. The vodka burns my throat as it goes down, and it sits in my stomach like an anchor, like a stone, like a bad memory you can't let go of. I put the glass on the ledger and say, "Can I have another?"

Yuri nods and pours again. We drink the next glass in silence.

I say, "We were selfish people, Patrick and I. It's what made us work in the beginning." I rub my nose with my fingers and smell vodka on my skin. The strings in my stomach loosen a little, and I know I'm going to vomit in the very near future. I say, "Someone had to stay behind. Someone had to cope, and Patrick was never good at that. He never learned to hide things, you know?"

Yuri waits, staring at me. Yuri and his terrifying eyebrows, his thick caterpillar of a mustache. I lose my train of thought and shrug, hold out the thimble for another shot. "You always need someone to stay behind," I say, "and he wanted to go more than I did."

"But you are not happy," Yuri said, pouring.

I remember Patrick's smile, every smile he ever smiled in my presence. They seem too few, looking back, and all I can do is shake my head. "No," I say, "not happy."

Yuri nods. "And there will come a time, yes, when you regret that he is gone."

I close my eyes to block the images that come. The vodka on my skin smells like antiseptic. My stomach boils and the strings seize their moment, pulling tight as I taste bile in the back of my throat.

"Yeah," I say, "almost certainly."

And Yuri hefts his bottle high and gives me a sad little grin. "Then we drink," he says, "and it will help."

And despite the feeling in my stomach, I agree.

I wake the next morning with a hangover, vomit coating the tile floor. I get up, wash my teeth, and shovel my belongings into a suitcase. Occasionally I stare at Patrick's things, the shorts and t-shirts strewn across the dusty floor. I don't want to take them, but I suspect I'll regret leaving them behind, living with the memory of Yuri walking away with things that had once belonged to Patrick. I know I will forget none of them, these articles of clothing. I remember every time Patrick ever wore them.

I shovel them into a duffel bag and pull it closed. I don't need to check the wardrobe to see if there's things I've forgotten.

Yuri doesn't work the morning shift. There's no way to say goodbye, no way to thank him or curse him for the pain in my stomach.

The airline sends a car to pick me up, a precaution to make sure I'll catch my flight. I'd cashed in Patrick's ticket, used it to upgrade my single ticket home, and there were people in the office who understood what'd happened. The citizens of V— have experience with these things. They've learnt to read the signs.

I wait outside until the car arrives. It's hot and dry and

I can hear the boat-calls from the river. When my car finally arrives it's small and black and out of style, driven by a short man best described by the same three words.

"Lot of luggage for a guy flying solo," he says.

"I like to be prepared," I tell him.

He nods, then sees the expression on my face. He sees the look in my right eye.

I sit in the back seat of the car. I say nothing as he starts the engine and begins the long drive home.

STORY NOTES

The Last Great House of Isla Tortuga

I've wanted to write fiction for as long as I could remember, but I came to it very late. Along the way, I wrote nearly everything else: poetry, scripts, advertising copy, essays, magazine articles, lectures, and RPG supplements.

This was the first story I finished after deciding to really put my focus on writing fiction, and I figured it would never get published given the subject matter. Instead, it was picked up for Jack Dann's *Dreaming Again* anthology in 2007, which served as a snapshot of Australia's established and emerging talent at the time.

This story has it's beginning in a second-hand bookstore, where I found a copy of the Wordsworth *Dictionary of Pirates* and figured I would need it for research one day.

On the Destruction of Copenhagen By the War-Machines of the Merfolk

This story began with something my sister told me. It's dangerous to admit this, because the lines between fiction and reality start to blur. Correlations are sought out between the sister in the story and my actual, living sister.

These correlations are largely superficial, and the story is definitely fiction. My sister did spend much of her twenties travelling, and it's largely thanks to this I learned that the Little Mermaid statue in Copenhagen harbor is one of the coldest places you can visit.

Beyond this, I will state on the record that I have no knowledge of my real-life sister living through an attack on Copenhagen, nor getting in trouble at an underground Korean casino. Having travelled with her, on one occasion, I can assure you her trips are carefully planned and only occasionally result in panicked phone calls from my parents.

The Seventeen Executions of Signore Don Vashta

I love the tale of Sir Gawain and the Green Knight, but I often find myself pondering how the magic works. That the Green Knight survives beheading doesn't bother me so much. That the Green Knight can still speak, while headless, confounds my admittedly shaky understanding of how lungs and vocal chords work.

This is the kind thing I start poking with a stick, figuring it will transform into a story before too long. This time it combined with research on the history of executions I was doing for another project, which led me to wonder how exactly you'd go about killing an immortal using the science available to us in the twenty-first century.

The magic used to withstand the trauma of a sharp sword might not be so adept at dealing with being thrown into a nuclear reactor, for example, or fired into the emptiness of space and left to asphyxiate.

It's Not A Bad Job, Really

This story owes a lot to my appreciation of the sparse, stripped-back realism of Raymond Carver's short fiction.

I frequently pastiche Carver's style when I'm stuck on a project, because there's something incredibly freeing about applying his voice and focus on the mundane to settings that are filled with fantasy or horror elements.

It's rare that it will go for more than a few paragraphs, but it's remarkably effective at getting me un-stuck.

I wrote this story when the process of getting un-stuck took considerably longer than usual, and I found myself with a finishes story at the end.

The Dragonkeeper's Wife

A friend made the mistake of saying, "there are no good stories with dragons in them," in earshot of me, which is rather like waving a red cape at a bull. I spent the next few weeks writing nothing but dragon stories, just to prove a point.

The story first appeared in Rob Santa's *Black Dragon, White Dragon* anthology, after he sat down to write the rejection letter and talked himself into including it while trying to explain why he was going to say no.

On The Finding Of Photographs Of My Former Loves

I wrote this back in 2007 as one of my first story submissions at the Clarion South workshop.

I had two reasons for going to Clarion. First, I went to spend six weeks around other writers, learning from the instructors, and developing a better understanding of how to make a living as a writer.

Second, I went because my then-fiancé and I had largely figured out we probably shouldn't be together anymore, but we wanted some time apart to be sure.

I wrote a lot of stories about being love, and what happens at the end, during those six weeks. This was the first of them to be accepted once I started submitting, taken up by Cat Rambo at Fantasy Magazine, although the timelines of publishing meant it would be the second story published.

The Clockwork Goat and the Smokestack Magus

I wrote this for Shimmer's *Clockwork Jungle Book* issue, which featured a series of steampunk stories about animals. I went with a goat because I figured very few other people would use one, and I wanted a very overt, conspicuous narrator for the story because that was the aspect of Rudyard Kipling's *Jungle Book* that always stood out for me.

Every writer gets a handful of stories that are something of a gift. You sit down with half an idea and a keyboard, then look up an hour or two later and there's something pretty-much finished in front of you.

This was one of those stories, and I remain extraordinarily fond of it. I keep meaning to go back and write a second story in Unden and Moloch Alley, featuring the Gallows Magus and the Queen of the Winter Seas, but there never seems to be enough time.

The Birdcage Heart

This started as a writing exercise about characters and their unconscious routines, because the things we do without thinking say an awful lot about who we are. Routines also give a writer patterns to break, which immediately escalate the tension and mark the moment that things start going wrong.

I started this with the most prominent unconscious routine in our lives - getting dressed - and I'd just finished the first paragraph when They Might Be Giant's *Birdhouse In Your Soul* came on the stereo. The rest of the story followed.

On the Cliffs, By the Sea

Years ago I collected the names of twelve people on my blog, promising to write a short story with each of them in mind. I warned people it would take a while, given that I'm a slow kind of writer, but I promised I'd get through everyone eventually.

This is the first of those stories, written for the Australian novelist Alan Baxter, who I first met at a conference many years ago.

Since then we run into each other semi-regularly, usually at a con bar or panel, and we'll end up talking comics, writing, and bad eighties action movies. It's largely because of Alan that I've seen the cult action film *Gymkata*, and I've almost forgiven him for that.

It turns out writing a story for a friend can be harder than I thought. I knew I wanted to do something with its roots in eighties action for this, and I wanted horror elements thanks to Alan's love for the genre.

It wasn't until it occurred to me that I could write the whole thing in the style of Angela Carter's *The Snow Child* that things truly came together.

Briar Day

There's usually a combination of things that come together to start a story. This one began with several things: a pre-occupation with the imagery from Disney's *Sleeping Beauty* that appeared in a childhood book; a break-up that resulted in a series of awful phone-calls; constant exposure to young men who believed that "chivalry" equated to feminism; an increasing interest in the things fairy tales teach us about masculinity, and how they're often as damaging as the messages about femininity contained within.

I wrote this in 2007 and it saw print in Ben Payne's *Moonlight Tuber #2: Captain Homunculus Dines With That Irascible Mizzen Mast, Part Three*, something I include in these notes because Ben never really got enough credit for the incredible name at the time of publication.

The version of this story Ben published is very much an artefact of it's time. It existed in a world where phone calls weren't flagged with caller ID, cell phones and text messages weren't yet ubiquitous, and social media is just starting to pick up momentum.

These days, the awkwardness of getting phone calls from your former partner have been replaced with the weirdness of Facebook memories and online conversations where the time stamp lets them see you've read their message and elected not to reply. I'm not entirely sure whether the situation is better or worse.

L'esprit de L'escalier

This is a story that ended somewhere very different than I expected. Originally I'd I intended to use the Kola Peninsula borehole and the urban myth about drilling a hole to hell as the setting. It turns out, neither of those things made it into the final version.

What led me astray was the title. I've been extraordinarily fond of this French term, which translates as staircase wit, ever since I first came across it. I'm frequently beset by the perfect thing to say long after its appropriate to say it, and I have a bad habit of conducting entire debates in my head long after everyone else has left a conversation.

This first appeared in Apex Magazine, where it became the subject of a blog post on the SF news site i09 that sent several thousand people over to read it. I've received more feedback on this story than anything else I've ever written.

On The Arrival of the Paddle-Steamer On the Docks of V—

I wrote very little in 2012 thanks to a combination of yet-to-be-diagnosed chronic sleep condition and my first real flirtation with full-time employment. This was one of three stories I finished, and it's one of the stories I'm proudest of over the last decade.

I spent a considerable amount of time in hotels that year, and that sense of being on the move seeped into this story alongside the references to *A Midsummer Night's Dream* and a fascination with cities steeped in the kind of history that Australia doesn't really have.

It was first published in Jonathan Strahan's *Eclipse*

Online in February of 2013, illustrated by my friend Kathleen Jennings, but trouble with the publisher meant the project was shut down two months later. In a world where stories first published online tend to be readable for years afterwards, it disappeared almost instantly.

The nicest thing about putting together a collection is giving it another chance to find readers who may enjoy it.

ACKNOWLEDGMENTS

These stories were written and published over a period of ten years, which means a complete list of all the people who should be thanked would be considerably longer than the meagre list who appears on this page. No writer truly works in isolation, and I owe a considerable debt to all the friends, editors, writers, co-workers, and housemates who offered support, feedback, and encouragement over the years.

Particular thanks go out to the following people:

- The inimitable Angela Slatter, write club buddy and one of the smartest writers I know
- The organizers, tutors, and fellow attendees of Clarion South 2007
- The staff and student body of the Griffith University Creative Writing program, who gave me the opportunity to both learn about the short story and teach others about them as well

(and really, teaching is just another kind of learning)

- The team of the Queensland Writers Centre
- My parents, Terry and Margaret Ball, and my sister, Sally Ball, who have put up with this craziness for far longer anyone else
- Sarah Blue, once the troll who lived under the stairs and now the mighty Sarahsaurus
- Adam Windsor, who let me camp out in his spare room for significantly greater period than was truly sensible
- All the editors and slush readers who worked on the magazines and anthologies where many of these stories first appeared, and those who have reprinted these works in the years since they first appeared.

PREVIOUS PUBLICATION CREDITS

Several of these stories have appeared elsewhere, in some cases in a different form:

"The Last Great House of Isla Tortuga," *Dreaming Again,* ed. Jack Dann (HarperCollins, 2008)

"On The Destruction of Copenhagen By the War-machines of the Merfolk," *Strange Horizons,* July 2009

"The Seventeen Executions of Signore Don Vashta," *Daily Science Fiction*, 21st February 2014

"It's Not A Bad Job, Really," is original to this collection

"The Dragonkeeper's Wife," *Black Dragon, White Dragon,* ed. Rob Santa (Ricasso Press, 2008)

"On Finding the Photographs of My Former Loves," *Fantasy Magazine*, June 2008

"The Clockwork Goat and the Smokestack Magus," *Shimmer #11 (The Clockwork Jungle Book),* January 2010

"The Birdcage Heart," *Daily Science Fiction*, 11 February 2011

"On the Cliffs, By the Sea," is original to this collection

"Briar Day," *Moonlight Tuber #2*, January 2011

"L'esprit de L'escalier," *Apex Magazine #16*, September 2010

"On the Arrival of the Paddle-Steamer on the Docks of V—," *Eclipse Online*, February 2013

ABOUT THE AUTHOR

PETER M. BALL is an author, publisher, and RPG gamer whose love of speculative fiction emerged after exposure to *The Hobbit*, *Star Wars*, David Lynch's *Dune*, and far too many games of *Dungeons and Dragons* before the age of 7. He's spent the bulk of his life working as a creative writing tutor, with brief stints as a  performance poet, gaming convention organiser, online content developer, non-profit arts manager, GenreCon convenor, and d20 RPG publisher.

He's the author of the Miriam Aster series and the Keith Murphy Urban Fantasy Thrillers, three short story collections, and more stories, articles, poems, and RPG material than he'd care to count. He's the brain-in-charge at Brain Jar Press, and resides in Brisbane, Australia, with his partner and a very affectionate cat.

Peter can be found online at:
www.petermball.com

facebook.com/Petermball

twitter.com/petermball

instagram.com/petermball

Also by Peter M. Ball

BRAIN JAR PRESS SHORT FICTION LAB

The Early Experiments

Winged, With Sharp Teeth

8 Minutes Of Usable Daylight

A White Cross Beside A Lonely Road

One Last First Date Before The End Of The World

SHORT STORY COLLECTIONS

The Birdcage Heart & Other Strange Tales

Not Quite The End Of the World Just Yet: Short Stories & Strange Futures

These Strange & Magic Things: Short Stories

KEITH MURPHY URBAN FANTASY THRILLERS

Exile

Frost

Crusade

MIRIAM ASTER NOVELLAS

Horn

Bleed

ESSAYS

You Don't Want To Be Published & Other Things Nobody Tells You When You First Start Writing